A TWIST AT THE END

A NOVEL OF

O. Henry

STEVEN
SAYLOR

SIMON & SCHUSTER
NEW YORK LONDON TORONTO SYDNEY SINGAPORE

SIMON & SCHUSTER
Rockefeller Center
1230 Avenue of the Americas
New York, NY 10020

Designed by Karolina Harris
Manufactured in the United States of America

1 3 5 7 9 10 8 6 4 2

Library of Congress Cataloging-in-Publication Data
Saylor, Steven, date.
A twist at the end : a novel of O. Henry / Steven Saylor.
p. cm.
1. Serial murders—Texas—Austin—Fiction. 2. Authors, American—
19th century—Fiction. 3. Henry, O., 1862–1910—Fiction.
4. Austin (Tex.)—Fiction. I. Title.
PS3569.A96 T85 2000
813'.54—dc21   99-089926
ISBN 0-684-85681-6

To Gary Coody,
good friend, generous host,
guardian spirit of Barton Springs

CONTENTS

These crimes have been of the most revolting character. . . . They are abnormal and unnatural, as compared with ordinary crimes among men. No one, not even the expert skilled in the detection of crime, can find a plausible motive. . . .

I have faith that the authors of these crimes will yet be uncovered. No human heart is strong enough to hold such secrets.

JOHN ROBERTSON, MAYOR OF AUSTIN
STATE OF THE CITY ADDRESS
NOVEMBER 10, 1885

Goddess of Liberty

1

*T*HE lady lies in pieces on the capitol grounds . . .

William Sydney Porter dreams. He lives in New York City now, but in the dream it is almost twenty years ago—back when he still lived in Texas, and worked as a draftsman at the General Land Office in Austin. He could look out the window above his drafting table and watch the tall cranes and the antlike workmen busily constructing the dome on the new state capitol building. It was on a day in February of 1888, not quite noon, when he and Dave set out from the land office and went for a stroll before lunch, and they came upon the lady lying in pieces on the capitol grounds.

In his dream, the lady lies there still.

She lies in four pieces. The most identifiable of these consists of her head, along with her left arm and the uppermost part of her torso. This part of the lady is situated face-up, and except for the separation from the rest of her body she might simply be a woman reclining on her back, staring up at the sky with her left arm thrown above her head, the elbow slightly bent. At the end of this upraised arm, her fingers and thumb are curled and joined as if to grasp something no longer there, some object with a cylindrical handle that has been plucked from her frozen grip.

Her mouth is shut, but her eyes are wide open, staring up at the sky through a winter canopy of naked branches.

Not far away, the lady's disembodied right arm lies against the trunk of a pecan tree. Nearby in the brown grass is another piece consisting of her legs and the lower parts of her anatomy. Next to that lies the bulk of her torso, from midriff to breasts.

Beyond her, up the hillside, looms the new, almost finished capitol building. Its walls of dusky rose granite seem to glow with warmth against the cold blue sky. The lofty central portico of the building and the three-storied wings are virtually complete, but a mass of scaffolding and a convergence of cranes indicate where the workmen, small as insects at such a distance, are still busy completing the dome.

The General Land Office is situated a little to the south and east of the new capitol building, at one corner of the grounds. A homesick German architect designed it before the Civil War. The German allowed for big windows to give the draftsmen plenty of light, and decorated the top with fanciful battlements to make it look a bit like a castle.

That was where William Sydney Porter worked in those days, toiling for hour after hour in a dusty, high-ceilinged office up on the third floor, unrolling maps on big drafting tables, placing glass weights to hold down the corners, using rulers and compasses and pens to calculate the longitude and latitude of various claims. A draftsman saw terrible things at the land office: widows and children who lost homesteads for lack of a proper claim, swindlers who grabbed vast tracts by legal trickery, fools who spent fortunes on worthless treasure maps and stormed into the land office determined to prove that the official surveys had to be wrong. But mostly the work was long and boring and tedious, just the sort of thing that people seem to have in mind when they speak of a "real" job, as in: "Now that you're married and have a baby on the way, you must think of getting a *real* job, Will." And so he had, and that was how he ended up at the land office, drawing lines and circles and scribbling numbers in ledgers, instead of sketching funny pictures and writing clever little poems and stories that nobody wanted to publish.

But in the midst of all that daily tedium there was the blessed oasis called lunch, and on the day he is revisiting in the dream, his friend Dave Shoemaker is treating him to lunch, because Dave has just received a raise in pay from the penny-pinching tyrant who owns the newspaper where Dave works.

In Will Porter's dream, just as it actually happened on that February day in 1888, the two of them descend the little flight of steps from the main entrance of the land office, walk past horses and carriages gathered in the forecourt, then cross the capitol grounds heading for Congress Avenue. Some spots are prettily landscaped, with shrubbery and grass and flower beds. Other areas are scraped or furrowed or piled high with dirt or gravel.

Though they do not know it, each step brings them closer to their discovery of the lady who lies in pieces.

Will is in his middle twenties. Dave is not quite thirty. Both are respectably but not ostentatiously dressed, wearing hats, vests, and long winter coats. Each has a mustache; Will's is ginger-colored and Dave's is black. Almost every man had a mustache in those days, or else a beard. Hair on the face was considered a mark of manhood and commanded respect. The older generation who ran things in Austin, men who were old enough to have fought in the Civil War, were given to wearing full, dense beards requiring the expert attentions of a barber. Young men of courting age were more likely to sport mustaches; a woman had to see a man's chin to judge his character.

Will and Dave stroll slowly across the grounds, nodding gravely, like two men discussing a matter of great importance.

"Will," says Dave, "I think you know my feelings on the subject."

"Do I, Dave?"

"Under no circumstances is a tamale a fit thing to put into a man's system in the middle of the day. That goes double for two tamales. Triple for three."

Will raises an eyebrow. "Millions of Mexicans swear by 'em."

"You'll hear me swearing, too, about twenty-four hours from now, if you persuade me to eat a couple of damn tamales for lunch."

Will licks his lips. "Mama Rodriguez makes a mighty fine tamale. She's only a streetcar ride away, down on Nueces across from the lumberyard. My heart was set on it, Dave."

"My stomach is dead set against it. Who's paying for this meal, anyway?"

"Touché, Shoemaker. What about the Iron Front?"

"Too greasy."

"The Blue Front, then?"

"Not greasy enough."

"Salge's Chop House?"

"Too crowded."

"Simon's?"

"Quiet as a graveyard."

"Roach's, then?"

Dave raises an eyebrow. "Never cared for the name."

"David Shoemaker," says Will in some exasperation, "I have just recited the entire list of decent eateries in the city of Austin, Texas, and you've vetoed every one."

Dave brightens. "I suppose the only remaining alternative is to take a liq-uid lunch down in Guy Town." He pats his vest pocket. "I even have a fresh deck of cards on me! Shall we wend our way down Congress Avenue and see what saloon we come to first?"

Will tugs at his ginger mustache. "You forget, Mr. Shoemaker, that I am now a married man! For me, Guy Town and its bachelor pleasures have re-treated behind a veil of mystery."

Their path takes a detour around a high mound of gravel. When they reach the other side, Dave comes to an abrupt stop. He wrinkles his brow. "What on earth . . . ?"

Will follows Dave's gaze to see what he's staring at. He steps closer, then steps back, turning his head this way and that, as if seeing the thing from the right angle will explain it. "Not a pretty sight, is it?"

Dave peers at the lady's tight-lipped, blankly staring face. He shakes his head. "I'll say it's not! When did this happen?"

"Don't know."

"Someone should cover her up!"

Will raises an eyebrow. "Don't see why. Decently dressed, ain't she? And it don't look like rain."

Dave nods vaguely. He walks from piece to piece, carefully observing each segment of the lady in turn. "Mr. Gaines at the *Statesman* will want to send a sketch artist," he mutters.

"Can't imagine why," says Will. "She's so very ugly." He walks up to the disembodied torso and gives it a kick. The blow reverberates with a hollow, metallic clang. "I suppose it's the perspective—nobody was ever meant to see this thing so close up. There's something grotesque about such an over-sized specimen of womanhood. What man wouldn't be unnerved at the sight of a woman three times bigger than he is, even if she is all in pieces! Now, at a proper distance—once she's all assembled and welded together and they set her on top of the capitol dome—I suppose everyone will rave about what a beauty she is. But this close up—well, if ever there was a face that could stop a clock . . ."

"She is indeed a harsh-looking lady," Dave agrees. "I suppose no one ever said that Liberty has to be beautiful. Now why do you suppose her left arm is raised up like that? It looks like she's holding on to a cylinder of thin air."

"Really, Dave Shoemaker! She's the Goddess of Liberty, ain't she? I imagine she's supposed to hold a torch of some kind. Or maybe a star."

"Ah, yes. A goddess. That explains why she's all dolled up in robes and drapery. And barefoot!"

Together, they study the various scattered pieces of the statue of the Goddess of Liberty, the crowning monument for the capitol dome. "She received quite a bit of coverage in the *Statesman* when the molds arrived from that catalogue outfit in Chicago," recalls Dave. "There's a foundry in the capitol basement where they cast her out of zinc. The workmen must have lugged her out here early this morning, getting ready to put the pieces together. A mail-order goddess—but from Chicago, not Olympus!"

Will laughs, but feels vaguely apprehensive as he continues to study the pieces of the statue. It's the monstrous scale of the thing, he thinks, and the fact that she's scattered all about, as if she'd been standing here on the capitol grounds minding her own business, doing whatever a goddess of liberty does, and some equally monstrous fellow had come along and chopped her to pieces with a monstrous ax . . .

The same thought seems to occur to Dave at that instant, because they exchange a look and see the same darkness reflected in each other's eyes.

They are thinking of *her*.

They are thinking of all the women who were so brutally murdered in Austin in the long, bizarre sequence of murders still fresh in everyone's memory. They remember one woman in particular. In light of those horrible crimes, it is no laughing matter to come upon a dismembered woman on the capitol grounds, even if she's only a statue made of zinc.

On that day in 1888, neither Dave nor Will acknowledged the thought. Instead they turned away from the dismembered statue, resumed their discussion of where to eat, and hurried off, giving no further thought to the lady lying in pieces on the capitol grounds. That was all there was to it, as it actually happened on that February day almost twenty years ago.

But in Will Porter's dream there is a sequel.

In the dream, as they walk away, Will glances back over his shoulder, gripped by a dreadful premonition of what he will see. His blood turns to ice.

The pieces of the lady are still monstrous, three times larger than life, but she is no longer made of zinc and no longer draped in robes. She is naked and made of pale white flesh. The places where she has been hacked into pieces are not clean and hollow and metal-bright, but streaming blood and quivering with gore.

Her mouth remains shut. Her blue eyes remain open and staring. Then she blinks.

Slowly, horribly, she lifts her head. The hugeness of it is uncanny and frightening, but she is no longer ugly. She is beautiful, the most beautiful

woman Will has ever seen. She looks straight at him. He says her name.
"Eula!"

It comes out as a sob. *Eula*—from the Greek word for "good" . . .

He wakes with a start.

His nightshirt is drenched with sweat. His head throbs. For a moment he
remembers nothing. All he can think is that the whiskey must have done
this to him. If he had any sense, he would give up the poison for good.

Then, in a flash, he remembers.

This isn't the first time he has had the dream. It comes around every so
often, this dream-memory of being back in Austin, strolling on the capitol
grounds with Dave Shoemaker and coming upon the Goddess of Liberty lying all in pieces.

It's occurred to him—because he is a professional story-writer after all,
and everything that crosses his path is grist for the mill—that there might be
a short story in the episode. He could give it a peculiar twist—trick the
reader into assuming at the outset that the lady in pieces is a real flesh-and-
blood lady, show the two unsuspecting men walking toward her, have them
come upon her and react as no two men possibly could at finding a hacked-
up body, but instead have them chat airily about how ugly she is, and then
finally have one of them give her a good swift kick, and with a hollow clang
let the reader see that the lady is only a metal statue . . .

But he has never written that story. What sane editor would purchase it?
A dismembered female, no matter what she's made of, is hardly a suitable
subject for fiction, not in the United States of America, not in the year
1906; nor in any place or year he can imagine.

He shakes his head, trying to clear it. He has dreamed the dream before,
but this time there was something different. This time, the statue became
flesh and blood at the end, turning a slightly disquieting dream into an outright nightmare. He shudders.

Suddenly his sweat-drenched nightshirt is intolerably binding. It clings to
him as he pulls it over his head, and extricating himself becomes a struggle.

What time is it? Just enough light from the street lamp leaks in around
the window shades to illuminate the clock on the dresser. Half past three!
He gets out of bed and walks naked across the big room, past the fireplace
and the writing desk, to the bay window. He raises the shade on the right-
hand side and lifts the sash. The fresh air chills the sweat on his bare flesh,
but he relishes the sensation. The street below is empty. The windows

across the way are dark. At half past three in the morning, even the great metropolis of New York is quiet.

He lowers the shade but leaves the window open to air the room. He switches on the electric lamp on his desk. A mug full of sharpened pencils stands beside a stack of papers, every sheet accusingly blank. Ever since he signed his contract with the *New York Sunday World Magazine,* his writing schedule has been relentless. He must produce a story for them every week—fifty-two stories a year! The challenge proved to be not so daunting after all, especially at a hundred dollars a story. In fact, he has found himself capable of writing even more stories, especially if a magazine offers a higher rate than the *World.* Sometimes he has finished a story the morning it's due for the *World,* decided it's good enough for *Munsey's,* run it by messenger to his editor there, had it accepted, and turned out something completely different for the *World* by his deadline that afternoon. He feels less like a writer sometimes and more like a traffic cop; the stories speed this way and that in his head, and his job is simply to keep them from colliding.

But sometimes, for no perceptible reason, the traffic comes to a standstill. The people inside his head stop moving, and fall silent. The sunlit phantoms of his Texas youth retreat into shadows. The well of his wit runs dry.

Fortunately, the void is always temporary. Soon enough the stories come rushing back, faster than he can write them. But this particular dry spell could not have come at a more inconvenient time. At the moment, he has four stories promised to four editors, two of them past deadline, and not a single plot has been hatched or a single word set down on paper.

Four stories, he thinks. Four stories amount to nothing! There must be four million stories in New York alone, one for every face on the street. The stories always come. But they must arrive at regular intervals, to keep the checks coming in. Checks to pay for the room, for the whiskey, for the doctors who prescribe for his insomnia and his constant backaches. Checks for his daughter's upbringing in Pittsburgh.

He opens the dresser. He slips a fresh nightshirt over his shoulders. He shuts the bay window, for the room suddenly seems chilly to him.

He sits at the desk and stares at a sheet of paper. Perhaps there's something to be used from the dream, after all, though he is not the sort of writer who typically uses dreams for inspiration. His stories are about the waking world, and any dreams they contain are daydreams, of the sort indulged in by bored shop girls and lonely office clerks. Supernatural fantasies do not interest him. Neither do allegories; in his stories, a duck is a duck, and if it opens its mouth, it quacks. Although, come to think of it, he did once write up a conversation between two lady statues—Diana atop the tower at Madison Square Garden and the Statue of Liberty in the harbor. But that was a parody, not a fairy tale. Diana, goddess of the hunt clutching her golden bow, her only garment a ribbon of copper floating behind her, made fun of the social scene at the cafés below. Liberty was so used to welcoming boatloads of immigrants from Dublin that she had picked up an Irish brogue.

He takes up a pencil, but instead of writing, he doodles. He has always had a penchant for drawing. Before he knows it, he has sketched from memory the Texas state capitol building in Austin, surrounded by squiggles meant to be trees. Atop the dome, he leaves the Goddess of Liberty unfinished, for he cannot remember what she holds in her upraised hand—a star, a scythe, a torch?

He decides that a nightmare is no place to go looking for inspiration. The dream of the dismembered lady has nothing he can use, and there is no use staying up. Perhaps a small glass of whiskey will help him get back to sleep.

2

He continues to doze until well past ten o'clock.

His room is on the first floor of a four-story brownstone. It was built for a single family to dwell in, but now, along with the landlady, it houses several boarders. His room was designed to serve as a front parlor; hence the generous dimensions, the big fireplace, and the bay window that affords a view onto Irving Place. Just off the parlor, a pantry has been converted into his private bath. These spacious quarters accommodate his bachelor needs.

At half past ten, he hears the sound of a knock on the brownstone's front door. After a moment the door opens. He vaguely hears a conversation between two feminine voices. A moment later, there is a quiet knock at the door to his room. The caller must be a visitor for him.

He is instantly awake, his chest tight with anxiety. Few women would call on him unexpected and unaccompanied. He knows at once who it must be: the last person on earth he ever wants to see again. He imagines sinking into the bed, being swallowed up by it, vanishing forever. A trapdoor, he thinks: every home should have one, for quick escapes.

Without waiting for an answer, the housemaid opens the door, steps inside, and pulls the door almost shut behind her. Her name is Lena. She is from somewhere in Eastern Europe. Her English is good, but her accent is thick. "May I coom een, Meeser Porter?"

He peers above the covers, blinking at the bright morning light that outlines the shades. "You appear to be in already!" he snaps. "Therefore you cannot 'come in' unless you go back out and do it over again."

Lena raises an eyebrow, not quite understanding. "There ees laddee ootside to see you."

"A lady? Who is she?" His mouth is dry.

"No nime, Meeser Porter. Sime as befoor. Sime laddee who cooms lass moonth."

His heart sinks. It was inevitable, of course. Having come once and obtained what she wanted, it was inevitable that she would come back for more. His face flushes hot with a violent combination of embarrassment, helplessness, and rage. He raises the bedcover to hide his face from Lena, who laughs, mistaking the gesture for modesty. In her own way, Lena is a woman of the world. Having grown up in close quarters with brothers and cousins, she has little understanding of propriety and not much respect for privacy.

"Shill I tell laddee to go way, Meeser Porter?"

"No! No, only ask her to wait a moment."

Lena nods and steps out of the room, shutting the door behind her.

He gets out of bed and pulls a robe over his nightshirt. He fumbles with the cloth belt, his fingers trembling, as he steps into his slippers. Passing the fireplace, he glimpses his face in the mirror above the mantel and is startled by the sight. Where he expects to see a grim jaw and a steely glare filled with anger, he sees instead two frightened eyes above a grimace like that of a man with a toothache. Is his fear of her that transparent? No wonder she presses him so hard!

He steps to the door. He reaches to open it, but has to steel himself for the task, as if the brass knob were red-hot. Even as he turns it, he glances over his shoulder, fancifully trying to imagine an escape, wondering where a trapdoor would be hidden. Under the rug? Behind the wardrobe? Where would it lead? Into the street? That would do him no good. The only trapdoor that might help him would be a trapdoor into the past. Isn't that where everyone would like to escape to? Now *that* might be material for a story, he thinks . . .

But no such trapdoor exists. There is nothing to do but turn the knob and pull the door open. His visitor, a woman of middle age but still with a good figure, is sitting primly on the little chair in the hallway. She looks at him with sad eyes as she stands, clutching a little handbag and smoothing the pleats of her long skirt. The black handbag, edged with red lace and pearls, matches her black gloves and her black hat. Her dress is black, piped with red in the pleats. She dresses very well for a woman who claims to be in desperate need of money.

"Mr. Porter, how kind of you to receive me." She still has the accent and the manners of a Texas belle, no matter that she was transplanted to New York many years ago. Such manners call irresistibly to his own upbringing, and he steps back automatically to allow her into the room. He shuts the door.

"I see I've arrived at too early an hour," she says. "I've disturbed your sleep. My apologies, Mr. Porter."

How absurd, that she should apologize for getting him out of bed, when her last visit has disturbed his sleep ever since! The woman's unctuous manner is indecent; he had rather be beaten up and robbed by thugs in an alley. He would like to shout at her but instead he clenches his jaw, forcing the fury to flow like hot iron down into his fists. He tries to make his face a blank, but when he again glances at himself in the mirror he sees the ashen features of a man caught in a trap. Behind her own melancholy facade, this woman must be laughing at him.

"What a pleasant room this is. I suppose that charming housemaid does the tidying for you," she says, noting an undershirt thrown across the back of his writing chair. "The light must be quite excellent when those shades are pulled up. It was in the evening when I visited you last, too dark to appreciate the light from the windows. Do you remember?"

"Yes." His mouth is dry.

"You were very kind to me on my last visit, Mr. Porter. Very understanding. And generous."

"Why have you come back?" His voice is flat. He wishes he could speak to her more harshly, but instead he echoes her stilted, meaningless politeness, reverting to the decorous manners of their youth.

"Oh, Mr. Porter, I fear that my circumstances have not appreciably improved, despite your previous kindness."

"For God's sake, woman, you're married to a Wall Street broker!" The anger finally wells up, but he keeps his voice low. Lena still might be in the hallway.

She flashes a melancholy smile and even manages a tear in the corner of her eye, as if to demonstrate how brave she is in the face of adversity. "Yes, Mr. Porter, I married a broker. You speak as if that wrote 'happily ever after' to the story, and perhaps it would, in one of your tales. Alas, not every broker is a rich man. And even men who are rich will not necessarily tolerate a wife who runs up foolish debts, and finds herself beholden to the wrong people." She sighs. "Austin was a hard place to live, I thought, but New York is much harder than ever Austin was, with harder people. Don't you agree, Mr. Porter?"

"Not necessarily. Though it may be that the city brings out the hardness in some people."

She flashes a wounded smile. "Oh, Mr. Porter, I assure you that I am the same person whom you knew in Austin, when we were both young. Do you remember, how you and your friends used to go about, serenading young ladies?"

"I never serenaded you," he says.

"No. But I must have heard you sing somewhere, because I remember your voice. A very rich bass, as I recall. Very deep and resonant. Oh, to be young, and to sing like a bird for the sheer pleasure of being alive! But I forget; in the end Austin was even harder on you than it was on me. How awfully things ended for you there." She wrinkles her brow with a look of concern. Her utter hypocrisy makes his blood turn cold.

"I can't give you as much as I did last time," he says.

"Oh, Mr. Porter, that you can help me at all is such a relief to me, I cannot tell you how great a relief!" She touches her throat as if to quell a sob of gratitude. The black glove looks very dark against her white skin. For a woman of forty-odd years, she is still quite attractive, and he has no trouble remembering the charm she exuded in their youth. How strange that they should both have ended up in New York, after all these years! From all outward appearances they have both, after grievous setbacks, achieved success. He has become a famous writer, she has married a prominent broker, yet for both of them success has not been enough. Now, after all the twists and turns of their separate lives, the two of them have ended up in the same city, in the same room, in circumstances as curious as one of the unexpected endings for which he has become famous.

Either her thoughts have taken the same course, or else she has simply decided that a bit of flattery is called for. "You know, I can still hardly believe it, that you are O. Henry. That the most famous writer in New York is actually Will Porter. I remember once when you waited on me in a drugstore back in Austin!"

"Bill."

"I beg your pardon?"

"It's Bill Porter now, not Will. My friends call me Bill, though I'm not sure what you should call me."

She blinks and flashes a brittle smile. "From Will to Bill—is that a part of the break you've made with the past? Let me see, what was it you did after that job in the drugstore? Eventually you married Athol, of course. And then you were employed at the land office; as a draftsman, wasn't it? That was a pretty good living, even with a wife and a little baby girl to look after. Then you started publishing that little newspaper with the pictures and stories that made everyone laugh, except the people you made fun of. What was it called?"

He can hardly speak. Why must she bring all this up? "*The Rolling Stone*," he says.

She nods. "But that was pure vanity, wasn't it? It cost you more to print the thing than you could ever earn from it. You started clerking at the bank at about that time, as I recall, handling all that money day in and day out. All that money, passing through your hands. And then came all the unpleasantness—Athol's terrible consumption, and your . . . what is that word? A legal term. *Indictment*, that's it. Your indictment, for embezzlement at the bank. And then off you ran to some place in Central America. Everyone was sure that you must be innocent, though people did wonder how you could abandon Athol when she was so ill and your baby daughter needed looking after. And Athol got sicker and sicker, until finally you did come back. And then Athol died. Poor Athol! And you went to trial. How awful for you! For embezzlement." She seems to take particular pleasure in saying the word, like a refrain in a poem. "Of course, none of your friends believed for a moment that any jury could ever find you guilty of such a terrible thing. But the world is a quizzical place, isn't it? They found you guilty. Guilty of embezzlement."

He manages to speak, but the stuttering words come out in a higher register than he intends: "How dare you? Have you no shame? You—your own past isn't—isn't exactly pure—"

"But we are not discussing *my* past," she says sharply. She sighs and strolls about the room. "We always called you Will. I suppose your fellow convicts called you Will, too. But now that you've served your time, and your transgressions are behind you, and you have a new life here in New York, it's Bill. I suppose that *does* make it just a little less likely that anyone will ever make a connection between your past and your present. Will Porter, Bill Porter—such common names, they could easily be two different people. Will Porter had a mustache; Bill Porter doesn't. Though there's not much you could do to disguise those wonderful blue eyes of yours. And of course you have a pen name to hide behind. But what *would* all those thousands and thousands of readers think of O. Henry if they knew he had been convicted of embezzling a bank in Texas? If they found out that he was a common jailbird?"

From the look on his face, she can see that she has pushed him almost too far. She betrays no signs of fear, but nonetheless retreats a few steps. "But all that's behind you now. You've had good fortune, Will—or Bill. Not all of us can say as much. You're famous. O. Henry is a household name—in New York, anyway, and that means you'll soon be famous everywhere. Everyone read 'The Gift of the Magi' last Christmas in the *World*—a wonderful story! And I see *Cabbages and Kings* in all the bookstores. The critics must wonder how you came to know so much about the tropics. What's the name of the mythical country where the stories take place—Anchuria? I don't suppose those critics know of the six months you spent as a fugitive from the law, down in Honduras. What would happen if one of your editors—or, God forbid, some unscrupulous reporter from a rival newspaper—got wind of your past? Contemplating that possibility must a terrible, terrible burden to you."

She shakes her head, the very picture of a woman consumed with worry for an old friend.

He is stunned. All the right angles in the room seem to slide off-kilter and he sways a bit, trying to steady himself. He dared to say a few cold words to her, and this is the result—she pays back ice with fire. He tries to swallow, but his throat constricts. "I already told you, I can't give you as much as last time."

"But you have stories in four magazines this month! I saw them—"

"That's not the way it works. The money comes in at odd times, sometimes before a story's published, sometimes after . . . and I have regular debts to pay."

"Ah, yes, supporting your little girl. I was curious about her. I asked a few questions here and there. I understand she's in Pittsburgh, being raised by some of Athol's relatives. So sad, that any girl should lose her mother at such an early age. And to have been separated at such a crucial time from her father, under such cruel circumstances. How old is she now, sixteen? She's almost a lady, ready to step out into the world. I imagine she would suffer even more than you, if ever—"

"For God's sake, can't you just leave me alone!"

She looks at him impassively, with neither malice nor supplication. "No. No, I cannot leave you alone, Mr. Porter. I need your assistance, and I must have it. My circumstances are such that I have no one else I can turn to. I need money, and I have no way to get that money, except by coming to you. When I came last time, I asked you for a thousand—"

"And I told you that was impossible!"

"Yet if you had given me what I asked for then, I might not have had to return, or at least not so soon. You gave me only one hundred and fifty dollars. I must have at least that much from you today."

"This is a crime. You know that. What you're doing is a crime."

"Is it a crime for a lady in distress to ask a gentleman, an old acquaintance, for assistance? I don't think so."

"It's blackmail. Again!"

"That's a very ugly word, Mr. Porter. Almost as ugly as another word: embezzlement. There is indeed a convicted criminal in this room, but that person is not myself."

He trembles. "I suppose I can write you a check."

She laughs. "Oh, that would never do! There must be no record of the transaction for my husband to come across. No, I must have the funds in ready cash. You had the cash on hand when I was here last time. You fetched it from your dresser, I believe. I remarked on what a sensible practice it is, to keep a few hundred in some easily accessible place. You may recall that I suggested, strongly suggested, that you make a habit of keeping such a sum on hand . . . for future contingencies."

He picks up his keys from the bedside table. They jangle in his shaking hand. He unlocks the top drawer of his dresser, where he keeps not only money but things too personal for prying eyes. There is an old picture of Athol from their courting days, and a picture of Margaret on a merry-go-round pony; most men would display such pictures proudly, but for him to do so would invite questions he had rather not answer. There are also letters and postcards, including some from friends he made in the penitentiary in Ohio. Lena regularly cleans his room, and the locked drawer is the only place inaccessible to her. How laughable it seems now, to think that he keeps secrets from the housemaid, who despite her humble station and mangled English is as decent and honest a woman as lives in New York, while the locked drawer is powerless to protect him from his visitor, a respectable broker's wife who goes to society balls, whom no one for a moment would suspect of the least impropriety.

He pulls out some folded bills. "Here, look for yourself. There's a little over a hundred, and that's all."

She sighs. "Then it will have to do . . . for now. Please lay it on the table." She will not take it directly from his hands. Perhaps she wishes to keep a judicious distance; she sees the way his fingers tremble, and perhaps imagines them around her throat. Or does she think that snatching the money from his grasp would be too grubby, too far beneath her?

He tosses the bundle on the table.

"Please," she says, "count them for me."

He does as she says, picking up the bills and laying them down one by one, counting aloud. "Ten, twenty, thirty . . ." Not until he lays down the last bill does he realize what she has done. She has tricked him into replicating his old role as a bank teller. Is it some sort of joke, yet another way to remind him of the job that led to his disgrace? What sort of monster is she, to keep torturing him even after he has acquiesced?

She scoops up the bills and deposits them in her handbag. "Thank you, Mr. Porter. Truly, I am grateful. You always were a gentleman."

He longs to say: *And you never were a lady.* But she has shown him that she will not brook casual insults, and that any deviations on his part from their absurd pretense of decorum will be punished with words many times harsher than any he can utter. She walks to the door, and actually has the gall to wait for him to open it for her. He resists for a moment, damning her with a silent curse, then walks to the door and pulls it open, unable to match wills and desperate to be rid of her.

"Thank you, Mr. Porter. I'll show myself out the front door. Have a good day. Write something clever! All New York looks forward to your wonderfully clever stories. We are so very proud of you, and your great success!"

She strides across the foyer. Suddenly, without thinking, he says, "I saw Eula last night!"

She stops.

"In a dream. Back in Austin. I saw Eula . . ."

Her shoulders twitch and her head jerks oddly, but she doesn't turn back. She steps to the front door, opens it, steps onto the stoop and slams the door behind her. He hears her descend the short flight of steps to the sidewalk.

He closes his door and goes to the window. He peers down at her from behind one of the shades, frustrated that he cannot see her face. She raises a hand to her brow. Weeping? Dazed? Or merely deliberating? After a moment she turns north and heads up Irving Place toward Gramercy Park, where the wives of brokers and bankers reside in grand houses.

3

At two o'clock that afternoon he has his first whiskey of the day, to help wash down a late lunch at Pete's Tavern.

After a wretched beginning, the day has stayed true to course. After his visitor left, he bathed, dressed, fortified himself with some of Lena's strong coffee and tried to write. For a couple of hours he scribbled nonsense, searching for the spark of a story, but in vain. He must have the plot in his head before he can make a proper beginning; then it all comes easily. But today there are no stories in his head, only a vague uneasiness left over from his nightmare, and the sharper anxiety caused by his visitor.

Pete's Tavern is his home away from home. The place is only a few steps from his room, at the corner of Irving Place and 18th Street. The staff reserve his favorite spot for him, the first booth inside the door, across from the bar. When he is in a talkative mood, the barman and the waiters are happy to converse, usually about his latest story in the *World*. ("Did such a thing really happen, Mr. Porter, or did you make it all up?" "Did you ever really know a fellow like that Texas Ranger? When did you live out West?" "That love story last week—I have a bet it was based on that young couple who always eat lunch in the next booth. Tell me I'm right!") When he wants to be left alone, they leave him in peace.

His only company today is a blank tablet of paper and a pencil, neither of which he has touched. His deadlines nag at him . . .

As if on cue, the door opens and an office boy, about fourteen years old, steps inside. He takes a few cautious steps and peers into the booth.

Porter peers back at him. "Don't tell me," he says. "You're from the *World*, aren't you?"

"Yes, sir. Are you Mr. Porter, sir?"

"That, young man, depends. I don't suppose that miser of a publisher has sent you here to bring Mr. Porter an unexpected cash bonus in gratitude for all his hard work?"

The boy frowns. "Well, no, sir."

"I see. Then I unequivocally am not Mr. Porter."

"Oh, but you must be. They said if you weren't at home, then you'd probably be right here, in the first booth. And here you are, sir."

"Am I to understand that you have already been to my . . . that is to say, to Mr. Porter's place of residence, looking for him?"

"Yes, sir. But as you weren't there—"

"As *Mr. Porter* was not at home, you mean."

The boy winces. "Please, sir, stop joking with me. The boss says I'm not to come back to the office until I get something from you."

"I foresee tomorrow's headline, then: '*World* Office Boy Goes Missing.'"

The Irish barman, drying glasses with a towel, glances up and chuckles.

"Just a page or two, then," begs the boy. "For the typesetters to get started on."

Porter tears a couple of blank pages from the tablet and offers them. "Tell them it's about spies who use invisible ink."

"Mr. Porter, please! Just a title, at least, so they can put it on the front page."

"Very well. The story will be called, 'Never Send a Boy to Do a Man's Job.'" The barman laughs out loud. Porter raises an eyebrow. "Not a bad title, actually. Sounds like an O. Henry story, don't it? Barman, another whiskey, please. To celebrate. We have a title!"

"Seriously, Mr. Porter, what shall I tell the boss?"

"Say that you tried your best. Here, show him this." Porter takes up his pencil and writes:

This will verify that the bearer of this document has duly discharged his editorial mission, braving the dangerous streets and potentially fatal intersections of the city of New York and enduring the hostile barbs of a weary wit, and is to be commended with the highest honors that the New York Sunday World Magazine *in its infinite wisdom can bestow.*

O. Henry

He reads the words aloud, then rolls the paper into a cylinder and presses it into the boy's hand. "And now clear out, young man, so that my muse and I may have our whiskey in peace!"

Looking utterly defeated, the boy lets out a sigh and leaves.

"If that kid has any sense—" begins the barman.

"Which he hasn't," says Porter.

"He'll keep that scrap of paper and frame it. Be worth something someday."

"It's worth almost two and a half dollars right now, if you figure four cents a word."

The barman hands the whiskey to the waiter. "This one's on me, Mr. Porter, for making me laugh. Glad to see the wee fellow cheered you up a bit. You've been looking a mite mopey ever since you came in."

"Have I? Can't imagine why." A shadow falls across Porter's face. The barman senses the change and resumes drying glasses.

Porter accepts the whiskey from the waiter, takes a sip and stares at the blank tablet. He glances up and notices that a customer at the bar is looking at him. It seems to him that he saw the same fellow standing across the street from 55 Irving Place when he left his room earlier that afternoon. A simple coincidence, he thinks.

He takes up his pencil and begins to sketch the man. The fellow's long

face, narrow lips, and high cheekbones lend themselves readily to caricature. He wears a tight-fitting, long black coat that makes him look very tall
and narrow, even seated on a barstool. He must be at least sixty years old,
but he sits very upright. A shock of white hair is swept back from his face in
the style of Paderewski, the famous conductor. He has a distinguished air,
but his shoes are scruffy. He has with him a bulging, brown leather satchel.
He seems out of place at Pete's Tavern.

Porter finishes the drawing and looks out the big picture window at the
front of the tavern. He notices a young man in a pin-striped suit on the far
side of the street, trying to cross. The young man steps off the curb and then
leaps back to avoid an oncoming automobile, looking flustered.

"Oh, no," Porter mutters under his breath, "not another one." The young
man is an editorial assistant at *Munsey's*, where he has another story overdue. His habits, he decides, are entirely too well known; he will have to find
some other establishment to patronize, unknown to his editors—if such a
place exists in Manhattan.

He slips out of the booth, leaving the paper and pencil and the empty
whiskey glass behind. The barman gives him a quizzical look.

"Tell this one that I was suddenly called away. To a funeral. In some
other state."

He hurries up the long, steep flight of stairs at the back of the room.
There are a number of doors off the hallway on the second floor, most of
them locked. He pokes about until he finds an open door to what appears to
be a meeting room. He sits in the nearest chair, wondering how long he
should wait before heading back downstairs.

Suddenly, in a flash, the elements for a story come to him: an office boy
sent to look for someone . . . a millionaire industrialist hiding incognito in a
tavern . . . an Irish barman . . . a stranger sitting at the bar. Where are his pencil and paper? He curses himself for leaving them behind. If he had them, he
could set to work here and now. He crosses his arms and legs and taps the air
with his foot, staring into space, his imagination suddenly at full throttle.

Then, faintly but unmistakably, he hears footsteps on the stairway. He
looks about the room. There is no possible place to hide; even if there were,
would he really want to be discovered by an editorial assistant, hiding himself as if he were . . .

A criminal.

Suddenly the story forming in his head seems ludicrous, too hackneyed
and contrived even for the readers of the *World*. Everything is ludicrous—
his writing career and the tiny morsel of fame it's brought him; the veil of

secrecy he so desperately struggles to keep drawn over his past; his daughter growing up a virtual stranger; his constant scramble for money. And now the blackmailer from his past, determined to pose a constant threat . . .

The footsteps reach the top of the stairs, then turn into the hallway. Every so often they pause and he hears doorknobs rattle; the man is trying the same doors he tried and found locked. Perhaps the man will be discouraged easily and turn back. However, if Porter's experience with editorial assistants is any indication, that is highly unlikely.

He crosses his arms and legs a bit more tightly and taps the air ferociously, awaiting the inevitable.

The footsteps arrive at the open door. A face peers around the corner— not the man from *Munsey's*, but the stranger who was sitting on the barstool earlier, looking at him.

They regard each other for a moment. Finally the stranger speaks. "That young fellow who came looking for you is gone. The bartender told him you had left, and the fellow believed him." The stranger's diction is very precise, with an almost imperceptible accent—German, Porter thinks.

"I see," Porter says, feeling ridiculous. The absurdity of the situation only deepens the blackness of his mood.

The stranger steps into the room. In one hand he carries his brown leather satchel. With the other he holds up the sketch Porter made. "You left this behind."

Seeing the subject and the caricature side by side, Porter laughs in spite of himself. "Not a very good portrait of you, I'm afraid. Certainly not very flattering."

"On the contrary, I think it is quite excellent. May I keep it? I have a fondness for such memorabilia."

"Certainly."

The man unlatches his satchel and carefully slips the paper inside. "You are, of course, Mr. Porter. Mr. William Sydney Porter. You write stories under the name O. Henry."

"I suppose there's no use denying it."

"Then I am very pleased to meet you, Mr. Porter. My name is Kringel. Dr. Kringel."

"And which magazine do *you* work for?"

The man looks surprised, then registers a smile as faint as his accent. "You've made a joke."

"I hope."

"Curiously enough, I *am* engaged in the field of publishing, though the journal I edit is not nearly so popular as the magazines where your own writing appears. Have you ever heard of *The Monist?*"

"Can't say that I have. Is that a Wall Street paper?"

The man laughs. "For better or worse, monism has nothing to do with money. Monism is a philosophical doctrine; from the Greek *mono*, meaning 'singular.' We monists hold that all reality is one organic whole without independent parts, that animate and inanimate matter spring from the same unifying principle, that there is really no difference between mind and matter. *The Monist* is our journal. It is rather more esoteric than the *World*, to be sure, but I can assure you that it is highly respected among scholars."

"I see. Tell me something, Herr Doctor: did I see you across the street from 55 Irving Place earlier today?"

The man looks chagrined. "Perhaps."

"And is it an accident that we both happen to have ended up here at Pete's Tavern?"

"Within the principles of monism, Mr. Porter, there is no such thing as an accident."

Porter sighs. "Dr. Kringel, I'm flattered, of course, but I can't possibly commit to writing something for your journal. At the moment, as you may have figured out, I'm spread pretty thin."

Kringel laughs. "Oh, Mr. Porter, no, no, no. Though I may someday ask you to write something, it would never be for *The Monist.*"

Porter raises an eyebrow at the man's condescending tone. "Then why did you follow me here?"

"I needed to talk to you."

"Why didn't you just introduce yourself on the street, or downstairs?"

"To be perfectly honest, Mr. Porter, I found the prospect of meeting you somewhat . . . intimidating."

"Intimidating?"

"O. Henry is perhaps more famous than you realize. For a man like myself, who labors in relative obscurity, to press himself on a man such as yourself, whom thousands upon thousands read every week—the prospect presents a certain challenge to the ego. And of course I wanted to make sure that you were indeed the William Sydney Porter, formerly of Texas, who is also known as O. Henry."

The mention of Texas makes Porter uneasy. "Why is the connection important?"

"Because I have a message for you, from an old, old acquaintance in Texas. He thought, but was not sure, that you had become—that is to say, were one and the same as—the famous New York writer O. Henry. Now I know for certain—or as certainly as a philosopher can—that you are the man I seek."

"An old acquaintance—from Texas, you say?" Once more, he mentally searches for a means of escape. Why is Texas haunting him today? His nightmare about the statue, blackmail before breakfast (now there, he thinks, is a title for a story: "Blackmail Before Breakfast"), and now this. Porter is not a believer in premonitions and portents, but he is a great re-specter of coincidence. "Who is this old acquaintance of mine?"

"He asked me to emphasize the word acquaintance, and not some other—confidant, intimate, colleague, or for that matter, friend. He says that the two of you met only once. Still, he thought you might remember him."

"What's his name?"

"Dr. Edmund Montgomery."

The name means nothing to Porter. Of course, such a common name could easily have slipped his memory . . .

Dr. Kringel reads his expression and is ready with more details. "Dr. Montgomery is an old Scotsman, though he's been in Texas for many years. A philosopher, like myself; we correspond, and I publish his monographs in *The Monist*. A brilliant mind, extraordinarily penetrating. Dr. Montgomery comprehends the relationship between animate and inanimate matter more fully than any other man I know."

Vague memories stir in Porter's head. "Keep going."

"You didn't meet him in Austin, but rather at his estate down in Hemp-stead. His plantation is called Liendo—"

"Ah, yes!" A memory springs to life. Porter sees a great white house sur-rounded by acres of woodlands and fields. The house is a mansion with stately columns and wide verandahs, but ramshackle and run-down, like a ghostly dream of the antebellum world that was dead before Porter was born. But who lives in the house? He tries to see faces, but cannot. It was all so long ago—even longer ago than the day he walked across the capitol grounds with Dave Shoemaker. "Keep going."

"Perhaps your memory of Dr. Montgomery's wife will be clearer. In many ways she is as extraordinary as her husband. German by birth, like myself. An artist, somewhat eccentric in her habits and dress. She kept her own name, despite her marriage, and so is still known to this day not as Mrs. Montgomery but as Elisabet Ney."

More memories stir to life. It is one of the peculiar side effects of growing older, he has discovered, to feel the fitful sparkings of ancient memories in his head—a teasingly evanescent sensation, like the tickle of champagne bubbles on the nose, or the intermittent flashing of fireflies on a summer night.

"Elisabet Ney," he says quietly. "A sculptress, wasn't she?"

The philosopher nods. "So you *do* remember?"

"Vaguely, vaguely." There was a train trip he took to Hempstead, with— Dave Shoemaker, of all people! They went to Liendo; they met Dr. Montgomery and his wife, Elisabet Ney. But what was the occasion? Something to do with Dave's newspaper work, probably, but he cannot for the life of him remember. Nor can he imagine why Montgomery would want to contact him again after so many years.

"Montgomery and Ney," he mutters. "Do they still live at Liendo?"

"Yes."

"I see. And is it common knowledge in that part of the world that I'm living in New York nowadays and writing under the name O. Henry?"

Kringel smiles and shrugs. "I couldn't say. But Dr. Montgomery knows all sorts of things that no one else seems to know." He taps his forehead. "He possesses great powers of deduction."

"A regular Shamrock Jolnes," quips Porter.

"I beg your pardon?" Kringel looks at him blankly.

"No, I beg yours, for indulging an author's vanity. I refer to one of my own creations, a parody of a certain literary sleuth. I don't suppose you happened to catch my story 'The Adventures of Shamrock Jolnes' in the *World*?"

"No, I'm afraid not."

"Just as well. So tell me, why have you, of all people, Herr Doctor, come here to Pete's Tavern to bring me a message from someone I barely remember from Texas?"

"I've sought you out purely as a favor to my colleague Dr. Montgomery. You see, by some means or other he learned of your whereabouts, and also that you were the man behind that famous *nom de plume*. I suppose I must be his closest contact here in New York. So he wrote to me, and asked that I should deliver his message to you in person. I could hardly refuse to grant such a small favor to such a great intellect, despite my initial trepidation."

"Trepidation?"

"It seems silly now, sitting here and talking to such an agreeable person as yourself, but I was a bit shy of imposing myself on you. Writers are only flesh and blood, of course, and I have known many, putting out *The Monist* as I do, but those men are primarily scholars and scientists, not—how shall I put it?—not Writers with a capital W, if you see what I mean."

"You're apt to give a fellow a swelled head," says Porter with a laugh, enjoying the moment. After the jolts of the day, his ego could use a bit of balm.

Kringel smiles. "In the same letter, Dr. Montgomery issued an invitation to visit him at Liendo. For myself, I must say that I am eager for the chance to finally meet him in the flesh; we are both growing old, and may never have such an opportunity again. And I have never been to Texas, which I should like to see. I have already made arrangements for the trip. The train will leave tomorrow morning."

"Then bon voyage, Herr Doctor. But you said that Montgomery sent a message for me. What on earth was it?"

"It was very brief and quite mysterious, at least to me. Here, I'll let you read it for yourself."

Kringel pulls a letter from his satchel and hands it to Porter. The letter is on printed stationery, with *Liendo Plantation* in handsome type at the top. Below that there is a date, and then the salutation, "My dear Herr Dr. Kringel," in a crabbed, stylized handwriting that was clearly learned in some ancient European academy, not at an American public school, where any child would have been rewarded with bruised knuckles for such penmanship; Porter finds it difficult to read. He scans the first paragraph, the content of which seems bland enough, inquiring as it does after the state of Kringel's health and alluding to mutual acquaintances, none of whom are known to Porter. Then he comes to the part about himself. Just as Kringel said, Montgomery tells his colleague of Porter's identity as O. Henry, and asks his colleague to seek him out.

Remind him, please, of our acquaintance, scant as it may have been and long ago (we were not intimates, confidants, or colleagues, not even friends, but bare acquaintances). See if you can refresh his memory with some details of my history and circumstances, but even if he fails to remember me, proceed to tell him that I believe I have come upon the solution to an old mystery. Say that I have discovered the person guilty of a most revolting crime, or rather a series of revolting crimes—I refer to those murders of young women in the city of Austin which began in the last days of the year 1884 and ended with the horrors of Christmas Eve, 1885, the responsibility for which crimes was never satisfactorily established, or not, at least, until now. (The details of my discovery are such that I cannot explain them here, but must deliver them in person.) If Mr. Porter's memory of those events of twenty years ago is hazy, or altogether blank, then mention to him the name . . .

Porter's mouth goes dry. The letter seems to come alive and tremble. He sees spots before his eyes, but through the spots he still sees the words on the paper:

> *. . . then mention to him the name* Eula Phillips. *I think he will surely remember her.*

The dream of the morning comes back to him with uncanny clarity. The dismembered goddess turns to flesh before his eyes, and her face is the most beautiful he has ever seen, and he speaks her name: *Eula*, from the Greek word for "good" . . .

"Mr. Porter, are you unwell?"

He does not quite hear the man, and looks up at him dumbly.

"Mr. Porter, you look distressed."

"No. No, it's only . . . only that this has been a very strange day. Very strange indeed."

"I'm sorry if there's something in the letter that's upset you."

"The letter is . . . of great interest to me. But it's a . . . great surprise. Completely unexpected." He gnaws at his lower lip. "You'll be seeing Dr. Montgomery soon, then? I suppose I should give you a reply to take to him . . ."

"A reply, Mr. Porter? Would you not prefer to deliver it yourself?"

"Myself? What, go to Texas?"

"Did you not finish reading the letter? Did I misspeak when I told you about Dr. Montgomery's invitation? It was extended to me, yes, but also to you. Dr. Montgomery wishes for you to come and see him at Liendo. He has wired money enough to pay for all your traveling expenses. As I said, I have booked accommodations on a train that leaves in the morning— accommodations for two. We shall travel to Texas together, you and I!"

As the day wanes and the shadows cast by the fifteen-story skyscrapers grow long, he walks south down Broadway in an agony of indecision.

He cannot possibly leave town on a sudden whim. He has deadlines to meet. He could claim a family emergency—say that his daughter has taken ill, that he must run off to Pittsburgh at once—but that sort of lie is always found out in the end. On the other hand, to disappear without any explanation to his editors would look even worse.

And what if the blackmailer returns, and discovers that he's suddenly left town? In such a circumstance, he tells himself, it would make no sense for her to make good on her threat to expose his past—but who knows how such a desperate, cruel-hearted creature might react?

Besides these practical considerations, there is the fundamental impossibility of ever returning to Texas, and especially to Austin. When he remembers the sweetness of his youth there, and how bitterly it ended, it breaks his heart. He lost everything in Texas: his wife, the wonder of seeing his little girl grow up, his dignity, his reputation, his freedom. He left the state a convicted criminal, in utter disgrace, a pariah to all who had known him. In New York, he has remade himself. He has become, by virtue of O. Henry, another man. He can never go back.

Everything is against the trip that Dr. Kringel has arranged. Off to Texas in the morning, indeed! There is no possible reason for him to entertain such a wild notion, not even for a moment, and every reason against it. Except . . .

Except for the mention of a certain name in Dr. Montgomery's letter. Had that name not been there, he could simply have folded the letter, returned it to Kringel with a bland smile, and said, "No thank you."

But the name was there. He even brushed his fingertips across the ink, to make sure he was not imagining it.

He is not a believer in dreams or portents. He puts no stock in intuitions or premonitions; even without such fanciful notions, life offers quite enough irony and confusion. But what does it mean, that he dreamed of Eula Phillips that very morning, jumbled though her image may have been, and on that very same day the blackmailer came—who knew Eula far better than he ever did—and then, within hours, he received a message from a man he has all but forgotten who claims to have some fresh solution to the mystery of Eula's death? Why do the day's events seem bent on haunting him with memories of Texas, and of her?

The day-to-day pressures of life have worn his nerves raw, he tells himself. Men under pressure jump at shadows, see faces in handfuls of dust, hear voices in the wind. He should be trying to think of a fresh plot, not looking for answers from the ether.

He reaches the foot of the island. Completely unexpected, a sign looms up before him. He could hardly miss her, standing as she does all alone out in the water, towering above the tugboats and steamers, her afternoon shadow lying long on the waves. She is the great incarnation of Liberty, holding up a torch for all the world to see.

What is it that her sister statue atop the capitol dome in Texas holds in her upraised hand? A star, a scythe, a torch? For the life of him, he cannot recall. The question nags—yes, nags at him quite intolerably.

He sighs, and blinks, and is suddenly at peace. His course of action is obvious: he must go and see for himself. In the morning, come hell or high water, he shall be on that train to Texas.

PART ONE

BLOODY

WORK!

Austin: December 1884 to January 1885

1

WILLIAM Pendleton Gaines, publisher and editor of the Austin *Statesman*, took a sip of scalding coffee and stepped onto his balcony.

The *Statesman's* editorial offices were located a block west of Congress Avenue in a grand, three-storied structure that might have passed for a Venetian palazzo. Gaines's penthouse office had tall windows on three sides and a door that opened onto a long, south-facing balcony. On days when the weather permitted—and Tuesday, December 30, 1884, was such a day, chilly but windless, with a clear blue sky—he liked to step outside and peer over the stone balustrade at the traffic down on Pecan Street. In summer, the dust and the smell of dung could be oppressive, notwithstanding the regular rounds of the mule-drawn street sprinklers. But on a still midwinter day such as this, the balcony was his favorite spot, as long as he had a steaming cup of coffee to keep him warm.

He stepped to the eastern end of the balcony and surveyed the skyline formed by the two- and three-story buildings along Congress Avenue. To the north, six blocks away at the head of the Avenue, rose the hill where construction of the new capitol building was set to commence in the spring. To the south, another six blocks away, he could just glimpse the topmost girders of the steel-canopied bridge across the Colorado River.

Midway between the capitol grounds and the river, Pecan Street crossed Congress Avenue at the busiest intersection in Texas. Both streets were lined with banks, hotels, tailors, stables, business offices, restaurants, and shops. Mule-drawn streetcars ran on glittering steel tracks laid into the packed earth, clanging their bells at each intersection. Horse-drawn hackney cabs and wagons clopped back and forth in a constant parade. Men in hats and coats and women in dresses with long skirts, cinched waists, and exaggerated shoulders strolled along the cement sidewalks elevated above the muck of the open street.

From his coign of vantage, Gaines viewed this vibrant prospect with a newspaperman's sense of possession. This was his town. He was its chronicler. He took a sip of scalding black coffee and felt the kind of deep satisfaction that other men got from looking at a favorite child, or a beautiful mistress, or a painting they had just purchased. This moment was a sort of apogee, he thought. Or was apotheosis the proper word? Whichever, life could scarcely get better than this.

His life had always been one of privilege. His father, who was now in his seventies, had been a great antebellum planter, growing sugarcane and cotton on vast tracts of the finest bottom land in Brazoria County. Gaines Senior had been a military hero as well, of both the Texas War for Independence and the Mexican War. When the Civil War began, Gaines Senior had been too old to serve and Gaines Junior too young. After the war, young Gaines was sent North, to a college in Pennsylvania for an expensive education in the classics. The students at Lafayette, reading the *Bellum Civilae*, argued almost as passionately about Pompey and Caesar as their fathers did about Grant and Lee, and Actium sometimes seemed as close to Gaines as Appomattox. "Unlike Father, I was born to be a wordsman, not a swordsman," he would say. He delighted in anagrams and could still, every now and then, pull off a sharp pun in Latin.

William Pendleton Gaines had been born to wealth without ever working a day. He had been raised in the reflected glow of his father's military glory without ever firing a shot. He had glimpsed the death throes of a society based on slavery and been educated in the values of another slave society dead for two thousand years. His was an elitist's upbringing, through and through. He had an elitist's means as well, being the sole heir (by right of surviving four siblings) to the family fortune.

When his father retired, Gaines delegated the day-to-day operations of the sugar and cotton plantations to his various foremen. With the profits, he pursued his own interests. He practiced law for a while, but his real desire was to own a newspaper. In 1882, at the age of thirty, he acquired the *Statesman*. After two years of successful operation, he felt he had already put his mark on the city, and was destined to make an even greater mark.

The year 1884 had been especially good for William Pendleton Gaines.

As befitted his rising social stature, he had moved into one of the finest houses in Austin, a stone aerie perched on a steep hillside just a short stroll west of his office. The house was named Bellevue, for its sweeping views south toward the river. There Gaines and his new bride, Augusta, had entertained Governor Ireland and Mayor Robertson, railroad builders and cattlemen, society ladies and professors from the new university. As editor of the leading newspaper in Austin, arguably the leading paper in the state, he was sought after by people from every walk of life, from glamorous actresses in touring plays to aspiring politicians, from local saloonkeepers eager to keep his office stocked with the finest whiskey, to temperance preachers eager to see their eloquent denunciations of liquor quoted in his columns.

Amid all this richness had come a gift that eclipsed them all. Four days ago, on Christmas morning, Augusta had given him the glorious news that she was expecting a child. From his office balcony above Pecan Street, Gaines looked out over the city of twenty thousand souls whose stories were his to tell, the city where his first child would be born, and felt a satisfaction that was surely as complete as any man could feel.

All this, and he was only thirty-three!

Gaines sipped the last of the coffee from his cup, then set it down on the wide balustrade and clapped his hands together, partly to keep them warm, but chiefly in anticipation. He pulled the gold pocket watch from his waistcoat, glanced for an instant at the beautifully engraved hunting scene on the cover, then flipped it open. The time was three minutes to eleven. His new business partners would be arriving at any moment.

He snapped the watch cover shut. The clicking seemed almost to act as a cue, for at that moment there was a sharp knock at the door to his office. He stepped from the balcony into the high, wood-paneled room suffused with winter light and elegantly furnished with an enormous mahogany desk, Chippendale chairs, and a cretonne sofa.

"Enter!" he called.

The door swung open, catching a bit on the deeply piled oriental carpet. It was one of the printer's devils, as apprentices were called in the publishing business, a red-haired boy named Tommy. Gaines had nicknamed him Mephistopheles. "Mr. Gaines, there's a couple of men to see you."

Gaines caught a glimpse of them in the anteroom beyond. "Dr. Terry! Dr. Fry! Come in! There's a stand by the door for your hats and overcoats. Would you care for coffee, gentlemen? I take it sweet—the sugar comes from cane grown on one of my own plantations on the Brazos River. No coffee, for either of you? Then run along, Mephistopheles, and get back to work! Now tell me, gentlemen, how have you enjoyed spending Christmas week here in Austin? Rather a milder climate than New Jersey, I'll wager!"

The two visitors made a curious pair. Dr. Terry was a thickly built man of about forty. He had big, meaty hands and quite possibly the largest head of any man Gaines had ever met. He wore pince-nez glasses and had a wide, bristling mustache. In the flesh, he looked exactly like his portrait on the labels of Dr. Terry's Liver Tonic and Ginger Aperient.

His companion, Dr. Fry, was a tall, narrow man with bony fingers and a long face. His jaw was clean-shaven but he wore large sideburns, which were more salted with gray than the flowing locks swept back from his high forehead. He reminded Gaines of the professor at Lafayette who had taught him Latin, but there was also something about the man that suggested an undertaker. In fact, Dr. Fry was neither a mortician nor a scholar, nor strictly speaking, so far as Gaines could ascertain, a medical man—imagine being treated by a blind doctor! In deference to this handicap, Fry concealed his eyes behind rectangular, cobalt-blue spectacles and carried a long thin cane for tapping his way. Like Dr. Terry, he looked in the flesh exactly like the image of himself which appeared in familiar newspaper advertisements for Dr. Fry, the Blind Phrenologist.

"Dr. Fry and myself have had a delightful week," said Dr. Terry. "We can only hope that the weather will continue to be as outstanding for the remaining week of our stay here. I shudder to think of what the snowstorms must be like back in New Jersey."

"Indeed, gentlemen, Austin is famous for its mild climate, as all the brochures will tell you." Gaines tried not to smile at Terry's outrageous Yankee accent; Gaines had not heard vowels so cruelly truncated since his college days up North. Dr. Fry, he had noticed, almost never spoke, but when he did there was a hint of a foreign accent.

"Gentlemen, if you have no desire for coffee, then can I offer you a stronger refreshment? It's a bit early in the day, but we do have something to celebrate." Gaines led them to a sideboard stocked with various liquors. He was especially proud of the whiskey, which was imported from Ireland. Gaines handed an empty glass to Terry, then hesitated, not sure how to offer one to Fry. Terry did it for him, taking the second glass and gently pressing it into his companion's hand. Gaines poured each of them a splash of whiskey, then offered a toast. "To the continuing success of Dr. Terry's miraculous tonic."

"And to the health of the people of Austin," responded Dr. Terry. "May they never suffer from catarrh of the bladder, weak spots in the liver, or de-

rangement of the kidneys. May they avoid the torments of female inflammation, manhood failure, stinging urination, spastic flatulence . . ." There
followed a long litany of human ills, until Dr. Terry finally concluded,
"May the good people of Austin be delivered from all these plagues—by
which I mean to say, may they have the good sense to treat themselves and
their loved ones at the first signs of distress to a course of treatment with Dr.
Terry's Liver Tonic and Ginger Aperient."

"Here, here!" said Gaines, and the three men emptied their glasses in
unison.

"And now, gentlemen," said Gaines, "to business. I presume you've had
time to read the final draft of the contract I sent to your hotel room yesterday?"

"Yes, Mr. Gaines. Dr. Fry and myself have reviewed all the stipulations,
and we see no further impediments."

The agreement was fairly straightforward. The *Statesman* would supply
free advertising space for Dr. Terry's tonic. Persons interested in purchasing
the tonic would be advised to mail or deliver their prepaid orders to the
Statesman office. Gaines in turn would send batches of orders (and a portion of the payments, retaining his share up front) to the tonic manufactory
in New Jersey, which would fulfill the orders and ship crates of bottled medicine to the *Statesman* for disbursement to the individual buyers. The
Statesman would also publish free announcements whenever Dr. Terry or
Dr. Fry happened to be traveling in the region and available for private con-
sultations. Besides questions of advertising space and guarantees of delivery,
the chief point to be negotiated had been the percentage of gross receipts to
be claimed by each party.

Terry and the taciturn Fry had been traveling by train for the last three
months, going from city to city and newspaper to newspaper setting up similar arrangements for the distribution of their tonic across the South. Pub-
lishers, they had found, were not always shrewd businessmen. Gaines,
despite a bit of haggling, had finally been willing to accept what they considered a minimal share of receipts.

"Well, then," said Gaines, "if we're ready to proceed, I'll send for a notary."

"Actually, there is *one* more point," said Terry, his tone almost apologetic.

"Yes?"

"A small point, but one which Dr. Fry insists upon. He has required it of
all the partners we have acquired across the country in our little enterprise."

Gaines raised an eyebrow. "If you're looking for a secret handshake, I should tell you right now that I'm neither a Mason, a Knight of Honor, nor an Odd Fellow."

"Oh, no, Mr. Gaines, it's nothing like that. Dr. Fry would simply like to examine your head."

Gaines looked from Terry to the blind phrenologist, who still had not said a word. Behind his dark blue glasses, the man's face betrayed no expression. "Examine my head? Ah, I see. Well, I suppose . . ."

Fry spoke at last. "Do you know very much about phrenology, Mr. Gaines?"

Gaines smiled. "Not much more than I've read in your own advertisements, I'm sorry to say."

"Phrenology is the science of reading a man's character by studying the shape of his head," said Fry. What *was* the faint trace of an accent in his voice? German, Gaines thought, and wondered if the name Fry had originally been Frei-something.

"How does a man judge the character of a new acquaintance?" continued Fry. "How do *you* judge whether to trust a fellow or not, Mr. Gaines? By looking into his eyes! The eyes are the window of the soul, the philosophers say. But I, alas, am at a certain disadvantage. I am unable to see you, Mr. Gaines; I cannot look into your eyes. Still, as a businessman, I should like—how to put it?—to take your measure. The best way for me to do that is to call upon my phrenological skills." As he spoke he flexed his hands and pulled at each of his fingers in turn, to limber them.

"Well, of course, when you put it that way," said Gaines, though he was not entirely comfortable with the idea. His first impulse was to decline such an odd request, but Terry had stated the stipulation quite emphatically. He thought of all the money to be made from sales of Dr. Terry's tonic, and shrugged. "What exactly does the examination require? How shall we proceed?"

"Just take a seat, wherever you are most comfortable," said Dr. Fry.

Gaines sat in the swivel chair behind his desk. Led by Terry, Fry circled behind him. A moment later, Gaines felt cold fingertips on the bald spot at the crown of his head. He shivered a little. "I'll try not to squirm. Rather like sitting for a shave at the barber's. Or being stuck in a dentist's chair!"

"Oh, not as bad as that, I assure you," said Dr. Fry soothingly. Dr. Terry remained behind the desk, out of sight. Gaines felt slightly ridiculous, sitting stock-still and staring at the tall windows across the room while a man he hardly knew commenced to knead the plains and ridges of his skull. Having a phrenologist run his cold, bony fingers over your head was a bit like disrobing before the steady gaze of a physician, he decided—it made a man feel rather naked, despite the professional decorum. Gaines actually felt himself blush, and wondered if Fry could feel the heat from his bald spot; the blind were said to have wondrous sensitivities in their fingertips.

The whole procedure was a little insulting, Gaines decided, as if his new business partners suspected him of some terrible character flaw and intended to discover it. Gaines was a gentleman, a Southern gentleman, and above all a Texan; what right had a Yankee doctor and a foreign head-reader to ask him to submit to a character examination?

As Fry's searching fingers crept down his forehead, tracing the ridge of his eyebrows with a butterfly touch, Gaines gave an involuntary shudder. He tried to calm his fidgeting by telling himself that the man's excuse for wanting the examination was perfectly reasonable, under the circumstances. Gaines had no faith in phrenology, but he was not particularly skeptical, either. If it was nothing but balderdash, like palmistry, then there was no harm in humoring the fellow. If it was a genuine science, what could it reveal about Gaines that he was not perfectly willing for his partners to know? He had nothing to hide. Even so, it was rather disconcerting to think that another man, a virtual stranger, might be able to read his character, which was practically the same as reading his thoughts, simply by laying hands on his skull.

Dr. Fry lifted his fingers away, and Gaines thought he was done. Then he felt the man close behind him, breathing on his bald spot, and felt the man's open hands cover his face, including his eyes, as if Fry were a sculptor and Gaines were made of clay.

At that moment there was a sharp rap at the office door. Tommy, the printer's devil, not waiting for an answer, stepped inside. "Mr. Gaines! The typesetter says—" Tommy stopped short, startled by the sight of his boss being handled in such a curious fashion by the strange man in cobalt glasses.

"Mephistopheles? What? Confound it!" Gaines shook his head and started forward in his chair, swiveling free of Dr. Fry, who snapped his hands away. Gaines blinked and scowled.

Tommy covered his mouth, suppressing an urge to laugh. Gaines's short, pomaded hair, kneaded by Dr. Fry, stood up in raggedy points.

"Get out, young man! Don't you know better than to bother me when I'm in a meeting?"

"But Mr. Gaines," said Dr. Terry, leading Dr. Fry to the center of the room, "surely you'll be wanting the young man to go fetch the notary for us?"

"What's that?"

"So that we can sign the contract."

"The contract? Yes, well, if Dr. Fry is satisfied . . ."

Dr. Fry, inscrutable behind his dark glasses, simply nodded.

"Yes, well then—don't just stand there gawking, Mephistopheles! Go fetch a notary!"

"Yes, sir!"

Gaines ran a hand over his head, smoothing his disarrayed hair into place. His head felt perfectly normal to him. He noticed no unusual bumps or ridges, nothing that could be called an irregularity. What could a phrenologist's hand detect that his could not? "You *are* satisfied, then, Dr. Fry?"

Dr. Fry nodded again. Gaines stared at him, then realized the futility of doing so.

"Did you find anything . . . unusual?" said Gaines at last.

"No," said Fry.

"Anything unexpected?"

"Not at all."

The situation was exasperating. Having submitted to the man's examination, surely Gaines deserved to be told the results, yet Fry seemed disinclined to elaborate.

"Well, then," said Gaines, trying to make light of it, "I've got a good head on my shoulders, have I?"

Once again, Dr. Fry merely nodded.

At length the notary arrived. The copies of the contract were laid out on Gaines's desk. A pen and inkwell were produced, and one by one the document was signed with the names William Pendleton Gaines, Ephraim Ebenezer Terry, M.D., and Frederick Augustus Fry, Ph.D.

2

A L E C Mack had nowhere particular to be that day.

Actually, he had nowhere to be the next day, or the day after that, or for the rest of his no-doubt short and miserable life for that matter, not unless 1885 was set to bring a big change in his luck. Last night, old man Sumpter had told him to move his sorry ass out of the shack in back of the Sumpter house and never come back. His job as Mr. Sumpter's runabout and handyman was over. And all because Alec had invited his new ladyfriend to come over for a visit.

Most white folk were reasonable enough with their help; a man, whatever his color, had certain needs. So did a woman. If a fellow should have a friend come over and visit for a bit behind closed doors, in the evening after his chores were done, it was nobody else's business. Old man Sumpter didn't own him; it wasn't like the old days, before Alec was born. Back then a white man could tell you when, where, and how much to piss when your pecker was soft, and where you could put it when the thing got hard. Alec shook his head and gazed at the tiny bubbles on the head of his beer, watching them pop one by one.

The bartender sauntered over. His name was Lem Brooks, Lem being short for William. Even though he wasn't much older than Alec, Lem didn't have a hair on his head. That shiny bald head plus a perfect set of pearly white teeth made him look like a grand piano when he smiled, which was most of the time. "Somethin' wrong with that beer, Alec?"

"Nope."

"Sure drinkin' slow."

"Gots to make it last."

"Plenty mo' where that come from."

"Cain't say the same about the nickel I just give you."

"What's the matter, old man Sumpter gettin' stingy?"

"In a manner of speakin'."

The Black Elephant was empty at the moment, except for Lem and Alec. In the middle of a Tuesday morning in the week between Christmas and New Year's, the white folk in Austin had plenty of work to keep the colored help busy, washing all the tablecloths and linens that had been soiled on Christmas Day, cleaning and shopping and fixing fancy meals for more visiting and more festivities to come. Alec himself would probably be chopping wood right that minute, or plucking another turkey for old lady Sumpter, if they hadn't run him off.

Mrs. Sumpter—she was the root of the problem. Always quoting from her Bible, always looking down her nose at him. She hated colored folk, and she wasn't the kind of woman to sympathize with a man's needs, not even her own man. No wonder old man Sumpter was always growling like a bad-tempered dog!

It was the old lady who caught them doing it, peering in through the little window of the shack. Alec had pulled the curtains shut, the way he always did, but the thin cotton panels were so tattered they didn't meet right, and anybody who made an effort could see in. Still, there would have been nothing to see if Alec had left the room dark, which normally he did. It was his new ladyfriend who wanted him to light the little oil lamp on the rickety table beside the bed. She said she wanted to look at him while they did it. Imagine that! And it was his ladyfriend who insisted, despite the cold, that they take off all their clothes to do it. She said they'd both work up enough of a sweat to forget the chill, and so they did. She looked at him and he looked at her the whole time. Remembering her face and the way the light had glanced across the sheen of sweat between her breasts gave him a shiver and made him feel a sweet ache between his legs.

But while they communed and looked at each other, someone else had been looking at them—old lady Sumpter. How long did she stand there, squinting and clucking her tongue, before she let out a whoop and screamed for her husband to come running? Alec and his ladyfriend pulled apart, not even finished yet and not sure what was happening.

They heard the sound of the screen door on the back porch slamming— the screen door Alec himself had put up the previous summer, and that

Mrs. Sumpter was so proud of, being the first in the neighborhood to own such a smart invention to keep the flies out. Then there was a heavy tread coming down the porch steps, followed by a fist banging on the thin door of the shack. The door had a lock of sorts—just a rectangle of wood nailed to the frame, not too tight, so that it could be pushed down to block the door. It wouldn't keep out a robber, but it was strong enough to keep visitors from barging in.

"Who's that?" Alec yelled.

"Open this door, Alec Mack!"

While his ladyfriend rushed to put on her dimity dress, Alec pulled on his trousers and shirt. He lifted the wooden block and opened the door. Old man Sumpter stood there holding his rifle. Old lady Sumpter was watching everything from the back porch steps, clutching her Bible like it was a brick she meant to throw at him.

"Somethin' wrong, Mistah Sumpter?"

The old man glowered at him. "My wife says you got a woman in there." There was no use denying it. The shack was too small to have a hiding place, and the lamp was still lit. Even with Alec's big frame blocking the door, Sumpter could see the lady standing at the far end of the little room, in the narrow space between the bed and the wall. "You know what I told you when I agreed to take you on here, Alec Mack. About fornication. What did I tell you?"

"You said . . ." Alec's mouth went dry.

"I said there'd be no such disgusting behavior taking place on my property. Why you people can't get married like decent folk, and control yourselves until you do, I'll never understand."

Alec gritted his teeth. "Mistah Sumpter, there was nothin' like that goin' on—"

"Don't lie to me, nigger! My wife saw you! Now gather up your things and get out of here. I won't have a lyin' fornicator living on my property."

"But Mistah Sumpter! There's a lot of work to be done around here. I's smack in the middle of replacing that section of fence—"

Mrs. Sumpter spoke up from the porch steps. "Always in the *middle* of your jobs, aren't you?" she said, a bitter, sarcastic edge to her voice.

Alec swallowed hard. "Mistah Sumpter, it's Christmas and holidays and all. Cain't you be forgivin'?"

The old man shook his head gravely. "Christmas indeed! You've besmirched the holy season with your behavior, and now you plead for Christian mercy. No, I will not have such degenerate activity on my property, taking place right in front of my wife. You see how you've agitated her? I mean what I say, Alec. Get out of here, and take that piece of trash with you. Right now!"

A voice called from the back porch of the house next door. "You having some trouble with your help over there, Mr. Sumpter?"

"Nothing I can't handle, Mr. Smith."

"You sure you don't need me to come over?"

"I'm sure, Mr. Smith."

"Well, you yell if you need me."

"I'll do that. Good night, now." Sumpter lowered his voice. "You hear that, Alec Mack? Are you happy? Shaming me in front of my neighbors! Not another word out of you! You gather up your things and get out of here, and don't ever come back."

Sumpter stood there watching, with the rifle in his hands, while Alec gathered up his few possessions in a small burlap bag he usually used for toting goods from market. There wasn't much—a second pair of pants and some socks, a leather pouch of chewing tobacco, his straight razor. From the corner of his eye he could see that his ladyfriend had started to cry softly. He would have gone to comfort her, but somehow he couldn't, not with old man Sumpter standing there watching everything and judging him. She put on her raggedy coat and he put on his and they left the little shack without saying a word.

A little away from the house Alec started to say something, but she cut him off.

"You cain't come to my place," she said, not looking at him. "I gots my little girl there. I never has a man in my place, never. The people I work for wouldn't like it, not any more than . . . than that ol' . . ."

She couldn't think of a word mean enough, and neither could he. They looked at each other and laughed.

"That's all right," he told her. "I'll get by."

"You got a place to go?"

He looked at the sliver of moon and the cold stars above. "My Mama lives over on the west side of town. Kiss me, woman."

The air around them and even the ground under their feet was cold, but her body felt warm. Back in her embrace, he didn't want to let go of her, but she finally pulled away. She ran off into the darkness without saying a word.

"Well," he said to himself, "I guess walkin' is one way to keep warm."

When he got to his mother's place, which faced an alley off Colorado Street, he spent a long time looking at the little unpainted house. It was even smaller than the shack he'd been living in. He didn't have the heart to wake her with such shameful news. Instead he just kept walking, up and down the streets of Austin, until he was too weary to go on and too sleepy to let the cold bother him. He fell asleep slouched against a tree in an empty field on the outskirts of town, with his burlap bag tucked over his feet to keep them warm.

When Tuesday dawned bright and cold, he went to Waller Creek on the east side of town to wash his face and hands, then bought himself a cheap breakfast at a colored eatery on East Pecan Street. After that he had nowhere to go, and ended up at the corner of Neches and Pecan, figuring a beer or two at the Black Elephant might go a long way to restoring his peace of mind.

"What the hell you doin' in here in the middle of the mornin', anyway?" said Lem, jarring him back to the present. "This be the time of day when I usually gets to take my standing-up nap."

"Go ahead. Don't let me stop you."

Lem shook his head. "You gone and got yourself run off from the Sumpter place, ain't you?"

"Looks like."

"I told you a couple of months back when you took that job, ol' man Sumpter was trouble. I ain't been in Austin long myself, but even I knows that sooner or later he runs off ever' colored man that works for him, then bad-mouths 'em to all the other white folks. What's he claimin', that you stole from him?"

"Never!" Alec slapped the bar, angry at the very thought. Then his face relaxed with a grin. "Had a ladyfriend over."

Lem put his hands on his hips and whistled. "Now don't tell me that ol' man Sumpter came sleepwalkin' into your room and caught you doing it!"

"Not zackly. Ol' lady Sumpter spied us through the window."

"She never!"

"She did, I swear to God."

"She was peepin' in your window? What time was this?"

"I don't know. After dark."

"Well, what the hell was she doin' looking in your room?"

"I don't know! Maybe she heard when my ladyfriend come in my door. Lord knows we kept quiet as mice."

"So what was the problem? The Sumpters just cain't stand the idea of colored folks makin' sugar?"

"I guess that's about it. He told me from the start not to have no ladies over, 'less I was to marry one, in which case he'd have to let me go, 'cause he wasn't gonna pay for two hired hands around the place."

"White folk!" Lem snorted. "Treat you like a barn animal, then 'spect you to behave like a Bible prophet. Who was this lady, anyway? Anybody I knows? Must have been pretty special to make you take the chance. How much you have to pay her?"

"Not a cent! I ain't never in my life paid a lady for pleasure."

Lem raised an eyebrow. He was used to hearing all kinds of lies on his side of the bar, but it was just possible that Alec was telling the truth. Alec was a big young buck, hardly more than twenty, with muscles in his limbs and chest that seemed always to be moving and stretching and about to come out of his threadbare clothes. He wasn't hard to look at either, with his wide, flat nose and his big innocent eyes, and the skin on his cheeks and forehead as smooth as a lady's black silk glove. All in all, as Lem's mother used to put it, Alec Mack was just the sort of candy box a choosy lady might pick off the shelf.

"Not a cent, huh?" said Lem. "Must be love, then."

"I don't know 'bout *that*." Alec made a face, but he remembered how she wanted to do it with the lamp burning, and the look in her eyes, and he wondered.

"So? What's the lady's name?"

Alec shook his head. "I never kisses and tells."

"You jus' want to keep her to yourself."

"Maybe."

"Well, don't worry 'bout *me* tryin' to steal her," said Lem. "I ain't even touched a woman since I moved to Austin. Livin' with Miss Mollie Smith back in Waco cured me of that cravin' for good." Lem clenched his perfect white teeth and shuddered like a dog shaking its coat. "I moved to Austin to get away from that woman, and damned if she ain't turned up here, over on the west side, cookin' and cleanin' for a Mr. Hall with a sickly wife. But I hear she gots a new manfriend, too, and that's a blessed relief. Lawdy, I'd move on to Dallas if I thought that crazy woman was after my bones!"

The tall, glass-paned front door opened with a gust of cold air. Alec, staring at the few bubbles that were still tadpoling upward in his glass, didn't take any notice of the newcomer until he glanced up and saw that Lem's face had gone grim. Alec looked over his shoulder and saw a tall figure silhouetted against the bright light from outside. The man's face was too shadowy to make out, but as he moved toward them, Alec could tell it was a white man just from the way he swaggered, slow and cocky. The door swung shut, and in the clearer light Alec saw that the man was wearing a city policeman's uniform—a long, blue serge jacket with gold braid at the cuffs, two rows of gold buttons down the front, and a badge with a star pinned on the breast. On his head was a round, flat-topped cap with gold braid across the base of the short brim, and a gold-embroidered emblem on the crest, composed of two laurel leaves framing the words CITY MARSHAL. Alec couldn't read. Lem could, but had no need to. He knew the man already.

Lem cleared his throat. "Good mornin', Marshal Lee."

"It's morning, Lem, but I'm not sure what's so good about it. I'm damned sick and tired of this cold weather. Pour me something to drink."

"You wants a beer, Marshal?"

The man snickered. "You ought to know by now that I never drink beer. Whiskey."

"Of course, Marshal, I knows that. A shot of the best whiskey in the house, sir, right away."

The marshal leaned against the bar a few feet from Alec. Alec glanced toward him and saw the man smirking at him, then looked at the bubbles in his beer again.

"Kind of chilly for a beer, ain't it?"

Alec fidgeted on his stool. "Cheaper than whiskey," he muttered.

"Wouldn't know. Never pay for the stuff myself." Before Lem could set the shot glass on the bar, Marshal Lee took it from him, threw it back and swallowed. He smacked his lips. "So, things staying pretty quiet around here, Lem?"

"See for yourself, Marshal Lee. Holiday season's a slow time at the Black Elephant."

"So what are you doing in here, boy?" The marshal turned his attention to Alec.

"Jus' havin' a beer."

The marshal nodded. "What sort of colored fellow sits around in a saloon drinking beer in the middle of the morning?"

"The man's a friend of mine, Marshal Lee," said Lem. "We was havin' a little talk, that's all. Woman trouble. You knows how it is."

"So what's your friend's name?"

Alec spoke up before Lem could. "My name's Alec Mack."

The marshal stared at him. "Alec Mack; I'll remember that. You heard what Lem called me. I'm the marshal. Part of my job is making sure that the decent people of this town aren't disturbed by what goes on in places like the Black Elephant. You don't ever cause trouble around here, do you?"

"I told you, Marshal Lee," said Lem. "Alec's a friend. He's a good 'un."

"Is he, now?" The marshal looked hard at Alec, and then at Lem. "I guess you'd know, Lem. You sure pour a good shot of whiskey."

"Always the best for you, Marshal Lee."

The marshal pushed himself from the bar and strode out of the saloon as cockily as he had come in. Alec glanced at Lem, who wouldn't meet his eyes.

A figure emerged from the storage room at the back of the bar. It was Hugh Hancock, the man who owned the Black Elephant and lived in the adjoining house out back. "What the hell was that about?"

"Mornin', Mr. Hancock," said Lem. "Jus' a visit from Marshal Lee."

"I could see that much." Hugh Hancock reached for a towel and started wiping off the bar, even though Lem had already cleaned it that morning. Hancock was a thin little man with white whiskers, and legs too short for the rest of him. He could never keep still. Lem found it comical sometimes, watching him scurry here and there on his bandy legs. But Hancock's nervous energy probably accounted for his success; not many black men owned their own business. Hugh Hancock was the first colored man Lem had ever worked for. It had spoiled him for working any other way.

"So what did the marshal want? Lookin' for somebody?"

"Lookin' for a free shot of whiskey, I figure."

"You give him the best?"

"I give him what you drink, Mr. H."

"Good. Las' thing I want is trouble from a ex-Ranger with a chip on his shoulder. That man's got a mean streak!"

Alec finished his beer. He didn't feel comfortable in the Black Elephant anymore. He stood up, a little light-headed, and made for the door.

"Take care of yourself," Lem called.

"You, too."

Alec stepped out onto Pecan Street, squinting at the bright, cold sunshine. He gave a start when he realized that Marshal Lee was only a few steps away. The man was leaning against the corner of the building with his arms folded and a smirk on his face.

"You know what I think?" said the marshal. "I think that a colored man with too much time on his hands is a fellow who's up to no good. I've got my eye on you, Alec Mack. You remember that."

Alec swallowed hard and walked on.

He wanted to think about something else, so he thought again about how his ladyfriend had looked at him last night, the way the lamplight had shimmered across her breasts and sparkled in her eyes, and the way she had said his name, silently shaping it with her lips and tongue. Out loud but only to himself, as if it were a secret that couldn't be shared, he whispered her name: "Rebecca. Miss Rebecca Ramey."

3

Got plans for tomorrow night, Will?" Dave Shoemaker put down his glass of whiskey and cut the end off a cigar with his pocketknife.

"For New Year's Eve?" Will Porter blew the head of foam off his beer, as was his habit to keep his mustache clean. Not every twenty-two-year-old could grow such a fine specimen of a mustache. To each side the ginger hair lay thick upon his upper lip, following the curve of his mouth to each corner before sweeping back above his cheeks and terminating in two painstakingly waxed and twisted points, gunfighter-style.

Will could hardly claim to be a gunfighter, though he didn't mind looking like one. He originally came from Greensboro, North Carolina, but at the age of nineteen, with a sickly disposition, his mother dead and his father of no account, he had been sent by his family to live with friends in South Texas, and entered his twenties on a ranch in rugged chaparral country. Will learned to ride horses, herd sheep, shoot jackrabbits, play poker, and speak cowboy Spanish. During the long days and nights on the range, he also read a great deal, for the family that took him in were bookish people with a substantial library. Will grew fond of Tennyson, and read a tattered copy of *Webster's Unabridged Dictionary* from cover to cover.

At twenty-one, in the spring of 1884, Will decided to leave the ranch for the city of Austin. He considered himself to be fairly well rounded, for a self-educated fellow. He could throw a lariat, quote from *Idylls of the King*, and grow an exceedingly fine mustache. Despite this résumé, once in Austin he had encountered some difficulties in earning a livelihood.

As a teenager back in Greensboro he had worked in his uncle's drugstore, where he did everything from running the soda fountain to dispensing prescriptions. His first attempt at gainful employment in Austin was a stint at Morley Brothers drugstore on East Pecan Street; but the Morleys rejected his informal qualifications as a pharmacist and took him on as a mere clerk. Making change for penny candy was tedious work after riding the range, and he quit after just two months.

Will at least had a place to stay, at a big boarding house up on Lavaca Street. It was run by Joe Harrell, another North Carolina connection who took him in out of pure kindness. After Will quit the clerking job at Morley Brothers, Mr. Harrell told him not to worry about paying rent, and said he could earn a little money working odd hours at his son's cigar store on Congress Avenue. Odd hours suited Will. When not studying beams of moving sunlight in his room, or aimlessly strolling the streets of Austin, or seeing how long he could made a beer last in some Guy Town saloon, he was able to devote adequate time to the care and grooming of his excellent mustache.

His occasional appearances behind the counter at the Harrell cigar store yielded little income but one great fringe benefit: his friendship with Dave Shoemaker. The store was near the corner of Congress and Pecan, just a short walk from the *Statesman* offices where Dave worked as a reporter. William Pendleton Gaines himself dropped in from time to time, though more often than not he sent one of his young printer's devils to fetch his purchases. Dave Shoemaker had acquired his boss's taste for fine Havanas, and one day when he dropped into the store, Will happened to be working. The two hit it off at once. They shared the same sense of humor, and they were both interested in the written word. Dave was only a couple of years older but seemed infinitely more experienced, at least to Will. He wrote for a living, and to hear him complain, hated every minute of it. Will thought being a writer must surely be the finest thing in the world, though so far his own literary endeavors had been limited to a few tall tales scribbled in notebooks, illustrated with his own sketches. These were exceedingly clever, at least in the estimation of everybody at Joe Harrell's boarding house.

The hour of twilight that Tuesday found Dave and Will sitting side by side at the bar of the Cabinet saloon, which was just across the street from the *Statesman* offices and a favorite haunt for the newspaper staff. Still flush with his Christmas bonus from Gaines, Dave had dropped by the cigar store after work to buy a couple of Havanas and found Will just finishing a shift behind the counter. The two of them headed for the Cabinet to start the evening.

"Tomorrow night is New Year's Eve," said Will thoughtfully. "Can it be

1885 already? Well, I thought I might use a small portion of my vast income to buy myself some fancy duds and go to the ball at the Governor's Mansion. All the right people will be there—university professors, cattle barons, captains of industry."

"And their eligible daughters," said Dave.

"Ah, yes, and their daughters." Will sipped his beer. Despite his precautions, a bit of stray foam got snagged in his mustache.

"I take it you have no plans for tomorrow night," said Dave dryly.

"Well, *if* that invitation from Governor Ireland *should* fail to arrive, I suppose there'll be something doing among the waifs at the boarding house. Joe Harrell might put out some fruit punch and ginger snaps. As long as they're free, that'll suit my budget. What about you?"

"Gaines has me working late tomorrow, to get out the New Year's Day edition. No holidays in the ink trade! Heaven knows there's bound to be a shooting or a brawl on New Year's Eve, and I've got to be on hand to write it up so people can chat about it over coffee on New Year's Day. Didn't I tell you? I'm the crime reporter now. My own special niche. Apparently, my shocking stories about confidence artists at the train depot caused such a stir that I now get to cover all the murders and mayhem in town. Gaines says I have a knack for the sensational."

"That's quite a compliment."

"It's quite an insult! I was born to be a poet. Instead—do you know what Schopenhauer called journalists? 'Professional alarmists and exaggerators.' I have a talent for exaggerating! And for alarming poor souls who are barely awake and only want a little breakfast and some coffee to start the day. I'm supposed to get their hearts racing. It's nothing to be proud of."

"This Schopenhauer fellow—does he write for the *Statesman?*"

Dave looked at his friend sidelong. It was sometimes hard to tell whether Will was joking or not. Of course there was no reason Will should know that Schopenhauer was a German philosopher, though he did seem to have read a lot of books. Dave let it pass.

"No New Year's Eve festivities for me," Dave said. "So I'm celebrating the end of 1884 twenty-four hours early. It's Guy Town for me tonight! Care to join me, Will?"

"I wish I could, Dave, but my only Christmas bonus was an offer to keep whatever loose tobacco they sweep off the floor of the cigar store this week. I don't think the natives in these parts still accept such stuff as currency."

"Then the evening shall be on me," said Dave.

"You're generous, Dave, but I couldn't accept—"

"Listen, I told you I got a fat bonus. Don't you know the good-luck rule for bachelors with a Christmas bonus? I mustn't enter the new year with a penny of it left in my pockets! You'll be doing me a favor, helping me get rid of it."

Will smiled. He sometimes wondered what it was about him that elicited such generosity from others, and whether it wasn't likely to spoil his character in the long run. It didn't seem right for a twenty-two-year-old man to be living off the kindness of friends, with no plan whatsoever of how to get ahead. Will's life in Austin, like the life he had enjoyed on the ranch, was pretty much one golden, lazy day after another, with the occasional interruption to do a few hours of work. Was something wrong with him that he liked it that way? Perhaps a man needed a mother to instill ambition in him, and a mother was what he'd never had. Maybe people could tell that Will was an orphan, and that was why they went out of their way to make his life easy.

Dave accepted his smile as acquiescence. "All right, then! First we'll have dinner. I'm in the mood for steak. Then we'll follow our noses to Guy Town."

They ate at Salge's Chop House, on the Avenue. The steaks were an inch thick, seared black on the outside and plump with blood inside, smothered with onions and served with mashed potatoes. Plentiful fresh meat was one of the advantages of living in cattle country.

Another particular advantage of living in Austin was the sheer number of saloons, far more than any man with a normal constitution could hope to patronize in a single night. Starting on the east side of the Avenue, Dave and Will decided to visit only their favorites. That meant a few minutes at the Mechanics Exchange on Brazos where Dave knew the owner's brother and could get their drinks for half price, followed by a hand of faro in the back room of the Bull's Head on East Pecan, which had a reputation for attracting innocents from out of town. Will sat the game out, having no money to wager, but Dave won enough to finance a round of drinks for the regulars at the bar. Such largesse was a career investment; as he had once explained to Will, "A reporter never knows who might be able to answer an important question someday. It behooves me to cultivate the widest possible circle of friends in the lowest possible places." Dave, though, had never been able to convince Mr. Gaines to pick up his bar bills and gambling debts as a business expense.

Eventually they boarded an empty streetcar headed west on Pecan Street.

The mule driver caught a whiff of their high spirits and laughed good-naturedly as they fumbled in their pockets to find nickels for the fare box. They spread out inside the streetcar, Dave sitting on one side and Will on the other.

Darkness had fallen, and a drop in air pressure hinted at the imminent arrival of cold winds from the north. The bustle of the day had died down. People who had a family to go home to—people unlike Dave and Will—had gone home already, seeking snugness and warmth. Carriages and pedestrians were so sparse that the streetcar driver didn't even bother to jangle his bell at the intersections. Will was glad that he didn't ring the bell. Perhaps the driver, too, sensed at such a desolate hour the strange peacefulness of the sound of the wheels turning against the steel tracks, and the steady clop-clop of the mules' hooves against the packed earth.

Will was almost of a mind to simply stay on the streetcar, to keep riding it to the end of the line and back, and then perhaps to take another streetcar running north and south, to sit huddled all night inside his wool coat and watch the world pass by at a mule's pace, to study men and women on the street, to peer at passengers huddled in hackney cabs, to wonder at the secret lives inside the lighted windows of passing houses, to see all these things up close for a moment and then watch them dwindle and vanish in the distance.

Will felt a sudden pang of sadness so poignant it took his breath away. He was relieved and thankful when Dave slapped him on the shoulder and jarred him back to the moment. The streetcar had reached their stop on the far side of the Avenue. It was time to go to Guy Town.

There were saloons all over Austin, especially along the commercial streets. There were secret and not-so-secret places to gamble scattered about town as well, along with houses of ill repute to suit every taste and budget. But nowhere were such establishments so densely concentrated as in the handful of blocks known as Guy Town. The area was located in the southwest quarter of Austin, with its borders set roughly a block south of Pecan, a block west of the Avenue, just north of the river and east of the big lumberyards along Guadalupe Street. The railroad tracks ran through it, and the geographical center of Guy Town was the train depot, where businessmen, farmers, and ranchers arrived daily from all over the state. In the shanty houses that fronted the railroad tracks, where no one would live if they could help it because of the noise and the filth and the smells, lived the poorer prostitutes, many of them unmarried Mexican and colored women who had to fend for themselves and their children. A block or two farther away from the tracks, one found bigger, better-kept houses, some of them quite respectable in every outward appearance, where the same business was conducted as in the shanties, but under more comfortable circumstances and at higher prices.

A man felt a sense of danger stepping into a Guy Town saloon, and at the same time a sense of freedom and possibility. As often as not, a saloon in Guy Town was connected with a neighboring brothel; when a saloon held a fandango, the women who offered themselves as dance partners expected to be paid. And while a man could find illegal places to gamble in other parts of town, the establishments in Guy Town attracted the most hardened and enthusiastic players and offered the widest range of games—faro, keno, monte, chuck-a-luck, or poker. A man could buy whiskey anywhere, but in Guy Town he could get absinthe or laudanum, the bitter taste sweetened with brandy. There were places where a man could buy morphine in bulk or try the mysterious new drug called cocaine, and it was common knowledge that there were opium dens behind the Chinese laundries. Such an atmosphere attracted all sorts of men, from those with the crudest appetites to those with the most refined. The wretched, too, had a place in Guy Town. A bum who might be asked to move along if he sat on the curb outside a shop on the Avenue attracted no attention if he took a nap in the alley behind a saloon in Guy Town.

Dave and Will started at a no-name establishment on Colorado Street, and from that point on the evening became a blur in Will's memory. When it came to vice, he could never keep up with Dave, and knew better than to try. He stuck to beer, and watched while Dave drank whiskey, puffed on a Havana, flirted with fandango girls, lost at poker and won at monte.

At one point Will saw a thing that was odd even for Guy Town. It was in one of the saloons with a covered back passage that led to a house next door. At a corner table in the rear, by the light of a lamp turned so low that the wick was sputtering, sat a couple of well-dressed men. One was tall and narrow. His broad-shouldered companion had a big mustache and wore a pince-nez, and looked familiar somehow. The two of them seemed to be engaged in friendly negotiations with a pretty blonde. That was ordinary enough, but the slender man wore dark blue glasses, almost black, which was very odd considering how dim the light was. Then Will noticed that the man held a cane in one hand. Even a blind man needed companionship, he thought; but would it matter if the woman was pretty?

Dave slid an arm over Will's shoulder. "I think it's time for me to go to bed. And not by myself!"

"What?"

"I mean to say, I'm in the market for companionship."

"You and that blind fellow!"

"What?"

"Never mind."

"How about you, Will?"

"Dave, you know my pockets are empty."

"So what? We'll get us one together."

"Are you serious?"

"I told you, the evening's on me."

"Dave, you've bought me beer and dinner, but there's some things I could never let you pay for. There's a principle at stake, I'm sure."

"You have the principles, but I have the capital."

"Each to his own."

Dave gave him a drunken, sidelong look and wagged his finger. "Well, then, if I'm going to spend all my whore money just on myself, then I'm not going to waste it in a place like this. I'll spend it all in one go on something really special."

Will laughed. "And where would you go for that?"

"Oh, I know a place. Not in Guy Town, either! On the other side of the Avenue, where the bigwigs go. Rich ranchers, and those jackasses who run the state government, and church types too good to ever be seen in Guy Town. They want the same things as everybody else, only for them it has to be the best. Well, tonight I'm treating myself to the best. I, sir, am going to May Tobin's."

"Where's that?"

"Never you mind. You're not coming, remember? A matter of principle." He laughed.

"Been there before?"

"No. But you can't be a reporter in this town and not know of the widow Tobin. May is the madam most discreet, with the freshest goods. They say her doves are still white—well, some of them have a few white feathers left, anyway. And they're so refined they can all recite Shakespeare. Sure you won't come along? You could teach 'em Tennyson!"

Dave found this enormously funny. He threw back his head, laughing. By the time he stopped, Will was gone.

Out on the street, a bitter north wind struck Will's face. It was a long, mostly uphill walk to his boarding house, but the streetcars had stopped running and he didn't have money for a hackney cab. If he walked fast, the exercise would keep him warm.

Why had he run like that, without even thanking Dave for the night out? He should go back and apologize, he thought, but how could he explain? He wasn't as worldly as Dave seemed to think he was. It wasn't a question of money or principles that kept him from letting Dave buy him a woman; when had Will ever said no to other people's generosity? It was something else. Deep down he had an image of what a woman should be, and the kind of women he saw in Guy Town didn't come close.

The wind was bitter against his face. Will shivered and broke into a run. Whiskey kept a man warm; beer gave him the chills. Dave did everything right, and Will was just a fool.

4

⚛

WHILE Dave Shoemaker was heading for May Tobin's, and Will Porter was running to his boarding house, Mollie Smith was finally drifting to sleep after a long day's labor.

The William Hall residence, where Mollie lived and worked, was a two-story house on Pecan Street nine blocks west of Congress Avenue, well beyond the bustling business district and just past the little iron bridge that spanned Shoal Creek.

The Hall household was not a cheerful place. Everything was shadowed by Mrs. Hall's illness.

Mollie, who kept house for the Halls and lived in a room at the back of the house off the kitchen, did not know exactly what was wrong with Mrs. Hall, and was not eager to find out. Mollie was young, only twenty-five, and had a great dread of sickness. She was glad that it fell to Nancy, the colored nurse who slept upstairs, to bathe Mrs. Hall, change her sheets, empty her bed pan, hold her hand, and sit with her when she had her moaning spells. Nancy was a big, heavyset woman, with the stamina of an ox and the patience of a cat at a mousehole. She had the temperament to be a nurse. Mollie, quick-tempered and perpetually dissatisfied, did not.

Mollie's work was to keep the place clean and to cook three meals a day for the men of the house, Mr. Hall and Mrs. Hall's seventeen-year-old brother, Tom Chalmers (Mr. Tom to the help). Her only direct dealing with the invalid was to take a bowl of hot broth up to her twice a day, whether the patient was well enough to drink it or not. Mollie dreaded even those brief moments of contact with Mrs. Hall. The poor woman looked more drawn and ghostly every day. That was hardly any wonder, since she couldn't eat solid food and seldom took more than a few sips of the broth Mollie brought her.

Earlier that afternoon, Mollie had been clearing lunch off the dining room table when the traveling medical man came to call. Mr. Tom answered the front door. A moment later, Mr. Hall came down from upstairs to greet the visitor. From the dining room, Mollie could peer around a corner and see through the parlor into the foyer, and as long as she kept the plates from clattering she could make out most of what was said. The caller's name was Dr. Terry, and he looked oddly familiar. Where had Mollie seen him before? Ah, yes, it was his engraved picture on the bottle of tonic that had recently appeared atop the dresser in Mrs. Hall's room.

Accompanying the doctor was another man, who was tall and thin and had lamb chop sideburns. He carried a long cane and wore little spectacles made of dark blue glass. Dr. Fry was his name, and even as Dr. Terry was introducing him, he suddenly turned his head in Mollie's direction. Mollie jerked back a bit, embarrassed to be caught looking, but the man seemed to see straight through her. That wasn't uncommon. Mollie was used to being invisible to white folks until they wanted something from her.

She lingered over her work in the dining room so as to overhear the conversation between Dr. Terry and Mr. Hall. It seemed that the doctor had not only patented his own tonic, but had successfully treated hundreds of cases similar to that of Mrs. Hall. Presently all four of the men headed upstairs. Along with the shuffling and stamping of so many feet on the stairs, there was a sharp tap-tapping noise.

Later, washing dishes in the kitchen, she heard them all come down again, and then heard muffled voices from the foyer as the two visitors took their leave. Mollie at once dried her hands and put on a shawl, then slipped out the back door. She reached the front of the house just as the front door was closing, and approached the two doctors as they were stepping off the porch. Dr. Fry, she noticed, took the steps slowly, tapping at them with his long cane.

"Dr. Terry!" she said, keeping her voice low.

Both men turned toward her. A bit of sunlight, breaking through the low clouds, glinted off Dr. Fry's dark blue spectacles. The naked pecan trees in the front yard shivered at a sudden gust of wind.

Dr. Terry smiled. "And who might you be, girl?"

"My name's Mollie Smith. I cleans and cooks for the Halls. Can you help her, Dr. Terry?"

The man's smile faded. "Mrs. Hall's case is difficult. Even double doses of my tonic seem not to revive her. I've given special instructions to the nurse. Only time will tell. It's kind of you to inquire so eagerly after the lady's well-being."

Mollie nodded. "An', I was wonderin' . . . "

Dr. Terry inclined his head. With his scraggly mustache and the little glasses that pinched his nose, he was a very wise-looking man, Mollie thought. "You have the well-being of someone other than Mrs. Hall on your mind. Am I right, Mollie? Is there someone else who's ill and needs to get better?"

"Not zackly. I mean, I's not sick like Mrs. Hall. But I gets these terrible headaches from time to time. They throb so, I cain't even sleep at night. I been feelin' one comin' on ever' since this mornin'. I just dreads it."

"Ah, a chronic sufferer of the megrim, I suspect," said Dr. Terry. "What sort of remedies have you tried?"

"Only what my Mama taught me. I wraps a long rag 'round my head and twists it tight to squeeze out the throbbin'."

The sun danced on Mr. Fry's glasses as he threw back his head and laughed. Mollie decided she did not like him as much as Dr. Terry.

Dr. Terry clucked his tongue. "Appalling, to think that such primitive and potentially dangerous measures are still so widely practiced in an age of science. We *are* in the hinterlands!"

"Oh, Doctor, I feels it comin' on right now, here 'tween my eyes. And I was wonderin'—I means to say, I knows you're a special travelin' doctor and all, and I cain't hardly pay you nothin'—"

"My girl, the practice of medicine is not purely for profit, and I am a tenderhearted fellow, am I not, Dr. Fry? I believe I can help you." He reached into the black bag he carried, and after a bit of shuffling he produced a little envelope only a couple of inches square. "I have here a powder which, God willing, will deal efficaciously with that looming megrim headache of yours. Before you go to bed tonight, take the entire contents in a glass of water."

"Before I goes to bed?"

"It may make you drowsy."

"It ain't ergot, is it? I heared of folks takin' ergot for headaches, only it s'posed to be poison if you takes too much."

"No, it's not ergot. It's only a mild soporific with anesthetic properties. It's perfectly safe."

Mollie nodded uncertainly but reached for the envelope.

Dr. Terry withheld it. "Ah, but can you afford my services?"

Mollie frowned.

Dr. Terry chuckled. "I think you can; unless you would begrudge a visitor from the northern climes a smile, the biggest smile you can spread across those pretty lips of yours—yes, exactly like that! That was easy enough, wasn't it? Here, take the powder, Mollie. Dr. Fry, I only wish that you could see the smile of gratitude on our patient's face."

Mollie's lips quavered a bit. She lowered her voice, though there really was no way to speak to Dr. Terry without the other man hearing. "Is he—I mean, can he really not—"

"Yes, Mollie, Dr. Fry is blind. And famous for it, I might add. He is Dr. Fry, the Blind Phrenologist."

"The *what?*"

"Dr. Fry studies the characters of men and women through a tactile examination of their occipital morphology."

Mollie's face went blank.

"He feels a person's head, and by scientific means is able to determine—"

"A skull-reader?" Mollie looked at Dr. Fry with fresh eyes, amazed to have met such a wonder in the flesh.

"He is indeed, and famously proficient at it. With his extraordinary insight into the nexus between personality and destiny, Dr. Fry can offer expert advice on matters of health, career, investment, travel—why, even marriage and romance."

"I never!"

"You shouldn't doubt him, Mollie. Dr. Fry is as much a scientist as I am. Here, bow your head."

"What?"

"Bow your head, Mollie. Permit Dr. Fry to make a cursory examination."

"Right here on the porch steps?"

"We must be off, Mollie. Now or never."

Mollie clutched the little envelope in her hand. "All right, then," she said, bowing her head. Dr. Terry reached for Dr. Fry's hands and guided them onto Mollie's head.

Dr. Fry spoke with an accent even odder than Dr. Terry's Yankee accent. "The girl's hair is reasonably short, but quite thick. Ideally, of course, the phrenological subject should be completely shaven prior to examination, to ensure a clear reading." Mollie stiffened. Dr. Fry chuckled. "Such ideal preparations are almost invariably impractical, of course, so an experienced phrenologist like myself learns to compensate as best he can."

The man's long, bony fingers moved over her head with surprising strength. Slowly but steadily, he kneaded his fingertips into the thin flesh of her scalp, smoothed his thumbs over her forehead, explored each hollow of her skull, assessed each plain and protuberance. He hummed knowingly, striking notes up and down the scale, and occasionally gave a little grunt of surprise.

"What is it?" said Mollie. "What are you feelin'?"

"Hush," said Dr. Terry softly. "Let him do his work."

Dr. Fry ended by running his fingertips from behind her ears down to the back of her neck, just above her spine. His touch gave her goose bumps. Then he lifted his hands and stepped back.

Mollie looked up, immediately dazzled by the winter sunlight reflected off the man's blue spectacles.

"Well, girl," said Dr. Fry, "I am not surprised that you have those blinding headaches. Your skull tells the whole story."

"It does, sir?"

"I'm afraid that you were born with a congenital predisposition to megrim. Even a beginning phrenologist could determine as much from those bony protuberances behind your ears."

Molly reached up and felt her head.

"Tell me, girl, are you married?"

She hesitated. "Not zackly. Not church-married."

"Ah. But you do have a fellow living with you, then?"

She nodded.

"Speak up, girl. If you merely nod or shake your head, I cannot see it."

Mollie cleared her throat. "Walter—that's my man—Walter and me lives in a little room out back, off the kitchen."

"I see. Are you satisfied with your circumstances, with things as they are?"

"I s'pose. Walter's nothin' special, but he works steady and does what I tells him." She laughed ruefully. "Not like my last man, that crazy Lem!"

"Ah, you have something of a temper, don't you, Mollie?" Dr. Fry wagged a long, bony finger at her, though his aim was a few degrees off. "I could tell as much from that faint ridge along your hairline. Temper often goes with megrim."

"It does? Well, sir, I reckon I does run a bit hot sometimes. 'Specially when a man rubs me the wrong way. Gets me in trouble now and then."

"I can imagine. You don't keep a gun about, do you?"

"Me, sir? Never!"

"Good. It would be most unwise, perhaps fatally so, to keep a gun close at hand when one has a ridge like that along the hairline."

"I never knew!"

Dr. Fry shook his head. "Few people do. We are awash in ignorance, up to our ears in it! Self-knowledge is the door; phrenology is the key. My skills are merely a means to reveal a subject's true nature, and from that knowledge all manner of heartache and tragedy may be avoided, God willing."

Just as the man's touch had given her goose bumps, so did the way he talked, in his odd foreign accent. Mollie shivered and clutched at her shawl.

Dr. Terry consulted his pocket watch and gave a cry. "The time, Dr. Fry, the time! We must be off at once. You have that powder I gave you, girl? Remember, take it before bedtime, in a full glass of water."

With that they departed, Dr. Terry bustling across the gray lawn and Dr. Fry tap-tap-tapping his long cane against the ground. They were surely the most extraordinary two men Mollie had ever met. She hurried back to the kitchen to finish washing the lunch dishes.

A little later, Mr. Hall and Mr. Tom had an argument in the parlor, talking so loudly that Mollie could hear every word from the kitchen, even with the door closed.

"Another damned quack!" Mr. Hall said. "And a damned expensive quack at that!"

"It was worth a try," Mr. Tom said. "Let's give it time. The tonic may yet do her some good."

"I have half a mind to pour the stuff into the nearest gutter!"

"You've half a mind, all right," said Mr. Tom. Mollie fought back a giggle. Young Mr. Tom could wield a sharp tongue on occasion, a trait Mollie admired. She certainly liked him better than Mr. Hall, who was always so stodgy and stuffy and usually looked right though her. Mr. Tom, on the other hand, occasionally cast an appreciative glance at her figure, and then would look away when she caught him at it.

Mollie was proud of her figure. Most men seemed to like the look of it, not just seventeen-year-old boys like Mr. Tom. Men liked Mollie. Mollie liked men, though they could be more trouble than they were worth. Her current man, Walter, had turned out to be a gem. Not a fast-talking charmer like bald-headed Lem Brooks. Lem had been fun, but Mollie needed a man who was more bendable. Walter, she had decided, was just about perfect: healthy and strong enough to keep steady work, but with a natural meekness. She had only to raise her voice to shrink him down to the size of a mouse. Mr. Hall had allowed Walter to move into Molly's room a couple of months ago. So far, there had been no trouble.

For dinner, Mollie heated up some ham left over from Christmas, and fixed sweet potatoes, biscuits, and a cobbler with canned peaches. All through dinner, Mr. Hall and Mr. Tom exchanged hardly a word. Mollie bustled back and forth between the kitchen, where Walter and Nancy ate, and the dining room. The headache kept building between her eyes. She thought about taking the powder, but Dr. Terry had said to wait until bedtime.

After dinner was over, she told Walter that she was feeling poorly and that he would have to help her wash up. He whined a bit about what a hard day he'd had, out doing chores for one of the neighbors, but he did as he was told. So different from Lem, who would rather die than do a lick of work in a kitchen, especially with a woman bossing him. Lem would wash whiskey glasses behind a bar all day long, but thought that washing a plate or a fork was strictly for women. Who could figure that?

After the washing was done, she poured the powder the doctor had given her into a glass of water and drank it, then stepped from the kitchen into her little room at the back of the house. It had been a porch originally, before it had been walled up to make a room. One door led into the kitchen and another door and a window opened onto the back yard. Inside was a chair, a bed, and a dresser that had a couple of drawers missing. An old, tarnished mirror atop the dresser was propped against the bare wood wall.

Walter followed her to bed and tried to crawl on top of her. When she rolled away, he pouted and said he had been hoping for a little sugar before he fell asleep, by way of reward for being so helpful in the kitchen, but Mollie's headache was too bad for that. Whenever Lem had pestered her that way, she had barked and snapped, but with Walter there was no need. She played pitiful instead, wrinkling her brow and mewling like a kitten. Lem had hated it when she did that, but Walter was what Mollie's mother called the feeling type; he wrinkled his brow and pouted right along with her. He held her hand, fetched a wet rag for her forehead, and hushed at once when Mollie complained that his talking was making her headache worse.

Walter really was a jewel. Mollie wondered if they should get married for real, instead of living as common-law man and wife. Then a warm, cozy feeling crept over her, and she was suddenly too sleepy to think about it.

"Blow out the lamp, Walter, and lie still," she whispered.

Walter lay quiet beside her, tired out from the day, disappointed but ready for sleep. A norther was blowing in, making the windows rattle. From the parlor at the front of the house, through the kitchen door and the dining room door, he vaguely heard the chiming of the mantel clock as it struck the hour. Ten chimes, he counted, and wondered where the day had gone.

5

$\mathscr{D}$AVE left the saloon shortly after Will and headed in the opposite direction. When he came to Congress Avenue, he strolled tipsily to the nearest streetcar track and attempted to walk atop the shiny silver rail, like a tightrope walker. He kept losing his balance, and blamed it on the cold north wind that blustered against his back, pushing him south toward the river. At one point he tripped and fell on the hard-packed earth. He staggered up, dusted off his knees, and yelled over his shoulder, "Stop shoving!"

The last few blocks of Congress Avenue, before it terminated at the toll bridge that spanned the Colorado River, was a desolate patch at night. The buildings were lower and more spread out than those in the commercial district to the north. Amid the darkened store fronts and empty lots, there was only one light to be seen, a lamp burning in the front window of a house on the east side of the street. Dave headed toward it.

The widow May Tobin's house was one of the few residential addresses remaining on Congress Avenue. For neighbors, she had a lumberyard located due south of her on the riverfront, and catty-corner from her across the Avenue, Zimpelman & Son's ice factory. During the day, while wagonloads of wood and carts of ice went back and forth before her house, along with plenty of other traffic taking the toll bridge across the river, the blinds at May's house were kept drawn and there was never a soul to be seen on the little front porch. People would pass by every day and hardly notice the place.

At night, when the ice factory and the lumberyard closed and the area became quiet, the blinds remained drawn except at the front porch window, where the glow of a lamp shone through lace curtains from dusk until dawn. The lamp was a beacon. There was not much cause for a man to come to that lonely block of the Avenue after dark, unless he was looking specifically for May Tobin's house.

The house presented an unassuming front of clapboard walls and simple gingerbread decorations painted white. From the street it appeared smaller than it actually was, for a number of rooms had been added at the back, well secluded from the street. A narrow driveway beside the house gave access to a small yard behind, where vehicles and horses could be hitched out of sight. The place was the size of a small boarding house, though only May Tobin and a couple of servants lived there. The extra rooms of May's house were often occupied, especially after dark, but no one actually lived in them.

May Tobin did not call herself a madam, nor was she one, strictly speaking; no prostitutes lived in her house, though some might conduct their business there. May ran a house of assignation. She made her rooms available to men and women who needed a place to meet in private. What they did in those rooms, and whether money changed hands, was none of May's business so long as someone paid for the room.

Some of her visitors were lovers who couldn't meet elsewhere; in those cases it was usually the man who paid for the room, though not always. Some of the women, who came often and met different men, were obviously prostitutes. Those women usually paid for the room themselves, though again, not always. May was flexible about such matters and drew no conclusions; calling one woman a lover and another a whore might make for neat categories, but May believed that the ways of the world were not as simple as that. There were degrees of prostitution and degrees of love, and plenty of room where the two might overlap. That she was never judgmental was one of the things that kept her customers loyal to May Tobin.

Within her small circle, May's house had acquired a reputation for civility and quiet refinement. Occasionally, May herself would facilitate an introduction. If a man who had been coming to her house grew tired of his regular companion, and if May happened to know of another woman who was available and seemed suitable, then May might arrange to bring the two together. She had a beautifully wallpapered parlor, with an upright piano and a crystal chandelier, which provided an ideal atmosphere for such meetings. If the two parties found no common ground, nothing was lost; but if they hit it off, they could move at their leisure to a more private room. May thought of herself as a matchmaker of sorts, and any gratuity she accepted from either party was no different than a matchmaker's fee.

Many of the men who came to May's house were what she called men of substance. She could tell from the way they dressed and spoke and carried themselves that they were above the common lot. Some worked for the state, as clerks or engineers. Some even held elected office, among them several legislators and at least one head of a governmental department. Some taught at the university. May never asked for more than first names, but in a town as small as Austin some of her customers were too well known to hide their identities from her even if they wished to do so.

Such men of substance, she had observed, often preferred more than beauty, willingness, and youth in a partner. Those things they took for granted; they could be purchased elsewhere. Men of substance sought quality. They appreciated the attributes of a cultivated woman—a sense of style, an educated wit, an aura of elegance or mystery. Such women were rare enough anywhere, and rarer still were the ones available on the open market, so to speak. But any such women to be found in Texas were likely to be found in Austin, and those in Austin were likely to be found at May Tobin's house.

Dave stepped onto the porch, tripping on the top step. As soon as he was out of the wind he heard the sound of music coming very softly from inside. Someone was playing the piano—not a sentimental love song or dance music, but Beethoven's *Moonlight Sonata*. That was appropriate, Dave thought, since the moon was full. He began to hum along, painfully off-key.

A brass knocker mounted on the white door frame caught gleams of blue moonlight. The knocker was such a pretty little thing that it made Dave smile: a doll-size hand sleeved in layers of lace. Dave raised the knocker and knocked three times. It was like shaking hands with a doll. He laughed.

The music abruptly stopped. Faintly, he heard the sound of a piano bench scraping against a wood floor. A moment later, the door opened an inch. He could see that it was barred with a chain inside. That was unusual, in a town where many people went to bed without even locking their doors.

A woman peered out at him through the narrow space, her face lit by the lamp at the window. From the little he could see—hair streaked auburn and gray and put up with tortoiseshell combs, a face that was lined despite its plumpness, a paperlike paleness about the four fingers which curled around the edge of the door—she appeared to be somewhere in the further vicinity of middle age. She also wore glasses, though the small oval lenses had no wire framing them, so that the light had to strike them just so before he noticed them.

"Do I know you?" the woman said.

"I don't believe we've had the pleasure," said Dave.

The woman studied him for a moment. "I believe you might be drunk, sir."

"I believe you might be right."

"Perhaps you should come back another time."

"But I'm here right now."

"So you are."

"Can't I at least come in? This is May Tobin's house, isn't it?"

"It is."

"And are you May Tobin?"

"I am."

"Well—may I please come inside, Mrs. Tobin?" Dave attempted a deep, gallant bow, but his arms swung a bit too far and he staggered sideways until he banged his shoulder against the porch post. "Ow! That hurt."

May Tobin raised an eyebrow. All men were little boys. This one, at the moment, was more little boy than most. It did not do to indulge such juvenile behavior too readily, but May smiled despite herself. She shook her head and lifted the chain. "Come in. I can at least supply you with some coffee."

"Coffee?" Dave stepped inside. He cocked his head thoughtfully, wondering if "coffee" was perhaps slang for a colored prostitute. He mulled over the possibility as he followed the woman down a dim hallway into a room where he promptly tripped over an ottoman and found himself sitting on a thick wool rug in a pleasantly appointed parlor. Overhead, a chandelier with crystal baubles cast a soft glow. A fire was burning. Hung above the fireplace was a large canvas in an ornate frame. A piano stood against one wall. A grandfather clock stood against another; watching the swinging pendulum made him suddenly queasy. Arranged about the room were pieces of overstuffed furniture draped with antimacassars, and little side tables set with doilies and ashtrays. Haphazardly stacked on one of the tables were a few books with gilt-edged pages. By newspaperman's force of habit he tried to read the titles, squinting and turning his head sideways. One of the books was called *What Can a Woman Do?*, which made him laugh, considering the nature of the establishment.

Nearer at hand, atop a little metal serving cart, he noticed what looked to be a humidor, and vaguely wondered what sort of cigars might be inside. He tried to get to his feet to have a look. After a couple of fumbling attempts, he decided that he was quite comfortable where he was and dropped back down on the rug.

May Tobin seemed to have disappeared. He gazed about the room and found himself staring at the painting hung above the fireplace. It was a curious choice for a whorehouse, he thought. A copy of a reclining European nude would have been the customary sort of thing, academic but prurient. The painting above May Tobin's mantel was a piece of purely indigenous art, showing a band of Comanche Indians attacking a family of Texas homesteaders. The boldly rendered details could be read at a glance, even from where Dave sat on the floor. A little farmhouse was in flames. The husband, bleeding from numerous wounds, was in the process of being scalped alive by three Indians with drawn knives; you could tell that the poor man was still alive by the look of shock on his face. The young wife had been stripped of her calico dress, which lay on the ground in tatters, and was trying to escape in her petticoats; her large breasts were ostensibly covered, but when Dave squinted he seemed to discern nipples beneath the thin wash of white paint that passed for an undergarment. Her face, with an expression of abject terror, was turned back toward the two Indians pursuing her, but her long, naked arms, as white as porcelain, were outstretched before her, as if in supplication to heaven, which hid behind a sky full of black rain clouds. Elsewhere, two naked blond children of indeterminate gender had been thrown like saddlebags across one of the Indian's horses, bottoms up; the Comanches obviously intended to abduct them, as they had been notorious for doing back in the days when Texas was a wild frontier. The Comanches were naked except for tiny loincloths which covered their genitals but not their buttocks. Their sleekly muscled limbs and flanks were the color of tanned hides. Their faces were painted with yellow stripes, and their bulging red eyes and gaping mouths made them look like demons from a nightmare.

It was quite an awful painting, Dave thought, awful in the most literal sense of the word, profoundly and at the same time ludicrously awful. Even a fellow who'd grown up in Hempstead, Texas, could see it was in the most wretched taste. Even so, there was no denying that the painting was likely to inspire terror and pity in anyone who looked at it, especially if they'd had a few drinks. The longer Dave studied it, the more awful and fascinating the painting became.

There was a movement at one of the doorways—not the one through which Dave had entered, he was fairly certain—and his hostess stepped into the room. She carried a steaming cup on a saucer.

May Tobin seemed unsurprised to find him still on the floor. She walked to the little serving cart, which along with the humidor held a tea service, including a creamer and a little silver urn filled with sugar cubes. "Do you take it black?"

"What's that?" Dave said, peering at the cup.

"Your coffee."

"But I don't want coffee. I didn't come here for coffee!"

"What did you come here for?"

He shrugged. "Why does anybody come to May Tobin's house?"

"Are you meeting someone? I wasn't expecting you."

"I'm looking for a woman."

"A particular woman?"

"I'm not too particular. Look, I have money. Plenty. I came here to spend it."

She looked at him steadily. "You never said whether you take it black or not."

"Sure, she can be black as coal, if that's what you've got!"

She offered him the saucer and cup. Dave stared at it for a moment, then finally took it. The brewed aroma was suddenly irresistible.

From where he sat on the floor, May Tobin looked rather intimidating, he decided, looming and staring down at him like a strict schoolmarm. She'd be pulling out a wooden ruler and rapping his knuckles next. He found the idea curiously intriguing. It was not exactly the sort of thing he had come for, but he was in a mood for almost anything.

"Look, Mrs. Tobin, they say you have the best girls in town—"

"'They'? Whom do you mean?"

"Come on, can you fix me up with a girl or not?"

"Such a vulgar way you have with words, young man. No, I cannot 'fix you up.' I'm afraid I have no accommodations for a single man this evening."

Dave smiled good-naturedly. "I'm plenty comfortable where I am. If all the girls are busy, well then, I'll just wait right here until one of them's free."

"I'm afraid you don't quite understand the way this establishment is run. Who sent you here?"

"Sent me?" Dave grinned. "My Mama sent me to the store to buy eggs—but I came here instead. I'm a very bad boy, Mrs. T."

"A very impertinent boy, to be sure. But I'll ask you again: who recommended my house to you?"

"Nobody. I just happen to know. I know things. Lots of things. That's my job."

She regarded him quizzically. "You don't work for the marshal, do you? I thought I knew all of you boys in the police department already."

"Not the marshal! Good God. I work for William Pendle . . . William Pendle . . ." He cleared his throat. "I work for William Pendle . . ." For some reason he was unable to get through the name, even with a running start.

"William Pendleton Gaines?"

"That's the one! You know him, too, eh? Sure you do. I'll bet Gaines himself comes here. Or used to? He's married and all settled down now, of course. He and the queenly Augusta live in a castle called Bellevue."

"Do I understand that you work for the *Statesman*?"

"Damn right! I'm the crime reporter, I am!"

From a hallway hidden behind a curtain, there came the sound of a door opening, then two voices, a man's and a woman's.

May Tobin raised an eyebrow, walked to the curtains and parted them an inch to speak to the people beyond. "Delia, don't bring your guest into the parlor quite yet. I'm seeing someone off."

Dave smiled. "Delia—I like the sound of that. Sort of like Delilah. Well, if Delia's through with her last one, then let's have a look."

May stepped to a yellow velvet rope that hung beside the piano and gave it a sharp tug. She walked to Dave, smiling, and took the cup and saucer from him.

A moment later, Dave was lifted bodily from the floor, his arms pinned to his sides. He couldn't see how or by whom; he could see only two enormous black hands gripping the front lapels of his jacket. Suddenly everything was spinning—the parlor, the dim hallway, the front door. Then the whole front porch lurched violently upside down, like a capsizing ship. Dave landed on his backside on the hard ground and everything came to a jarring halt.

He sat stunned and confused, and might have sat there indefinitely had the wind not been so cold. Eventually he picked himself up, shaking a bit, and looked back at the unassuming little house with the lamp in the window.

"Not good enough for May Tobin!" he muttered to himself, and then laughed at the absurdity of it. "Kicked out on my ass! And in the middle of the holiday season. Where's her Christian charity, I ask you? Kicked out of May Tobin's house, and not a single soiled dove quoted Shakespeare to me. If that don't beat all!"

He trudged up Congress Avenue, limping a little and beginning to feel slightly nauseous. After a while he heard the clopping of hooves behind him and turned to see a buggy turning into the street from May Tobin's drive. Delia's customer was leaving, so why had Dave been ejected? As he stepped aside to make way for the buggy, he decided to take a look inside and see if he knew the man, but a sudden wave of nausea sent him staggering to the gutter instead.

By the time he recovered himself, the buggy had passed. Dave stood and wiped his mouth on his sleeve. He felt considerably more sober, and also considerably stiffer from his tumble on the hard ground. He watched the buggy's slow but steady progress against the north wind as it headed up Congress Avenue, all the way to the end. Just before it would have reached the capitol grounds, the buggy pulled to the left and came to a halt in front of the big building that housed temporary offices for the state government. The norther had rendered the air crystal clear, and beneath the bright moonlight, even at a distance of almost twelve blocks, Dave could dimly see someone step out of the buggy, pause—to hitch his horses, no doubt—then vanish into the state building. There were two things government men could never get enough of, Dave thought: women and work. Imagine a fellow dropping by his office at such a time of night, between leaving a whorehouse and heading home to his wife!

Dave walked up the deserted avenue, leaning into the wind. He kept his eyes on the distant buggy. Just as he was reaching Pecan Street, the halfway point, the man emerged from the state building, paused to unhitch his horses, and stepped back into the buggy. The wind carried the clopping of hoofbeats down to Dave as the buggy continued on to the end of the Avenue, then turned west and disappeared from sight.

Back at the house at the foot of the Avenue, May Tobin had resumed her interrupted *Moonlight Sonata*. When she reached the end, she pressed the foot pedal and let the final note reverberate in the room. The note gradually diminished, until the only sounds were a gentle crackling from the fireplace and the tick-tock of the grandfather clock. May sat on the piano bench for a while, then closed the music book and got up.

As she was crossing the room, she noticed something on the rug. She stooped to pick it up. It must have fallen from the coat pocket of her unwanted visitor while he was being ejected. She held it to her nose, inhaled the aroma, and looked at the band. It was indeed a Havana. May Tobin had a nose for quality, in tobacco as in other things.

She opened the lid of the humidor, intending to add the cigar to her own store, then reconsidered. She took a small pair of scissors from a little drawer in the humidor and snipped off one tip of the cigar, then lit a taper from the fireplace and held its flame to the other end. She puffed until the flame caught, then tossed the taper into the fireplace and settled back among the plump cushions on the sofa, her head wreathed in cigar smoke.

A low chuckle came from an overstuffed chair near the fire. May tapped her cigar against the rim of a crystal ashtray. "What are you laughing at, Delia?"

A young woman turned and looked at her above the back of the chair, showing two green eyes below a mass of jet-black hair. "How can you stand to smoke those things?"

"Don't begrudge your elders their pleasures, young lady. You're young and haven't yet exhausted all your vices; this is about the only one I have left. You'll also find that a cigar is considerably more reliable than a man. You might try one sometime."

Delia laughed. "May Tobin, May Tobin, what a corrupting influence you are!" She turned back to the fire. "What was so wrong with that fellow that you had to throw him out? Don't tell me you finally met a man too ugly to be entertained in your parlor."

"Oh, he was handsome enough. Quite good-looking, in fact."

"Drunk?"

"Yes, but not rowdy; that wasn't the problem. He's a reporter for the *Statesman*."

"Ah. You think he was up to no good?"

"No, I think he came here just to have some fun. But I imagine some of my guests—your new friend among them—might prefer not to be observed by a newspaperman while they're in this house."

Delia chuckled softly and stared at the fire. A log cracked open with a small explosion of cinders.

May set the cigar aside for a moment to unlace her high shoes. "How did it go, with your new friend?"

Delia shrugged. "Well enough. I'll see him again, if he wants."

"Oh, he'll want to see you again, Delia. I could tell by the look on his face. You should cultivate young Mr. Shelley. He's a rising star, you know."

"Oh, I'm sure he is. But they're all just men, aren't they? When you see them naked, I mean."

May sighed. "Yes, Delia. When all's said and done, a man is nothing but a man." She put her feet up on the sofa and puffed on her cigar, letting the clouds of rich, aromatic smoke envelop her.

6

*O*n the same night that Mollie Smith went to bed with a megrim headache, and Dave Shoemaker paid a call on May Tobin, Lem Brooks attended a ball on the opposite side of town.

Ordinarily on a Tuesday night, Lem would have been tending bar at the Black Elephant. But Mr. Hancock owed him a night off, and Lem, who had a reputation among the colored folk of Austin for being the best prompter in town, had been asked to call the figures at a ball.

It was one of the biggest events of the year for the young colored folk of Austin. Many of them would be working on New Year's Eve itself, attending to the white folk at all their parties, so they threw their own New Year's celebration a day early. The party was held on the east side of town in the parlor of a big boarding house on Sand Hill, close to the Tillotson Normal and Collegiate Institute, which offered instruction to colored students. Most of the boarders, guests, and members of the band were Tillotson students. There was a piano player, a trumpeter, a drummer, and two string men who switched between fiddles and banjos. The crowd was full of pretty girls and handsome young men dressed in their Sunday best.

Lem had a few beers that night, but not too many; he had to keep sharp to call the figures. Standing at the corner of the elevated bandstand, he clapped his hands and stamped his feet and announced changes in the dances, leading the men and women through curtsies and do-si-dos and lining them into squares and circles and rows, telling them when to approach and how to mingle:

"Swing yo' partner, don't be shy,
Look yo' lady in the eye!
Throw yo' arms around her waist,
Take yo' time—there ain't no haste!"

Calling a quadrille was a little like telling folks when and how to make love, he thought, and like giving them the beat to do it by.

He cast his eye on several of the girls as they passed by, but they all seemed satisfied with their partners and didn't look back, or else glanced away shyly when he gave them his grand piano grin. Tillotson girls were more tender buds than the full-flowered ladies he was used to. It was just as well; after all, Lem had sworn off women.

The dance continued well into the small hours. Lem kept drinking beer, and calling figures, and the night became one great swirl of laughing faces and spinning bodies.

The woman who owned the boarding house and was hostess of the party finally got up on the bandstand to announce that the next dance would be the last. It was an old-fashioned reel, and Lem called the figures for all he was worth.

Afterward, as the crowd dispersed, the hostess paid the band for playing and Lem for calling. It wasn't much, but calling was the easiest work Lem knew of, and the coins made a nice jingle in his pocket.

Outside on the street, he fell in with some friends who were heading his way. From the house on Sand Hill to Congress Avenue was a good eighteen blocks in a straight westerly line, and from the Avenue it would take another few blocks of zigzagging to get to Rosie Brown's house on Lavaca Street, where Lem boarded. It would take a sober man at least twenty minutes of steady walking. Lem and his friends were not exactly sober, and the night was cold, with a stiff norther whipping up.

The four men walked along East Pecan, keeping a steady pace to ward off the cold, laughing and singing and trading comments about some of the women who had been at the ball. Lem tried to shush them when they got close to the Black Elephant. The saloon was closed, but there was a light on inside, which meant that old Hugh Hancock was probably still up, cleaning the place. If he saw Lem pass by, he might try to corral him into helping, so they skulked past the saloon like thieves, giggling and shushing each other, then broke into a run that turned into a race to Congress Avenue. At every intersection the wind buffeted them from the north, hard enough to make them veer off course. Lem got to the

Avenue first and stood laughing and gasping for breath while his friends caught up.

There at the corner of Pecan and Congress Avenue they parted ways, Lem heading north, his friends heading south. Lem waved farewell and walked into the wind, squinting. The norther was beginning to blow leaves and dust and all manner of debris down the wide thoroughfare from the direction of the capitol grounds.

Running had been a good idea. He no longer felt either cold or drunk. The wind stinging his face invigorated him. He hummed a dance tune. He didn't feel tired. He felt manly. Watching the pretty girls at the dance had worked on him more than he realized. Or maybe it was the full moon; people said that could stir a man's loins. Whatever the cause, all at once and out of nowhere he found himself carrying a log between his legs. It tugged at his britches and felt warm against his thigh.

It seemed a shame to lug the thing back to his room at Mrs. Brown's house, where there was nobody to help him with it. For an instant he pictured what might happen if he woke old Rosie Brown and asked her to lend a hand. He threw back his head and laughed out loud. He shouted to a hackney cab that was passing by, "Lawd, I mus' be drunker than I thought!" The driver didn't hear him because of the wind and the wool muffs pulled over his ears.

Lem felt the coins in his pocket, sliding cool and slick against his fingertips. Together with the money he'd managed to save up in a jar back at his room, he probably had enough to hire some company for the night. Guy Town was only a few blocks away. But on a cold night like this, the girls weren't likely to be out strolling the streets; instead they'd be snug and warm in their beds, waiting for customers to come calling. Some establishments in Guy Town would welcome a colored man and some wouldn't. Lem wasn't so worldly as to know one such place from another, and he was in no mood to have a door slammed in his face by some snooty white madam.

His best bet for a warm reception was Fannie Whipple's place. Fannie was colored and kept colored girls, but her house was back the way he'd come, over on Red River. By the time he got the money from his jar and trudged halfway back to Sand Hill, the fire in his log would likely have burned out. Besides, it seemed ridiculous that a fellow as charming and handsome as himself should have to pay for something that he ought to be getting for free.

Then he thought about Mollie.

He and Mollie Smith had practically been man and wife for a while, over in Waco. Mollie was the best cook in the state of Texas, and not just in the kitchen, as Lem used to brag to friends.

Of course, as Lem knew only too well, a man could also get burned hankering after Miss Mollie. She was impossible to live with, determined always to have her way and given to awful fits of temper. Lem and Mollie had worked for a widower on a little farm outside Waco. They'd even had a little house all to themselves. But when Mollie went on a rampage you could hear her all the way into town. One night she broke a bottle and threatened to cut Lem's face with it. That had been the last straw for the farmer, who said that one of them would have to go, and he didn't mean Mollie. The farmer didn't want to do without that fine cooking, Lem thought; and he had to wonder, too, if the old widower wasn't keen to try Mollie's cooking outside the kitchen. While Lem gathered up his things, Mollie told him she never wanted to see him again, and Lem said that was quite all right with him, as he hoped never to meet another woman as domineering and bossy as Miss Mollie Smith.

Lem had moved to Austin, which turned out to be the best thing he'd ever done. He loved tending bar at the Black Elephant, working for a black man and serving black customers. Sometimes there were whole days when he hardly saw a white face! As for women, he had so far successfully avoided the whole lot of them.

Then, a couple of months back, Mollie moved to Austin. It seemed that the farmer had taken a new wife, and the bride wanted to do her own cooking, with no assistance from a pretty young mulatto. The first time Lem saw Mollie on the Avenue, he gave a start, then couldn't help but flash his grand piano grin and tip his hat. Mollie looked prettier than ever, but all she'd given him back was a smirk before she hurried on, not saying a word. The last few times their paths had crossed, Lem had made a point of saying a few words, and even trailed after her a bit, wooing her in a good-humored way. Mollie seemed to like the attention, although her manner stayed aloof. She told him she was cooking for a family named Hall, and living in a room behind the kitchen at the back of their house over on West Pecan, just past the little iron bridge across Shoal Creek. The place was outside Lem's usual rounds, but since then he'd made a point of strolling by a few times, just to see where it was.

What was to stop him from traipsing over there right now and paying a call on Mollie? She'd be surprised to see him, might even be a bit alarmed to hear somebody tapping at her window in the middle of the night, but she'd calm down as soon as she saw his face. In the middle of the night had always been when she liked it best, provided she wasn't having one of her terrible headaches. "I bet she's in the mood for it right now," Lem said to himself. "Such a cold, windy night, be a shame for a woman as pretty as Mollie to pass it all alone."

Lem turned his back on the norther and headed back down the Avenue until he came to Pecan Street, then turned right.

Suddenly he remembered that he had heard about Mollie taking up with another man. That was hardly surprising, considering how pretty she was. What if she and her new man were living together? What if Lem got to the Hall house and found the fellow sleeping right there in Mollie's bed? The evening could take an unpleasant turn.

On the other hand, could any man possibly put up with Mollie's temper day after day? "Dogs'll hang around if you whup 'em, but most fellas ain't that stupid," he said to himself. If Mollie had taken up with a new man friend in Austin, the fellow was probably already gone by now, in which case Mollie would almost surely be in the mood to see him.

Lem's route skirted the northern reaches of Guy Town. West Pecan Street was as quiet as a graveyard, with no one about but a few ramblers like himself, walking with heads bowed and hands in their pockets, minding their own business.

He came to the little iron bridge. Shoal Creek splashed quietly below. He walked onto the span. His footsteps made a muffled clanging. He wondered idly if the noise was loud enough to wake anybody who might be sleeping under the bridge. Lem himself had resorted to sleeping rough a time or two in his life. On a cold night like this it was best to find cover so the morning frost wouldn't settle on you. Under a bridge could be reasonably comfortable, if you had a blanket and kept your hands and feet wrapped up.

Lem thought of his friend Alec Mack. Where was Alec tonight? he wondered. Probably sleeping rough somewhere, maybe under this very bridge. And all because the folks who'd hired him didn't like the idea of two colored people doing what everybody else in the world does from time to time. The world could be mighty unfair. One mistake and a man could find himself with no work, no money, no place to stay, and his good name turned to mud . . .

Perhaps paying an unexpected call on Miss Mollie in the middle of the night wasn't such a good idea after all, Lem thought. What if she wasn't so glad to see him, and she yelled and raised a ruckus? Lem didn't know anything at all about the Hall family. Some folks were mighty quick to pull out a gun if they heard a noise in the night. The log between his legs could be steering him straight into trouble.

At the middle of the bridge, Lem hesitated for just a moment, then pressed on. The Hall house was almost in sight.

Then Lem saw the dog.

The creature was sitting back on its haunches in the middle of the road at the far end of the bridge, not thirty feet away. From the size of the thing, Lem figured it must be some kind of hound. But there was something strange about the dog.

Lem blinked. The dog must have blinked, too, because suddenly Lem saw two flashing points like little balls of fire where the creature's eyes should be, as if there was a furnace inside its head and Lem could see straight through to the bed of coals inside.

The dog began to growl, a sound Lem could hear even above the wind in his ears and the gurgling of the stream. Then the dog sprang to its feet, baring its teeth and staring at him with fiery eyes, its lean body so tense it quivered like a boiling pot.

Lem knew in a flash that this was no ordinary dog at the end of the bridge. The thing was not a dog at all.

It was a dog ghost.

He had never encountered a dog ghost before, but all his life he had heard about them, beginning with stories Grandma Sooty told him when he was little. When he got older and accused her one day of making up all those stories, she swore that every word was true and gave him no biscuits and jelly as punishment for doubting her. Lem partly believed her and partly didn't—just as, at this moment, a part of him believed what he was seeing and a part of him did not.

By rights, a man wasn't supposed to fear a dog ghost, as long as his conscience was clean. A dog ghost wasn't really a dog at all. It was the ghost of someone you had known; it just took the shape of a dog. And unless you'd done something truly terrible, like killing a man, it generally showed up for a helpful reason—to give warning, or steer a man from danger, or help him find something he'd lost. Lem swallowed hard and told himself he had nothing to be afraid of.

Still, it was hard not to be frightened of a dog that was growling and baring its fangs, and staring at you with eyes like two balls of flame. Maybe it was just a trick of the moonlight that made its eyes flash like that. Maybe it was the full moon that was making Lem imagine things. Probably the creature was nothing but a common hound dog, after all.

"Hey! Git! Run along!" Lem yelled and waved his arms. He stamped his foot and sent a clanging shudder through the bridge. That should have been enough to send any normal dog running with its tail between its legs.

Instead, the creature started to walk slowly but deliberately toward him, its whole body quivering with tension. It blinked again; the fire in its eyes went out for an instant, then flared back up. Silvery moonlight gleamed across its bared fangs.

Lem swallowed hard. The thing had to be a dog ghost. But if that were so, whose ghost was it? And what had it come for?

Lem's legs twitched. He opened his mouth. His throat was dry. "Grandma?" he whispered.

The ghost dog stopped in its tracks, not fifteen feet away.

"Grandma Sooty?" Lem's voice cracked.

Suddenly the creature gave a great leap and landed right in front of him. Lem spun around and started running.

The barking behind him had a hollow ring to it. Sharp fangs nipped at his heels, cutting through his wool socks and scraping his flesh. Lem ran faster than he had ever run before.

7

*I*N the middle of the night, Tom Chalmers was awakened by a noise at his bedroom window.

He had been sleeping fitfully, his mind in turmoil over his sister's declining health and his growing dislike of his brother-in-law. His dreams were strange and uneasy. In them, a dark brown medicine bottle as large as a man was moving through the house; its head was a giant label with a picture of Dr. Terry, the doctor who had come to call on his sister that afternoon. Traipsing along behind the giant medicine bottle was Dr. Fry. The giant tonic bottle moved forward like a doll propelled by a giant hand, its flat bottom rapping against the floorboards, while the blind man followed behind, tapping with his cane. Rapping and tapping, rapping and tapping . . .

The noise finally woke him. For a confused moment Tom was uncertain where he was, or whether he still dreamed.

A norther had blown in. Gusts rattled the house. In his half-sleep, he thought that the rapping must be a tree branch knocking against the window frame. He snuggled beneath the covers. At seventeen he was no longer a boy, and it was nonsense to be afraid of noises in the night.

From the parlor he heard the mantel clock chime the half hour. He could vaguely remember having heard it chime three times a little while before. Three-thirty in the morning, and there he was, lying in his bed imagining things!

The rapping began again, sounding for all the world like knuckles deliberately knocking on wood. Tom lay very still, completely awake. Along with the rapping, he heard another sound. Perhaps it was only the wind, but to Tom it sounded like a moan. Perhaps it was an animal—but what animal could make a sound as wretched and miserable as that?

Tom jumped out of bed and stood in his flannel nightshirt, facing the long, heavy drapes pulled shut over the window. He walked to the drapes, then reached out and clutched them. Against his fingertips he felt the cold air trapped between the windowpanes and the thick fabric. He imagined the nightmarish act of wrenching the drapes apart and confronting whatever stood outside his window. Surely it was nothing, he told himself—the wind, a branch, an animal—and yet he could not make himself open the drapes.

Then he heard a low, hoarse voice from outside, muffled by the glass and almost drowned by the gusts of wind. The voice called his name. "Mr. Tom! Mr. Tom! Oh God, wake up, Mr. Tom!"

Very slowly, he parted the drapes until a vertical slit appeared. He pressed one eye to the gap. The world outside was a mass of jumbled shadows and silhouettes tossing in the wind. Abruptly, the closest mass of shadows resolved into the shape of a man who stood below the window with his shoulders stooped and his head bowed, tightly hugging himself. The man reached up to rap at the windowsill. Tom gave a start. Through the glass he heard a muffled sob. "Mr. Tom . . . oh God . . . wake up, sir!"

Tom took a deep breath and pulled open the drapes. "Walter! Good God, you scared me half to death!"

"Oh, mercy, Mr. Tom, help me, please . . ."

"Wait a minute, while I strike a match." Tom stepped to his bedside table and lit a hurricane lamp, then carried it to the window. He undid the top latch and pulled the sash open, letting in a gust of cold wind. "Good Lord, Walter, it's freezing out there!"

"I think . . . somebody . . ."

"What on earth's the matter?"

"I think somebody musta nearly killed me, Mr. Tom." Walter's speech was slurred. Tom had to strain to understand him.

"What's wrong with you, Walter? Are you drunk?" Tom stooped a bit and held up the lamp to get a better look. Patches of Walter's closely shorn hair glistened unnaturally in the light, as did some slick, wet substance on his face. Tom made a noise of disgust and drew back. Walter was covered with blood! The man's face was lumpy and swollen, with a great clump of clotted blood on one side of his head and a deep gash under one eye. Tom put a fist to his mouth and swallowed hard.

"My God, Walter! Where have you been? Who did this?"

"I jus' been here . . . in the room out back."

"Where's Mollie?"

Walter looked confused. "I think—I think she be gone."

"She's not in bed?"

Walter shook his head. "No. Oh, Mr. Tom, I'm hurtin'! I'm cold. Please, can I come in the house?"

"No! You know you're not allowed anywhere in the house except Mollie's room and the kitchen."

"But Mr. Tom, I gots to have help! I think I mus' be dyin'!"

Tom tried to think. It would appear that Mollie's hot temper had gotten the better of her once and for all. She must have taken a knife and a skillet to Walter to mess him up so badly. If she wasn't still in her room, she must have run off, afraid of the law. What would they do for a cook?

At least Walter had sense enough to walk around the outside of the house and knock on his window, instead of tramping through the dining room and the parlor, getting blood on the furniture and carpets. Mr. Hall slept upstairs, as did Nancy the nurse, in rooms adjoining Mrs. Hall's. Tom was the only one on the ground floor, so it was Tom to whom Walter had come for help.

But what was Tom to do? He tried to think, but the cold air from the open window was cutting through his nightshirt and turning his feet to ice. He could run upstairs and wake his brother-in-law, but if he did that it was all too easy to imagine the shouting and arguing that would follow, which would surely wake his sister. Whatever had happened between Walter and Mollie, it was hardly worth turning the whole household upside down at half past three in the morning. Besides, Tom was old enough to handle such a problem himself.

But what should he do? By rights, no one in the house owed Walter a thing. Walter worked for himself. He was neither a boarder nor a hired hand. He was allowed to stay in Mollie's room free of charge strictly as a favor to Mollie, and only so long as he caused no trouble.

This was trouble.

Walter shuddered and groaned. "Mr. Tom, please, cain't you take me to see a doctor? You could take me in the buggy."

"I'm not even dressed, Walter."

Walter clutched his head. "Cain't you wake up Mr. Hall, then?"

"I will not! Mr. Hall is no more responsible for you than I am. Good God, Walter, look at the windowsill—you've got blood all over it!"

"Please, Mr. Tom, help me! I needs a doctor."

Steven Saylor

Tom took another look at the wounds on Walter's face and swallowed hard. "All right, listen. Go see Dr. Steiner. Tell him Mr. Hall sent you. You know where Steiner lives, don't you?"

Walter nodded.

"I don't suppose you're up for riding a horse. Mr. Hall wouldn't want you to take one, anyway, if Mollie's not here to vouch for you. You'll have to walk. It's not that far. Go on, now—I'm freezing!"

Walter said nothing coherent, but stood shaking his head and mumbling. Tom eventually stopped waiting for him to leave, and shut the window. Walter remained where he was, his head bowed, hugging himself, his image framed by the window sash. Tom blew out the hurricane lamp. Finally, Walter turned and walked slowly away. Tom shook his head and closed the drapes. His feet were like blocks of ice. He slipped back into his warm bed with a grunt of satisfaction, rather pleased at the decisive way he had handled the crisis.

Walter returned the way he had come, walking along the side of the house to the back yard. He passed the fallow vegetable plot, the toolshed and the outhouse. He came to the back fence. The gate to the alley stood open.

Surely Walter had been the last person to come in through the gate that afternoon. He distinctly remembered shutting it and latching it, just as always, because Mr. Hall insisted that it be latched so that no dogs could get in. Yet the gate stood open. Dully, Walter thought that Mollie must have gone out into the alley, leaving the gate open behind her. He had better leave it that way, then; if she came back and found it shut, and had a hard time unlatching it in the dark, that was just the kind of thing to set off her awful temper.

The trip to Dr. Steiner's house seemed endless. The cold wind cut through his thin coat and his worn shoes, but Walter kept moving, putting one foot ahead of the other. The moonlight was so bright that sometimes he grew confused, and wondered why it was so dark in the middle of the day. He no longer felt the pain in his head quite so sharply, but occasionally it came over him in a throbbing wave that made him feel as if his whole face might cleave open like a split melon. How had it happened? He couldn't remember. He remembered going to bed. He remembered waking up in terrible pain, groping blindly about the dark room, calling for Mollie, then finally pulling on some clothes and going to beg Mr. Tom for help.

Dark houses loomed up around him, then passed like ghostly ships.

Something in his head was not right. Suddenly he was lost, even though the houses around him looked familiar enough. He knew the houses, but he couldn't remember where they were, or where he was going, or what he was doing in the street.

He needed to rest. He sat down on a tree stump beside a hedge that blocked the north wind. He shivered. His hands and feet felt numb. For a while he seemed to sleep, though he never shut his eyes. Finally he got up and started walking again. He needed to see Dr. Steiner; that was it—he was on his way to Dr. Steiner's house.

He was confused about which direction to take. He recognized the house of a colored man he knew, and rapped on the door. The man saw his condition, made a terrible fuss, and told him to come in, but Walter said he only needed directions to Dr. Steiner's house. The man insisted he borrow a wool overcoat before sending him on his way. Inside the coat he began to feel a bit warmer. If he could only keep the cold out, he could at least think straight.

When he finally got to the doctor's house, he had to knock a long time. The colored maid who finally opened the door looked sleepy and cross, then gasped when she saw him. Walter collapsed at her feet.

It was Mollie's job to be the first one up in the Hall household, to light the stove and the fireplaces and to cook breakfast. But the next morning the fires remained unlit and the house was still cold when Mr. Hall and Mr. Tom got up. When they met downstairs, the dining room table was still bare.

"Where the hell is that girl?" said Mr. Hall.

"Probably back in Waco, or halfway to Hempstead by now," said Tom.

"What do you mean?"

Tom told his brother-in-law about his nocturnal visit from Walter.

"Was he really hurt?" said Mr. Hall.

"Covered with blood, I'm telling you. Mollie must have nearly killed him."

"I didn't hear a thing."

"Neither did I, until Walter woke me. I guess, with the way the wind was howling—"

"So Mollie's run off?"

"Walter said she'd disappeared. She's probably afraid of the law. When you see what she did to Walter, you'll understand."

"Well, if she's that violent, we're lucky to be rid of her, and she'd better not come back." Mr. Hall grabbed a poker and some matches and set about starting a fire in the dining room. "I swear, the impossibility of finding decent help these days! Your sister had a knack for it, before she got too sick to run the house. It's too much, for a man to have to manage servants on top of everything else! Back in my father's time, when a man could buy and sell his help and discipline them the way he saw fit, things were different, I can tell you. You and I have grown up in a different world! To think, there are people even now who'll argue that making the coloreds into free labor somehow advanced the cause of civilization!" Mr. Hall poked at the fire and frowned. "I wonder if our nurse Nancy can at least make a decent pot of coffee? Where the hell is *she*?"

"Here I is!" Nancy bustled in from the parlor. "I knows, I knows, I slept late, but Mrs. Hall kept me up half the night, tossin' and turnin'. But what are y'all doin' here with no breakfast in front of you? Why ain't there no fire in the parlor? It's cold this mornin'!"

"My wife kept you up last night?" said Mr. Hall.

"Oh, she was agitated somethin' fierce! It was that norther blowin' in. Sick folks is extry sensitive to changes in the weather."

"Did you hear any noises from downstairs?"

"What kind of noises?"

"A fight between Mollie and Walter."

Nancy frowned. "No, I didn't hear nothin' like that. Jus' the house shakin' from the wind."

"Well, they must have had quite a row. Walter showed up at Tom's window in the middle of the night, blood all over his face, and Mollie appears to have run off. That's why there's no fire and no breakfast."

"Good Lawd! Oh, I knowed that girl had a temper. And Walter Spencer is too sweet and soft for his own good."

"I don't suppose you could brew us up some coffee, and maybe scramble a half dozen eggs?"

Nancy sighed, causing her considerable bosom to heave up and down. "Would that be *before* or *after* I empties Mrs. Hall's bedpan, sir?"

Mr. Hall made a face. "Nancy, I know you're here to nurse my wife, not to clean and cook, and I pay you accordingly. But just this once, under the circumstances—"

"I hears you! Cain't you hear my stomach growlin', too? Jus' sit yo'selves down and I'll fix up somethin'."

"We would be obliged," said Mr. Hall wearily.

Nancy went into the kitchen and set about kindling the stove. She cracked eggs into a bowl, measured out some grits, and poured water in a pan to boil. Soon the kitchen was warm and the windows were covered with condensation.

Nancy looked at the door to Mollie's room; it was shut tight. She shook her head. So much for Mollie, so much for Walter. It would be a shame if Mollie had ruined Walter's face, though, because he was not a bad-looking man, if a little slow. Nancy only hoped it wouldn't take Mr. Hall too long to hire another cook. She had quite enough work to do already, looking after Mrs. Hall.

The grits came to a boil and Nancy started stirring. She looked at the door to Mollie's room again. Now wouldn't it be something, she thought, if the little vixen was in there after all, sleeping like a baby the whole time everybody was wondering where she was? Probably Mr. Hall and Mr. Tom hadn't even bothered to look. Nancy could just picture Mollie snuggled under her blanket, smiling in her sleep. She could also picture herself pouring a cup of cold water over the silly girl's head and dragging her into the kitchen to finish cooking breakfast.

Nancy set the grits off the burner to stop them boiling, then walked to the door and opened it.

A few moments later, she appeared in the dining room. Mr. Hall looked up and smiled, anticipating coffee. The look on Nancy's face made him sit upright. "Nancy, what on earth—"

"You look like you've seen a ghost," said Tom.

Nancy's voice came out at an odd pitch. "Mr. Hall, I think you better come see. This cain't be right. Mollie may have cut Walter's face some, but this cain't be right."

They followed her through the kitchen to the little back room. Nancy stepped back while the men looked inside.

The first thing they saw was their reflection in the old tarnished mirror that had been propped on the dresser. The mirror had toppled to one side and was wedged crookedly between the dresser and the wall. Tom and Mr. Hall saw themselves reflected at a disorienting angle, their images obscured by streams of dried blood spattered across the mirror's surface.

The chair had been overturned. The bed was a shambles, with the mattress partly pulled off the frame, the pillows scattered, and the sheets twisted. There was blood everywhere.

The blood on the mattress and sheets was thickly pooled in some places, where it was still reddish and barely congealed, and thinly smeared in others, where it had dried to a brown crust. Spatters of blood had been flung upon the walls. Pools of blood lay on the floor. There were bloody finger marks on the back doorsill.

For a long moment no one moved or said a word. Then Tom covered his mouth and bolted out the back door. He staggered down the steps, clutched the rail with one hand and his stomach with the other, and bent double.

Mr. Hall was aghast. "Could this . . . could all this blood have come from Walter? For God's sake, she must have nearly cut his head off. Unless . . ."

Unless the blood was Mollie's blood, he thought. But that was impossible. Who could imagine Walter doing such a thing? Docile, obedient, slow-witted Walter . . .

Tom wiped his mouth on his sleeve and called from the yard. "There's more blood out here. All over the steps!"

Mr. Hall started to cross the room. His foot struck something hard near the foot of the bed. With the toe of his shoe he pushed aside a rumpled bit of sheet. Nancy huddled behind him. Together they peered at a bloody ax on the floor.

"Oh, Lawd!" whispered Nancy, shivering from the cold and beginning to weep. "What's become of Mollie?"

Mr. Hall dropped to the floor, swallowed hard, then peered under the bed. "She's not here," he said. "Not in this room. And surely not anywhere in the house . . ." He went to the back door. As Tom had said, there was more blood on the steps leading down to the yard.

Standing on the top step Mr. Hall surveyed the back yard, which was fenced all around. There was a bare clothesline strung between two wooden uprights, a big iron barrel for burning rubbish, the muddy furrows of the vegetable garden, a pile of compost. The padlock on the toolshed was securely in place. Beyond the toolshed was the outhouse. With a twitch of irritation he noticed that the gate to the back alley was open. Walter must have left it that way when he went off to see the doctor. Mr. Hall had told him time and again that the gate was always to be kept shut, lest dogs get into the yard and scatter the compost and the rubbish.

Shaking his head and muttering, Mr. Hall descended the steps and strode across the yard to the gate, intending to pull it shut. But as he reached out and laid his hand on the top of the gate, from the corner of his eye he glimpsed something lying on the ground, wedged in the narrow, weedy strip between the outhouse and the back fence.

Even before he turned his head he knew what it must be. He could sense the presence of death.

8

A gruesome way to end the year, that's for sure," said Marshal Lee. "Ever seen a dead body, Shoemaker?"

Dave swallowed hard. "Sure, I have. I'm the crime reporter for the *Statesman*, ain't I?"

"Just thought you looked a mite green."

"You referring to my tender years, or my complexion?"

The marshal laughed. "Green's green, Shoemaker. You got a face a couple of shades paler than a baby lima bean."

"You'd be green, too, if you had a hangover to match mine."

The marshal snorted. Horatio Grooms Lee was by no means green. He was thirty-five, ten years older than Dave, and had seen quite a few dead bodies in the years he'd served as a Texas Ranger.

Service in the Rangers brought out the best in some men. Out on the raw frontier, experiencing the bare-boned struggle for existence, a man could learn to taste fear and swallow it whole, appreciate the true worth of loyal comrades, see the fading light in the eyes of a dying Indian or a worthless outlaw and glimpse the fact that every wretched human has a soul. But with some men, the same experiences had the opposite effect; the stark ugliness of death and the sheer meanness of the struggle winnowed away anything sweet or gentle in a man's disposition, leaving behind only what was hard and bitter. Grooms Lee had been hard when he left for the Rangers, and was harder still when he came back.

The marshal was a man of prospects, of whom a great deal was expected.

He was the only son of his father's first marriage; his mother had died bearing him. His father was Joseph Lee, a power in Texas politics for decades, who had most recently been appointed to head the commission in charge of building the new state capitol. The younger Lee's service as marshal of Austin was seen by most as only a stepping stone on his way to greater things. With his father's connections and his own reputation as a lawman, Grooms Lee might someday be elected to the state legislature, or go to Washington, or perhaps even make his way to the Governor's Mansion.

The city council had appointed Grooms Lee marshal largely because of his father's influence, but with due confidence in the man's own experience and temperament. He appeared to possess the traits people wanted in a lawman, like tenacity and judgment. But there was another side of Grooms Lee that the politicians in their council chambers never saw. He showed one face to those above him and another face to those below. His peers saw a fine fellow with an even temper, Joseph Lee's boy, retired from the Rangers with honor, now pledged to maintain law and order for the good people of Austin. Others, especially if they crossed him, saw a man with a mean streak as wide as the Colorado in flood.

His meanness could be petty. To Grooms Lee, a squeamish man was a weak man, and he liked to needle men weaker than himself, the way he needled Dave Shoemaker as they stood over the lifeless, mangled corpse of Mollie Smith.

The body of the dead woman had been dragged by the marshal and a deputy from the narrow space between the back fence and the outhouse into the yard. She was nearly naked. Scraps of a tattered nightdress clung to her here and there, the blood-soaked cloth pasted to her flesh. She had stiffened in a suggestive position, with her arms above her head and her legs as far apart as the space between the fence and outhouse allowed. Her face had been so brutally damaged that it was impossible to read any expression there. Not for the first time, Dave held a fist to his mouth and swallowed hard to fight back nausea.

He had indeed seen dead bodies before; the marshal's question was just short of an insult. Dave had grown up in Hempstead, a town known all over the state as Six-Shooter Junction on account of its endless family feuds and gunfights. He had been five years old the first time he saw the bloody corpse of a man killed by gunfire. Since then, growing up in Hempstead and later working for the *Statesman,* he had witnessed the results of death by stabbing, falling, smoke inhalation, runaway carriage, poisoning, and all manner of disease, and twice he had seen black men accused of rape lynched by mobs. None of those sights had been pretty, but none of them had been quite as hard to look at as the body of Mollie Smith.

Some of the nausea, he told himself, was on account of the liquor he drank the night before. He would have been queasy that morning no matter what. It was a miracle he hadn't thrown up the moment the marshal and his deputy pulled the mangled body into sight from behind the outhouse.

He clutched his pencil and notepad and scribbled random details and impressions. Keeping his mind busy helped to quell the nausea.

Except for the bedridden Mrs. Hall, he had already talked to all the residents of 901 West Pecan Street, including the much-bandaged and hardly coherent Walter Spencer, for whom the family had begrudgingly set up a folding cot in the kitchen. Dave had looked at Mollie's blood-spattered room and had made a sketch of it. He had paced the yard, so as to measure how far the body had been dragged, and had drawn a detailed plan of the property.

Dr. Burt, the city physician, was on his way to have a look at the body before it was carried to the dead room at the city hospital. Dr. Burt would also perform an official examination of Walter Spencer. Dave scribbled a note: "Ask Burt for expert description of all wounds, cause of death. Was woman outraged?" *Rape* was not a word Gaines would allow in the *Statesman*.

Dave looked up from his notepad. He cleared his throat. "So, Marshal, have you got any suspects yet?"

"I hope to make an arrest within the hour."

Lee's blunt answer surprised him. "Who?"

"Think I'm gonna tell *you* before I make the arrest?"

"Walter Spencer?"

The marshal sniggered. "Not likely. Maybe you didn't interview the folks in the house as closely as I did. Walter Spencer was the proverbial bull with a ring through his nose. Where Mollie Smith led, he followed. Besides, Spencer was damned near killed himself."

"He's a pitiful sight with all those bloody bandages on his head, that's for sure. Then you don't think there was a fight between him and Mollie?"

The marshal raised an eyebrow. "I suppose you think the two of them took turns hitting each other in the head with that ax?"

"We don't know for certain that Spencer's wounds were caused by the ax," Dave noted.

"Sure, and we don't for certain know that Mollie's head was smashed in by the ax, either. We'll let Dr. Burt render a professional judgment. But when I see two people with their heads cracked open and there's a bloody ax on their bedroom floor, I think I can figure it out. The question is, where did the ax come from?"

Dave nodded. "Mr. Hall says he doesn't keep an ax on the premises. He buys his firewood ready-cut."

"So think it through, Shoemaker. Do you really imagine that our tame bull premeditated such a crime? Bought or stole an ax, sneaked it into the house, waited till after dark, then whacked his bossy sweetheart a few times in the head, dragged her outside and did to her what he could have been doing inside under the blankets? Makes no sense." Marshal Lee tapped his forehead. "Try to think like a detective for a change, Shoemaker, instead of like a newspaperman."

Dave gritted his teeth. "Then how do you see it, Marshal?"

"It's the oldest story there is. You've just got to ask yourself, who's the third man in the triangle? This fellow brought his ax with him, found the lovers in bed, tried to kill 'em both. Probably thought he finished Spencer off; must be walking around this morning, thinking Spencer and Mollie are both dead. Hated Mollie bad enough to crack open her head, loved her bad enough to still want to take his pleasure with her after he'd done such a thing. Imagine crawling on top of that." Lee looked at the corpse with disgust.

"We don't yet know that she was raped."

The marshal snorted. "Dr. Burt'll tell us. Unless you'd like to have a look for yourself. Go ahead, take a peek. I won't tell. See if they're the same down there as a white woman. See if black men squirt out the same stuff we do." Lee's deputy guffawed. Dave felt his face flush in spite of himself.

"So this was a crime of passion? Seems awfully messy."

"Don't forget, we're dealing with colored folks here."

"You're sure it was a colored man?"

The marshal shook his head at Dave's simplemindedness. "You think a white man could have done this? This fellow was more animal than human."

"But you're sure it wasn't Walter Spencer?"

"Spencer's one of the tame ones. Look, Shoemaker, maybe you come from a family that never had the wherewithal to own slaves. I guess you're too young to remember those days, anyway. You don't understand the coloreds like I do. They're different from us, closer to the animal kingdom, and as with all animals, there's two categories: the ones who give you trouble and the ones who don't. You can't always tell by looking, but you can acquire a practiced eye. Some of 'em are wild and won't ever be tamed.

They're too dangerous to be allowed near decent people—they simply have to be got rid of. Most of 'em are pretty docile, and as long as they do what they're told, you might as well feed 'em and give 'em shelter. But even the docile ones can turn feral. You have to be vigilant. That's one of my jobs, to keep an eye on the coloreds, to judge which ones are trouble and which ones aren't."

"I guess you were looking the other way when this happened."

Lee stared back at him grimly. "Keeping track of their mating habits and heading off their little jealousies is *not* part of my job. Hasn't been anybody's job, since Mr. Lincoln had his way. They're out of control. You see here what can happen. Still, somebody's got to clean up the mess and see justice done, to protect the peace of decent folks like the Halls." He looked down at the naked body of Mollie Smith. "They say she was pretty, for a colored girl. You'd never know that now. You can still see why they liked her below the neck, though."

Dave looked elsewhere and swallowed hard. "So, Marshal, who's the suspect?"

Grooms Lee smiled. "Tell you what, Shoemaker. Trail along behind me, like a good newshound, and see for yourself."

All over Austin that day, news spread of the murder of Mollie Smith.

At first, only a small circle of people—the Hall household and their immediate neighbors—knew of the event. When Tom Chalmers telephoned the marshal from a nearby store, the owner overheard and called his friends. Meanwhile, someone in the marshal's office telephoned William Pendleton Gaines at the *Statesman,* and so Dave Shoemaker was dispatched to cover the story. Dr. Burt, after examining the corpse and Walter Spencer, called upon Dr. Steiner to inquire about his treatment of Spencer's wounds, and so the overlapping circles of both medical men soon learned of the crime. Mollie's body was taken to the city hospital, where rumors of what had happened spread rapidly among the staff and beyond. When the marshal made an arrest that afternoon, news of the event fanned out from the workers at the city jail.

Rumors began to proliferate. A person learning of the murder late in the day might hear a detail from one source, another detail from a second source, and then a third detail that contradicted the first two. Few private houses had telephone connections, but many a boarding house and business did, and the wires helped to spread the various stories. By sundown, thousands of people knew something about the murder, though as often as not the details they had heard were naggingly incomplete or only half-true and occasionally outright fantastical. Some heard rightly that a colored servant girl had been killed; some heard that both the girl and her lover had been murdered; and some heard that the two of them together had killed a member of the Hall family. Sooner or later, everyone heard that Marshal Lee had arrested a colored man at the Black Elephant saloon. A reliable account of the murder would have to wait for the next morning, and the New Year's Day edition of the *Statesman*.

That night, at family dinners and at New Year's Eve parties all over town, some people talked openly about the murder, but many deliberately avoided discussion of such an unsavory subject, especially in mixed company. At the stroke of midnight, the year 1884 was as dead as Mollie Smith.

9

⤳

$\mathcal{W}$ILL Porter passed the whole of New Year's Eve knowing nothing about the murder on West Pecan Street.

Had he worked a shift at the Harrells' cigar shop, he surely would have heard about it, for a steady stream of customers talked of little else; but Will's services had not been required. Had he spent the day loitering in the parlor of the boarding house, he would have gotten an earful of rumors from the other residents, who came and went all flush with the news. But the day was glorious, with a snap in the air and a pale blue sky scrubbed clean by the norther of the previous night, and on such a winter day Will could hardly stay inside. Had he dropped into a coffee shop on Congress Avenue, he would almost certainly have been drawn into a discussion about the strange events on West Pecan Street; Will however, was so low on spending money that even coffee seemed an extravagance.

While Dave Shoemaker was investigating the murder and all Austin was buzzing with rumors, Will spent the final day of 1884 "tramping," as he called it—seeking the company of tramps, who were plentiful enough around Austin, if one knew where to look for them.

From the boarding house, Will headed west on Mesquite Street. After five blocks or so, just past the three-story high school building with its handsome mansard roof, he descended into the shallow, wooded valley along Shoal Creek, where a network of trails crisscrossed and ran alongside the water.

In some places the paths were so narrow and closely hemmed with vegetation that a man could imagine himself in a forest miles from civilization. Gnarly scrub oaks were festooned with parasitic clumps of mistletoe and ball moss. Prickly pear, spiny yucca, berry-studded spice bush, and pale winter grasses sprouted amid the interstices of broken, bone-white limestone underfoot. The winter had so far been mild, and even now, brightening the palette of umber bark, gray-green foliage, and white stone, there were little patches of upright purple asters with delicate, spiky leaves, and weedy, unkempt goldenrod resplendent with bright yellow flowers.

Lacy ferns grew along the water's edge. In places, the limestone ledges along the bank had tumbled and worn so as to form natural steps down to the creek, with tree roots intertwined among the stones. Limestone boulders littered the creek bed, like furniture for giants. At one such spot Will came upon a group of tramps warming themselves like lizards on the sun-heated rocks. Will found a place and joined them. He spent the rest of the day listening, against a background of trickling water, to the rambling tales of threadbare wanderers and half-wits.

Quite a few of the tramps arguably belonged in the State Lunatic Asylum, but lacked a family to commit them and had so far escaped the attention of the marshal. Others seemed merely to have run out of luck. Most of them Will knew already, at least by name. A newcomer among them was a handsome colored fellow who called himself Alec Mack. Whites and coloreds mixed more freely at the tramp level of society.

Among the old-timers was a grizzled Civil War veteran who called himself the Colonel. He wore a stained and patched gray uniform decorated with medals that dangled from tattered ribbons. The Colonel had an inexhaustible supply of stories about the Lost Cause. Some of his tales seemed far-fetched, but they were seldom dull, and sometimes they were hairraising. Will had no doubt that the old man had fought in several engagements; of his claim to have won a battle or two virtually single-handed, Will was more skeptical. He could listen to the Colonel's stories for hours, especially if he could lie back against a warm rock with a pile of ball moss for a pillow, studying the sky through a skein of oak branches and sun-dappled leaves.

The day waned. Sunlight faded from the treetops, and even the Colonel ran dry of stories. Will grew hungry. He hiked south along the creek until he came to the Pecan Street bridge, then scrambled up the steep eastern slope out of the creek bed. He crossed Pecan Street at the exact spot where the spectral dog had nipped at the heels of Lem Brooks the night before.

He headed for a little house on Nueces Street, close to the railroad tracks and across from a lumberyard, where a woman named Rodriguez sold tamales for a penny a piece. Sitting on a stool on her back porch, Will ate a plate of tamales and a bowl of pinto beans, washing them down with a glass of Lone Star beer. There were several other diners on the porch, all Mexicans. Their Spanish was too quick for Will to follow, but he overheard several mentions of *"una mulata muerta"* and wondered about the dead woman they were discussing with such animation.

He arrived back at the boarding house at twilight. The parlor and kitchen were deserted. The upstairs was quiet. The Harrells were planning to see in the new year elsewhere and had already left. The various boarders were either out taking dinner or napping in their rooms in preparation for a late night ahead. Will retired to his room and settled onto his bed, feeling pleasantly tired from the long day outside. He felt inspired to make some sketches of the Colonel from memory and to write down some of the old man's stories. The work carried him deep into the night. Just before the clock downstairs struck midnight he fell asleep on his bed, his notebook on his lap.

So it was that Will Porter woke on New Year's Day, 1885, among the small minority of Austinites who still knew nothing at all about the murder of Mollie Smith.

He woke ahead of everyone else at the boarding house except the cook. She had started a pot of coffee but told him that breakfast wouldn't be served for at least another hour. "Everybody else sleepin' late," she said. "No sense me makin' a bunch of breakfas' that'll turn stone-cold 'fore it's et." Will poured himself a cup of coffee, then stole the newspaper from the front porch and took it up to his room.

The *Statesman* consisted of eight pages of small type laid out in narrow columns, with headlines only slightly larger than the text. The format never varied. The front page featured news of the nation and state compiled from Associated Press dispatches. The back page had market reports, including a column called "Cattle Clatter." In between, there were regular spots for social announcements, meetings of the city council, proceedings of the state legislature when in session, court reports, railroad timetables, "Texas Tidings" (items from other newspapers around the state), a catch-all column headed "Local Short Stops — Newsy Nuggets and Pungent Items Caught on the Fly," odd bits of international news, and a long column in which William Pendleton Gaines pronounced his editorial opinions on everything from the Chinese labor problem in California to the latest trends in ladies' fashions.

There were also advertisements for various restaurants and stores around town. Some featured illustrations and fancy type, but many were written as stories, as short as a sentence or as long as a paragraph, and interspersed among the news reports so as to be indistinguishable from them. Having no money, Will had no use for advertisements, but often read one in spite of himself, drawn in by the headline and not realizing that the item was an advertisement until the end. He had once complained to Dave Shoemaker about such trickery. Dave only laughed and told him that was exactly what the advertisers intended. Sometimes they even asked for their pieces to be written up by someone on the newspaper staff. Dave himself had written more column inches of advertising copy than he could count. With the same people writing the news and the advertisements, it was no wonder that readers could hardly tell one from another.

Sometimes Will read the front page, sometimes not. If a story was about an address on Indian policy by President Cleveland, or a congressional debate about railroads, Will would skip it. An account of a bloody clash between police and labor anarchists up North would more likely draw his attention, and he always read every word of any story—and there were plenty of them—about lynchings, murders, outlaw gangs, or lovelorn suicides.

To judge by the *Statesman*, lynchings were as common as trials, at least in the South. Usually a colored man accused of rape or murder was the victim, but not always. Sometimes, if a feud between neighbors erupted into shooting and murder, a mob of local people would seize the killers and hang them on the spot. Murders of every sort were commonplace—stories of shootings, stabbings, poisonings, and bludgeonings came from every state; Will sometimes imagined that a man walking from Texas to Maine would trip over one dead body after another. Quite a few of the outlaw stories came from various places in Texas. There were still whole towns run by gangs, and in some places in South and West Texas, virtual warfare had been going on for years between clans of outlaws and companies of Texas Rangers.

But of all the lurid stories on the front page, the suicides fascinated him most. There seemed to be so many of them, men and women alike. Except for the ones who hanged themselves or jumped off a bridge, they invariably used morphine. Back in Greensboro, where Will had been allowed to dispense drugs at his uncle's store, he had sold plenty of morphine to customers. He soon spotted the ones who were addicted to the stuff, because they came in again and again. But thinking back, he now wondered about the ones who had come in only a few times—just enough to buy up an adequate store of morphine for a calm, quiet death. Had he ever sold morphine to a suicide? He had been so young then, he had never really thought about it. Now, every time he read of a suicide by morphine, he wondered.

There were no suicides on today's front page, nor much else of particular interest. He turned the pages and scanned the columns at random. His eyes caught on a brief item.

BE GENTLE WITH CHILDREN
"Now quit your crying, sir, or I'll give you something to cry for." When such words are spoken to a weeping little boy, he don't know whether to stop crying or go on. But he does know that the cross old aunty who says them is a hateful creature. What makes her hateful? Possibly dyspepsia; or maybe liver complaint. In either case, give cross aunty a bottle of Dr. Terry's Liver Tonic and Ginger Aperient and tone her up so that she may be healthy and happy.

He laughed out loud. Tricked again! He wondered if Dave had written the piece.

Will was ready for a second cup of coffee—and did he smell bacon from downstairs? He was refolding the paper when a headline caught his attention.

BLOODY WORK!
A FEARFUL MIDNIGHT MURDER ON
WEST PECAN—MYSTERY AND CRIME.
A Colored Woman Killed Outright,
and Her Lover Almost Done For.
In the very early hours of yesterday morning, there occurred in the city one of the most horrible murders that ever a reporter was called upon to chronicle—a deed almost unparalleled in the atrocity of its execution.

The account was full of lurid details—the discovery of Mollie Smith's corpse ("nearly nude," the story said), the finding of a bloody ax, a description of her room "bathed in blood," and a gory description of the wounds inflicted on Walter Spencer. Will read on.

Marshal Lee arrested William Brooks, alias Lem Brooks, a young colored man employed as a bartender at the Black

Elephant saloon on East Pecan. When called on at the county hall by this reporter, Brooks made the following statement:

"I knew the woman Mollie Smith in Waco but parted ways with her there and have had nothing to do with her here in Austin. I knew she had taken up with another man and I did no more than speak with her when we met by chance on the street. I am completely innocent of her murder. I can prove by any number of witnesses that I was at a ball on Sand Hill till 4 o'clock in the morning, and was the prompter. They have got hold of the wrong man."

Going to the boarding house where Brooks resides and where he said he went after leaving the ball, the reporter asked of Rosie Brown, the colored woman who runs the establishment, at what hour Brooks came in. "Between 2 and 3 in the night," she answered. "Are you certain of that?" She was asked. "Yes sir, I am, because he woke me when he came into the foyer downstairs, as he knocked over an umbrella stand, so that I presumed he was drunk, and he was talking to himself in a very agitated way. I had trouble going back to sleep and looked at my clock and saw that it was just half past 2."

It will be remembered that Brooks claimed it was 4 o'clock when he left the ball. It would have been at least 20 minutes past 4 ere he got to his room, had he gone directly home. A number of Negroes confirmed that he stayed through the dance, and it may be that the landlady was mistaken about the hour.

Will put down the paper with a shiver.

He could most definitely smell sizzling bacon. He carefully folded Mr. Harrell's newspaper, picked up his empty coffee cup, and followed his nose downstairs.

10

*L*EM stood on tiptoes to peer through the window of his cell. The window was small and crisscrossed with iron bars. The cell was on the top floor of the two-story jailhouse, and the window was set so high that all he could see was a patch of sky and a corner of the General Land Office. If he grabbed the bars and pulled himself up, he could see a bit of the capitol grounds across the street.

Lem shivered and hugged himself. The day was sunny, and from the people he could glimpse walking on the grounds and the way they were dressed, without long overcoats or gloves, it looked like New Year's Day had warmed up nicely. Inside the cell, it was as cold as a meat locker. The sunshine skirted the north face of the building, never penetrating inside to warm the stones and iron bars and concrete. Lem was more cold-natured than most young men, on account of his head being bald.

There had been a wool blanket on his cot, but it was filthy and stank of piss. Lem had tried to sleep wrapped up in the thing, but finally couldn't stand the smell. In a fit of anger, in the middle of the night, he had stuffed the blanket between the bars of his cell and thrown it into the hallway beyond, then yelled for the night jailer. When the man finally trudged up the stairs and asked what he wanted, Lem told him the blanket stank and asked for another. The man smirked and shook his head. "Should've settled for what you was given," he said, then went back downstairs.

The stinking blanket was still where Lem had thrown it, in a crumpled heap on the floor. It looked to be just beyond his reach, but Lem didn't know for sure; so far he had been too proud to try to reach for it.

He spent a long, sleepless night on the hard cot. The dark hours passed as slow as cold molasses, and he had plenty of time to wonder how he had landed in such a place. Eventually the room lightened, and the first full day of his captivity began. What a way to mark the new year!

Somebody had killed Mollie Smith.

They had tried to kill her new lover, too, from the look of things. With an ax! It made him queasy to imagine such a gruesome sight—beautiful Mollie with her head split wide open. The jailer said that she had been dragged into the back yard after being hit with the ax, and then raped. What sort of man would do such a thing to a woman who was dying or already dead? Certainly not Lem. It made him shudder to think of it. Dead things frightened him, and the idea of carnal union with a corpse was about the most awful thing he could imagine. Anybody who knew him would realize that Lem Brooks was the last man on earth to do such a thing.

Besides, the marshal said that Mollie had been killed sometime before four o'clock in the morning, because between three and four o'clock, Walter Spencer woke Tom Chalmers to show him his wounds. And where was Lem before four o'clock? There were dozens of witnesses who could swear he hadn't left the dance much before four, and then spent at least twenty minutes walking home. Caesar Barrow, John Tom Jackson, and Henry Soloman had walked along with him down East Pecan, past the Black Elephant all the way to the Avenue.

It was his crazy landlady who had made all the trouble. It seemed that he had awakened Rosie Brown when he came in and went upstairs to his room, and she had looked at her bedside clock, and for some reason she had gotten it into her head that the clock showed it was between two and three o'clock. She had told Marshal Lee as much, and on the strength of her word he had arrested Lem. A sleepy old lady who'd been awakened by a noise in the middle of the night—why put any stock in anything she had to say? Rosie Brown probably couldn't even see as far as her clock without her glasses. She wouldn't deliberately lie, Lem thought, but she could be mistaken. If a person mistook the little hand for the big hand, then ten minutes after five o'clock—which was probably when Lem actually got home—could look just like twenty-five minutes after two!

Lem had thought about explaining as much to Marshal Lee, but there was a problem. If his friends left him on the Avenue shortly after four, and Lem didn't arrive home, just a few blocks away, until after five, then how could he account for that missing hour of time? The last thing he could do was tell the whole truth.

That had been a big mistake—instead of going straight to his room on Lavaca Street, he had thought of Mollie and headed for the Hall house. What were the odds that on the very night he decided to pay a call on Mollie Smith, someone else should have murdered and raped her? That was not the kind of coincidence that was likely to impress the marshal, or a judge, or a jury.

What if someone saw him walking down West Pecan Street in the direction of the Hall house, with the full moon bright enough to show his face? He couldn't remember passing anyone that close, but that didn't mean it hadn't happened. In the story Lem told the marshal, he headed straight to the boarding house after he parted ways with his friends on the Avenue. It wasn't completely a lie, but it wasn't completely the truth, either. What if there was a witness who could point up the lie? What use was his alibi then?

Trapped in his cell, unable to sleep, fretting endlessly over every moment of the last two days, he kept coming back to the same horrible fantasy. It was like poking at a sore tooth; he couldn't help it. His thoughts led him in a circle that always ended with the worst possible thing that could have happened that night.

What if he *hadn't* turned back at the Shoal Creek bridge? What if he had crossed the bridge and done exactly as he intended, sneaking up on the Hall house to try to rouse Mollie?

He dwelled on the idea so much that he could picture it almost as if it had happened, as if it were a memory instead of a morbid fantasy. He could see himself tapping on the back window and peering into the dark room, trying the back door, finding it unlocked, stepping inside, into Mollie's room, feeling his way in the dark, getting something wet and slick and warm on his hands—because everything in the room was drenched with blood, they said, blood all over the floor and the walls. He imagined a door swinging open, a lamp blinding him, a voice screaming "Murder! Murder!"—and him standing there with blood all over his hands and a bloody ax at his feet.

What would it have mattered then that he had an alibi, that a hundred dancers at the Sand Hill ball could vouch for his whereabouts at a certain hour? If he had pressed on as he intended, and made his way into Mollie's room, and been caught there—he envisioned the scene so vividly that his whole body gave a jerk, he sucked in his breath and sweat poured off his forehead.

But something had stopped him from crossing the Shoal Creek bridge.

The dog ghost.

He had laughed at himself when he got back to his room at Rosie Brown's house, had a good chuckle at the notion that the ghost of his dear Grandma Sooty had made herself into a dog and chased him halfway across Austin, nipping at his heels. He woke up grinning at his foolishness hours later, and was still smiling when he stole into Rosie Brown's kitchen to forage for some late breakfast.

And then the marshal came looking for him, and all hell broke loose.

He had no doubt now about what had happened on the Shoal Creek bridge. He met a dog ghost. He was heading for a dangerous place, and the dog ghost chased him away. That the dog ghost was really Grandma Sooty, he was almost certain. She had reached out from the world beyond and had done what she could to save him. But was it enough?

Lem shivered and hugged himself. He'd never known a man could be so miserable. He stared at the blanket out in the hallway. He walked to the bars, never taking his eyes off the blanket. He dropped to his hands and knees on the cold, dirty floor. He caught a whiff of the stinking piss. The lower he went, the stronger the smell became. He dropped onto his side and pressed his shoulder between the bars. He extended his arm. The tip of his middle finger barely grazed the rough wool. If he could reach it with two fingers, he might be able to pinch just enough of the blanket to pull it toward him. He wrinkled his nose and pressed harder against the bars. He wiggled his fingers, but his middle finger only pushed the blanket a tiny bit farther away.

It was no good. The blanket was out of reach.

He pushed himself off the floor and got to his feet, brushing off dirt and grit. He was filthy now, and lying on the frigid stones had made him even colder, and the stale smell of urine had settled in his nostrils. He glared at the blanket, furious at himself for having thrown it out of reach, ashamed of himself for having tried to get it back.

He turned to the window and gazed at the cloudless patch of blue crisscrossed by iron bars. He would have wept, but his face was too cold. "Why'd you even bother, Grandma Sooty?" he whispered. "Why'd you even bother?"

"The damned thing is, Justice Von Rosenberg won't let any damned reporters into the damned courtroom!" Dave Shoemaker banged his empty beer stein against the tabletop. He was holding court himself, at Scholz's Beer Garden, northeast of the capitol grounds on San Jacinto Street.

Scholz's was a sprawling establishment, with dining rooms, meeting halls, a bar, and a kitchen, but its most popular feature was the courtyard out back, a festive place with gurgling fountains and exotic cockatoos on display in gilded cages. While a brass band played oom-pah-pah music, waiters in long white aprons delivered vast quantities of beer, treading back and forth among the crowded tables and occasionally scattering the peacocks who roamed freely in the gravel-strewn courtyard. More than a dozen men, Will Porter among them, had pulled their wooden folding chairs into a semicircle at Dave's table, knowing that if anyone had new information on the murder inquest, it would be Shoemaker.

It was late afternoon on Monday, the fifth day of the new year, which was also the fifth day of Lem Brooks's captivity.

"Damnable!" said Will, to add his outrage to Dave's. He banged his stein on the table.

One of the other men shushed him. "Watch your language, whelp!"

The little crowd laughed, but the rebuke was at least half-serious. Scholz's prided itself on being a true German biergarten, not a saloon but a wholesome establishment where women and children could venture without encountering coarse language or brutish conduct. It was run under the auspices of the local Germania Society, which regularly convened in the meeting hall. In the warmer months, along with concerts in the courtyard, the society sponsored daytime balloon ascensions and nighttime fireworks. As their advertisements in the *Statesman* stated, "No improper characters will be allowed on the grounds, and visitors may be called upon at any time for references." Scholz's was a long way from Guy Town, geographically and otherwise, but there was no better place in Austin to enjoy a stein of German beer, so long as a man watched his tongue and kept his temper.

"Of course, I don't happen to see any ladies in the garden at present," said the man who had chided Will, "so I don't suppose a 'damn' or two will get us evicted. But I do think that Shoemaker had better watch the careless manner in which he besmirches the name of Justice of the Peace Von Rosenberg. Within these gates, we're on German soil, you know."

"As if a Shoemaker wasn't as German as a Von Rosenberg!" said Dave. "My folks just didn't know how to spell."

"And they passed the trait down to you, to judge by the atrocious spelling I see in the *Statesman*!" said the man. Everyone laughed, but in fact most of them were slightly in awe of Dave's literary prowess. Every man in the group was under thirty and most of them were clerks, either for a bank or a business or the state. They spent their days in offices, tallying up columns, writing out orders, answering correspondence. Dave's life seemed adventurous by comparison.

The strongest personality among them was William Shelley, the man who had shushed Will and was now needling Dave. His family had connections in the state government, which explained how Shelley at the age of twenty-seven had the plum job of a clerkship working for Comptroller Swain, making $1,300 a year. He was unmarried and lived at his father's house on the bluff west of Shoal Creek called Castle Hill, so named for the military academy with a crenellated turret that perched on the hillside. Shelley had attended the academy as a boy, and between his lawyer father and his early military training he had acquired a crisp, authoritative manner that served him well at the comptroller's office. Will Porter found him intimidating. Dave, on the other hand, seemed to enjoy a bit of verbal sparring with Shelley.

Will loosened the scarf at his neck. The afternoon was just mild enough to sit bundled outdoors in the sun and enjoy a tepid beer. He watched two of the resident peacocks strut to a nearby fountain for a drink. The male gave a shake and unfurled his plumage. The female shrieked and stalked off. The male strutted after her.

"Closed hearings!" said Dave. "Von Rosenberg didn't waste a minute. He impaneled the jury of inquest on New Year's Day, kept them working Friday and Saturday, broke for the Sabbath, and has them back again today, and not one official statement of what's been discovered. No reporters allowed into the courtroom—nobody allowed in at all, except the clerks and the witnesses and the jury of inquest!"

"Twelve-man jury?" asked Shelley.

"Six."

"Any colored fellows?"

"None in the draw. But it does have an odd tilt to it—half of the fellows are hack drivers!"

"Probably make for good jurors; ought to be pretty good judges of character," declared Shelley. "Who else did Von Rosenberg round up for the jury?"

"A railroad watchman, a carpenter, and a deputy sheriff, Bill Pace; he's the foreman."

"Can't you talk to some of these fellows outside the courtroom and find out what's going on?" asked Shelley.

"You sound like Gaines! Of course, I waited like a cat at a mousehole and cornered each one as he came out of the courthouse."

"And?"

"I couldn't squeeze a peep out of them! Von Rosenberg's sworn them all to secrecy—witnesses, jury, the lot. He must have put the fear of the law in 'em, because they're all keeping their mouths shut. I should be inside, damn it, seated in the front row, looking over the stenographer's shoulder and taking notes. The *Statesman's* the eyes and ears of the people. It's an outrage!"

"Damnable!" said Will, banging his stein on the table again. William Shelley gave him a withering glance.

A waiter strutted up to the table. He shook his head, causing his drooping mustache to sway. "*Meinen Herren!* You must vatch your language, please!"

"Our language?" Will piped up. "It's . . . called . . . English," he said, enunciating like a tutor. Dave kicked him under the table.

The waiter huffed and wagged his finger disapprovingly at Will. "For you, *mein Jugend:* no . . . more . . . beer! And for der rest of you gentlemen?"

"More beer all around!" said Dave. He held up his stein and the others did likewise.

"*Ja, ja,* I bring it right away." The waiter scurried off, deftly sidestepping a rampant peacock that suddenly trotted across his path, only to avoid a near-collision with a redheaded boy in knee britches who shot around him and ran to Dave's table. It was Tommy, the printer's devil, clutching a scrap of paper.

"Mr. Shoemaker!" the boy called.

"Why, if it isn't the devil himself. What's up, Mephistopheles?"

"Mr. Shoemaker, the inquest is finished. Justice Von R. just issued the verdict! I got a copy for you!"

"It's not a verdict, you silly boy. Give me that!" Dave snatched the paper from Tommy's hand. The other men huddled closer, but Dave warded them off with his elbows. He peered at the handwriting on the ruled paper, then shook his head. "Not a damn scrap of new information. They didn't find out any more than I did!"

"What's it say?" asked Will.

Dave read aloud. "'We, the jury of inquest over the remains of Mollie Smith, find that she came to her death between 10 P.M. on the night of December 30th and 3 A.M. on the 31st, from injuries on her head inflicted with an ax, and we believe that said injuries were inflicted by one Lem, alias William Brooks.'" He flipped the paper over, as if looking for more. "And that's it! All this time I was afraid they were going to pull some big surprise out of a hat and make me look bad to Gaines for not conjuring up the murderer myself."

"So it *was* this colored fellow Lem Brooks, after all," said Shelley.

"Nonsense!" said Dave. "He's got witnesses and an alibi that put him miles away until well after three in the morning."

Shelley crossed his arms and leaned back, making the gravel crunch under his chair legs. "Maybe the jurors know some things you don't."

"I seriously doubt it. They just followed the marshal's lead and went after the first colored fellow whose name popped up. They're as lazy as he is."

Will sucked his breath between his teeth and nudged Dave, who looked over his shoulder to see Marshal Lee.

The marshal touched the brim of his hat. "Hello, Shoemaker. I just saw your junior colleague run in here." He cast an eye at Tommy, who fidgeted. "I suppose he's brung you the word. Now you can run back to Gaines and write up the news for everybody to read in tomorrow's edition."

Dave studied the man for a long moment. "'News' would imply something new, Marshal. Seems to me that the findings of the inquest are pretty stale."

"You think so? Well, in these parts, things are run by judges and juries, not newspapermen."

The waiter returned, balancing a big tray on one hand and carrying a folding chair in the other. There was a frothing pitcher of beer on the tray, along with a full stein which Grooms Lee accepted without even a nod of acknowledgment. The waiter deftly unfolded the chair with a jerk of his wrist and set it on the gravel behind the marshal, but Lee remained standing.

"I think it's pretty evident that you're holding an innocent man in jail," said Dave. "And the fact that you've convinced three hack drivers, a watchman, a carpenter, and a deputy sheriff to agree with you isn't particularly persuasive. The inquest's finding isn't a verdict. It's the opinion of six men, and nothing more. That's the way we'll present it in tomorrow's *Statesman*."

"Suit yourself." Marshal Lee shrugged and took a sip of beer. "But you're overlooking the obvious."

"How's that?"

"First of all, consider where Lem Brooks's alibi comes from—a bunch of drunk colored folks having a dance over on Sand Hill. They protect their own."

"Wasn't Mollie Smith one of their own?"

The marshal pursed his lips. "Even you ought to be able to see that I did Lem Brooks one hell of a favor by putting him in jail, where he's safe. We haven't seen a lynching in Austin in quite a while. I intend to keep it that way. People are pretty upset—a servant girl axed to death on her employer's premises, right inside the house. It could have been Mrs. Hall. Six respectable citizens have mulled over the evidence and stated for the record that I did the right thing when I arrested Lem Brooks. If I hadn't, he'd either be long gone or else hung from a tree. Somebody has to act responsibly in this town, Shoemaker, whether the daily press chooses to or not."

Dave put his empty stein on the table and stood. "Speaking of responsibilities, Marshal, I have a deadline to meet. If you fellows will excuse me—"

"Now wait a moment, Shoemaker," said William Shelley. "As I recall, you ordered the last round of beer! Who's going to pay?"

"Pretend you're in church, gentlemen, and take up a collection!"

There was a round of laughter as Dave and Tommy left. While everyone's stein was refilled, the marshal, ignoring the chair the waiter had brought for him, took Dave's seat at the center of the group.

Several of the men started talking at once.

"When do you think they'll have the trial, Marshal?"

"How soon will they hang the nigger?"

"Splendid job, Marshal."

"Done like a true Texas Ranger!"

When the pitcher passed by, Will shook his head and covered his stein with his hand. Amid the commotion he excused himself and headed for the gate. With Dave gone, he didn't feel quite comfortable in the group. Marshal Lee intimidated him even more than William Shelley. Besides, Dave had been paying for his beer, and Will didn't care to be embarrassed when it came time to pitch in for the latest round.

11

L E M was sleeping fitfully when the jailer woke him by banging his billy club against the bars. Lem gave a start and sprang upright on the cot. It was Tuesday morning, one week since the last day of Mollie Smith's life.

The sullen jailer had become a familiar sight, but there was someone else with him, a portly colored man with a broad, balding forehead and a salt-and-pepper beard. The man wore a Sunday-best suit and tie. His shoes were polished to black mirrors.

"Well, there he is," said the jailer. "Give me a yell if he spits at you. I'll be downstairs." He gave Lem a final smirk and left.

Lem rubbed the sleep from his eyes. "Do I know you, mister?"

The man shook his head. "I don't think we've met. My name is William Holland." The man extended his hand through the bars. He had a deep voice and a genteel way of speaking.

Lem walked to the bars. "I'm Lem Brooks."

"Yes, I know." The man gave him a firm handshake, then looked past him into the cell. He lowered his voice a little. "How are they treating you, son?"

"Decent enough, I guess. Nobody's beat me, if that's what you mean."

"Are they feeding you enough? Keeping you warm? I don't see a blanket on that cot."

"The one they give me stank. I th'owed it in the hall. They won't give me 'nother one."

"Well, perhaps we can do something about that."

Lem looked at him quizzically. "Who are you, anyway? You a preacher?"

Holland chuckled. "No, just a schoolteacher. I don't suppose I ever had you in one of my classes?"

"I didn't go to no schools in Austin."

"Oh, I've taught in colored schools all over Texas. But I don't think I ever taught you; I'd remember. But you must have had some schooling. You make change for the customers down at the Black Elephant, so you must know your numbers."

"Sure, I can add and take away. And I can read and write some. But I don't remember ever seein' you in the Elephant. Did Mr. Hancock send you?"

"No. But I went down to the Elephant to have a talk with him. Hugh Hancock says you're an honest man and a hard worker."

Lem wrinkled his brow. "Whatfor you talkin' to Mr. Hancock?"

The man didn't answer, but looked at him appraisingly. "Do you have family in Austin, Lem?"

"No sir. I come from Waco. Ain't got much family left there, either. Jus' about all of 'em done passed over."

"I don't suppose you've had many visitors here in jail."

"Hardly none at all. Man from the *Statesman* come the first day. Mr. Hancock come by coupla times, brung me some decent food. My landlady, Rosie Brown, sent me a change of clothes. And my friend Alec come once. Being inside this place shook him up so bad I don't reckon he'll be back."

William Holland nodded. "It's a terrible thing that's happened, Lem, that young woman being killed like that. I understand you knew her pretty well."

Lem shrugged, suddenly suspicious.

"You lived with her in Waco, didn't you?" said Holland.

"So what if I did?"

"The marshal thinks you killed her. So does the jury of inquest."

Lem looked at his feet. "I never!"

"Look me in the eye, Lem, and say that."

Lem raised his eyes. He still didn't know what the man was doing there, but looking into Holland's eyes, Lem couldn't help but trust him. "I swear I never killed Mollie Smith. Never would have, never could have. No way. I didn't do it, Mr. Holland."

Holland held his gaze for a long moment, then reached through the bars and grasped his hand. "You stay strong, son. You may feel like everybody's forgotten about you in here, but they haven't. Think of better days. And I'll see if I can't get that jailer to give you a clean blanket."

Holland smiled, gave Lem's hand a final squeeze, and then departed.

William Holland was a man with a most unusual history.

His mother had been a slave. William and his two younger brothers were born into slavery in Texas. About the time they reached adolescence, their mother died. A white man named Bird Holland, a hero of the Mexican War, purchased the three boys. As was customary, the boys acquired their new master's last name.

In short order, Bird Holland freed the brothers. He took them into his home, bought them good clothes, seated them at his dinner table. Bird Holland never legally acknowledged that he was their natural father. Nor did he deny it.

Emancipated young black men had no prospects in Texas in the 1850s. Eventually Holland sent them north to Ohio to be educated at a colored academy. While his sons pursued their studies in Ohio, Bird Holland settled in Austin and entered a career in politics. In '61, the year the Civil War broke out, he resigned as Texas secretary of state and joined the Confederate army. Meanwhile, two of his sons, including William, enlisted in the Union army.

In '64, as the war was drawing to a close, William Holland was twenty-three. He fought with the Sixteenth U.S. Colored Troops in the battles of Nashville and Overton Hill. His younger brother Milton had an even more notable military career, and received the Medal of Honor for bravery.

Bird Holland was killed in action that same year, fighting for the Confederacy at the battle of Mansfield, Louisiana.

After the war, William Holland returned to Ohio and attended Oberlin College. A deep chord was struck inside him by the motto of his teachers: "Live largely and unselfishly." He decided to move back to Texas, to see if he could make a place for himself.

His peculiar pedigree and the peculiar times in which he found himself gave William Holland a wide but often uneasy acquaintance with the ways of the world. His father had been white, but by all social and legal standards, William was colored. His father had defied society to care for William and his brothers, but had also been willing to die for the Confederacy. William had known slavery and freedom. He had lived in the North and the South. He was by training and inclination a scholar, but he had also been a soldier.

He began his career in Texas by teaching in colored schools all over the state. Organizing the first statewide convention of colored men drew him into politics, and in '76 he was elected as a Republican to the Texas legislature, where he sponsored a bill establishing the first state college for colored students, near Hempstead. Many in the state government still remembered his father; the open secret that he was Bird Holland's son unsettled some of his colleagues but also gave him a certain covert prestige.

For a while he held a position at the Austin post office, a federal appointment made under a Republican administration. Eventually he returned to teaching. He was now principal of Austin Public School Number 5.

After seeing Lem Brooks, Holland hurried back to the east side of town, to his two-room schoolhouse on Mesquite Street. He arrived just as his assistant, Mr. McKinley, was ringing the bell for the students to take their places inside. Holland was relieved. Meeting Lem Brooks had been important, but it would never do for him to be late for the beginning of the school day; William Holland was forever preaching punctuality to his students, and considered it incumbent on himself to set an unwavering example. He strode to the front of the classroom, a little out of breath.

"Good morning, students!"

The boys and girls sang out in unison: "Good morning, Mr. Holland!"

And so the day began.

While Mr. McKinley taught letters to the beginning students in one room, Holland taught arithmetic to the more advanced students in the other. He loved nothing better than to teach, and the morning passed swiftly. After the noon break, Holland put away his chalk and slate. For the rest of the day he taught grammar and reading.

When Mr. McKinley rang the dismissal bell, the students left in a stampede, including some rowdy boys whom Holland would ordinarily have kept after school for discipline, but to whom on this day he granted clemency. He told Mr. McKinley that he could go home early.

A few minutes after McKinley left, a carriage pulled up to the hitching post in front of the school. Two white men stepped out. They were both large of frame, bearded, well dressed, and in their early thirties. They looked alike enough to be brothers, and in fact they were. John and James Robertson were respectively the mayor of Austin and the district attorney of Travis County.

The brothers strode up to the schoolhouse door. Holland opened it before either of them could knock.

It had been a delicate matter, deciding when and where the Robertson brothers could meet with Holland to discuss the case of Lem Brooks. Holland had requested the meeting in a letter which he posted to the mayor early on Monday morning, even before the jury of inquest announced its findings. The mayor called on his brother at the courthouse to discuss Holland's letter, and while they were talking a messenger arrived with the jury's statement. The Robertsons decided to confer with Holland as soon as possible, but where? To meet an acknowledged leader of the colored population at either the mayor's or the district attorney's office would invite speculation and ears at the keyhole. To meet him socially, for a meal or a drink, was simply not possible. The brothers decided to pay a visit to Holland's schoolhouse the next day, and sent a reply to that effect. Who could spin any gossip out of an informal visit by Mayor Robertson to a city school? That the mayor should be accompanied by his brother, who happened to be district attorney, would surprise no one, as the two of them often went out and about together.

"Thank you for coming, Mr. Mayor, Mr. District Attorney," said Holland.

"Thank you for the invitation, Mr. Holland," said John Robertson dryly. He surveyed the starkly furnished classroom. "As mayor and an ex officio member of the school board, I seem never to have time to visit the free city schools often enough, especially the colored schools. This place appears to be immaculately kept."

"Thank you, Mr. Mayor."

James Robertson cleared his throat. "Can we speak freely?"

Holland smiled. "After the afternoon bell is rung, none of my students remains here by choice. I sent my assistant home early. There are only the three of us here, gentlemen."

The attitude of the Robertson brothers toward William Holland was obscure, even to themselves. Any white man who was the son of a former secretary of state would have commanded their instant respect; but Holland was not a white man. Like Holland, though a few years later, both of the Robertsons had served a term in the Texas legislature; but they could never seriously regard any colored man as a colleague and a peer.

Above and beyond all other differences, Holland and the Robertsons had been on different sides during the war. The two brothers had grown up in Tennessee. James had bitter memories of his widowed mother's struggle to survive, including a humiliating episode when she had to plead with Union soldiers not to take the family's last horse. John had been old enough in the war's last years to enlist for the Confederacy; it was even possible that he and Holland exchanged fire at the battle of Nashville.

Nevertheless, William Holland was a man of undeniable intelligence, impeccable manners, and unimpeachable integrity, and no man in Austin had a better claim to speak on behalf of the colored citizenry.

The mayor strolled slowly about the classroom. "Your letter indicated that you wished to discuss the effects of the terrible crime that occurred last week. This thing has left everyone with jangled nerves. The people of Austin are understandably upset."

"The colored folk of Austin as much as the white folk, if not more so," said Holland.

"That goes without saying," said the mayor.

"Rest assured," added his brother, "I know how badly the people of Austin want to see the guilty party prosecuted for the crime. The coloreds as well as the whites."

"Whoever killed Mollie Smith must be found out, and tried, and hung. A crime so atrocious cries out for justice," said Holland.

"We can all agree on that," said the mayor.

There was a lengthy silence, during which the two brothers contemplated a group of framed portraits on the nearest wall.

"Rutherford B. Hayes, James Garfield, and Grover Cleveland," noted the mayor. "I believe it's customary in most schools to display only our current chief executive, Mr. Cleveland—an outstanding Democrat, if you'll pardon my partisanship."

Holland smiled. "The portraits of President Hayes and President Garfield are my own personal property. Mementos, actually. I was a delegate at the national Republican conventions where they were nominated. When I teach the children about citizenship, I find it instructive to share those experiences. I can point to the portraits and say, 'In my own small way, I helped to make those men president.'"

"Ah, yes," said the mayor, somewhat chagrined.

An uneasy silence followed. Holland laced his fingers behind his back, as was his habit when addressing students, legislators, and fellow delegates. "I suppose we can save some hemming and hawing if I'll simply be blunt. Do you intend to prosecute William Brooks for the murder of Mollie Smith, Mr. District Attorney?"

"Just as bluntly, I'll tell you that I haven't yet decided."

"Meanwhile the young man languishes in the city jail."

"If he *is* the murderer, it would be irresponsible to let him out."

"Yet there doesn't seem to be a bit of evidence against him."

"Marshal Lee disagrees with you. So does the jury of inquest. Six honest citizens decided there was good cause to suspect Brooks of the crime."

"Mr. District Attorney, I don't know how the inquest arrived at its opinion, but I've been making some inquiries of my own, talking to various colored folk who know Lem Brooks, including his landlady and his boss and his friends and customers down at the Black Elephant. Now, so far as I can gather, the only evidence, if we can call it that, which weighs against Brooks is the purely circumstantial fact that he and Miss Smith once cohabited when they lived yonder in Waco. That previous relationship might provide a motive—I say it *might*—except that not one of the people I spoke to can remember ever having heard Lem Brooks express anger or animosity or ill will toward Miss Smith or toward her new man, Walter Spencer. When he did express his feelings on the subject—and this was generally leaning over a bar, in a setting where men are apt to speak openly—Lem Brooks seems to have expressed only a feeling of relief at being rid of his association with the young woman."

"Many a man broods over a wounded heart in secret," noted James Robertson.

Holland shook his head. "I do not think Lem Brooks is the secretive sort, sir. Go and speak to him yourself. Just as surely as there's not a hair on his head, there's not a lie in him. But the facts of the matter are even more convincing of his innocence. Consider, sir: whoever did that crime surely got some blood on himself. Yet Brooks's landlady showed me his room, and there was no blood to be seen anywhere. She says she can account for every stitch of his clothing—she does his washing—and there was not a drop of blood on any of that, either. There's no ax missing from her premises, or from the Black Elephant. And if the crime was committed before three in the morning, as the inquest itself determined, then Lem Brooks has a hundred people who can swear to his presence elsewhere. He was calling the dances at the ball on Sand Hill."

"Brooks's alibi does complicate the matter, I'll allow you that," said the district attorney.

"If you bring him to trial for the murder, it will be an injustice, sir, and not only against William Brooks," said Holland.

"What do you mean?"

Holland took a deep breath and grimaced thoughtfully. "How can I put this, gentlemen, other than bluntly? The colored people of Austin are very upset about this whole affair—more upset than you realize, I suspect. A young woman has been murdered in a most horrible way. A young man has been accused of the crime, but not one of the people I spoke to thinks he could have done it."

The district attorney shook his head. "All of this was taken into account by the jury of inquest."

The mayor looked aggrieved. "Mr. Holland, do you think that we feel the urgency of this matter any less than you do?"

Holland sighed deeply, stumped by the impossibility of explaining himself. Men like the Robertsons simply could not imagine how powerless he felt, how powerless every colored person in Austin felt in the face of what had happened. How he envied James and John Robertson, though not for their wealth, or their fine houses, or the deference others showed them. He envied the power they wielded and took so much for granted. They could make justice happen. Make justice happen! How godlike that was! They could see to it that wrongs were righted, that the guilty were punished and the innocent set free. No colored man could do such things. A colored man could vote and serve on a jury among white men, to be sure, but there was not and in William Holland's lifetime there would never be such a thing as a colored district attorney or a colored mayor of Austin.

Every shred of real power was in the hands of the Robertsons and their kind. Holland was merely a beggar at their table; that was the hard truth of the matter, and all his education amounted to nothing, except that it allowed him to grovel more eloquently. The Robertsons knew this; they would not even meet with him openly in their offices, yet here stood the three of them, doggedly maintaining the pretense that he was a constituent like any other, that the powerless people he spoke for carried some weight in their scheme of things.

The absurdity of the situation suddenly overcame him. Pretense crumbled, and for a brief moment Holland lost his nerve. The naked reality of how things stood was as crippling as a blow to the solar plexus. The Robertsons cared nothing for Mollie Smith, except insofar as her murder on a white man's property had outraged the white people of Austin. They cared nothing for Lem Brooks, except insofar as his orderly destruction by a jury might bring a satisfactory conclusion to a regrettable episode. They had deigned to call upon Holland merely as an indulgence, a sop, and his role was to be pacified, accept their better judgment, hold his tongue and tell others to do the same. He had intended for something else to happen, but now saw that his hopes were impossible.

He literally stooped a bit, as if bending from a blow. His face flushed hotly, his hands turned sweaty, and spots swirled before his eyes. This loss of nerve was a familiar ordeal, though he had not felt it for some time. It had struck him almost daily when he was in the legislature, facing the animosity of men who called him a Republican puppet and treated him like a perverse curiosity of nature, no more their equal than a cigar-smoking monkey. Less often but just as acutely he had experienced the same loss of nerve when he worked behind a desk at the post office, and when he moved as a presumed equal among the white delegates at the Republican conventions.

He sucked in a breath. That was the trick—to catch his breath, to calm his racing pulse, to remind himself that his flesh, though lighter than many black men's, was dark enough not to show a telltale blush. They must never see how shaken he was. He must maintain his dignity. He must endure the moment, exert his intelligence, earn their respect. And yet, in the end, wasn't it merely another acknowledgment of their power, another instance of his groveling, this tacit presumption that respect was theirs to give and his to earn?

Politics had once infected him with grandiose, cruelly impossible dreams. In recent years he had withdrawn from that world, and even as a school principal he had dealt as little as possible with those who ran the city. How much simpler and more gratifying it was to stay with his own kind, to invest his energies in teaching young colored boys and girls, to better the life of one person at a time. And yet, if he did not stand up now and speak for the colored people of Austin, using all the advantages of his birth and hard-won education, who would?

The critical moment passed. It was only that: a moment. He looked at the Robertsons' faces and saw that they had perceived nothing of his crisis. If they noticed anything, it was merely a shadow crossing his face, a flicker of unease. His breath returned, his heart steadied. His optimism (surely a gift from God, for there was no other way of accounting for it!) reasserted itself. These men could never be his friends, but what good was there in presuming them to be his enemies? They were men, as he was a man, and could be moved by reason and every man's natural love of justice. When he spoke, they listened. If he could find words plain enough, they might even understand.

"Mr. Mayor," he said slowly. "Mr. District Attorney. The ball on Sand Hill that night was held in a boarding house not far from my own residence. I could hear the music and the laughter until far into the night. I didn't attend, but I happen to know quite a few of the guests who did. Some of them are former students of mine. Some of them are colleagues, teachers at the Tillotson Institute. These are respectable people, responsible citizens. They all saw William Brooks call the dances until the ball was over. If you insist on bringing him to trial, despite the unanimous objection of those people, you will essentially be calling every man and woman at the Sand Hill ball a liar or a fool."

The district attorney was taken aback. "Now see here, Mr. Holland, there's no need to perceive personal insults in the impartial workings of the courts!"

Holland raised his hand. "But more important than that, gentlemen, is the fact that the fiend who killed Mollie Smith is still at large. Are you genuinely satisfied with Marshal Lee's efforts? It seems to me that he settled for arresting the first colored man touched by the least taint of suspicion, then called it quits. Would he have done as little if the victim had been Mrs. Hall instead of Mrs. Hall's cook? If you settle for trying William Brooks, if you pursue his conviction, you do more than torment an innocent man. You might as well tell the colored people of Austin that a young colored woman can be murdered in cold blood, then violated while she lies dying, and no one in power gives a damn about it!"

In the quiet that followed, James Robertson cleared his throat. He turned and paced slowly down the middle of the classroom, then turned and paced back. He looked at his brother the mayor and exchanged a glance that indicated they would discuss the matter privately between themselves, later.

It was the mayor who finally spoke. "As always, Mr. Holland, you have stated your concerns in a clear and forthright manner."

The district attorney nodded, not quite meeting Holland's gaze. "The colored folk of Austin are fortunate to have a fellow who can speak on their behalf so . . . forcefully."

"Thank you, gentlemen, for taking time from your busy affairs to meet with me."

The mayor looked relieved that the interview was drawing to a close. "It has been a pleasure, sir. It's always good to pay a personal visit to our city schools. The spotless disposition of your classroom reflects a high level of organization and discipline."

"Yes, a pleasure," concurred the district attorney, averting his eyes.

Holland smiled. "There is one other small matter which I wanted to discuss with you gentlemen before you go . . ."

That night at the jailhouse, Lem Brooks slept snugly beneath a clean wool blanket.

12

⌒⇁

$\mathcal{T}$ H E baby started to cry again.

They were all standing on the platform, waiting for the train—Eula and the baby and her husband, Jimmy, and to see them off, Jimmy's parents and Jimmy's sister, Delia, who was Eula's dearest friend in all the world. They were waiting for the afternoon train that would take Eula and Jimmy and the baby up to their new life on the McCutcheon farm in Williamson County. They were leaving Austin; they were moving to a farm. Jimmy was going to be a farmer—a farmer! Eula would have laughed, but she was too tired, and besides, the baby was crying again, and something would have to be done about it.

The train should have been at the platform already, but the man at the International and Great Northern window said there was a delay, something about the mechanics refitting a gasket on the engine. At least the sun was out.

The baby fell silent for a moment. In the quiet that followed, Eula could hear the murmur of conversations all up and down the platform. So many people waiting for the train! Where were they all going? The train followed a northerly line from Austin to Texarkana, with twenty stops in between, then it continued on to St. Louis, eight hundred and fifty miles away. Eula knew, because she had looked at the timetable posted outside the ticket window. If only *they* were going to St. Louis, or Chicago, or some other big city hundreds and hundreds of miles away, where life was exciting and there were interesting people to meet! Instead, she and Jimmy would be getting off at the third stop, Hutto, twenty-eight miles from Austin. George Mc-Cutcheon would meet them with a wagon and take them to his farmhouse. Eula felt as if she had been sentenced to prison.

The baby began to cry again. Jimmy's mother drew up to one side of Eula and Delia drew up on the other, both of them clucking like hens. Every woman on the platform pricked up her ears at the sound. Some of them even started edging a bit closer to Eula and the baby while continuing to talk among themselves, not even conscious of what their feet were doing, drawn by the sound like filings to a magnet.

Their reaction was perfectly natural, of course. Every woman there was simply responding as any woman should to the sound of a baby crying; every woman but Eula.

Her body responded, to be sure; she was fairly aching to feed the baby. It was her spirit that was strangely inert. She felt only a numbness inside, and a great weariness.

She had thought that the baby would make her happy, and it had, for a while, as long as everyone left the two of them alone. She had been perfectly content in their little room at her in-laws' house on Hickory Street. The baby had been part of her happiness. So had Delia—dear, sweet Delia, closer to her than a sister. That had been perfection, then: Eula and her baby, and Delia helping her and making her laugh and clucking over the baby. Even Jimmy's parents had been tolerable, as long as Mrs. Phillips didn't intrude too much. Even Jimmy had been tolerable for a brief while after the baby came, saying he had a reason now not to drink and would never do it again. That promise had lasted for about a week, and then things had gone back to normal, except with the added burden of the baby. And now they were off to a farm in the middle of nowhere, and her whole life was being turned upside down, and she was simply too tired and too miserable to deal with another moment of it.

Still, the baby would have to be fed. Her breasts insisted on it. The bosom of her dress was already beginning to blossom with little patches of moisture, which she hoped would not be noticeable against the dark fabric. "Delia, come with me," she whispered. They left Mr. and Mrs. Phillips and Jimmy without a word and went inside the station. The ticket agents behind their barred windows looked up at the sound of the baby crying. The women standing in line for tickets turned their heads as one, all looking alert and concerned. Delia found the door labeled LADIES and opened it for her. They stepped into a small lounge furnished with a tall mirror and a settee upholstered with faded purple velvet.

Eula sat. She tried to undo the top buttons of her dress, but the baby was wriggling and her fingers moved awkwardly within her kid leather gloves. "Delia, help me, sweet!" Delia undid the buttons for her and even reached inside to help her free one breast. The baby seized it and eagerly began to suckle.

Delia leaned back against the opposite corner of the settee and laughed.

Eula narrowed her eyes and looked at her sister-in-law glumly. "What is so very funny, Widow Campbell?"

"The look of relief on your face! It must feel quite extraordinary. And don't call me that. You know I hate it."

"I call you that because I envy you. The childless widow—how lucky you are!"

"Now, Eulalia—"

"And don't *you* call me *that* . . . or else I shall call you Adele."

"Better that than Widow Campbell. Except that my name was never Adele. It was always Delia, beginning in my crib. They're not the same name, you know. Adele and Adelaide and Della all mean 'noble,' which anyone could tell you I'm not. Delia is from the Greek, 'of Delos.' It refers to the moon goddess Artemis, the Roman Diana."

"You're not noble, then, just divine," said Eula wryly.

"Something like that."

"And what does Eulalia mean?"

"It's from the Greek, too. 'Fair speech,' I should think. 'Eu' in Greek means good."

"Then it hardly suits me, does it?"

"Now, Eula—don't cry."

"I can't help it."

"First the baby, now you. A couple of crybabies! That's better, now you're laughing. You're still crying, but you're laughing, too."

"Oh, Delia, you make me laugh!"

"That's what I'm good for."

"How shall I ever get on without you?"

The two of them regarded the picture they made in the mirror: the petite, almost childlike blond mother, radiantly beautiful despite her glistening eyes and sad demeanor, dressed in blue and nursing her baby, and her slyly smiling, raven-haired companion all in black—no longer dressed that way because she was a widow but because during her period of mourning she had discovered that black suited her so well. Eula was much the smaller of the two, short and slender but with a full bosom. Delia was tall, like her brother.

"Oh, don't worry, sweet," said Delia, "you know I'll come visit you at the farm as often as I can. It's only thirty miles away."

"It might as well be the end of the earth."

"It's only three stops on the train. Austin to Duval, Duval to Round Rock, Round Rock to Hutto. And then a wagon ride to the farm. The train will run late today, but I'm sure the agent at Hutto will tell Mr. McCutcheon to wait."

"I hope he doesn't. Then we'll simply have to catch the next train back to Austin and forget this crazy idea of Jimmy going off to be a farmer! Why can't he be a carpenter, like his father? Why can't he find work in town?"

"You know the answer to that, Eula. Jimmy can always find work; he just can't keep it. My dear brother is a slave to drink." Delia's face in the mirror was no longer smiling.

"But what's to stop him from being just as much a drunkard on Mc-Cutcheon's farm as he is here?"

"Mr. McCutcheon is to stop him, I presume. You must know the man better than any of us, Eula; he's your father's friend. Is McCutcheon a staunch moralist? A Bible-quoting Baptist? Did he vote prohibitionist in the last presidential election?"

Eula laughed. "Heavens, I don't know! All I know is that he's a good friend of Father's. Father stays at McCutcheon's farm sometimes, and Mr. McCutcheon stays free of charge at Father's hotel whenever he comes to Austin." Eula's father, Mr. Thomas Burdett, was proprietor of the Capitol Hotel on Congress Avenue.

"And so, as a favor to your father, Mr. McCutcheon is taking Jimmy on to work at his farm. A pity your father couldn't employ Jimmy himself, at the hotel." Delia shook her head. "But that would only have been asking for trouble, hiring a son-in-law who drinks. There's a bar right off the lobby, isn't there? No, it would never do for Jimmy to work at your father's hotel."

"So we've been swept under the carpet!" said Eula. "Off to the farm we go, where Jimmy can still drink himself into a stupor every night, but where no one will have to see it. No one but me."

Delia leaned toward her, suddenly earnest. She circled Eula with one arm and laid her hands over Eula's where they held the baby. "Maybe not, sweet. Maybe the change will do Jimmy good. Open air, honest hard work, you and the baby there to give him a reason to stay sober."

"No saloon right around the corner . . ."

"Exactly, no saloons! Maybe this move to the farm is just what he needs, Eula, to straighten himself out and do right by you and the baby."

"Maybe." Eula sighed deeply. The rise and fall of her breasts, together with the suckling of the baby, caused a curiously pleasant, calming sensation to spread through her. She closed her eyes. "Oh!" she said dreamily, "I do know something else about Mr. McCutcheon . . ."

"Yes?"

"The poor man's a widower now. Lost his wife, just last month. Sad. I suppose my father thinks he'll appreciate Jimmy's company. I shall have to cook and clean for *two* men, now, besides taking care of the baby . . ."

"A widower, you say?" While Eula's eyes remained closed, Delia openly pondered her friend's face. Perhaps it was not the best idea, she thought, to send a beautiful, unhappy young woman like Eula to lodge under the same roof with a recent widower. Whatever else George McCutcheon might be, he was a man—and Delia knew men. She knew what men liked. Eula, with her bright blue eyes, her golden hair, and her rose-petal skin—what man would not find her beautiful? What a fool Jimmy was, choosing to blind himself with drink when he had Eula at home to look at!

Feeling Delia's breath on her cheek, Eula blinked and opened her eyes. Delia drew back a little. Eula wrinkled her nose, then grinned.

"Delia, that smell!"

"What? It's only my toilet water."

"Oh no it's not! You smell of cigars!"

"Oh, dear . . ."

The two of them laughed. The baby momentarily lost its hold on Eula's nipple and began to cry again until Eula maneuvered him back into place. She shook her head in mock disapproval and lowered her voice.

"Delia, Delia, what nasty habits you've picked up from that Tobin woman! Never mind how I shall manage without you—how shall you manage without me?"

"What do you mean?"

"To cover your deceptions. Delia, last week, your mother almost found you out. You said you were going to sit the night with your sick friend Matilda across town, when actually you spent the night at May Tobin's. It was almost midnight when your mother suddenly took it into her head to run over to join you at Matilda's. I told her she was crazy, that she would only wake the sick woman, but it was all I could do to keep her from going. But, Delia, what if she *had* shown up at Matilda's and asked where you were?"

"Matilda would have thought of something to tell her, I'm sure. Just as I'd have done the same for Matilda; Matilda is another of May's regulars, as I've told you. But my mother would never have pushed the matter that far. She suspects I'm up to something, but she doesn't know what it is. Nor does she want to know, really. I'm sure she had no intention of going to look for me that night; she was just testing you, Eula, seeing if she could trick you into telling her something. And I'm sure she was greatly relieved when you didn't. My mother frets, and can't help fretting, but she'd sooner go deaf than hear the truth. She's the same about Jimmy; she's always asking me why he can't keep work, but if I tell her that he drinks too much, she changes the subject. She doesn't have a clue as to what I'm up to at May Tobin's, but I'm a widow, and so she worries, because she thinks that any widow under the age of thirty must be prone to wickedness."

"And so you are!" Eula said with a laugh.

"And so I am," Delid replied quietly.

Eula was suddenly earnest. "But you're not wicked, Delia. No one could ever call you that. You're good, and sweet. And lucky! I envy you. You have no husband, no child, and all the lovers you want."

"Eula, keep your voice down!"

"But it's the truth," Eula whispered. "You're free. You come and go as you like. And you make your own money, and you don't have to wash other people's clothes or cook for other people's families to get it. You have a secret life. You smoke cigars like a man!"

"A vice I've picked up from May. Apparently I need to splash on more toilet water afterward!"

"And you meet such interesting men! For the rest of my life I'll be stuck with Jimmy and farmer McCutcheon, while you're flirting with millionaires who run the state."

Delia laughed. "I don't think there are any millionaires in Texas, my dear. All the millionaires are back East, running steel mills and such."

"But if any millionaires ever do come to Austin, they're sure to visit May Tobin," said Eula.

"Probably! But do you know, I did meet the most interesting fellow at May's recently." Delia's green eyes sparkled.

"Well?"

"May says his name is Shelley, one of the sons of old man Shelley who has that big house over on Castle Hill. William Shelley; not Bill, but William—he's awfully formal. And not the least bit shy; he told me he works for Comptroller Swain and practically runs the department for him. Said the path's all clear for him to make a big name in the state government. He even claimed he was going to drop by his office to do a bit of 'catching up' after he left May's house that night! I told him I was insulted; I thought I'd exhausted him for sure. Of course he's awfully young; couldn't be thirty yet. No beard, just a mustache. But he must be important, because some man from the *Statesman* came barging into May's parlor that night, drunk as a skunk, and May had him booted out of the house rather than let him get a look at Mr. Shelley."

"Handsome?"

"Mr. Shelley? Quite! And unmarried."

"No ring?"

"No, but you can't always judge by that, because a lot of them slip off the ring when they come through May's door. Still, I could tell with him. No ring, *and* he wanted to talk afterward. The married ones already have a wife to talk to. It's only the other business they're looking for."

"Oh, Delia, I hate you! Jimmy hasn't touched me since the baby came."

"Do you want him to touch you?"

"I don't know. But it doesn't seem right. Am I so ugly since I had the baby?"

"Eula, don't be ridiculous. You're more beautiful than ever! I mean that. Oh, it *is* cruel, for you to be stuck with Jimmy. Sweet, lovely Eula and my dear, dreadful brother. What a mess he's made of everything. It's so unfair."

"That's why I envy you."

"Don't, Eula. My life is harder than you think. I joke about it, because I like to see you laugh. And I tease you with my tawdry conquests because . . . oh, I don't know why! I shall miss you so!"

"Now *you're* crying, Delia."

"Why not? We both deserve to cry."

They sat in silence, wiping their tears and looking at each other in the mirror.

The door swung open. Mrs. Phillips bustled in. She regarded them for a moment, then smiled. "Look at the two of you—just like sisters! Only my Delia is dark, and you're so very fair, Eula dear. I think the baby shall take after you. Is he done nursing?"

"I think so," said Eula. She sniffled and wiped a gloved finger under her nose.

"Oh, and I missed it! I waited on the platform with the men on purpose, to give you girls a chance to say good-bye."

"That was thoughtful of you, Mother," said Delia.

Mrs. Phillips nodded, then clapped her hands. "But now the train is finally boarding. Come, it's time for Eula to go!"

Within minutes the train began to pull away from the platform. The great black engine puffed clouds of smoke and vapor into the cold air. Eula poked her head out the window and watched as Delia and Mr. and Mrs.

Phillips waved and rapidly receded in the distance. Finally she settled back into her seat, holding the baby on her lap. Jimmy sat close beside her. He reached for one of her hands and clutched it. With his wavy black hair and green eyes, how like Delia he looked!

Eula began to cry again.

Two well-dressed gentlemen were seated across from Eula and Jimmy. One of them was a big, thickly built man of about forty with a very large head and pince-nez glasses. He looked vaguely familiar. When Eula began to sob, the man politely turned his attention to the copy of the *Statesman* on his lap.

The other passenger wore the cobalt-blue glasses of a blind man. His face remained tilted rather disconcertingly in Eula's direction. "Excuse me," he said after a moment, "but is there a window open? Perhaps someone could close it. Or am I the only one who finds it a bit chilly in here?"

Jimmy began to rise from his seat, but Dr. Terry motioned for him to stay where he was. "I'll take care of it, young man." He gave Jimmy a commiserating look, as if to acknowledge that comforting a weeping woman was the more pressing task. Dr. Terry shut the window, then returned to his seat beside Dr. Fry and recommended perusing his newspaper.

Jimmy held Eula and leaned close. He whispered in her ear, "Don't cry, sweet. It'll all be different on the farm. You'll see. Everything'll change for the better. I promise you!"

Eula was certain she could smell whiskey on his breath.

That evening, Dave Shoemaker worked late helping to put the final touches to the next morning's *Statesman*. Gaines had wanted another story on the Mollie Smith murder. Dave told him there were no new developments. "So what?" Gaines had barked at him. "If there's nothing to report, then report that!"

After everything else was done, Dave went to the office telephone and asked the operator to ring the police. Fortunately, it was someone other than Marshal Lee who answered. A little later Dave sent a last item to typesetting, to be run on the local-interest page:

> Tonight, as the *Statesman* goes to press, telephonic information from police headquarters reports all quiet in the city of Austin.

The Journey Back:

*D*o you mind if we close the window?" Dr. Kringel puts down the book he's reading. "I feel a bit of a draft."

"Not at all. Here, I'll do it." William Sydney Porter gets up from his seat. They are traveling first-class and have the compartment to themselves.

Porter grips the window frame on either side and pushes upward. The effort sends a dull pain through his lower back. He grits his teeth. What does it mean, that his back is always hurting, so badly that sometimes he can't sleep at night? Recently he looked up his symptoms in a medical manual — he learned to do that when he worked in the drugstore in Greensboro as a boy, and later, when he worked in the prison dispensary in Ohio, he became quite adept at diagnosing his fellow prisoners' complaints. He has just about concluded that he suffers from Bright's disease, an inflammation of the kidneys. How ironic, he thinks, that such a foul condition should have such a lovely name.

His doctors, however, dismiss his diagnosis. They tell him not to worry. They say he suffers from overwork and nervous agitation. They order him to stop drinking, and prescribe dope to help him sleep. The chronic aches in his abdomen and back are nothing but advancing old age, they say. Every man's back gives out sooner or later. But he's only forty-three! Surely he shouldn't be falling apart quite yet . . .

The pain subsides. He takes his seat across from Dr. Kringel and manages a smile. "Is that better, Herr Doctor?"

"Yes, thank you, Mr. Henry."

"Shh! Mr. Porter, if you please. You know I'm traveling incognito."

Kringel smiles. "A slip of the tongue. Funny, that to travel incognito you use your real name. Perhaps I should take a false name, so as to travel incognito with you." He laughs.

"Oh, I think 'Herr Doctor Kringel' sounds quite fanciful enough."

"Does it?"

"As should any name worth calling oneself."

Kringel smiles and takes up his book again. The publisher's name on the spine catches Porter's eye: S. S. McClure. He does a double take and leans forward. "Good Lord!"

Kringel lowers the book and looks at him quizzically.

"You're reading *Cabbages and Kings!*"

Kringel laughs. "I was wondering how long it would take you to recognize your own book, Herr Porter."

"My surprise is exceeded only by my gratification, Herr Doctor. It's the high point of any writer's day, to see his work being read by a gentleman on a train. Here, let me inscribe it to you!" Porter deftly lifts the volume from the doctor's hands. "But what's this? The title page is missing!"

"Is it?"

"Look here, you can see where it's been torn out along the spine. My book, mutilated!"

"I assure you, I didn't do it," says Kringel apologetically, running bony fingers through his mane of white hair.

"Where did you get the book?"

Kringel seems to hesitate. "At a book stall in Manhattan. I thought, as we would be traveling together, that I should read it. The stories are quite delightful."

"I see." Porter wonders darkly if the doctor shopped about until he found a secondhand copy—how else to explain the torn-out title page? His royalties are scant enough without people buying used copies! "Ah, well, I shall inscribe it to you anyway." He turns to the half-title page and writes, *To Herr Doctor Kringel, my traveling companion— While the train conveys us to Texas, may these tales transport you to tropical Anchuria and safely back again— O. Henry.*

He hands the book back to Kringel, who reads the inscription with a smile and slips the book into the brown leather satchel always at his side. "What is the origin of the name 'O. Henry,' pray tell?"

"Damned if I know, though everyone else seems to have a theory."

"What does the 'O' stand for?"

"Nothing. Literally nothing, as in zero. It's a naught, not a letter."

"Surely not."

"No, surely *naught!*"

Kringel's face is impassive for a moment, then he laughs. "You've made a pun!"

"Actually, I believe it was you who made the pun, Herr Doctor. I merely pointed it out. But I won't judge you too harshly; punning is a congenital, not congenial, defect, more deserving of pity than scorn. But to answer your question seriously, it's always been just 'O. Henry,' though I did have an editor a few years back who insisted I give him a first name for the byline. I told him the 'O' was for Olivier."

"And is it?"

"No. I suspect it might be Omar, as in Khayyam."

"Ah, 'A loaf of bread, a jug of wine, a book of verse, and thou beside me in the wilderness.'"

"Sounds swell, don't it? Omar had all that; I've got soda crackers, a pocket flask, a railroad timetable, and you in the opposite seat."

"But we are headed for the wilderness, are we not, Mr. Porter? I must confess that the idea of going to Texas makes me feel quite the intrepid explorer."

"Manhattan it isn't, but it's not exactly Borneo."

"I have images of gunfights and rattlesnakes."

"You might well see both, just as a man might well see labor riots and pickpockets if he visits New York. But you'll agree there's more to New York than that, and likewise there's more to Texas. When I think of my years there, it's the big sky and big hearts I remember." He gazes out the window. "People think Texas is all flat desert or grazing land, but around Austin it's hilly, with green meadows and wildflowers and oak forests. Austin's not a big town, but it takes itself seriously, having the state capitol and the university and all. It's the kind of place where most of the people were born somewhere else, and came there by choice. Most of Texas is like that; it's the frontier, or at least it was when I was there. People tend to be freer in a place where the roots don't go so deep. They have room to move about. And they move slower, especially come summertime, when it's hot as hell and the only thing that'll cool you off is a dip in cold spring water. Come August, grown men go down to the swimming hole at Barton Springs and splash each other like little boys."

"You sound nostalgic for the place."

Porter smiles. "It was a good place to be a young man in his twenties. But then, I suppose it's good to be in your twenties just about anywhere."

"Why did you leave?"

Porter looks out the window again. "Circumstances."

"Have you ever gone back to visit?"

"No." He shifts uncomfortably. His back is bothering him again. It's because of the seats, he tells himself. They're harder than he's used to. The long train trip will be even longer if his back is aching all the way. "What about you, Herr Doctor? Where do you hail from?"

"Oh, a tiny village in Bavaria that no one has ever heard of. I've been in America for many, many years."

"So I presumed, from how faint your accent is. Ever get homesick?"

"For Germany? Of course."

"Ever go back?"

"No." Dr. Kringel seems no more eager to discuss his origins than Porter, who wonders vaguely if the doctor, too, has things in his past he'd rather not discuss.

He gazes out the window. They are passing through farmland somewhere in New Jersey. It's madness, he thinks, to be taking such a trip. Madness! This thought occurs to him every thirty minutes or so, but has yet to compel him to pull the emergency brake. A feeling of inevitability has settled over him, stronger than the feeling of absurdity that he should be traveling all the way to Texas on a whim.

He yawns. Last night in his room on Irving Place he amazed himself by turning out not two but *three* completed stories, so as not to leave town with obligations unmet. His wrist aches still from so much writing. His head is dull from lack of sleep. He left the manuscripts with his landlady, along with notes to his editors explaining that he will be out of town for a while but giving no specific details.

He is off on a lark, as free as a bird. If he were twenty, this would be a great adventure. Instead, it is something else, though he is not quite sure what.

The characters in his stories are always doing the unexpected, or having the unexpected done to them. That's why readers love his stories; most of life is so drearily predictable that everyone yearns for strokes of serendipity, unforeseen developments, surprise endings. Now he finds himself on a journey which he could never have anticipated even twenty-four hours ago. He ought to feel thrilled, and he does, but mixed with the exhilaration is a vague uneasiness. He has the sensation of being drawn toward something terribly sad, of having been summoned by ghosts. Dr. Kringel calls him nostalgic, and so he is—but nostalgia can have a dark side, as cold and empty as death itself.

The doctor seems to follow his thoughts. "Forgive me for prying if it's none of my business, but I can't help but be curious about the events to which Dr. Montgomery alluded in his letter—the 'revolting crimes,' I believe he called them."

"The work of the Servant Girl Annihilators," mumbles Porter, with an ironic edge to his voice.

"I beg your pardon?"

He clears his throat and speaks up. "'The Servant Girl Annihilators'—a little name I came up with back then, back when it all happened. It was sort of a joke." He lowers his eyes. "Seems odd now that I ever could have made a joke about such a thing."

"I gather there was a series of murders in Austin, back in '84 and '85?"

"Yes. But you see, that's in retrospect, when you put it like that: 'there was a series of murders.' It neatens it up somehow. It says, here's where this thing started, and there's where it ended, and there you have your series of events. But at the time, when such a thing is actually going on, especially at the beginning, you don't see it that way. You don't see a beginning, middle, and end. You don't see all the connections." He shakes his head. "I haven't thought about all that for years. It's like . . . like a manuscript you put away because you were never quite satisfied with it, even though you put your heart and soul into it; it just finally became too much of a vexation to you. And years later you find it in a box and take it out and look through it, and parts of it are familiar and ring true, but other parts you can't even remember, not at all, as if some other person had written them . . ."

Dr. Kringel nods thoughtfully. "I think I know what you mean. If the past is too painful to discuss—"

"No, it's not that. It's too dull to be called a pain. It's just that so much happened, all in such confusion and so long ago, and there was never a resolution to it. Of course, there's never a resolution to anything, is there? Not really. One thing leads to another, and another . . ." He is thinking about the blackmailer now—thank God that every clickety-clack of the train wheels puts a bit more distance between him and that women! How curious that Dr. Montgomery in his letter should have invoked the name of Eula Phillips to summon him back to Texas, because the original link between Porter and the blackmailer was Eula Phillips . . .

"Forgive me," says Kringel. "I can see that the subject distresses you."

"No, no, if I'm grimacing, it's because my back is bothering me a bit. It's only natural that you should be curious when someone mentions 'revolting crimes.' Contemplating mayhem at a safe distance is the universal pastime of the age. Just pick up any newspaper for a daily dose. Shipwrecks, bomb-ings, executions, murders—"

"You sound disapproving, Mr. Porter. Yet you write for those same news-papers, don't you?"

"Yes, but my stories are a kind of antidote to all that poisonous mayhem. I'm the page the readers turn to for a quick bromide." Porter smiles ruefully. "So—what do you want to know about those 'revolting crimes' in Austin?"

"When did they start? Who was the first victim?"

"Well, it was around New Year's Eve of '84, as I recall. A colored girl with a common sort of name, Mollie or Maggie or Mary, Smith or Jones or John-son. I wonder if anyone nowadays, even back in Austin, remembers the name of that poor girl!" He muses for a moment, then laughs. "I remember Dave Shoemaker told me he was always writing it down wrong and had to rely on the typesetter to catch the mistake."

"Dave Shoemaker?"

"Friend of mine who wrote for the newspaper. And the person, coinci-dentally, who introduced me to Dr. Montgomery and his wife that spring. It was a mighty small world back then."

"It still is," says Dr. Kringel, "for here sit the two of us, born a world apart yet with so many links between us—perhaps more than we realize."

"Well, we shall certainly have time to discover them all between here and Texas."

"Yes, that gives us something to look forward to during the journey." Kringel clears his throat. "I believe you mentioned having a pocket flask of whiskey a moment ago . . ."

"Good idea! Especially if I'm going to reminisce about murder and may-hem." He pulls the flask from his waistcoat. He locates a little cabinet be-neath the window that contains glasses for their use. He pours a finger for each of them.

"A toast," says Dr. Kringel. "To the past."

Porter hesitates. "Very well: to the past."

The whiskey warms his throat. "Let me see what I can remember. It seems there was an ax—yes, an ax was used in all the murders, that was the most gruesome thing. After the first one, poor Mollie Smith or Mary Jones or whoever, they arrested a young colored fellow, claimed it was a crime of passion. They had no idea, you see, of what was to come . . ." He shakes his head. "Then there was a respite, if I remember correctly."

"A respite?"

"No more murders for a while, at least not like that one. Life went on pretty much as usual, that spring. Nothing of significance occurred . . ." He shrugs, but there is an odd glimmer in his eyes and a furrow in his brow. He sighs, feeling the ghostly twinge of a pain inflicted long ago, a wound to his heart from a springtime almost forgotten.

Clickety-clack, the train carries them farther from New York and closer to Texas every minute. Porter reminisces and Dr. Kringel leans forward, listening intently, occasionally interrupting to ask a question. It seems odd that a philosopher should be so fascinated by such sordid stuff as those murders in Texas, long ago; but then, Porter thinks, why not? Even incognito, O. Henry is a storyteller of unusual gifts, and what is a philosopher but flesh and blood, as hungry for sensation as the next man?

PART TWO

AMONG THE
BUSHMEN

❦

Austin and Liendo: January to May 1885

13

Enjoy your breakfast?" the jailer said, collecting the tray from the slot.

Lying on his cot facing the wall, Lem grunted. "Lumpy grits. Skinny piece of rancid bacon. And was that s'posed to be coffee or dishwater?"

"Insult my cooking, will you! Well, too bad you didn't enjoy it. It's the last meal you'll be getting in this place."

Lem rolled over to face the bars. The jailer's scowl broke into a grin. "You mean—" Lem's mouth went dry.

The jailer threw back his head and cackled. For a moment, Lem thought the man had made a fool of him. Then the jailer sighed and wiped a tear of laughter from his eye and sorted through the jangling keys on the big ring until he found the one he wanted. The lock made a clanking noise. The door swung open.

Lem cocked his head. "What's so funny?"

"The look on your face! Well, come on. What are you, deaf? They're letting you out. Guess they decided you didn't hack up that poor girl after all."

Lem slowly got up and walked across the cell. Three steps and he was across the threshold. The jailer slammed the door shut. The clanging echoed up and down the hall.

The jailer led him down the stairs. The man sorted through his keys and opened a metal lock box that sat on a counter in the lobby. Inside were the things they'd taken from Lem's pockets on the day Marshal Lee brought him in: a few coins (the pay he'd received for calling the dances at the ball on Sand Hill—that night seemed ages ago), a pocketknife, his key to Rosie Brown's front door, a cloth pouch with some tobacco in it.

The jailer produced a printed form and a fountain pen. "It says you got all your things back. There's the date, Monday, January 12th. Make your mark and I'll witness it."

"I knows how to sign my name," Lem said quietly, but his hand shook so badly that the W was an illegible squiggle, and making the *i* he pressed too hard and obliterated both letters with a discharge of ink. He took a deep breath and started over, concentrating on each letter of *William Brooks*.

"Now you're free to go. Keep out of trouble!" The jailer scooped up the paper, slammed the box shut, and plucked the pen from Lem's hand. He threw back his head and cackled again. "Oh, the look on your face!"

Lem walked across the little lobby and out the front door. He paused on the steps. He felt a little like he had felt on his first day in Austin, stepping onto the train platform, a stranger with no one to greet him and no place to go. He was facing the capitol grounds. The General Land Office loomed on the hill across the street, like a giant cake frosted to look like a castle. The day was overcast, with stacks of pearl gray clouds and here and there a bit of yellowy white where the sun almost broke through. The soft, hazy light made everything seem not quite real. Lem silently prayed that he wasn't dreaming. He even shut his eyes for a moment and opened them again, but nothing changed. He was free.

His first impulse was to head straight to the Black Elephant. Hugh Hancock had promised to hold his job for him, and a beer would certainly hit the spot—no, a shot of whiskey! And not the cheap rotgut, but the best in the house, the label Mr. Hancock himself drank, the kind that Lem always served to Marshal Lee . . .

The air was chilly. He slid his hands into his pockets and fingered his house key. Perhaps he ought to go to the boarding house first, to make sure everything there was all right. A long hot bath in the tub would be heaven! But he didn't relish the prospect of seeing Rosie Brown.

A stroll down Congress Avenue might clear his head, but Lem wasn't sure he wanted to confront so many faces all at once. Who knew what folks had been saying about him, or how they might react when they saw him out on the street again?

He turned away from the Avenue, vaguely thinking he'd head for the Elephant; a few blocks east and then due south on Neches Street would get him there, skirting the busier parts of town. But when he came to Neches, he went ahead and crossed. It was a strange thing, but his feet seemed to know where they were going even if he didn't. He came to Red River Street; Fannie Whipple's place was on Red River. A bit of womanly comfort was something he could surely use! But his feet kept walking. He crossed the little bridge over Waller Creek, and then the broad expanse of East Avenue. The way grew steeper. The climb taxed his breath a bit, but it felt good, so good to feel the muscles in his long legs pulling and stretching after so many days of being cramped inside the cell. He drew in lungfuls of cold, crisp air until his chest ached and his head felt light as a balloon.

When he saw the place, he knew it at once, though he couldn't remember having noticed it before. He crossed the gray lawn to one of the windows and rose on tiptoes to peer inside. He couldn't quite see the boys and girls sitting in their places, but he could see their teacher pacing slowly back and forth at the front of the classroom, holding an open book in his hands and reading aloud in his deep, genteel voice:

"Who are you, dusky woman, so ancient hardly human,
With your woolly-white and turban'd head, and bare bony feet?
Why rising by the roadside here, do you the colors greet?"

William Holland paused to look up and scan the faces of his pupils, who were following every word with rapt attention. Then he noticed the man peering in through one of the windows. Holland removed his reading glasses and blinked several times, then broke into a smile.

"Please excuse me for a moment, children. I have a visitor. Eudocia, would you continue reading Mr. Whitman's poem in my absence?"

A girl near the front of the classroom obligingly stood and took the book from him. She cleared her throat and commenced reading in a high, singsong voice:

"Me master years a hundred since from my parents sunder'd,
A little child, they caught me as the savage beast is caught,
Then hither me across the sea the cruel slaver brought."

Lem Brooks awaited him on the doorstep. Lem's shoulders trembled and his voice was choked with tears. "Thank you, sir!"

Holland clutched his shoulders. "What does this mean? Did they let you out? Are you free?"

Lem tried to speak, but was unable and nodded instead. "Your doin'," he finally managed to say. "Wasn't it?"

"I did what I could," Holland said.

"Thank God for you and Grandma Sooty!"

Holland smiled quizzically. "I thought you had no family, Lem."

Lem shook his head and sobbed. Holland stepped forward and circled him with his arms.

The children must have heard, because there was a silence from the classroom. Finally, Eudocia continued to read:

> "What is it, fateful woman, so blear, hardly human?
> Why wag your head with turban bound, yellow, red and green?
> Are the things so strange and marvelous you see or have seen?"

That morning, Marshal Grooms Lee was busy elsewhere. Normally he would have taken charge of freeing a prisoner himself, but in Brooks's case he had no stomach for it. He signed the necessary papers and let the jailer handle the rest. The district attorney was a fool to let Brooks go. Lee practically said as much to the man's face, but Robertson had insisted. No matter; Lee knew where Brooks lived and where he worked. The marshal would keep his eye on him.

But for the moment, Lee had other business in another part of town, on a street of humble little houses and shanties just to the northeast of the capitol grounds. A little past North Avenue he stopped his horse and dismounted. The house had no proper yard, just a plot of packed earth that merged imperceptibly into the street, but it did have a cedar hitching post. Marshal Lee hitched his horse and stepped onto the porch, his heavy boots making loud footsteps. The house was sorely in need of paint. The spot where he knocked on the door frame was worn to bare wood.

A middle-aged colored woman answered the door. When she saw his gold-braided cap and blue uniform, she wiped her hands on her apron and pulled it off.

"Is this 1511 Brazos Street?" said the marshal.

"Yes, sir."

"You don't have any numbers showing."

"They was painted 'bove the do'frame, once 'pon a time. Wore off, I reckon."

"Are you Cynthia Spencer?"

"I is."

"Is your son here?"

"I gots three sons. They's all livin' here now. The two youngest is out workin'."

"It's Walter I'm looking for."

"He's here, but he's feelin' awful poorly. He's lyin' in his bed right now."

"No I ain't, Mama." A hulking, shadowy figure stepped up behind her. "Who's at the door?"

"You know me, Walter," said the marshal. "Step out here on the porch."

His mother moved out of the way, but Walter hung back. "The light hurts my eyes."

"Step out here anyway. You run along, Mrs. Spencer. Or is that Miss Spencer?"

The woman gave him a sour look and withdrew. Walter stepped out. His head was bandaged. Part of the dressing drooped down to cover one eye.

"So you moved back with your Mama," said the marshal.

"Yes, sir. Never was a real boarder at the Hall house. Never paid rent. When Mollie passed, I had to go."

The marshal cocked his head. "You had a nice arrangement there for a while, though. No rent and a warm bed. You must miss Mollie something awful."

"I do, sir!"

"So you're not back to working yet?"

"Not yet, sir. I tried to do some liftin' for a fellow just yesterday, but my head cain't stand it. Awful headaches! Just like Mollie used to git, I reckon. She'd git headaches so's she couldn't see straight. Lie flat on her back and snap at me if I so much as made the floorboards creak. I'd make faces when she wasn't lookin', 'cause I didn't think they could be that bad, but Lawd I believes it now. I figure she left me her headaches when she passed over, kinda spiteful like."

The marshal looked at him darkly. "Did Mollie have some reason to spite you, Walter?"

"No! Never had one reason to be the least bit spiteful, but that never stopped her." Walter chuckled softly, then gritted his teeth.

"I had to let Lem Brooks out of jail today, Walter. The district attorney's not going to charge him with Mollie's murder."

"He ain't?" Walter made a crooked face.

"You understand? Lem's free to come and go. I figured I ought to tell you, Walter. If it *was* Lem Brooks who murdered Mollie and did that to your head, who's to say he won't try to finish what he started?"

"You mean, come at me with a ax again?"

"Maybe. I figured you ought to know."

Walter shook his head. "I never did nothin' to hurt that fella."

"Maybe he doesn't see it that way." Marshal Lee shrugged. "Or maybe I'm wrong about Lem Brooks, and the district attorney is right. But if Lem didn't take an ax to Mollie, who did?" He gave Walter a long, hard look. It was a rare man who didn't squirm a little when Grooms Lee fixed him with that look, but Walter's grimaces made it hard to gauge his reaction. The marshal leaned closer. "You say Mollie passed her bad headaches on to you. Could be that's another way of saying it was Mollie who hit you in the head with that ax. She could be a mean bitch, couldn't she? You never did a thing wrong, but she still took her spite out on you, day after day. Had a big man like you walking on tiptoes, afraid to make the floorboards creak! If a woman like that up and hit me in the head with an ax, I figure I might grab it away from her and hit her right back, without even thinking. Is that the way it was, Walter?"

Walter's jaw quivered. He clutched his head with both hands. "I gots to lie down," he whispered.

Marshal Lee shook his head. "Mollie had you by the balls, didn't she? Liked to give 'em a hard yank now and then."

"Don't talk bad about Mollie!"

"She figured you weren't man enough to do anything about it. She was wrong about that, wasn't she?"

Walter pulled his hands from his head and held them rigidly at his sides, his fingers spread wide apart and quivering. He hunched his shoulders and a wild look came into his eyes. Grooms Lee experienced an unaccustomed sensation, a tremor that was something like fear. He felt the color drain from his face, but he managed not to blink.

"I don't like it that there's nobody in jail for killing Mollie Smith," he said evenly. "Makes me look bad. And I don't think you're nearly as simple-minded as you make out. This thing's not over. You're smack in the middle of it. You try to slip out of Austin without me knowing, and I'll hunt you down with bloodhounds. Understand me, Walter?"

"He understands you." Walter's mother stepped onto the porch and took her son by the shoulders, pulling him toward the door. She slid her palm under the bandages, against Walter's forehead, feeling for fever. "He ain't goin' nowhere, Marshal. Where would he go? Jus' leave us alone!"

She pulled Walter inside and closed the door in Lee's face.

She shouldn't have done that, the marshal thought, especially when meek, mild Walter was just beginning to show what he was really made of. But the marshal was satisfied; he had made his point.

He stepped off the porch, unhitched his horse, and hoisted himself into the saddle. He peered up and down Brazos Street, then decided to ride up north a ways, around the new university grounds, just to see how things were faring in that part of Austin. Then he would double back around the capitol grounds and canter down the Avenue. By noon or thereabouts he would have worked up a good appetite. He figured the Iron Front was just about due to treat him to a free steak.

14

⤳

$\mathcal{T}$HE printer's devil came running through the office. From the corner of his eye, Dave perceived him as a streak of red hair. "Gaines coming through!" Tommy cried.

Like matching bookends, Dave Shoemaker and his fellow reporter Hiram Glass swung their feet off their desks and onto the floor, each rotating in his swivel chair. Idle jabbering, compulsive doodling, and even staring into space Gaines could abide, acknowledging as he did that part of a reporter's job was to ruminate and discuss, but the one thing he could not tolerate was a pair of feet propped on a desktop.

William Pendleton Gaines came swaggering up the aisle between their desks. His hair was sleekly pomaded and swept back from his balding forehead, and his mustache was well waxed and pressed into curlicues. He was wearing his best gray suit, which his wife, Augusta, had ordered for him from a New Orleans tailor, taking the measurements and choosing from among the swatches of gabardine herself. He carried a folded document in his hand.

"David Shoemaker!" he said, practically shouting. He swatted the document against the desk at the very spot where Dave's feet had rested a moment before. "What word on the Mollie Smith case?"

"The last I heard, she was still dead."

Gaines looked down his nose. "Very amusing. Perhaps we'll run that for our lead item! What in blazes is the marshal doing to find the killer?"

"Damned if I know. Whenever I ask, he just smirks and nods, like he knows a nasty secret."

"And does he?"

"I doubt it. If you ask me, Grooms Lee is just a mean little—"

"He's Joseph Lee's boy is what he is, and don't you forget it!" said Gaines. "Once construction starts on the new capitol this spring, Joseph Lee is going to be king bee in this town. He's head of the building commission, from which shall pour a great river of largesse, like the Nile overflowing its banks."

"That doesn't make Grooms Lee any less a bastard and a bully."

Gaines tilted an eyebrow. "David Shoemaker, you pretty much say whatever you please right to my face, don't you?" He put his fists on his waist and raised his chin. "And that's why I keep you on, damn it! Pay attention to this young man, Hiram Glass. You would do well to emulate him."

Hiram nodded. He was a slender, monkish fellow with graying temples and a receding hairline, fifteen years older than Dave. He had been at the *Statesman* longer than anybody else, including Gaines. Along with editing the state and national wire reports, his specialty was political reporting.

"Well, there we are, Mollie Smith is yesterday's news," muttered Gaines. He waved the document in his hand. "*Here's* tomorrow's news. Something in your purview, Glass."

"What is it, Mr. Gaines?" Hiram's eyes appeared to be half shut, but that was his typical expression.

"Gentlemen, I have just come from having lunch at the Governor's Mansion. I carry with me the text of the speech which Governor Ireland shall deliver tomorrow at the opening of the Nineteenth Session of the state legislature."

"Bless us all, the politicians are about to convene again!" said Dave.

"No shortage of news once that happens," said Hiram morosely. For Dave, the influx of legislators and their staffs meant that overnight it would become impossible to find an empty barstool in Guy Town. Crime-wise, there was always the prospect of a politician or two being caught in a gambling scandal, or fistfighting in a saloon, or perhaps even engaging in a gunfight. Members of the legislature were known to be lively. But for Hiram Glass, the new session meant long hours listening to boring speeches and poring over reams of proposed legislation. Few men were as well versed in the workings of the legislature, or had as sure a grasp of the personalities involved. But Hiram's knowledgeability came from diligence, not passion; politics bored him profoundly, which was one reason he had succeeded as a political reporter. He had no strong preferences or points of view, and hence no difficulty deferring to the opinions of William Pendleton Gaines on any given issue, and slanting his stories accordingly.

"So tell me, Hiram," said Gaines, "what issue is likely to cause the biggest stir in this upcoming session?"

Hiram leaned back and pressed his fingertips together. "I imagine it shall be whatever issue the *Statesman* reports on most stirringly."

Gaines laughed. "Well put, man! That's the spirit! The *Statesman* separates the wheat from the chaff, the silver from the dross. It's up to us to say what matters and what don't! Well, then, I'll tell you one thing to keep an eye on. A few evenings back, Mrs. Gaines and I had the Moores to Bellevue for dinner. You know Taylor Moore, our state representative for Travis County. Brilliant lawyer, wonderful fellow all round! His wife's a charmer, thick as thieves with my Augusta. Anyway, Moore told me about a piece of legislation that's going to raise the roof down at the state building. When he told the ladies, you should have seen Augusta's eyes light up."

Hiram laced his fingers together. "Might you be referring to the bill requiring employment of female clerks in the state departments?"

"Exactly! The upshot is this: women can't get a toehold in clerical positions in the state government, and Moore and some colleagues in both houses intend to change that. Now, there's no law preventing a department from taking on women clerks. In fact, a couple of sessions back the legislature passed a law specifically stating that it was legal to hire women. Plenty of women have applied for state jobs since then, and how many do you think they've hired? Not a single one! The ladies have been systematically excluded. Representative Moore has a phrase for it, calls it—now what was it? Ah, yes! The 'invisible shield' that keeps women out. But if he and his allies in the legislature have their way, the state of Texas will remedy the situation overnight. The bill he's backing will *compel* department heads to hire women clerks in equal numbers to men, and not in some far-off future but right away—*bang*, get rid of half the male clerks and hire women to take their places. Overnight parity of the sexes! Did you ever hear of anything so bold? Augusta was ecstatic. 'The cause of women shall be advanced by fifty years with the stroke of a pen,' as she put it."

Dave cocked his head. "What you've just described is about the most farfetched notion I've ever heard of! Do I understand that the *Statesman* is going to support this outlandish bill?"

"Outlandish? Epoch-making!" said Gaines.

"I had no idea women's suffrage was one of your causes," said Dave.

"Suffrage? Nonsense! No woman shall ever have the vote during my lifetime, and thank God for that. But I have always supported the right of any woman to enter the workplace, if her circumstances demand it."

Dave peered about. "I don't see any women in this office." He raised his eyebrows in mock horror. "You're not going to replace Hiram and me with lady reporters, are you?"

Gaines gave him a withering look. "Only if you persist in vexing me, Shoemaker. Glass, I take back what I said about emulating this fellow. Now then, I've wasted enough time chatting with you two. Get back to work!" He headed for his own office, then abruptly turned back. "And keep your feet off your desks!" He raised an eyebrow shrewdly. "I doubt that I'd have such a problem with women reporters."

As soon as Gaines was gone, Dave swung his legs up onto his desk. He leaned back in his swivel chair with his hands behind his head. "Fire half the men and take on women! Taylor Moore must be as crazy as Gaines."

"The word is, it's liable to pass," said Hiram.

"You kill me, Hiram Glass."

"I'm deadly serious."

"Never in a million years."

Hiram made no reply. He opened the large bottom drawer of his desk and pulled out a brown glass bottle and a measuring spoon.

"What now?" said Dave. Hiram was famous for his consumption of patent medicines. Other men might keep a flask of whiskey or a half-smoked cigar in their desks; he kept a store of tonics. Dave tilted his head to peer into the big drawer. "Good Lord, Hiram, you've accumulated a whole pharmacopoeia in there! There must be twenty bottles."

"Each and every one of them has its purpose. I use them only as needed." Hiram poured a spoonful from the brown bottle and inserted it into his mouth. On the bottle's label Dave spied the engraved countenance of Dr. Terry.

"Our master's new business partner! You got that poison for free, I hope."

"Indeed I did." Hiram smacked his lips and made a sour face. "From the good doctor himself, while he was in town promoting his wares."

"Taste good?"

"The flavor is irrelevant. It's highly effective at calming my nerves."

"What the hell are you talking about, Hiram? There isn't a nerve in your body."

"In point of fact, dear colleague, I have been afflicted with nervous complaints all my life. If you have observed no outward signs of distress, that's a testimony to the efficacy of my tonics."

"Just look at all them bottles! Honestly, Hiram, I believe you must try every patent medicine that comes down the pike."

"One of the few advantages of working for this newspaper is that I get to see advertisements for all the newest medicines in advance. There's a specified tonic for virtually every possible complaint. Even, if I may mention it, odoriferous wind"—Hiram reached into the drawer and held up a slender green bottle—"the cure for which might be of particular interest to *you*."

Dave harrumphed. "No medicine for me, thank you very much. I'll just stop eating beans for breakfast."

Hiram smiled serenely. "Ah—I feel my nerves being steadied even as we speak. I have a feeling we're in for a grueling legislative session."

15

⌘

$\mathcal{I}$N the rush of the new year, the murder of Mollie Smith was largely forgotten. The first weeks of January passed swiftly.

For Eula Phillips, the new year meant adjusting to life on the Mc-Cutcheon farm. As anticipated, she missed Delia. She missed the hustle and bustle of Austin. Still, the move did seem to mark a change for the better in Jimmy. Away from the saloons and his regular drinking pals and his doting parents, his head seemed to clear.

George McCutcheon promised him regular wages and, depending on how the crops and livestock fared, a small share of any profits at the end of the year. All Jimmy's previous jobs had come from friends of his father in the Austin building trade, men who, knowing Jimmy's reputation, took him on begrudgingly as a favor to Mr. Phillips. They expected little from him and he fulfilled their expectations, showing up for work drunk or late, and sometimes not showing up at all, always eventually getting himself fired. But on the farm there was no question of slacking off; animals had to be fed, firewood had to be toted, fences and walls and roofs had to be mended— not tomorrow, but today. Jimmy's constitution had always been hardy, even when he was drinking, and working in the cold outdoors seemed to invigorate him. He worked hard, ate heartily, and slept soundly. A week after they arrived on the farm, he reached for Eula in the darkness one night and made love to her for the first time since the baby came.

As for Eula, she had more work than she had ever thought herself capable of. McCutcheon's late wife had hired a colored housemaid, and the woman was competent enough, but there was far more work than she alone could handle. Eula cooked, cleaned house, ordered provisions from the nearest general store, washed and mended Jimmy's clothes. She took care of George McCutcheon's clothes as well, a responsibility she found oddly unsettling. It seemed improper somehow that she should put her hands inside McCutcheon's long johns to turn them inside out. Handling his undershirts, she could smell the strong sweat of his body, different from Jimmy's. One night, stitching the frayed inseam of McCutcheon's denim pants, a short, wiry hair—it had to have come from between his legs—somehow became wrapped around her forefinger. The sudden intimacy of it made her flush. Rather than touch the hair, she held up her hand and blew it away, but afterward it seemed that she could still feel it, very faintly, where it had circled her finger, like a ring.

McCutcheon, whom she had barely met before coming to the farm, was younger than she had thought—older than Jimmy to be sure, with flecks of gray in his hair, but younger than her father. The recent loss of his wife had burdened him with a great sadness. Because he never smiled, Eula was not sure whether she thought he was handsome or not. She did know that he was strong and fit, for one day in the hallway she caught a glimpse of him without his shirt. His shoulders were broader than Jimmy's and his chest had more hair on it, curly dark hair like the one in his pants.

To add to all her other work, there was the baby, whose demands were unending. Eula continued to be disappointed and puzzled over her reactions to the baby. It seemed to her that there must be some maternal instinct natural to other women that was stunted in her. To be sure, on some days the baby was a pure blessing, for he kept her company and without him she would have wept from loneliness. On those days, when McCutcheon and Jimmy were off working with the hired hands and the house was quiet, and she had caught up with her work, she might sit for a whole hour and do nothing but play with the baby, giving him a finger to clutch, cooing at him and kissing him, telling him he was her perfect angel. In those moments it seemed to her that she loved him in exactly the way that she should, and that she was as good and natural a woman as any other.

But on some days—and this was such a day—she never caught up with her work, the baby never stopped crying, and the hired woman did nothing but try her patience. At lunch, McCutcheon and Jimmy arrived at the back door and came into the kitchen without bothering to stamp their boots, and left mud all over the floor she had just mopped. Both of them were surly about something and said hardly a word. After they finished eating and went off again, she spent the whole afternoon blinded by tears. Her marriage to Jimmy had been a mistake from the beginning, she told herself. The baby was a goblin changeling. The colored housemaid secretly hated her, and so did McCutcheon. She was stranded and doomed to grow old on a lonely patch of earth miles from everything that mattered to her.

She opened the private drawer in her bedroom dresser, the place where she kept letters and mementos. She pulled out a worn, folded piece of stationery. It was a list she had started the day after they arrived, headed *All the Things I Shall Miss About Living in Austin:*

> *Delia*
> *~~going to church on Sundays~~*
> *dressing up to go to church on Sundays*
> *all the fancy hats with feathers at Mrs. Boddy's millinery shop*
> *afternoon tea and cookies at the Oriental tea shop*
> *Lundberg's bakery (the smells!)*
> *strolling on Congress Avenue*
> *browsing among the secondhand books at Rydell's*
> *tamales at Rodriguez's*
> *oysters at Simon's!*
> *plays at Millett's Opera House*
> *summer concerts at Scholz's Beer Garden (the day we went up in the balloon!)*
> *picnics with Delia ~~and Jimmy~~ at Swenson's Ruin*
> *the mill at Barton Springs (dipping my feet in the COLD spring water on a HOT summer day!)*
> *strolling along Shoal Creek ~~with Jimmy~~*
> *the gardens on the lunatic asylum grounds*
> *the waterfall on the Colorado River*
> *~~our room at the Phillips's house~~*
> *having Mrs. Phillips to do the shopping and cooking and Sallie Mack to clean up after us!*
> *the view from the roof of Father's hotel*
> *the view from Mount Bonnell*

She lay on the bed, the list in one hand and her handkerchief in the other. The baby was quiet in his crib. She closed her eyes and let her thoughts wander. She began by picturing the places on the list, then found herself recalling the train ride from Austin. She remembered the two curious characters who sat across from them, the blind man and his doctor friend with the strangely familiar face.

The familiarity, it turned out, was because she had seen him in newspaper advertisements. He had patented a medicine. He was very friendly. He even gave Jimmy a free sample of his tonic, right after introducing himself. What had become of that sample? She could remember watching Jimmy uncork the tiny bottle, take a sniff, then slip it into his coat pocket. What had Jimmy done with it? The answer was painfully obvious to her now: the tonic must have had alcohol in it. Jimmy probably drank the whole thing in secret. Yes, she remembered now that he got off briefly at the Round Rock station. "Need to stretch my legs," he said.

The blind man had been a doctor, too, or at least introduced himself as one, though Eula had wondered at the time how a blind man could practice medicine. The thought now occurred to her that perhaps he received his education and degree and then lost his sight. Perhaps that was why he became a phrenologist—because he had gone blind and could no longer work as a doctor, yet could still make use of his hands. He, too, had been very friendly. He offered to give them both a reading . . .

Lying on the bed, Eula floated between memory and dreaming. She was on the train leaving Austin, with the baby in her lap and Jimmy beside her and the two men across from them.

"A phrenological examination!" said Jimmy, only it came out slurred together, *phrenologizamination!* "That would be excellent! Wouldn't it, Eula? Only, I'm afraid we couldn't afford to pay you anything."

"Jimmy" she said, embarrassed. She sniffled and wiped her nose and wondered if her eyes were terribly red from crying.

"Payment? Perish the thought!" said the blind man in his faint German accent. "Anything to help pass the time! Dr. Terry and I have such a long journey ahead of us."

"How far are you going?" asked Eula.

"To St. Louis. Then to Chicago, I think. Dr. Terry and I travel a great deal."

"St. Louis and Chicago," whispered Eula, trying to imagine such places. "I'm afraid we shall be on the train for only a little while. Hardly long enough for a . . ." She hesitated, not trusting herself to pronounce *phrenological* any better than Jimmy had done.

"How far are you traveling?" said Dr. Terry.

"To a place called Hutto. The third stop."

"Hutto!" Dr. Fry laughed. "What a curious name. Isn't that the word the Bedouins shout to their camels? 'Hutto! Hutto!'"

Eula laughed a little, in spite of herself. "I think it comes from an Indian tribe."

"Well, then—shall I begin with you, young man?" said Dr. Fry to Jimmy.

"How can you tell that he's—" Eula began, then caught herself.

"What's that?" said Dr. Fry.

"Nothing."

"No, please, ask."

"I was only wondering, how can you tell that Jimmy's young?"

Dr. Fry laughed. "Someday in a room of strangers, Frau Phillips, try closing your eyes and see what you can tell about the people, just from their voices. You might be surprised at how much a person can 'see' without eyes, especially with practice. Your husband has a young voice. So do you. And is that not a very small baby I hear? I think you are both quite young, to have such a little one. Now, if I can tell all that with just my ears, imagine what I can tell with these!" He held up his hands and wriggled his fingers, like a pianist limbering up.

"All right, then!" said Jimmy. "As long as it doesn't cost anything. How do you want me?"

Dr. Fry proceeded with what he called a limited examination, having Jimmy lean forward and bow his head. It seemed to take a long time, while the doctor hummed and clucked his tongue and made little exclamations. When he was finally done, Fry sat back and nodded pensively.

"I think . . ." he began. Jimmy hung on every word. "I think you are a man of hidden talents. You have ambition, yes? That much is evident from the prominence of your organ of approbativeness—here." He indicated a spot on the top of his own head. "Yet you complain of having little money, and indeed the organ of acquisitiveness is not of corresponding prominence—here." He pointed to a spot near his temple. "This imbalance, I suspect, may have frustrated you in finding the correct means of fulfilling your ambitions. Yes?"

Jimmy nodded gravely.

"The organ of calculation, located over your eye, indicates that you have a good head for numbers, but you're also clever with your hands, as I can tell from the breadth of your organ of constructiveness, in the region of your temple."

"Yes! Eula, this fellow knows me!"

"I should think a clever fellow like you would prosper in the city, yet you're headed for the country."

"I'll be working on a farm," said Jimmy, with considerably less enthusiasm.

Dr. Fry nodded thoughtfully. "I see no reason why a fellow with your manifest skills shouldn't prosper on a farm. You must be fit enough for working outdoors. That pronounced curvature along the occiput, at the lower back of your skull—that indicates a robust set of internal organs. You have a stout heart and a strong liver."

"In that case, as you hardly seem to need it, perhaps I should take back that sample of tonic!" exclaimed Dr. Terry with a laugh. He even leaned toward Jimmy and playfully reached inside his coat.

Jimmy drew back, laughing. "That's enough about me. Now you, Eula."

"No, Jimmy. I'm holding the baby."

"I'll hold him. Let the man read your skull. Afraid of what he'll find out?"

"I just don't want to, Jimmy."

"If Frau Phillips wishes to decline . . ." The blind man shrugged.

When the train stopped at Round Rock, Jimmy announced that he wanted to stretch his legs. As soon as he was gone, Dr. Fry cleared his throat. "Young lady?"

Eula looked up from the sleeping baby. "Yes?"

"I did not say quite everything that I discovered from my examination of your husband."

"Oh?"

"I think he has a problem with drink. Am I right?"

Eula looked down at the baby. "If you smelled a bit of whiskey on his breath—"

"I use my hands, young lady, not my nose! I find evidence of a serious weakness in your husband."

"Weakness?"

"A flaw in his character. A lack of willpower. I knew at once from certain . . . anomalies . . . to be found in his organs of continuity and firmness. Any trained phrenologist could tell that this is a young man with a proclivity to alcohol slavery."

Eula kept looking at the baby. She did not speak for a long moment. "I think you're very presumptuous, sir."

"Frau Phillips, you misunderstand! I would say nothing, except that I detect in his character another flaw. His organ of destructiveness, located just above the ear—so prominent I think you must be able to see it if you look. I think your husband could be a very violent man, yes? When coupled with a slavery to drink—"

"Jimmy, violent? You don't know what you're talking about."

"He loses his temper, yes? Yells and throws tantrums?"

"Jimmy may be weak, but he's never hurt anyone. He's just a little spoiled, from living with his parents."

"Young lady, I say these things only as a caution to you and the little *Säugling*."

"I beg your pardon?"

"The *Säugling*—the suckling, the little one. I think—" Fry was about to say more, but at that moment Jimmy rejoined them.

They reached Hutto. Eula and Jimmy said good-bye to the doctors. Mc-Cutcheon was waiting for them on the platform. He and Jimmy went to fetch the bags, which were being unloaded from the train, but there was a problem. When Jimmy reached into his coat pocket to produce the claim tickets, his pocketbook was missing.

The station agent allowed them to claim their bags anyway, for there were only a few people getting off at Hutto and there was no question of ownership, but the loss of the pocketbook was a blow. Mr. Phillips had given Jimmy twenty dollars to see them off that morning.

McCutcheon suggested a pickpocket. "It happens all the time around trains and train stations. Wherever you have railroads, you have pickpockets. And confidence men! They can eat a man's lunch from under his nose."

"Perhaps it fell out of your pocket," Eula suggested. "Remember, Jimmy, when Dr. Terry made a joke and pretended to reach inside your coat—"

"No, I don't think so. He was reaching for the bottle of tonic, anyway."

"Is the bottle still there?"

Jimmy didn't answer.

And he never did find his pocketbook . . .

Eula opened her eyes. She was not sure whether she had been asleep or not. What had she been thinking about? Her reverie vanished, beyond recall. She was fully, starkly awake, lying on their bed in the farmhouse, and from his crib the baby was crying for her.

A few days later, something occurred to lift her mood.

McCutcheon announced that he would soon be going into Austin for a few days, to tend to some business. He wanted Jimmy to stay on the farm to look after things in his absence, but he said there was no reason why Eula and the baby shouldn't come with him, if she wished. The hired woman could look after Jimmy.

Back in Austin, if only for a few days! Eula wrote a letter to Delia at once to tell her the good news.

16

A month after the death of Mollie Smith, her murder had faded from public concern. There was not a word to be found in the *Statesman* about the crime or its aftermath. Had a trial loomed, it might have been otherwise. As it was, the people of Austin, having experienced a collective shudder, went about their business. The talk of the town now revolved around the doings of the legislature.

As William Pendleton Gaines had foreseen, the sharpest debate was sparked by Senate Bill No. 79, with the long-winded title, "An act requiring the Comptroller of Public Accounts, Commissioner of the General Land Office, and State Treasurer to employ females, when their services can be had, to fill one half the clerkships in the several departments under the control of these officers." In a town which thrived on politics, the "Female Clerks Bill" (as SB 79 popularly became known) was the controversy of the season.

Senator Evans of Bonham, who introduced SB 79, noted the precedent for hiring female clerks established in Washington, D.C., and the fact that in some places women had been appointed to the job of postmistress. "In every such instance," extolled the senator, "women have proven not only equal but superior to men. Their work is more neatly done and more accurate. Their presence throws around them a moral influence that makes the male employees better men. They are willing to work for less wages than males, for instead of wasting their income in dissipation, they spend wisely, and so it takes less money to do them. We believe it would be economic to employ women even at the same wages paid to males, because they would be so much more prompt and efficient that more work would be done and fewer clerks would be required."

The Senate voted to consider the bill. The *Statesman* urged the women of Austin to attend the debates: "Ladies, go up to the senate chamber, and by your presence and smiles encourage the gallant legislators who are going to do battle for your sakes!"

On the morning of January 27, a large crowd assembled at the state office building at the head of Congress Avenue. It was an undistinguished structure of three stories, without ornament on the outside, cramped inside, and woefully inadequate to its purpose. Pending construction of the new capitol building, the temporary state building not only housed government departments but, with the legislature in session, had to accommodate the staffs of both the House and the Senate. To make room, offices had been partitioned and hallways turned into offices. File cabinets and crates of office supplies, normally stored in the musty meeting chambers, had been carted up to the attic. On this morning, even the narrow sidewalk outside was inadequate, with the crowd overflowing onto Congress Avenue.

Dave Shoemaker, approaching the outskirts of the crowd, took a deep breath and plunged in. Muttering, "Excuse me, excuse me!" he elbowed his way to the narrow doorway, where he had to raise his arms above his head in order to sidle through. Not until he was well within the little lobby did he pause to look over his shoulder. "Still with me, Will?"

"Barely! If it's a mortal sin to step on people's toes, like Mrs. Harrell says, then I'm headed straight for hell."

"Shh! Watch your language. Ladies present!"

"I'll say!" Will peered about and grinned.

It was a rare thing to see a woman in the lobby of the state office building, but not on this day. The crush of would-be spectators looked less like the usual male herd of reporters and lobbyists, and more like an intermission crowd at Millett's Opera House; millinery feathers and flowers mingled with bald pates and bowler hats. Feminine voices and laughter echoed above the rumble of men's voices. Some of the men in the crowd were clearly unnerved by the spectacle of so many females invading their preserve. Others, like Will, found it exhilarating.

They made their way to the gallery entrance, Dave leading and Will following in his wake. The door was shut. "All full!" snapped a frazzled sergeant at arms, who then muttered, "Oh, it's you, Shoemaker. But it's still full up. Got reporters from every paper in Texas in there, and some from out of state."

"But you can't keep out the *Statesman*." Dave reached for the door.

The sergeant blocked it. "The *Statesman* is already inside. Hiram Glass got here an hour ago."

"I know. He's saving seats for us."

The man laughed out loud. "Don't see how."

"You don't know Hiram!"

"*You* don't know what it's like in there."

"Let us in and we'll see for ourselves."

"You and who else?"

Dave hooked his thumb. "This is Will. He's a writer, too." It was not a lie, exactly.

The man glowered at them. His expression softened when Dave reached for something in his coat pocket, and he smiled when Dave slipped something into his hand. He opened the door barely enough to let them slip through, then closed it behind them, shouting at the crowd to stay back.

"What did you give him?" whispered Will.

"My last Havana."

"Dave!"

"Well, my last Havana *label*. The cigar's the cheapest Harrell's sells, but that lummox will never know the difference."

The spectator's gallery ran along one side of the senate chamber, cordoned off by a long wooden railing. Long rows of chairs rose on a succession of low tiers. Dave and Will scanned the seats, looking for empty spots. It took only a moment to realize that every seat, without exception, was taken by a woman. All the men in the gallery were standing, either against the back wall behind the last row of chairs, or up and down the steps along the walls at either end.

"Look, there's Hiram, standing way over there at the far end, down by the railing," said Dave. "Best spot in the house! Looks like he even managed to save some space for us."

Will saw the man Dave indicated, but looked in vain to see any spare standing room, unless six inches on either side of Hiram Glass constituted enough space to squeeze into. Nevertheless, he followed obediently as Dave began to make his way between the long wooden bar and the first row of seats. Dave kept tipping his hat. "Excuse me, ma'am—Sorry, miss—Watch your toes!—No, please don't get up—Coming through!"

Will was dazed by the roar of voices, the mingled smells of ink, shoe leather, and women's perfumes, and the dazzling array of colors and patterns displayed by the women massed in their finery; the ranks of men standing in dark suits formed a sort of frame around them on three sides.

And the hats! Bristling with plumage, ringed with silk bouquets, piled with tulle and spangled with sequins, bejeweled like bird nests—some even with little birds perched on them! The women who had come to watch the debate looked less like aspiring clerks and more like fashion plates. Young and old, dark and fair, pretty and plain—all were dressed in their finest. Will found it at once exciting and intimidating to see so many women gathered in one place, all so animated and wearing such purposeful expressions.

At last they reached the corner where Hiram Glass was standing. Somehow, Dave found a way to squeeze in. Hiram remained closest to the bar, with Will wedged between him and Dave, their backs to the wall.

"Hiram Glass, meet Will Porter."

Will and Hiram exchanged nods. "I try to read your 'Legislative Notes' column in the paper . . . whenever I can," said Will.

Hiram gave him a sardonic look. "Do you also drink castor oil when you get the chance?"

"Where are our seats, you dog?" said Dave. "You were going to save us each a seat!"

Hiram cleared his throat. "So I did—until all the women started arriving and all the men started giving up their seats."

"Well, tarnation, Hiram, you didn't have to follow the pack. You're a professional, here to do your job."

"So are these other fellows. If I'd kept my seat, it would be in all their columns tomorrow. 'The reporter from the Austin *Statesman* was the only man of the press not gallant enough to stand for the ladies.' I'd never hear the end of it from Gaines!"

"I see your point. Well, we've still got the best spot in the gallery—close to the podium so we can hear the speeches, and a clear view of all the senators so we can watch their beaming faces. Oh, this is going to be quite a show! If you've come to see politicians make fools of themselves, Will, I don't think you'll be disappointed!"

"What politicians? I came to look at the ladies." Will demonstrated by craning his neck and peering up and down the long rows of the gallery.

"We've got the best spot for that, as well!" crowed Dave. The atmosphere of the place had excited them both, in contrast to Hiram Glass, who stood with his arms crossed, clutching a pencil and notepad, looking desperately bored.

Will nudged Dave. "Look who else is here—your friend from the comptroller's office."

"Where?"

"Up against the back wall. See that knot of fellows all talking to each other? In the middle: William Shelley."

"So it is," said Dave. "A gaggle of government clerks all clucking at once, and him the head clucker. I saw him at Scholz's yesterday, holding court."

"I thought *you* held court at Scholz's."

"Not lately, Will. Not enough murders in this town since that poor colored girl. Right now, all anybody wants to talk about is the Female Clerks Bill, and everybody wants to hear what Shelley has to say about it, since he claims to be the comptroller's fair-haired boy."

"And what does young Mr. Shelley say?" inquired Hiram, tilting his ear toward Dave. The pencil twitched in his fingers.

"Says Comptroller Swain is dead-set against it; doesn't intend to let the legislature tell him who he can and can't hire in his department, especially as pertains to the gender of his clerks. Shelley's up in arms himself, seeing as he has a personal stake. He hasn't much seniority. Isn't even married— can't plead he has mouths to feed. If this cockeyed bill passes, half the male clerks are out on their backsides to make room for the ladies. William Shelley's likely to find himself out of a job."

"Shouldn't he be upstairs in his office right now," asked Will, "comptrolling something or other?"

Hiram barked out a mirthless laugh. "There's not a clerk in this building who'll get a lick of work done all week, or for the rest of the session. They're all too busy plotting how to do in this bill, so as to save their jobs, which they don't seem particularly eager to tend to in the first place."

The senators drifted into the chamber, singly or in small groups. Some pointedly ignored the gallery, but most at least glanced at the rows of women. At length the gavel was struck, the roll was called, and a quorum of the thirty-one members declared present. The chaplain addressed a prayer to the deity and the business of the day commenced.

Reports of various committees were submitted, motions were made, points of procedure discussed. To Will it all seemed quite Byzantine, not to mention boring, though he noticed that Hiram Glass was constantly scribbling and flipping the pages of his notepad, as were a number of men in the gallery. At last it was announced that the body would consider Senate Bill No. 79.

There was a hush of low whispers in the gallery as the spectators shifted about, like passengers settling in for a bumpy ride.

Senator Evans opened with a speech in favor of the bill. He was a lackluster speaker, but the ladies applauded him enthusiastically.

Senator Randolph was a firebrand by comparison. Woman's place, he insisted, was by the hearthstone; he quoted from a Bible to make his point. He argued that labor-saving machines were already throwing thousands of men out of work, so that there were no longer enough jobs for men, let alone women. To solve the problem of impoverished females, he advocated strong laws compelling men to support their womenfolk.

Senator Terrell's style was less self-righteous and more sarcastic. "If women are fit to be made clerks, why not elect them to the legislature? Don't laugh, gentlemen! Perhaps Senator Evans can induce them to serve for $1.50 a day, and save the state a considerable sum!" There was a great deal of laughter from the men in the chamber, and some boos from the women.

Temple Houston, the son of Sam Houston and the youngest and hand-somest member of the Senate, pledged his support of the bill. He delivered an eloquent discourse on the superior virtues of the female sex, playing shamelessly to the women in the gallery, who applauded and blew him kisses throughout his speech.

Not as charming but no less ardent a supporter of the bill was Rutabaga Johnson of Collin County, the Senate's most notorious eccentric. "I listen to these other fellers opposin' this bill, and I tell you what, if they'd been left lack I was to the care of a pore widdered mother, and growed up deprived of a good eddication, they'd stop to consider! Give the women a chance to earn theirselves a honest livin'! Some of these fellers got a wife or a sister at home, practically chained to a washtub, and they oughta know better. As for these little squirrel-headed clerks all piled up at the feeding trough, I say, turn 'em all out! Some of these ladies got twice the smarts of them gimlet-headed fellers. Just lookit all them dude clerks loiterin' in the gallery and out in the lobby, 'stead of gettin' some work done—they's all wrought up cuz some fe-males who'll drink less and work harder are ready to take their places!"

There were titters of laughter throughout Rutabaga Johnson's speech, which ended to thunderous applause from the ladies and hoots from the clerks. After the uproar died down, there was a motion to cut off debate. The vote on the bill commenced.

Nineteen senators voted yea. Ten senators voted nay.

There was a flurry of celebration among the women. The gavel was banged and the Senate adjourned until the next day. With a great deal of hubbub, the gallery began to empty.

"By a margin of two to one!" said Dave, stunned.

Hiram Glass snapped his notebook shut. "Mr. Gaines shall be pleased."

"Is it a law yet?" asked Will.

"Oh, hardly," said Hiram with a wry laugh. "There are many steps to go.

Engrossment, amendments, further debate. Eventually it may be sent to the House, which will go through the same rigmarole and then send it back to the Senate for final passage, whereupon the governor may sign it into law—or veto it. There's many a hurdle before SB 79 becomes law. But the vote today is an impressive show of support, especially in the face of so much opposition from the department heads, like Comptroller Swain."

Will nodded and scanned the gallery. There were some very pretty women in attendance. Some of them caught him looking; he smiled crookedly and looked away, feeling rather foolish, as he often did when confronted with the opposite sex.

Then he saw a face that took his breath away.

How was it possible that he hadn't noticed her before? His pulse quickened. His chest constricted. He blushed. The experience was immediate, overwhelming, extraordinary. That a man should go weak in the knees at the sight of a beautiful woman was the stuff of penny dreadfuls and the worst sort of plays at the opera house—yet here it was, happening to him!

Her blond hair was pulled back and done up tightly, capped by a little green hat with a high plush crown and a yellow velvet stripe. The green color matched her dress with lace ruffles at the neck and cuffs. As Will watched, she put on a pair of brown suede gloves. Her hands were small and rose-white, like the tender flesh of her throat where it showed above the high neck of the green dress.

She turned and spoke to the taller woman next to her, who wore a dark blue dress and a troubadour hat, its tall crown decorated with black ostrich feathers. They were easily the two most beautiful women in the gallery, but they looked nothing alike. The black-haired woman had more pronounced features and a darker complexion; in her green eyes there was a predatory glint, a vixenish quality that some men would find attractive. Her blond friend was more like a dove, delicate and demure. It made him ache to look at her.

The darker woman noticed someone at the back of the gallery and nodded, then whispered to her blond friend, who responded by glancing at the nod's recipient. Will followed her gaze and saw none other than William Shelley, returning the same barely perceptible nod!

The two women began to move toward the exit, as did Shelley. For a moment it appeared they would meet at the door, but Shelley hung back and seemed purposely to avoid looking at the women as they passed through the doorway into the lobby. The dark-haired woman and Shelley obviously knew each other, yet made no effort to speak. What did it mean? Will wondered.

He moved to follow them. Dave called after him, "Where are you off to?"

"Someone . . . in the lobby," Will mumbled.

The lobby was jammed. He caught sight of the green plush hat amid a sea of other hats and headed toward it, brushing against shoulders and bosoms and treading on toes. He lost sight of her, then spotted her again off toward the main entrance, with her dark-haired friend in the troubadour hat. They slipped through the doorway side by side.

He followed. The narrow sidewalk was as crowded as the lobby, with a jam of carriages and hackney cabs drawn up in front. They seemed to have vanished—then he caught sight of them in the street, making their way between the parked vehicles. They had been joined by a man in a farmer's slouch hat and dungarees. Will drew up behind them, close enough to hear the darker woman call the blond by name. Eula. She called her Eula.

The farmer hailed a cab. He helped the dark woman to step up into the seat, then the blond, then stepped in after them. The cab driver snapped the reins and they were off, heading south down the Avenue.

Who was the man? He looked older than the women. An uncle, brother, father? That he might have been a husband, *her* husband, Will did not care to consider, even though, as she was disappearing into the cab, he had glimpsed on her finger a glint of gold which was almost certainly a wedding band.

He watched the cab dwindle in the distance for a while, then returned to the lobby. The crowd had thinned. Those who remained were gathered in little groups, talking and laughing. He found Dave and Hiram with half a dozen other men at the foot of a staircase gathered around William Shelley, who was performing a rude imitation of a certain senator.

"Now, if'n you all had growed up lack I did, with a pore widdered mother and not a lick of eddication what to speak of—"

Dave was laughing so hard he had tears in his eyes. Even Hiram Glass looked on with a wry smile.

"Shelley!" Will grabbed his sleeve.

William Shelley blinked and glared at him. "What? Oh, it's you, Porter. What do you want, whelp?"

"The woman in the gallery—the one in blue, with dark hair. Who is she?"

"I don't know what you're talking about."

"But she nodded to you, and you nodded back. There was another woman with her—a blond in a green hat and green dress."

"Sorry. Can't help you. Now if you're done interrupting me—"

"But I know you saw them. I think the blond's name is—"

"You're mistaken," Shelley said sharply. Then he chuckled and raised an eyebrow. "Really, how could I have noticed mere females when I was riveted by the address of Senator Rutabaga?" He mimicked a facial expression which convulsed Dave with fresh laughter. "Anyway," he said, addressing his fellow clerks, "*some* of us have to get back to work. We must leave it to these gentlemen of the press to make sense of the day's spectacle." He started up the staircase.

Will stepped after him and grabbed his arm. Shelley spun about so forcefully that Will lost his balance and fell on his backside. The clerks hooted and giggled. Even Dave laughed. Hiram Glass shook his head.

Shelley gave him a look of such animosity that Will sat motionless on the floor, stunned into silence. Then Shelley turned about and ascended the stairs, followed by the coterie of laughing clerks.

The clerks were still laughing and chattering among themselves, rather like the squirrels that Rutabaga Johnson made them out to be, as they filed through the door on the third floor labeled COMPTROLLER OF PUBLIC ACCOUNTS. They drifted to their various desks and cubbyholes, where piles of paperwork awaited them. Since the beginning of the legislative session and the uproar caused by the Female Clerks Bill, the normal routine of the office had been completely disrupted.

"Can you imagine such a thing?" said one of the men to William Shelley. "A woman in this department? Working right next to you? Or worse— one on either side! The endless gossip—who has the cleverest children or wears the prettiest dresses or keeps the messiest house. They'd drive a man loco! Nothing would ever get done." The man sat down at the desk across from Shelley, leaned back in his chair, and peered out the window at the capitol grounds across Mesquite Street.

Shelley nodded. He didn't stop at his desk but walked on, past a long row of file cabinets, and knocked at the door to Comptroller Swain's private office.

A voice sounded through the thick wood. "Come in!"

Shelley slipped inside and closed the door behind him.

William Jesse Swain was a generously proportioned man who required a generously proportioned office. His desk was an enormous thing made of solid oak. His chair was larger than most, as it had to be to accommodate his girth. His bookcases had capacious shelves to hold all the big ledgers and reference volumes with which he surrounded himself. He was a man of large ambitions, and he thought large thoughts.

"How did it go down there?" he asked Shelley. Even when he lowered his voice to a confidential tone, it had a booming quality.

"Nineteen to ten, sir."

Swain made a disgruntled noise. He asked for the names on each side of the vote. Shelley recited them from memory.

"So that's how they want to play it!" Swain huffed. "Half of those fellows who voted yea today have no intention of seeing this thing passed into law. They're just as against it as I am, but they want to be *seen* to be for it. I did my time in the legislature; I know how that game works! Female clerks — over my dead body!"

Swain lit a cigar and puffed at it. "I'm halfway through my second term as comptroller. I've made my mark on this department, and I intend to leave it in a condition that reflects suitably on my achievements. I damned sure don't intend to let those grandstanding fools in the legislature fill this place half full of females before I go. I'll resign first! Or I'll stick around and make life so miserable for the first batch of women that there won't be a second batch. So — nineteen to ten." He shook his head. "How'd the debate go? Details, son, details!"

Shelley stood with his arms clasped behind him, rather as he had done when reciting as a boy at the military academy on Castle Hill, and described the various speeches. He ended with his imitation of Rutabaga Johnson; his performance for the crowd downstairs had merely been a dress rehearsal for his report to Swain. He soon had his boss laughing loud enough to startle the clerks in the office outside.

Shelley finished. Swain sat quietly for a while, puffing on his cigar. "I shall have to schedule private meetings with certain members of the Senate — discreetly. Can I depend on you to handle the details, Shelley?"

"Of course, sir."

"You're a good man, Shelley. You come from good stock; your father's a damned good lawyer. He did the right thing, sending you to the academy. Doesn't look like young men your age are likely ever to see a war, but military discipline gives a man character. That'll see you a long way; maybe all the way to a job in the Governor's Mansion, if you stick close to me."

"That would make my father very proud, sir."

"Damned right! You know how many votes I received in the last election, son?"

"Over two hundred thousand, sir." Shelley had been asked the question before, and knew the precise figure; he also knew that his boss preferred to recite it himself.

"More like two hundred forty thousand, son! Damn near a quarter of a million votes—the largest number of votes ever cast for any man running for any office in the state! It can be argued that I am the most popular elected official in the history of Texas. John Ireland can't make that boast."

"It's rumored, sir, that Governor Ireland is planning to run for the U.S. Senate."

"Let him! That way, come '86, the Governor's Mansion will be up for grabs. Stick with me, son! Stick with me!"

"I'll always do my best for you, sir."

Swain puffed on his cigar and looked at him thoughtfully. Shelley had learned to read the changes in his boss's moods. There was a change now—the whole character of the room seemed altered—but Shelley could not quite make it out.

"So, son, what was it like down there in the gallery today?"

"Crowded, sir."

"Mmm, yes, I assume there must have been a considerable number of women in attendance."

"Enough to take up all the seats! The clerks and reporters were left to stand."

"No man should have to *stand* through a speech by Rutabaga Johnson!" said Swain, grimacing. "Any pretty ones?"

"I beg your pardon, sir? Pretty speeches?"

"Hell, no! Enough about the speeches! Were there any pretty ladies in the gallery?"

"Ah! Well—yes, sir, I suppose there were." Shelley lowered his eyes, thinking of Delia, the woman he knew from May Tobin's house. He had never expected to see her in the gallery, yet there she had been, laughing and applauding along with the respectable women, in the company of an equally striking young blond—another of May Tobin's girls, he wondered, or just a friend? He would have liked to talk with Delia and to have met her blond friend, but not in a public place, and certainly not in the building where he worked. To her credit, Delia had been discreet—yet even so, that whelp Will Porter had noticed the nods they exchanged! Shelley wrinkled his brow at the memory of Porter badgering him in the lobby.

Swain leaned back in his chair. "Don't be coy with me, son. I'll bet you have quite an eye for the ladies."

Shelley shrugged uncertainly. Where was Swain leading him? "As much as the next fellow, I suppose."

"You being such a hearty young fellow, and not married yet, I'll bet you know all the best places for a fellow to have a good time in this town. Say, if a man wanted to spend some time with a pretty lady, with no strings attached."

Shelley wrinkled his brow even more. "Honestly, sir, I'm not sure what you mean. I assure you, on my own time away from the office, my conduct would never bring discredit—"

"For God's sake, son, I'm not judging you! I'm asking for your help."

Shelley's brow slowly unknitted as he began to comprehend.

Swain puffed at his cigar. "You're discreet, son. Lord knows, a fellow in my position has need to be discreet. And you're loyal to me. Lord knows, I'm depending on that. And I figure from the guilty way you act, you know exactly what I'm talking about!" Swain laughed and slapped his desk. "So, can you help an old codger like me find a bit of relief in this town, without everybody talking about it behind my back, or not?"

Shelley returned his smile. "Actually, sir, I just might happen to know of a place . . ."

Shelley left his boss's office with a smile on his face. Of all the men over whom Swain reigned in the department, of all the bigwigs with whom Swain lunched and dined, *he* was the one the old man had come to for advice, man-to-man, *he* was the one the old man had decided to trust. From now on, Swain would be his mentor and Shelley would be the old man's protégé. They would be closer than father and son, for they would share secrets few fathers and sons ever shared.

The man who sat at the desk across from him was still leaning back in his chair, idly looking out the window. "What the hell were you and the boss man talking about all that time?"

Shelley picked up a pile of papers and straightened the bottom edges against his desktop with a crack that gave his fellow clerk a start. "That's quite a backlog piled up on your desk," he said sharply. "Hadn't you better get to work?"

The man frowned at him, then pulled his chair up to his desk and reached for his ledgers.

Shelley tried to keep a stern look on his face, but a grin kept breaking through. William Jesse Swain was a cannonball headed straight for the Governor's Mansion, and he, William Shelley, was hitched to that cannonball, set to ride it all the way!

17

$\mathcal{I}$N the month since old lady and old man Sumpter had turned him out, Alec Mack still had not found regular work or a place of his own. The Sumpters had spread word that he was immoral and not to be trusted.

After a week of sleeping rough in the cold, Alec finally knocked on the door of his mother's little house. She knew from friends that Alec was in some sort of trouble, and had been waiting for him to show up. She had a place made up for him to sleep on the floor in the corner, close to the fire. She hardly said a word to him, but the way she shook her head cut him to the quick.

There were small things to be thankful for. The weather had been mild for January, with plenty of sunshine and no sleet or snow. His friend Lem Brooks, after some fretful days in jail, was back tending bar at the Black Elephant. And Alec's mother seemed to be doing well for herself.

Sallie Mack was an industrious woman, blessed with a sturdy constitution. She could wash and wring clothes, clean house and scrub floors. Mostly she worked for Mr. and Mrs. Phillips, who in return let her live on their property.

The Phillipses owned a whole quarter of a block at the northwest corner of Hickory and Lavaca. Mr. Phillips was a builder by trade and fancied himself an architect. He had kept adding to his original house until the result was a family compound. The main house faced south onto Hickory, and annexes were joined to it by covered verandahs. One annex contained a workshop, another an apartment to let. The Phillipses' widowed daughter, Delia, lived in her own annex, and until recently their son, Jimmy, and his wife, Eula, had lived in another.

The little house where Sallie lived was at the back of the lot, unconnected to the main house and not as well tended. It faced north, onto the alley. Sallie sometimes thought of the little house as a stepchild among the other structures, raggedy-clad and pushed to the back and made to face the other way. Still, it was not a bad situation, for Sallie's front window looked across the alley into the back yard of the Hirshfeld estate, where one of the most successful merchants in town was building a grand mansion. Sallie Mack lived in lowly circumstances, but surrounded by opulence. That fact kept her humble, but also made her rather proud of herself. Plenty of people she knew had done worse. She thanked God every day that He had given her a strong back.

She was less thankful for the tribulations He had sent her way with Alec. The Lord had given her son a handsome head, but then He hadn't bothered to put any sense in it. Every time Alec struck out on his own he always came back with a tale of woe. One of these days he would get himself into real trouble, the sort that coming home to his Mama couldn't fix—that was Sallie's greatest fear, and sometimes at night she couldn't sleep for worrying. Until that happened, though, what could she do but keep taking him in?

Mr. and Mrs. Phillips wouldn't mind, or so she hoped. They might have heard rumors about Alec getting into trouble, but they surely wouldn't make her turn him away. The Phillipses had their share of trouble with their own son. Everybody knew Jimmy Phillips drank and couldn't hold a job. By rights, the Phillipses should sympathize with her problems with Alec. Mr. Phillips might even be persuaded to find some work around the place for Alec, now that Jimmy had gone off to the farm with his pretty young wife.

There was a couple Sallie wasn't sorry to see go! Jimmy could be a charming fellow, and Eula was pretty as an angel, and their new baby was a sweet thing. But when he drank, Jimmy tended to break things, and it was Sallie who had to clean up the mess. As for Jimmy's wife, Sallie had a feeling that her daddy must have spoiled her something awful. Mr. Burdett owned a hotel on the Avenue. What white man with that kind of money and a girl as pretty as Eula wouldn't make a fuss over her? It wasn't that Eula turned out mean or shrewish; she was all sensitive and touchy, like a cat that didn't like petting. Little things peeved her and she was always crying. Once, back when Eula was expecting, and right after Sallie had scrubbed the floor in the couple's annex, Eula had knocked a big clay pitcher off the bedside table. Milk ran all over the floor and under the bed.

Eula had wept for an hour. Sallie figured *she* was the one who ought to cry, since she had to do the mopping!

Jimmy and Eula! Doing a chore for those two always seemed twice as hard as it ought to. With them gone, there seemed to be a lot less work around the place.

Jimmy's sister, Delia, was another character. Sallie had never known a woman who enjoyed being a widow so much. Delia came and went just as she pleased, at all hours of the day and night. With her husband dead, you might have thought she'd have to account to her father, but her parents doted on her just as blindly as they did on Jimmy.

Thinking of the Phillips children made Sallie feel better about Alec. He would turn out all right in the end, she told herself. Still, she couldn't help but fret.

Now that he had a roof over his head, Alec had another, rather immediate concern. It had been a month since the night the Sumpters caught him in bed with Rebecca Ramey, and he had not been alone with her since.

Rebecca—that was a Bible name, and Alec liked to imagine her clothed in some ancient costume, glittering with jewels. He could close his eyes and remember how the sweat had shimmered on her breasts, and in his mind's eye the beads of sweat became pearls decorating her nakedness. He thought about her constantly.

She wouldn't allow him to visit her, even in broad daylight. She worked for Mr. Valentine Weed, who owned the biggest livery stable in town. The Weeds had a big house at the corner of Cedar and San Jacinto, where Rebecca did the cooking and cleaning and lived with her ten-year-old daughter. Her previous job had been at the big steam laundry on East Pecan. She had hated it and never wanted to go back. She also had seen how the Sumpters kicked out Alec, and she had no intention of giving the Weeds any excuse to do the same to her and her little girl.

Had it been summer, perhaps Alec could have persuaded her to meet him out of doors, at some secluded spot along Shoal Creek—the idea of seeing her naked with dappled sunlight across her breasts was one of his favorite daydreams. But it was winter. They needed a place to meet.

So that day, instead of making the rounds looking for work, being peered at by old white men and talked about in low voices and sent away empty-handed, Alec headed to the Black Elephant. He planned it so that he would arrive at the quietest hour of the day. Hugh Hancock was taking a nap. Lem

Brooks was alone behind the bar, and the only customer was an old drunk dozing in the corner.

They chatted for a while, about the weather, Alec's mother, how nicely folks had treated Lem since he got out of jail. Alec was saved the trouble of bringing up his lady friend; Lem did it for him.

"What 'bout that woman who got you into all this trouble? You still seein' her?"

"You see, Lem, that's my problem . . ." Alec explained his predicament. Lem nodded sympathetically while he polished glasses, but shot him a quizzical look when Alec explained about Rebecca's daughter.

"She got a chile *ten years old?*"

"Eleven next month."

"Eleven? Hell, man, this woman old enough to be yo' mama!"

"No she ain't!"

"She got a kid half your age! Too old for a frisky tadpole like you."

"I don't know how old she be," said Alec. "Never thought 'bout it. Neither would you, if you seen her like I seen her! Thing is, she live just a coupla blocks f'om here, and I cain't even drop by the back door to say hello. I s'posed to sit across the street, waitin' for her to leave the place to do some shoppin' for whatever, before I can so much as talk to her."

"And talkin' *ain't* zackly what you got in mind!" Lem laughed, showing off his dazzling teeth. "Sound to me, Alec, like what you needs is to set you up some place to ron-day-voo."

"That's jus' what I was thinkin'!" Alec slapped the bar. "And I's wonderin', knowin' how sometimes you work the late shift, and Mr. Hancock let's you close up the place, if some night, you know, after ever'body be gone, you might jus'—jus' leave the back door unlocked for me . . ."

"Let you do it *here?*" Lem stared at him.

"I know it's askin' a lot, what with Mr. Hancock livin' just back of the place—"

"Hell! Sure, I'll do it."

"What?"

"I said, sure. Why not? Jus' 'cause I done washed my hands of womenfolk for good, don't mean you has to."

"I'd fix it with you in advance, of course, and you can always back out if there comes some change—"

"Hell, name the night! Wednesday? Thursday? There's that old settee in the storage room for takin' naps, be perfec' for you. Take a lamp in there, shut the door—there's even a lock on the inside. Jus' right for what you got in mind."

Alec could hardly believe it. Deep down he'd never expected Lem to agree, and certainly not without some pleading on his part. Now if only Rebecca would go along so readily . . .

"Only one thing," said Lem, his face suddenly grave.

"What's that?"

"When you and yo' ladyfriend be on your way over, walkin' in the dark, if'n ever you sees somethin'—somethin' that puts you off . . ."

"Like what?"

Lem no longer looked at him, but stared into space. "Somethin' like—I don't know. Like a dog, maybe. A snarlin', angry dog with flashin' eyes . . ."

Alec grinned. "Hell, I sees a dog in my way, I pick up a stick and run him off. Th'ow a rock at him—"

"No!" Lem leaned over the counter, his eyes wide. "Don't you *never* do that, 'cause you never know. Might be a dog ghost."

Alec laughed. "You funnin' me."

Lem grabbed him by the shoulder and looked at him so hard it was scary. "Didn't your Mama ever tell you 'bout dog ghosts?"

"Sho she did. But I never seen one."

"Well, I did! And if you ever gets a warnin' like that, you take it. Understand?"

"Sho, Lem, sho." Alec gingerly pulled himself from Lem's grip. He had never seen Lem act in such a way. It had to be something about going to jail that had changed Lem somehow. He'd get back to being himself again, sooner or later. Seen a dog ghost, indeed! Like there ever was such a thing!

The important thing was, Lem was agreeable to his idea. It was going to happen. Alec was going to see her naked again, and touch every inch of her. The thought made his head spin. How he loved to say her name silently in his thoughts, where no one else could hear: Rebecca! Rebecca Ramey!

18

⌘

M R . Taylor Moore, formerly district attorney, currently representing Travis County in the Nineteenth Legislature, rose early on the morning of February 11, as was his habit.

He left Mrs. Moore sleeping and slipped into the adjoining room where they kept their wardrobes. He stripped off his long johns. His bathing water had been set out in the basin the night before and was frigid, as he preferred it. He scrubbed himself with a soapy rag, rinsed, then briskly dried himself.

His ablutions done, Mr. Taylor Moore stood still for a moment. By the cold morning light he took a long, hard look in the full-length mirror that stood between the massive oak wardrobes. It behooved a man, Moore thought, every so often to observe his naked figure. Mrs. Moore, once sleepily walking in on this ritual, teasingly accused him of vanity. Indeed, the appearance of his nude physique did not particularly displease Taylor Moore. But it was not mere vanity that prompted his scrutiny. "Know thyself!" the philosophers said. Surely, he thought, that knowledge must necessarily include an unflinching acquaintance with the portion of mortal clay which a man has been given by the Creator to house his spirit.

That clay, which starts out so firm and resilient, was malleable stuff. Moore found it appalling, the degree to which a man's flesh could sag and stretch over time. He was still relatively young, only thirty-eight—for a politician, not yet in his prime. Some fellows thought it acceptable, even fashionable, to become portly after the age of thirty, as if jowls connoted sagacity and a projecting belly manifested material success. Taylor Moore, however, did not agree. He wondered sometimes if certain of his colleagues ever seriously observed themselves in a mirror. Surely not, he'd decided, for how could they then display themselves before crowds of voters, knowing full well how they must appear to their fellow man?

He saw in the mirror a physique not much different, in general outline, from the one he had sported when he was twenty. Taylor Moore was tall and long-limbed but with an ample chest and adequate shoulders, and a belly as flat as an iron. The bow-shaped curves of his abdominal muscles were as clearly etched as those of a swimmer in a Thomas Eakins painting. Despite a full beard with hints of gray, he looked younger than his years. His face was long and rectangular. His nose was perhaps on the large size, his mouth small. His eyebrows curved upward toward each other in a way that gave him a pensive, vaguely melancholy expression, even when he smiled. Though he had never considered himself handsome, most women seemed to hold a different opinion.

His best suit was neatly laid out for him, his black leather shoes polished and buffed, his collar crisply starched. Once clothed, his face took on greater prominence. He had trimmed and shaped his beard the night before; that was too big a job to be left for the morning.

He observed himself from head to foot. He saw a man who made his living by his intellect, yet who sported the physique of an athlete. Here was a fellow who knew how to take care of himself, who gracefully combined maturity with youthful vigor—just the sort of man who could stand up before a body of lawmakers and deliver a speech full of wit and authority, commanding their respect, compelling their agreement. On this day, that was just what Taylor Moore intended to do.

The House chamber in the temporary capitol building was larger than the Senate chamber, so as to accommodate the much larger body of 106 members. The gallery was larger as well, but still not large enough to accommodate the great crowd which gathered that day to hear the Female Clerks Bill debated.

Will, Dave, and Hiram arrived so early that they actually found seats, which they eventually surrendered as more and more women arrived. A row of young clerks in the back steadfastly refused to budge, however. One of them quipped, rather loudly, "They want only half the clerkships—why should we give them *all* the seats!" The remark prompted a number of women to stand and vacate their seats, but this resulted only in congesting the aisles, as no men were willing to take the empty seats. The women eventually returned to their places at the insistence of the fire marshal.

"A strange mood in the gallery today," remarked Hiram Glass to his companions. They had ended up in correspondingly the same place as before in the Senate gallery, all the way to one side and at the very front.

Dave nodded. Will made no response; he was scanning the gallery, searching for a particular face.

"Fallen in love yet?" asked Dave.

"What?" Will blushed, taken aback.

"Look at him!" said Dave. "I think he *is* in love. Which lady is it? I'd say the most striking is that matron in the front row with the purple hat—Augusta Gaines, the queen of Bellevue and my boss's wife. She happens to be with child, though you can't tell yet by looking. Unless the prize goes to the smiling beauty next to her—Mrs. Taylor Moore, who's come to watch her husband orate today. But they're both too old for you, lad."

"Don't be silly," said Will. "I was just—" He stopped short, for he suddenly saw the *other* woman, the brunette who had been with the blond that day in the Senate gallery. But she was alone; the woman she had called Eula wasn't with her.

The chamber filled slowly. The sheer number of representatives gave the proceedings both a grander scale and a more circuslike atmosphere than the occasion of the Senate's debate. After the formal opening of the day's business, the speaker ordered a clerk to read the text of the bill. A flood of amendments were proposed. Motions were made to amend the amendments. One, echoing the amendment to the U.S. Constitution which granted voting rights to former slaves, would have added language to the effect that women should be eligible for employment "without regard to previous condition of servitude." The clerks in the gallery laughed heartily at the joke.

All the proposed amendments were rejected, and debate on the bill commenced. It was opposed on various grounds—that it would impair the efficiency of the departments; that it was unconstitutional for the legislature to dictate the hiring policies of department heads; that it would ultimately benefit brazen "Yankee women" and "Susan Anthonys" who would swoop down from the North and snatch the clerkships away from the more demure ladies of Texas. (This prompted a cry of "Stuff and nonsense!" from Augusta Gaines.)

One representative proposed that half the frontier battalions of the Texas Rangers be composed of women; why not, if women were the true equals of men and employment by the state was merely a question of fairness? Another suggested that voting on the bill be suspended so long as the gallery was full of women, since the presence of so many "pretty, pink-cheeked damsels" was likely to cast a mesmeric influence upon the legislators. Another moved to transfer the discussion to Millett's Opera House and charge twenty-five cents a head for admission.

If the Female Clerks Bill were to become law, asked Mr. McKinney of Walker County, what would come next? Would the bill's supporters propose in the next session that women be permitted to vote? Such logic would ulti-mately allow women to serve on juries, and to hold elective office—any of-fice, including that of judge, or state representative, or even governor of Texas! "Such a logic draws woman too far from her natural sphere for me to countenance," he concluded. "Home is her sphere. Keeping the hearth is her office. God has said it!"

Mr. Bergstrom of Bexar County objected that the bill was an egregious example of unconstitutional class legislation. "This bill contains a veritable Pandora's box of trouble. Some of the members, out of misplaced chivalry, would open that box. But do so for the women, then it follows that the col-ored people will have the right to put in *their* claim for a share of state jobs. Imagine a colored quota, to be enforced by law! Where will it end?"

Mr. Cochran chided opponents of the bill for raising the specter of woman's suffrage. "The purpose of this bill is as far removed from woman's suffrage as heaven is from earth. The spirit of chivalry that prompted the introduction of this bill would cry down with derision the slightest intima-tion that our women should be sent to the ballot box. The idea that women should be clothed with political power was born of political insanity, an abortion of a diseased mind which would attempt to unsex our women by dragging them into the muck of the political arena. The opponents of this bill are trying to defeat one measure by confusing it with another!"

Mr. Taylor Moore of Travis County was next to speak. There was a cheer from the gallery, initiated by Augusta Gaines. Beside her, Mrs. Moore ap-plauded quietly and held her chin high. Taylor Moore cast her a smiling glance, cleared his throat and began.

"Mr. Speaker! At the heart of this bill is a supposition, that in the matter of employment by the state, there exists and has existed blatant discrimina-tion against a group of citizens, namely the entire female sex of the state of Texas—and this, in spite of the doctrine of the majority party, my party, the Democratic party, of 'equal and exact justice to all and exclusive privileges to none.' This bill is intended to remedy past discrimination against women and to stop the perpetuation of that discrimination in the future.

"The opponents of this bill rather coyly point out that there is no law *pro-hibiting* the employment of women by the departments. If there were such a law, debarring half the population from the pursuit of a livelihood, what a shameful blot on our civilization that would be! Even more coyly, the opponents remind us that a law specifically *permitting* the employment of women by the state was passed by a previous legislature. Good for our predecessors, I say! But they did not go far enough, and it is incumbent on us to take the next step.

"We must go further, Mr. Speaker, because the injustice being perpetrated against women is not to be found in statutes, but in custom and daily practice. Custom bars the admission of women clerks into the department as effectually as an iron door, and that door will not be broken down until the law speaks! Custom, perpetuated year after year, is the invisible shield that protects the male inhabitants of Texas from fair competition in the departments.

"The opponents, after proudly pointing out that the law permits the hiring of women, then wring their hands and complain that hiring a woman, even in the respectable profession of a clerk, will inevitably strip her of her womanly grace and refinement. Mr. Speaker, I am thoroughly sick of this maudlin and inconsistent sentiment that goes into ecstasy over the delicate virtues of womanhood, even as it denies the possessors of those virtues the means to feed and clothe themselves! These opponents would put woman on a pedestal, and then let her starve there!

"Despite the opponents' sentimental view of home and hearth, the fact of the matter is that there are many women, all too many, who do not merely wish to work, but *must* work if they are to have decent lives. What man here would not be overjoyed to see every woman in Texas the queen of a hearth, able to devote herself to the care and nurture of her loved ones without a single care for monetary concerns? But that, Mr. Speaker, is a picture from a child's book, not the way things actually are!

"There are many women who need to work. We can chart the reasons for this situation, if we wish. Consider all the fine men who were killed or maimed in the War Between the States. Almost a generation has passed since that great tragedy, but its consequences are still felt in many a household and by many a woman who was left orphaned or widowed or bereft of the son or brother who should have been her mainstay and support in these latter days. Instead of being supported, many a woman was forced to become the support of a man whose body was broken by the sacrifices he made on the battlefield.

"Add to this the curse of drink and the general loosening of morals in our time, and spare a thought for those women who are worse than widows, who find themselves wedded to drunkards and vagabonds and must call upon their own resources to feed their children and themselves.

"Consider, too, the trend in modern society for power and wealth to become concentrated into fewer and fewer hands. Society has become divided into virtually two classes, the employers and the employed, those who live upon what they have already acquired, and those who must daily acquire what they live upon. Men and women alike are thrown upon their own resources, and for some, the poorest, there is an actual struggle for existence. This is the harsh reality which has so disturbed the sacred sphere of the hearth and forced many women of our day, no less feminine and virtuous than their mothers and grandmothers, into the pursuit of a livelihood. The gentlemen who assert that God has ordained woman for household cares and nothing else, neglect the reality that our schoolrooms and shops and, yes, our offices are populated more and more by honest, heroic women who are driven there not by unnatural ambition but by stern necessity. Those pious gentlemen forget that there are women who have no homes, who are too proud to be pitied and too noble to surrender their independence. Will they agree that no woman should ever feel compelled to enter into matrimony merely to gain a means of material sustenance?

"What would the opponents have such a woman do? Must she restrict herself to the backbreaking labor of the washtub? Must she beg for alms? Or must she sink even lower? Mr. Speaker, we are only too aware of the channels of *illegitimate* commerce open to a woman. We know the temptations that may beset a woman in need and the depths of degradation into which she may fall. Once fallen into that abyss, will she find the gentlemen who oppose this bill springing to her assistance, extending helping hands to pull her from its depths? I say, better to keep her from falling into that abyss in the first place! Better to enact legislation, like the bill before this house, which guarantees her a fair, fighting chance to support herself by honest labor. Surely that is no less than should be given to every man, and every woman, in this great state!"

Taylor Moore struck the podium with his fist. The women in the gallery spontaneously rose to their feet, applauding and cheering. Mrs. Moore, her face beaming with pride, wiped a tear from her eye. Her husband took a bow. As he rose he touched his fingers to his lips and blew a kiss. It was meant for his wife, but not a few of the women in the gallery seemed to think it was intended in a general way for them all, and they enthusiastically returned the gesture; imaginary kisses sprinkled the hall. Will Porter craned his neck and peered between the hats and lace. The dark woman was still alone; Eula had not joined her. Curiously, she remained seated while all the other women rose to their feet cheering. She seemed to be lost in thought as she pondered the words of Mr. Taylor Moore.

19

If the so-called Female Clerks Bill had been a human child, its tombstone might have read: *Here lies Senate Bill No. 79, born January 19, died February 19, 1885; though it lived but a month, it shook the state of Texas.*

After several days of debate, the House of Representatives passed the bill by an overwhelming margin. Significantly, two minor amendments had been added. The amended bill was sent back to the Senate.

Because amendments had been added, the Senate was required to debate those amendments. Senator Terrell, the bill's archenemy, moved to postpone such debate indefinitely. His motion passed by a vote of fifteen to eleven. Some of those who had voted for the original bill now voted to postpone considering it again.

Debate on the amended bill was never scheduled. Senate Bill No. 79 fell into legislative limbo. Despite majority votes in both houses, the bill was effectively dead.

May Tobin had attended none of the debates, but had listened attentively to Delia Campbell's firsthand accounts. "Men are so devious!" May remarked to Delia, when she learned that the bill was kaput. "Those hypocrites never intended to let that bill become law. It's a pity for women everywhere—but then, if the thing had been successful, it might have put me out of business."

"How so?" asked Delia.

"Why, all the bright, attractive young ladies like yourself would go find legitimate employment as clerks. You wouldn't have to resort to the livelihood you earn here. I'd have to shut the house down."

"I can't speak for anyone else," said Delia, languidly removing the cigar from her lips, "but I, for one, shall *never* become a clerk."

The legislature turned its attention to other matters—appropriations for the university, relief to war veterans, a move to disband the Texas Rangers ("a costly body of official barnacles" according to those who believed the frontier force had outlived its usefulness). On March 2, amid gala festivities, the cornerstone of the new capitol building was laid. The month of March blew through central Texas in typical fashion—wet, wild, and windy.

By now, except by those most directly affected, the murder of Mollie Smith was virtually forgotten.

Springtime at the farm in Williamson County meant birthing infant livestock and planting crops. Jimmy Phillips and George McCutcheon worked from dawn until dusk. Eula was lonelier than ever. Delia, responding to the misery in her letters, came for an extended visit.

With Delia there, the farm seemed a new place to Eula. Springtime seemed truly to have arrived; the depression that had gripped her all winter loosened. Her chores seemed lighter. Caring for the baby became a source of comfort instead of a burden. The very air she breathed seemed sweeter and more wholesome.

The two women cooked and sewed and tended the vegetable garden together. Eula had feared that Delia would quickly grow bored, but her sister-in-law seemed to enjoy her respite from the city. "Don't you miss Austin?" said Eula one day. They were in the garden, setting out poles and tying strings for the beans to grow on. The baby slept in a crib set in the shade nearby. "Don't you hate it here as much as I do?"

"Hate it? It's lovely."

"You say that because you don't have to live here. You can leave whenever you like."

"Well, I won't be leaving anytime soon, Eula. I intend to stay with you for quite some time. When I do go back, you know you can come and visit anytime you like."

"And stay with your parents? Last time, they hovered over me the whole while. They seemed to think that the fact that I came to Austin without Jimmy meant there was trouble between us."

"Is there?"

Eula gazed at the long furrows of the garden. "No. Things are going well. Better than I thought they would. Jimmy stays sober, *most* of the time. Demon rum! Why must we put up with it? I sometimes think the prohibitionists are right."

Delia shook her head. "I don't see how outlawing alcohol would make men stop drinking it. What they do at May Tobin's house is illegal, but the law doesn't stop them. A man will do what he wants. A woman's only asking for heartbreak if she thinks she can stop him."

"Delia, you've picked up the most cynical notions from that Tobin woman."

Delia smiled. "You've never even met her."

"I'd like to, someday."

"Never! A respectable young wife and mother has to be careful about the company she keeps."

"I worry about you sometimes, Delia." Eula suddenly looked so somber that Delia had to laugh and give her a kiss.

"Shall you lecture me then, and try to shame me into abandoning my wanton ways?"

"No. But perhaps I ought to."

"You don't sound very convincing. You shall have to hurl more fire and brimstone than that if you mean to scare me."

Eula smiled. "Would I be more convincing if I could orate like those fellows we listened to in the Senate?"

Delia laughed. "They were truly dreadful, weren't they? Croaking like puffed-up frogs. Do you suppose such a band of old frogs could ever be elected if women were given the vote?"

"Never! We would run them off with a stick."

"Only I'm not sure that we could find better fellows to replace them."

"Fellows?" said Eula. "What makes you think any man would ever be elected again, if women had a say?"

"Eula, you're right! That's what they're afraid of, isn't it? If they allow us to vote, they'll have their mothers and wives making laws over them."

"And their mistresses," said Eula.

"Well, I hardly think—"

"If the men who patronize May Tobin's house are fit to run the government, then why not the women at May's house, too?"

"Eula! I had no idea you were a radical suffragist."

"I suppose it's all the time I spend here alone, day after day, thinking. A lot of things don't make sense to me."

Delia laughed. "Well, women running the government shall never happen in our lifetime, so I suppose you can paint the fantasy any color you wish. The state of Texas run by fallen ladies—I think that even Rutabaga Johnson would draw the line at that!"

"Does *he* ever visit May's?"

Delia shrieked with laughter. "Heavens, no! Oh, dear, there's a thought to keep me here on the farm!"

Eula looked at her keenly. "What about that fellow you pointed out to me in the Senate gallery?"

"William Shelley? That's a different story."

"He still comes?"

"Regularly. Even though I gave him a bit of a start that day, in the gallery. Politicians—they're all so fearful for their reputations! But he keeps coming. Not only that, but . . ."

"What, Delia?"

"You must never, ever breathe a word of this."

"Of course I won't, Delia."

"Only a couple of weeks ago, he brought his boss to May's house."

"His boss?"

"The comptroller. Mr. Swain!"

"Should I be impressed?"

"Only because he's going to be the next governor of Texas."

"Really?"

"It's a sure thing. Mr. Shelley says so, and so does May—and May knows everything. I've never seen her so excited by a visitor in the house."

They tended the garden for a while, until Delia saw that Eula was shaking her head.

"What is it, sweet?"

"Nothing, really. Only—we're taught as children that the world is such-and-such, and then we grow up and find that it isn't that way at all, but completely different."

"Is that so terrible?"

"It makes me sad."

Delia reached for Eula's hands. "Maybe it's sad only if you keep wanting the world to be something it's not. Maybe if you see the way things really are, that makes you . . . *free,* in a way."

"But if you see everything as it is, and it's all so small and ugly, then what is there left to dream for?"

"Oh, a million things, Eula. You never have to stop dreaming."

Eula looked at the farmhouse and the barn, at the outhouse and the little toolshed, at the sheep in the pasture and the field where the men were plowing. "I'm not sure what my dream is," she said quietly, "but this surely isn't it."

20

*A*PRIL showers bring May flowers," declared Dr. Terry with a wry smile. He stood, along with Dr. Fry and scores of others, along the railing of the Congress Avenue bridge, looking west, upriver. Few of those on the bridge intended to cross to the other side, yet all had gladly paid the toll, in order to better view the devastation.

Directly below them, masses of debris had accumulated against the pilings of the bridge. More masses of debris were scattered all up and down the muddy, ravaged shores on either side of the Colorado. The storms of March and April had culminated in a flood which had swept down the river in a great wall of water.

"The flood has inspired our friend and colleague Mr. Gaines to wax most poetical," noted Dr. Terry. "Shall I read to you from the *Statesman*, Dr. Fry?"

Dr. Fry stood with his back to the rail, facing east so as to enjoy the morning sunlight on his face. He nodded, causing the sunlight to glimmer across his cobalt-blue spectacles. "Please do."

Dr. Terry cleared his throat. He read loudly enough for everyone within thirty feet to hear. "'The Colorado has been on the biggest boom since the famous flood of '39. The cruel, devastating waters swept down on a dreadful holocaust of swollen turbidity, surging and dashing in a mad fury which has never been equaled in human history.'"

"Or at least not since 1839," noted Dr. Fry.

"A dam!" Dr. Terry abruptly proclaimed, less to Dr. Fry than to those whose attention had been captured by his reading. "A dam is what this city needs, not only for its benefits to industry and agriculture, but to put an end to such devastation."

There were shouts of "Hear, hear!" and "Smart fellow!" and "Damned right!"

Dr. Terry lowered his voice. "It seems, Dr. Fry, that we have returned to the town of Austin at a most timely juncture. Fortune smiles on us. This flood is a positive godsend! The advantages of a dam shall be on everyone's lips. And here we are, returned for the very purpose of investing our hard-won capital in just such a project." He raised his voice. "Oh, Dr. Fry! I only wish that you could see with your own eyes the churning brown vortices, the flotsam, the jetsam, the poor souls lining the treacherous, crumbling banks!"

Dr. Fry assumed a grave expression.

Dr. Terry raised his voice even more. "Gentlemen! Do you see those haggard wretches down there, standing forlornly along the bank? Scores of them—men who have lost everything to the flood: their homes, their meager worldly possessions, their livelihoods! Before, they lived in little shacks on the waterfront or slept on makeshift rafts. They fished for food and profit. Gone the shacks! Gone the rafts! Gone the fishing poles and the nets! Those men are lucky to be alive.

"Gentlemen of Austin! I am new to these parts, but the fierce civic pride of this great capital city has already captured my allegiance. I feel compelled to do something for those unfortunates. I must take action! I will! I propose to take up a collection for those beleaguered victims, right here and now." He took off his hat and held it before him. "Dr. Fry, beginning with you! There, there, reach into your pockets. A nickel, man? I'll settle for nothing less than a dollar! Here, I shall reach into my own waistcoat and put in two dollars myself. You, there, sir? What will you give? Think of those men going hungry and naked, victims of the awful, unsparing ravages of nature! And you, sir. How much? Very well, a nickel then, if you cannot spare more for your fellow man, but that much at least! And you, sir? And you?"

Like the flooding Colorado, Dr. Terry carried all before him. By the time he was done, his hat sagged with a considerable weight in coins, with a few bills spilling over the top like the green froth on the river. He loudly thanked the generous citizens of Austin, then left the bridge and made his way down to the riverbank, proceeding slowly so as to assist Dr. Fry in the descent. There he disbursed a portion of his charitable collection to the bewildered drifters and vagrants who stood gawking at the river. The portion which he kept for himself (by causing some of the coins and bills to vanish through a small tear in the silk lining of his hat) was, as he figured it, a reasonable commission to compensate his efforts on behalf of the needy.

That night, he and Dr. Fry dined on the thickest steaks the Iron Front had to offer, and discussed the exciting possibilities of doing business in Austin.

"Hiram Glass! What . . . on . . . earth—?"

Hiram, who had arrived at his desk in a whistling mood, stiffened and flinched. "Shoemaker! Didn't your mother ever teach you that it's rude to stare? But I forget, you were raised by cows. Well, better get your hooves off your desk. Gaines will show up any minute."

"Hiram! My God . . ."

"Do you have a problem, Shoemaker?"

Dave laughed. "Well, at least I know my up from my down."

"What are you talking about?"

Dave kept staring at him with an expression of wonder. He shook his head. "All I can figure is that you must've stopped this morning for a shoeshine from old Sam down in the lobby. But Hiram—you're supposed to put your *feet* on the block, not your head! The polish is for your shoes!"

Hiram's face seemed to crack like a walnut.

"Either that," Dave went on, "or I'm thinking you must have got your head stuck in one of the presses while they were loading the ink!" Dave slapped his desk and started laughing so hard he lost his balance and very nearly fell backward in his swivel chair.

Hiram set about repairing his cracked countenance. He clicked his teeth, stiffened his jaw, compressed his lips, narrowed his eyes. "I take it that you are referring to my hair."

"Are you certain that's your hair? I thought it might be—"

"Enough of that, Shoemaker! The fact of the matter is that I have joined the thousands of others, men and women alike, who have turned to Hale's Hair Renewer in order to revivify their scalps."

"Golly, Hiram, everybody knows that stuff is just black shoe polish in a bottle, thinned with printer's ink and ammonia and topped off with a squirt of French perfume."

"It most certainly is not! Hale's Hair Renewer is a scientific combination of costly ingredients, especially formulated to restore brittle, colorless hair to its original shade and texture."

"Hiram, you're hardly an old graybeard." Dave's eyes suddenly lit up. "I know what this means! You have a new lady friend, don't you?"

Hiram gave no answer. He sorted through a stack of papers on his desk. "Terrible thing, this flood," he said crisply.

A few moments later, William Pendleton Gaines came sweeping through the office. He came to a halt in front of Dave's desk and thrust a newspaper clipping under his nose.

Dave peered at the text cross-eyed, then pretended to sniff. "Smells like . . . Bratwurst? Sauerkraut?"

"So, you *do* recognize German when you see it," said Gaines.

"I grew up speaking German."

"Yes, but can you *read* it?"

"Of course I can! I told you I could read German when you hired me."

"So you did." Gaines raised an eyebrow. "But I've never had occasion to test you—until now."

"What is this?" Dave took the clipping.

"From some German newspaper. A friend of Augusta's is over there visiting family. The lady noticed this story, saw the Texas connection and figured I might be interested. Came in yesterday's mail. I read enough German to make out the gist of it, but that Gothic type gives me eyestrain, so I want you to translate. Besides, you come from Hempstead, don't you?"

"Sorry to disappoint you, boss, but Hempstead's not in Germany. It's not that far east. Past Manor, but this side of Houston—"

"I know where Hempstead is, damn it! Just read the thing. Good Lord, Hiram, what the hell have you done to your hair? Did you fall in a tar pit, man?"

Dave scrutinized the text before him. He smiled broadly for no apparent reason, then began to read aloud haltingly, translating in his head. "From the Dresden *Tagblatt*: 'The Mystery of Elisabet Ney—Whatever Became of the Noted Sculptress?—The Woman Who Softened the King's Cold Heart Said to Be Living Among Savages in America.'" He threw back his head and laughed.

"You can laugh *after* you've read the story," said Gaines. "Get on with it!"

Dave squinted. The headlines were easy enough to decipher, but the main text with all those long compound words in tiny type was indeed enough to induce eyestrain. He paused between each sentence, having to reorder the syntax into passable English, and frequently gestured with his hands to indicate his degree of satisfaction with a particular choice of word. "'Almost fifteen years have passed since the leave-taking of Elisabet Ney for the New World, with no news of her whereabouts. . . . The once-famous artist has once again become a subject of conversation, due to the increasing turbulence surrounding the royal court of King Ludwig II. . . . As matters come to a head between the beleaguered monarch and the agents of unification, there has in the daily presses been much speculation about the king's famously erratic character. . . . It is universally asserted that Ludwig is now and has always been a notorious woman-hater, completely averse to the female sex.'"

"Must be why they call him Mad Ludwig!" asserted Gaines.

"'Contrarily, it will be remembered that it was Elisabet Ney, in 1869 only thirty-five years of age but already a noted artist, who successfully induced the king to sit for a life-size marble statue, which now stands in Munich.'"

"*Induced* him, or *seduced* him?" asked Gaines. Hiram Glass rolled his eyes.

"Sir, either you trust me as a translator or you don't!" said Dave. "Now then: 'The youthful monarch consented to sit only after much persuasion, and then only if Miss Ney would agree not to speak to him or take measurements of his head or in any other way lay hands on him. . . . He showed up for his first sitting in an irascible mood. . . . Miss Ney, unable to use him in such an attitude, begged permission to read to him aloud. . . . Her selection was Goethe's—'" Dave made a face. "'*If a genie*'?"

"*Iphigenia*." The classically educated Gaines corrected Dave's Greek.

"As you say. Well, whatever that is, that's what she read to him. To continue: 'In her studio garb of a trailing robe of white wool with wide open sleeves folded back, Ney must have looked something like an ancient Greek princess herself. . . . Listening to the stanzas, the king's sullen features became lofty and noble. . . . Miss Ney finished reading and sat still. . . . "Why don't you begin?" Ludwig asked her sharply. . . . "I am studying Your Majesty," the artist answered. . . . Baffled, Ludwig looked back at her, and from then on was her willing subject and sent her massive floral arrangements in advance of every sitting. . . . There were four sittings in all, and each time Miss Ney read from Goethe to soothe the royal breast; the sublime result can be seen in the masterpiece which stands in Munich.

"'When the sittings were finished, the young ruler sent an inquiry to Miss Ney asking if she would accept a gift of jewelry, or if she wished for any other gift. . . . "Only flowers, as I have no time to look after valuables," she replied. . . . Ludwig, having never encountered such a sentiment among his circle of sycophants, held her in the highest esteem from that day forward.

"'Then, under mysterious circumstances, Miss Ney and her husband, the British physician Edmund Montgomery, abandoned their elegant villa in Munich. . . . It is thought that they emigrated to the United States of America. . . . Shortly before she departed, Miss Ney, who had sculpted men such as Bismarck and Garibaldi, made this remark: "After so many great men of the civilized world have sat for me, I would like now to model the greatest of the wild men."

"'Some time after her departure, an item appeared in several German newspapers, to the effect that a tribe of wild North American Indians had captured and carried off a German sculptress who had dared to enter into their territory. . . . This story was roundly dismissed as the wildest sort of rumor. Nevertheless, Miss Ney has never been heard from again. . . . Has she voluntarily drawn a veil of obscurity about her life these last fifteen years, or has some dire misfortune overtaken her? . . . Whatever the truth may be, as the heirless king's power struggle with his republican ministers becomes increasingly dire, Elisabet Ney is remembered here as the only woman who was ever able to warm, if only for a little, his frigid heart.'"

"That's a hell of a story," said Hiram Glass, without expression. "But where's the Texas connection?"

"Well," said Gaines, beaming, "as Augusta's friend over in Germany happens to know, this Elisabet Ney is living right here in Texas—in the vicinity of Hempstead! She and her husband are pretty much hermits, but they have connections in high circles. I'm told they're bosom friends of Oran Milo Roberts, our former governor as now heads up the law school at the university. Well, Dave, you come from Hempstead, don't you? You must have heard of this lady, at least."

Dave nibbled his fingertip and made a pretense of looking thoughtful. "Maybe. I wonder—could she have been the strange old lady who lived back of the railroad station with all the cats?"

"Don't be ridiculous, man! She and her husband live on a plantation outside of town."

"Ah! This does begin to sound familiar . . ."

"Good! Because this is what I have in mind: since you speak German, and since you come from Hempstead, I want you to head over there and bring me back a story about this woman."

"I see. Ask her what it was like being captured by Indians and all that?"

"David Shoemaker, you are treading on very thin ice. Can you handle this story or can't you? It's bound to be interesting—famous lady artist, friend and confidante of the greatest statesmen and crowned heads of Europe—and somehow or other she ends up in Six-Shooter Junction! That kind of story practically writes itself! Besides, Augusta is still in a holy snit over what happened to the Female Clerks Bill. She says we don't run enough stories of interest to the lady readership, beyond the occasional piece about hanging drapes or making hatboxes out of egg crates. So what do you say, Shoemaker? Think you can make a story out of this?"

"I don't know, boss. It'll mean being away from town for, oh, at least a day or two—maybe longer if this Ney woman's really a hermit. You know how seriously I take my responsibility to stay abreast of the day-to-day crime situation in Austin . . ."

"I think the con men and prostitutes in Guy Town can get along without you for a few days, Shoemaker."

"But what if there's a real crime?"

Gaines snorted. "Not counting the graft in the legislature, there hasn't been a real crime in this town—a crime worth reporting on—since that colored girl was murdered back around New Year's Eve. Hell, if something like that happens again, I'll send you a telegram and tell you to haul your rear end back to Austin pronto."

Dave nodded thoughtfully. "Well, then, boss, if you're certain you can do without me—sure, I'll go to Hempstead for a few days. Even a week, if I have to."

Hiram Glass rolled his eyes.

"Good," said Gaines. "That settles it. You'll leave tomorrow, Dave. And, Hiram, you can take up any slack while he's gone. But good Lord, man—what have you done to your hair?"

21

⚜

Explain to me again why we're off to Hempstead, and on such short notice," said Will Porter, watching the landscape pass by outside the railcar window.

"It's perfectly simple," said Dave Shoemaker. "*I* am headed there by order of His Majesty William Pendleton Gaines, or 'Mad Bill' as we peasants call him, as an emissary to the great European artist in exile, Miss Elisabet Ney. Ostensibly, I'm to seek out her life story for purposes of journalistic exploitation—but frankly, just between you and me . . . ." He lowered his voice. "I suspect Queen Augusta has a hankering to see her husband immortalized in marble. She's thinking what a fine finishing touch it would provide for the grounds at Bellevue, if only she had a life-size nude of Gaines striking a heroic pose."

Will wrinkled his brow. "I'm not sure that Austin is ready for naked statues. Couldn't Gaines wear a loincloth?"

"I'm sure Miss Ney could come up with an artistic solution."

Will gazed out the window. The Houston and Texas Central Railway was carrying them eastward out of the rugged Hill Country into the flatlands. Dense stands of conifers alternated with meadows full of wildflowers—Indian paintbrush, bluebonnets, and red and yellow fire-wheels. "I understand why *you're* going to Hempstead. What about me?"

"You, Mr. Porter, could use a small vacation."

"From what? The three or four hours a week I put in at the Harrells' cigar store?"

"No, from the humdrum routine of your lackadaisical existence."

"I've been plenty busy lately," said Will defensively.

"Doing what?"

"Singing, for one thing. Someone at the boarding house overheard my bathtub rendition of 'Jeanie With the Light Brown Hair'; next thing you know, I've been drafted to sing in every charity minstrel show in town. A fellow who can sing bass is always in demand."

Dave smiled wryly. "I hear you've also been showing off your talents in church. Found religion, have you?"

"I'm strictly nondenominational; I'll sing for any church that'll have me. You might be surprised, Dave Shoemaker, how many girls—*nice* girls—a fellow can meet when he sings in a church choir."

"I understand you serenade as well."

"True, some of the fellows and myself have formed a serenading party. By night we load a small organ in a rented hack and travel hither and yon, making sweet music outside the windows of young ladies. Sooner or later one of them either invites us onto the porch for lemonade, or else threatens to call the police, and we call it a night."

"I take it all this strain to your vocal chords is paying off in romantic dividends?"

"I've made the acquaintance of one or two nice young ladies and earned the goodwill of many a doting mother. My eye is on the long term, Dave. I don't aim to be an old bachelor like some fellows I could name."

When it came to marriage, Dave thought, having a steady job was what impressed the mothers; but he didn't say that. "Then you haven't pinned your hopes on a particular lady yet?"

"Not at all," Will said. Something changed in his voice. He was thinking of *her*, the woman called Eula. Every Sunday when he sang, it was his secret fantasy to glimpse her face in the congregation. On the nights when he serenaded, his unspoken hope was to look up and see her standing at a window, illuminated by a halo of lamplight. He spoke of her to no one, not even to Dave.

And yet Dave sensed something. "There!" He sprang forward and pointed at Will, who started back. "Right there! That look that just crossed your face. *That's* why you need to get out of town for a few days."

Will laughed uncertainly. "I don't know what you mean."

Dave looked at him slyly. "Maybe you do, and maybe you don't. I can't put a finger on it—it's not a twitch, not a frown. Something about your eyes, like a cloud that crosses the sun. When a fellow starts getting that look, it means he's due for a change of scenery."

Will gazed out the window at sunlight flickering through the pine trees, and changed the subject. "I still don't understand why Gaines is paying for you to take a trip to your hometown and visit with friends."

"That's the rich part! Gaines doesn't realize that I already know the Doctor and Miss Ney! He thinks he's sent me off to beg for an audience with some reclusive European artist. I told him it might take me a few days just to wangle an interview out of her, and he went for it! Two minutes after he gave me the assignment, I went down to the telegraph office and sent a wire to Hempstead, asking the Doctor and Miss Ney if I could spend a night or two at Liendo on such short notice. They wired back to say I was welcome, and invited me to bring a friend. So here I am, off to stay with old friends for a while, at Gaines's expense!"

"How did a fellow like you ever get to know such highfalutin folks?"

Dave looked at the passing countryside with a wistful expression. The train was passing through a meadow where a vast expanse of bluebonnets spread in all directions like a shallow lake. "I was a kid when the Doctor and Miss Ney moved to Hempstead. Must have been the year I turned thirteen; wasn't long after my mother died. The big house out at Liendo Plantation needed a lot of fixing and cleaning up. The foreman hired some boys from town to help tote and haul. I'd never seen such a grand house—big columns in front, with a big wide porch and a balcony upstairs. Even broken down, to me it looked like the grandest mansion in Texas.

"We weren't supposed to go inside the house, but I sneaked in through the kitchen and went exploring. The new owners hadn't finished unpacking yet, and boxes and crates were stacked all over the place. There didn't seem to be anyone about, so I kept wandering, all the way upstairs into Dr. Montgomery's study. There were books all over the place, crammed into shelves and stacked on the floor—big books with leather bindings and gilded edges, filled with mathematical formulas and diagrams and drawings of plants and animals, some in English and some in German and some in other languages I couldn't recognize. Over against one wall there was a long table with all sorts of laboratory equipment—retorts and beakers and test tubes, even a microscope. Can you imagine the effect of a room like that on a thirteen-year-old boy who'd never been more than fifteen miles from Six-Shooter Junction? It was like some sort of wonderland.

"I was sitting on the floor, looking through one of the books, when I heard somebody come in. I looked up and saw this gentleman with long sideburns and spectacles. I'd figured that whoever owned the things in that room must be an old man with white hair and whiskers, but this fellow was slender and spry-looking and handsome. I just sat there, waiting for him to yell at me, but instead he strolled over, humming to himself. He looked down at the biology book in my lap. He started asking me questions. Did I know what protoplasm was, or a protozoan? Had I ever seen a cell through a microscope? Had I ever *looked* through a microscope?

"He led me over to his worktable. He didn't let me touch his microscope, mind you, but he let me put my eye to it. It was just a drop of swamp water on a bit of glass, but to me it was a whole new world.

"Dr. Montgomery said I could come back and look at his books again sometime. I went back the very next day, and he actually let me borrow one. He and Miss Ney had all sorts of books, not just about science. They had novels and poetry and biographies. They even knew some of the authors. Back in Europe she'd been a sculptress and he'd been a philosopher. They showed me a picture of the house they'd lived in, and it was even grander than Liendo.

"That was my education—not what I learned in the schoolhouse at Hempstead, but going to their house, borrowing books and listening to them talk about the places they'd been and the people they'd known. Didn't you ever wonder, Will, how it came about that a poor boy from Hempstead like myself, with no college education, knows Plutarch from Petrarch?"

"Sounds like they practically adopted you," said Will.

Dave shook his head. "I only visited now and then. I'd borrow a book, finish it a week or two later, and drop by to borrow another one. We weren't close like family. Nicer than family, in a way; never any yelling." Dave cocked his head. "I look back now and I think they must have been glad to have someone in the town who appreciated them, even if it was just a kid with a yen for book-learning. Most folks in Hempstead thought the new owners at Liendo were mighty peculiar. Everybody assumed they were living in sin, because Miss Ney never referred to the Doctor as her husband, but as her 'best friend.' She called herself Miss Ney, never Mrs. Montgomery. She was proud of her name and wouldn't give it up; there was a Marshal Ney who served Napoleon.

"They had a hard time, especially that first year. I don't think they had any notion of how to run a plantation; but then, nobody did after the war. One of their baby boys died that first summer, of diphtheria. She made a death mask and they cremated the body. Dr. Montgomery said that was the scientific thing to do, on account of the microbes. People thought that was strange, even suspicious, and it started a round of awful rumors. But the Doctor and Miss Ney finally settled in. I guess they must have made something of the plantation, since they're still there. Their other little boy must be about thirteen by now, the same age I was when they came to Hempstead."

"How long has it been since you've seen them?" said Will quietly.

"Must be getting on four or five years. I don't get back to Hempstead much since my father died. It's not much of a place to visit. You must know the joke."

"What joke?"

Dave smiled. "Drunk gets on the train at Houston, headed for Austin, and falls asleep. First stop out of Houston is Hempstead. Pretty soon the conductor comes through to collect tickets. He wakes up the drunk. The drunk confesses he hasn't got a ticket. Conductor says, 'And where do you think you're going, mister?' Drunk says, 'Goin' to hell, I reckon.' Conductor says, 'Well, then, get off at the next stop!'"

Will laughed. "You just made that up!"

"I swear I didn't. That joke's as old as I am."

"So this train's taking us straight to hell, is that it?"

"Some of us, I imagine," said Dave.

Past a mile marker that read 119, the train pulled into Hempstead station.

On the platform, a voice called out behind them. "Mr. Shoemaker!" The man was tall and burly, with coarse black hair haphazardly cut, as if with a bowl and pruning shears. His ruddy skin was so weathered that it was impossible to judge his age. "Mr. Shoemaker, don't you know me?"

Dave studied him for a moment, then smiled. "Not if you're going to call me 'Mr. Shoemaker,' Horace. I'll think you mean my father."

"Hey, but I can't hardly call you Davey Boy no more, can I? You're a big fellow writing for the newspapers now."

"I'll answer to Dave. And this is Will Porter. He's a writerly sort of fellow, too, though not as famous as yours truly. Will, shake hands with Horace of Liendo Plantation."

The man's callused fingers were as weathered as his face. Will figured he must be part Indian.

"Miss Ney sent me with a buggy to pick you up."

"I always used to walk from town."

"Walk?" Horace snorted. "It's four miles from here to the front gate. Nobody walks it, except for kids—and Miss Ney. Hell, she come back one night from a trip, train was real late and nobody at the house knew. She wouldn't wait at the hotel, walked all the way home in the pitch dark. Carried her six-shooter with her, you bet. Fired it a couple of times, just to scare off the cows." Horace grunted. "Give me them satchel bags."

The buggy took them out of Hempstead and immediately into the countryside. The road was rutted, with few houses along it. Dave became quiet. Will conversed with Horace.

"Why do people call it Six-Shooter Junction?"

Horace kept his eyes on the road. "Oh, lot of people get shot around here. Family feuds, mostly. You stay at Liendo, you'll be safe."

"Are there are a lot of workers on the plantation?"

"Must be twenty families, all colored. Some of 'em been around since they was slaves on the plantation. Sharecroppers, now. Miss Ney feeds and clothes 'em." Horace made a grunt which passed for a laugh. "She don't think much of 'em. Calls 'em deadheads. Says they're worse than the Irish. Keeps saying she's gonna bring over some Germans to farm the place right."

"What sort of crops?"

"Tries to grow cotton. Tries to grow corn. Had better luck with cattle— got a hundred head now, plenty of milk and butter. Sells off some lumber every now and then. That lady's tried every way there is to make ends meet. If it wasn't for that batch of money they get from Europe once a year, we'd all be starving. I reckon they'd sell the place if they could, you bet, but they couldn't get half what they paid for it."

"Does Miss Ney do everything? What about Dr. Montgomery?"

"Oh, he stays busy. Totes little bottles of water up from the pond to look at under his 'scope, makes drawings of all the little critters. You remember him doing that, don't you, Dave? That man can sit for a solid hour watching a dung beetle roll a ball of dirt across the road. He knows everything about spiderwebs and bird nests and ant beds and tadpoles. Got a name for every part of a crawdaddy, even the ones so small you can't see 'em. He's got the soul of an Indian. Make a lousy farmer, you bet. Lets Miss Ney run the place while he reads his books and writes his letters. But he can get a thing done when he sets his mind to it. Helped to get that colored college started, just down the road at Prairie View. He was real proud of that."

Dave suddenly spoke up. "What about Lorne? Which one does he take after?"

Horace grunted. "Good question! No good for farming, like his father. Stubborn, like his mother. Don't care much for books, though. Rather go off and play with the Hempstead boys. Oh, that burns Miss Ney! Remember how she used to dress him up like a little prince? Put him in tunics and sandals, and long white flannel robes. Dressed him in a Blue Boy suit one day, a Scottish kilt the next. Now he gets his clothes all torn and dirty playing with those town boys—'hoodlums,' she calls 'em. Pretty soon she'll send him off to some fancy school back East where they make a boy wear a uniform, you bet."

The road grew rougher, with high grass on either side. Beyond the grass grew stands of cedar and dogwood. They passed through a thicket of yaupon holly, and when they emerged into sunlight they had their first sight of Liendo a hundred yards away.

With a little imagination, Will could see it as it must have been in its glory days before the war, when the grand lawn had been immaculately kept and the house had gleamed with fresh paint and spotless windows. With a bit more imagination, he could see what the Doctor and Miss Ney must have seen when they decided to purchase the place—a grand house in the middle of the Texas wilderness, dilapidated but full of potential.

Steps led up to a generous porch enclosed by four square columns. Above the porch, enclosed by the same columns and surrounded by a low wooden rail, was a balcony. Both the porch and the balcony gave access to the house through tall, wide doors flanked by shuttered windows. To either side of the central pediment, the house extended in wings that ended in tall chimneys. As they drew closer, Will noticed the decorative semicircular niche cut into the center of the pediment, enclosing a wooden star and the numerals 1853.

It was a classic Greek revival plantation house, sturdily built of wood on a red brick foundation to withstand the fiercest coastal storms. It was only a little more than thirty years old, yet had the look of having always been there. But Liendo looked down-at-heels. The grounds were poorly kept; weeds alternated with patches of bare earth, and the towering oaks with moss trailing from their limbs had a shabby, neglected look. In the middle of the grounds there was a small fountain, apparently broken, for the basin was dry and strewn with leaves. As for the house itself, there were broken balusters in the railings of the balcony, missing slats in some of the shutters, and cracks in some of the windows, all of which were liberally coated with dust. The white paint was cracked and peeling.

Horace stopped at a spot where a footpath bisected the grounds and led from the road to the porch steps. "You can get out here," he said. "I'll drive around to the stable in back and bring up your bags."

Will and Dave descended from the buggy. As they walked toward the house, the front door opened and a woman stepped out. Her hair, chestnut brown streaked with gray, was as short as a man's, parted in the middle and combed back from her face. Instead of a blouse she wore a long smock which rested loosely on her shoulders, baring her throat. The smock hung almost to her knees. Underneath, she appeared to be wearing some sort of bloomers made of a fabric sturdy enough for outer wear. Will had never seen such a thing, but after all he had heard about Elisabet Ney, he could hardly be surprised at the sight of the woman wearing pants.

22

*M*ARSHAL Lee surveyed the mayhem.

He stood alone in an upstairs room in the brick building at the corner of Hickory Street and Congress Avenue. The entire second floor was occupied by Dr. O. B. Stoddard, who used several rooms for his dentistry offices and the rest for his private residence. Dr. Stoddard was a bachelor who lived alone, save for his caged mockingbird.

Here, in the spacious, elegantly furnished reception room, the fire had done its worst damage. The tall mirror that occupied most of one wall was scorched and cracked. The mirror had hand-cut Venetian glass borders decorated with elaborate curlicues, and must have been imported from Italy, Lee thought; his father had a similar mirror in his office at the capitol building commission, and it had cost a considerable sum. This one was ruined, though it still gave back his smoky reflection as he poked about the room.

The rug was also ruined, as much by water as by fire. It must have been a beautiful thing, with riotous arabesques in red and purple and yellow. Now it was scorched through in places and blackened by wet soot and muck. Some of the black spots were Lee's own boot prints, laid down as he crossed and recrossed the room, searching for anything that might indicate who had been here the night before and set the fire.

Against one wall stood a tall bookcase with rows of big, bulky volumes, their spines charred. Half a dozen elegantly upholstered wooden chairs had been partly or totally destroyed. The grand piano in the corner was intact though badly scorched; large patches of varnish had bubbled up and cracked like molasses candy. Lee opened the keyboard cover and banged out a few notes, unable to tell whether the piano was still in tune. He was famously tone-deaf, as his fellow Rangers had frequently reminded him whenever he tried to sing around the campfire.

"What a god-awful racket," said a morose voice behind him. Lee turned from the piano to see a dapperly dressed man at the doorway. His face was familiar. The man tipped his bowler hat. "Hiram Glass, of the *Statesman*."

Lee banged the keyboard cover shut, sending a discordant reverberation through the room. "What the hell are you doing up here?"

"I suppose you were expecting my colleague, Mr. Shoemaker." Glass gazed about the room. "He's away for a few days, off doing the paper's business elsewhere."

"To hell with Shoemaker, and to hell with you! I don't want any damned gawkers from the *Statesman* nosing around up here until I've finished taking a look."

"What is there to see? It's all too obvious, isn't it?" asked Hiram as he pulled out a notebook and began scribbling. "Someone set a fire, though it seems to have been contained rather quickly."

Marshal Lee scrutinized the reporter for a long moment, considered kicking his skinny backside down the stairs, and then decided not to. The fact was, he felt rather spooky, poking about the room alone. "Good thing they put out the fire as quick as they did," he remarked, running his fingers over a bit of charred wallpaper. "This is a brick building, fairly fireproof, but the bottom floor is a sewing shop. If the blaze had spread down there, imagine all that calico and muslin going up in flames! Might have spread up and down the Avenue. Good thing the Hook and Ladder crew got here so fast."

Hiram raised an eyebrow. "I thought Colorado Engine Company No. 1 would be responsible for any fires in this vicinity."

Lee snorted. "The Colorado boys went to the wrong location. Hook and Ladder beat 'em here by half an hour. How the hell did you get up here, anyway? I posted a man at the foot of the stairs to keep everybody out."

"And he's doing an excellent job," said Hiram. "There's quite a crowd gathered out there. Most are curious about the fire, but some of them came by because they've got toothaches and want to see Dr. Stoddard."

"Stoddard won't be seeing patients today. He's lying unconscious in his bedroom down the hall. So how the hell did you get past my man and up the stairs? I should sandbag that idiot."

"Don't treat your deputy too harshly, Marshal. He successfully kept out a crowd of gawkers, and let only one experienced newspaperman slip past him. I'd still have been stumped if I'd found the door at the top of the stairs locked, but someone seems to have cut a hole through the wood close by the knob, rendering the lock useless. It looks as though they drilled four holes in a square and then used a knife to cut out the space between the holes, and so were able to reach inside and unbolt the door, allowing access to Dr. Stoddard's chambers here on the second floor. I suppose that must have been the work of the arsonists. Would you agree with that assessment, Marshal?"

"Hiram Glass, you're every bit as weasely as Dave Shoemaker."

"I'm only doing my job; or Dave's job, in his stead. My excitable employer seemed to think that this incident might warrant calling our so-called crime expert back from Hempstead, but I assured him that I could handle the situation. Nevertheless, Mr. Gaines thinks this may be a big story—Dr. Stoddard, a prominent citizen, a respected dentist, knocked unconscious by an unknown assailant or assailants, and his offices set on fire. Mr. Gaines thinks this may be the biggest crime story in Austin since—well, since the West Pecan Street ax murder last winter. The one that was never solved." Oblivious to the hostile look Lee shot him, Hiram walked to the piano, opened the keyboard cover, and tapped at middle C. "In this case, it may help that Governor Ireland plans to issue a reward of two hundred dollars for the apprehension of the guilty party."

"What?"

"Oh, it hasn't been announced officially yet, but Mr. Gaines spoke to the governor by telephone this morning. Ireland doesn't want Austin gaining a reputation as a lawless city, not while he's in the Governor's Mansion."

"Lawless, hell! If there's a problem in this town, it's the politicians who go talking to the press behind my back."

"May I quote you?" asked Hiram sweetly. He was rather enjoying this break from the monotony of covering political issues. Having met and been unimpressed by every governor since Reconstruction, he was hardly to be intimidated by a blusterer like Marshal Lee. Hiram idly tapped out a melody on the piano: *But it stopped—short—never to go again when the old—man—died* . . . "This piano is done for. The heat must have warped the wires." He closed the keyboard cover. "This whole place reeks of kerosene."

"They scattered burning rags in the operating room, through that door," said Lee, "but the damage was worst here in the waiting room. They weren't expert arsonists, I'll tell you that. Did a pretty haphazard job. Even so, if Hook and Ladder had taken much longer to get here, the whole second floor, including Dr. Stoddard's private quarters, might well have gone up in blazes, along with Stoddard."

"Incinerating the only witness! Though, as a witness, Dr. Stoddard seems rather confused," said Hiram.

"Confused? The man's unconscious."

"Actually . . ." Hiram paused judiciously. "Not any longer."

"What are you saying?"

Hiram cleared his throat. "After I slipped up the stairs, before I came in here, I tiptoed down the hall and had a peek into Dr. Stoddard's bedroom. The nurse sitting with him said he came to only a little while ago. She didn't seem to mind if I spoke to him a bit."

"Hiram Glass, you're *more* of a weasel than Shoemaker!"

Hiram felt flattered. "Stoddard seemed baffled at first; kept thinking he must have fallen off a streetcar and hit his head. Then he started remembering details. Says his caged mockingbird woke him up in the middle of the night, then he heard someone fiddling with the door at the top of the stairs—that must have been the arsonists cutting through the wood. He says he got out of bed and padded down the hall in the pitch dark, came into the waiting room and heard noises in his operating room beyond. He saw shadows moving about and headed back to his bedroom, but they must have followed him. I understand he was found lying unconscious on his bedroom floor. The odd thing is, the nurse says that there's not a bump on his head. What do you make of that, Marshal?"

"What I make of it, Hiram Glass, is that you've tried my patience enough for one day. You're interfering with the law. Now get out." There was a change in the marshal's voice, from bantering sarcasm to something harsher, but Hiram seemed not to notice.

"I'll tell you a thought that occurred to me, Marshal. A dentist like Stoddard must keep a fairly large store of chloroform, don't you think? And the chloroform would be in his operating room, wouldn't it? Perhaps these arsonists were clever enough to use some of that to render Dr. Stoddard unconscious. I imagine a heavy enough dose, poured into a rag and held over his face, would render him unconscious for hours. What do you think of my theory, Marshal Lee?"

Hiram Glass was utterly unprepared for the violence of the marshal's assault. He was suddenly backed against the wall, his notepad and pencil scattered on the floor, his collar clutched so tightly in the marshal's fist that he could hardly breathe.

"What did I just say to you, Hiram Glass?"

Hiram grunted and wheezed. "You—asked me—"

"I *told* you to get out, didn't I?"

Hiram nodded, unable to speak.

"Then do it!" Lee spun him about and pushed him through the door, then followed him into the hallway and shoved him toward the stairs.

"My notes!" Hiram protested.

Marshal Lee did what he had been wanting to do since he first set eyes on the man. He kicked him squarely in the backside. Hiram gave a small scream and went staggering down the steep stairway. At the bottom he collided with the startled deputy, who had stepped in from the sidewalk to see what the commotion was about. After a brief scuffle, Hiram ran out the door and through the crowd on the sidewalk.

The deputy, puzzled that anyone could have slipped past him into the building, quailed under the marshal's gaze and retreated to his post outside the door.

Eventually, the damage to Dr. Stoddard's insured fixtures and furnishings would be assessed at nearly eight thousand dollars; the piano alone was valued at six hundred. There were indications of theft, though hardly enough to justify the scale of destruction. The arsonists had taken fifty dollars which Dr. Stoddard kept as ready cash in a drawer, but his safe was unmolested. The only other item of any value for which Dr. Stoddard could not account was a large bottle of chloroform—enough chloroform, as Dr. Stoddard noted, to render unconscious a considerable portion of the city's population.

23

Dr. Montgomery and Miss Ney were not unpleasant hosts, but they were so different from anyone Will had ever known, so *foreign*, that he could not quite connect with them. At Liendo he felt always on the outside looking in, making one self-conscious blunder after another.

His blundering began in the first half-hour of the visit, when Miss Ney conducted Dave and Will from the front porch into the grand foyer and up the staircase to the balcony. The European housekeeper brought tea and shortbread while they took in the view of the shimmering woods and flower-spangled fields beyond the poorly kept grounds. It was the brief season of Texas spring, before the sweltering heat of summer, and every so often a mild breeze blew across the balcony.

Miss Ney's manner struck Will as eccentric and formal, relaxed and stilted all at once. The seeming paradox resulted from her peculiar way with the English language, which she forced into German sentence structures. Her native accent was mixed with a hint of a Scottish burr picked up from her husband, along with diphthongs that were decidedly Texan.

She seemed genuinely impressed that Dave had made a success of himself as a newspaperman. "When your telegram I received, and with the end of interviewing *me*, when my career is nonexistent and my history as an artist is vanished, well, it is absurdity, I think, no one will care to read such a story. But proud of you I was! To think that little Davey Boy of Six-Shooter Junction is now a journalist in the capital! All about your activities must you tell. Do you the legislature attend?"

Dave shook his head. "I'm afraid politics isn't my specialty."

"Good! Politics is a cesspool! Even in this country is it so. Politics from Europe drove us—all the wheels within wheels and the little cliques one against another all conspiring. Bismarck!" She said the word in such a way that Will thought it was a German epithet. "Wagnerians and anti-Wagnerians! Nationalists and monarchists! Enemies all of the free spirit. If you do not move among politicians, good for you. What then do you write about, besides expatriate Europeans here in the Texas wilderness?"

"Actually, I'm the crime reporter."

Miss Ney looked at him blankly. "Such a thing is there?"

"I assure you there is. Our readers have an insatiable appetite for every detail of every crime, and my job is to feed that appetite. Alas, I have become a true journalist—a 'professional alarmist.'"

Will remembered Dave quoting the same phrase once before. "It was a fellow named Schopenhauer who said that," he piped up, "about journalists being professional alarmists." Will smiled at his hostess, feeling rather clever.

"Oh, yes, I know." Ney smiled back at him. "'Exaggeration to newspaper writing essential is, to make as much as possible of every occurrence, as if one a play were writing. So that all newspaper writers by trade professional alarmists become.'" She touched Dave's hand apologetically. "Not very flattering, I am sorry, but never a man to flatter anyone was he, the wise and always so witty Herr Schopenhauer. Very good to me he was, but most trying and difficult also could he be!"

Will wrinkled his brow. "You . . . *know* this Schopenhauer fellow?"

"Of course. A bust of him I executed."

"You . . . sculpted him?"

"Like mentor and protégée were we. Though because of my gender, of course, he had much to overlook. Still, a great thinker, as you will agree? *The World As Will and Idea* is a book that will outlive us all, yes?"

Will stared back at her blankly. "I thought he was . . . a reporter." He looked helplessly at Dave.

Dave cleared his throat. "The misunderstanding is my fault. It was from Miss Ney that I learned of Schopenhauer."

Miss Ney laughed. "Ah, something else Herr Doctor Schopenhauer said I am remindful of, looking at you two young men with your mustaches so outstanding. When one day I was modeling him, staring at me most intently was he, and so I asked, 'Why are you looking at me so, Herr Doctor?' And to me without a smile he answered, 'I am just trying if, perhaps, I can discover on your lip the tiniest mustache, because it becomes to me each day more impossible to believe that you are a woman!'"

She laughed and shook her head, and in that moment looked quite feminine, Will thought, despite her oddly mannish costume. "Of course, with strange notions about facial hair he was positively obsessed, and himself would not wear a beard. What did he say? Ah, yes! 'The beard is a half-mask, and by the police should be forbidden. As a sexual symbol in the middle of the face, *obscene* it is. That is why it so pleases women.'"

Will flushed warmly and gazed out at the view. He had never heard a woman speak in such a frank manner, and was uncertain what to make of it. No woman had ever made him feel embarrassed about his mustache! He suddenly realized that he was tugging at it, and drew his hand away.

He did not know what to make of Miss Ney. Nor did he know what to make of her house. The rooms with their lofty ceilings and fine wood floors had furnishings that seemed bizarrely out of place. Everything—tables, chairs, benches—looked homemade and crudely finished, some of it apparently made from old planks. Miss Ney, with apparent pride, referred to her furnishings as "rusticated." The Harrells' boarding house had finer machine-made stuff in the parlor!

Dr. Montgomery seemed normal enough, and his English, when he chose to speak, was as elegant as Miss Ney's was peculiar. But he seemed to be a man of few words, at least around Will. The Doctor took frequent walks with Dave, during which they presumably spoke, and contributed occasional utterances at the dinner table, but he addressed no more than half a dozen words directly to Will during the entire visit.

Their son, Lorne, was decidedly surly, though perhaps not unusually so for a thirteen-year-old. His mother doted on him whenever he was in her presence, which he seemed to resent. He displayed no interest whatsoever in the two visitors.

For considerable periods, while the Doctor and Dave strolled and Ney saw to the business of the plantation and Lorne went off on his own, Will was left to amuse himself. There were plenty of nooks and crannies to explore at Liendo, but he found the atmosphere of the place oppressive. In a shed behind the house he discovered an amazing collection of what he presumed to be Miss Ney's sculpting apparatus—hammers and chisels, metal shims and armatures, much of it rusty and all of it covered with dust. Stacked against the walls were a number of variously sized, strangely amorphous objects which Will realized must be clay molds, for each had a split down the middle. He pulled apart one of the smaller molds and saw within it the clearly defined impression of a hand. He did not inspect any of the others for fear that he would break something, though he was not sure it would matter if he did. It looked as if nothing in the shed had been touched in years.

On another occasion he explored Dr. Montgomery's study. It was smaller than he had been led to expect from Dave's account, and certainly more crudely furnished, with pine shelves, a chair, and a plank sleeping cot as primly made up as a soldier's barracks bed. There were many books and journals in various languages; the ones in English were scarcely easier to read than the others. There were no tales of adventures, no western romances or detective stories — not a single book of the sort Will would care to take on a long train journey.

The Doctor's worktable was covered with instruments, including a microscope of German manufacture. Montgomery had left a drop of pond water on the slide, with the mirror below adjusted to catch the light from the windows. Out of idle curiosity, Will put his eye to the tube and adjusted it until something came into focus. The transparent creature he beheld was the shape of a crumpled sombrero, with a fringe of busy little feelers. "The monster of the pond!" Will muttered. Another creature floated into view, then another. They must be as common as cows, he thought; thank God they were invisible to the naked eye! The sight of a field full of such deformities would scare a man to death, or drive him crazy. He wondered if the microscopic stuff inside a human being was as repulsive to look at.

Part of the long table served as a writing desk. There was a pen and inkwell and a blotter, and several stacks of manuscripts which appeared to be articles the Doctor was writing. Will picked up a page. Doctor Montgomery's handwriting was precise and elegant, with bold strokes and slender serifs. The words were easy to make out, if not the meaning.

TO BE ALIVE, WHAT IS IT?
by Edmund Montgomery

That matter-quickening something we call life, in what does it consist?

The mere mention of its name conjures up a vision of all that is most marvelous in the sense-revealed universe. Life is regarded as a *mystery*, an alien influx into nature, baffling scientific interpretation. Eminent scientists, satisfied that spontaneous generation nowhere occurs, have conjectured that the germ of life meteorically descended on our planet from the skies.

The scientific spirit revolts against the facile subterfuge of attributing any occurrence in nature to miraculous intervention. It irresistibly urges toward *unification,* toward a *monistic* interpretation, and the firm belief that *nature is all-embracing* and that her phenomena without exception are interdependently connected, forming part of *one all-comprising cosmos . . .*

Will leafed listlessly though a few more pages. The words made vague sense to him, but left no clear impression in his mind; each sentence slipped out of his head as soon as he read the next, like a tune that wouldn't catch. Inserted among the pages was a drawing of something seen under the microscope, labeled, "Figure 1 — An Amoeba with Long and Broad Processes." The thing was even uglier than what he had seen under the microscope!

On another occasion, his restlessness drove him to go snooping in Ney's bedroom, to his regret. The room was as crudely and almost as sparsely furnished as the Doctor's study, except for an incongruously elegant walnut vanity surmounted by an etched mirror, and, even more incongruous, a hammock stretched between two corners. The bed was apparently a place for stacking books and folded laundry and such. The hammock was draped with a sheet and a thin blanket, and was evidently where Ney slept at night. Will spied, atop the fireplace mantel, a small brass urn and an object made of white plaster. He smiled as he stepped closer and saw what the object was, for here was comforting evidence that Ney was indeed a woman like any other, with the sentimental instincts of all women. The object, made of plaster from a mold, was the face of a sleeping child, perhaps two years old. It was an image of such innocent repose that it made him sigh to look at it. It must have been sculpted from life, from Ney's son Lorne, he thought; what a difference between the baby and the boy!

Then, with a chill, he remembered that Dave had told him there had been another boy, a baby who had died of diphtheria soon after the Doctor and Miss Ney came to Liendo. They had burned the body, to prevent the germs from spreading. The plaster cast was not a sculpture, but a death mask. The urn beside it surely held the baby's ashes.

Will sucked in a breath and retreated from the room. He stole into the hallway, shutting the door quietly behind him.

* * *

On their fourth day at Liendo, which turned out to be their last, Will went for a morning stroll through the woods down by the creek. The day was already quite warm. He came upon Miss Ney sitting on a rock, her bloomers pulled up almost to her knees and her feet in the water. He would have turned back so as not to disturb her privacy, but she looked up and saw him, and her steady gaze invited him to approach. She made no effort to cover her ankles and calves. He found a place to sit on a nearby rock.

"I thought it was your husband, ma'am, who liked to come down and study the pond life."

"So he does, young Will. To cool my feet I prefer, and simply to gaze at the rushing water. Foaming and plunging, ever changing. The form of it, no sculptor could ever master. I think that is why we humble artists our statues surround with fountains. The water to our will we cannot shape, so endlessly it fascinates us. Easier to capture the quicksilver of a smile than to capture the water. Do you see? Life and motion, stillness and stone—opposites are they, and yet together we try to blend them. To be an artist, very difficult is it! Do you agree?"

Will nodded uncertainly.

"This way of talking, about art and life, is it not the way you also see the world? Do I make no sense to you?"

He shrugged self-consciously. "I guess I'd have to think about it for a while. I'm not as swift as Dave."

"Ah, but I think you are. He tells me you are a writer, too, yes?"

"Not like Dave. Maybe someday."

"No! A writer you are, or not. No in-betweening! It does not matter if in the given moment you write or do not write. The writer is you, not the writing. Just as I am a sculptress, even when I do not sculpt; even not for many a year. It is the way that we see and hear and touch. This water I sculpt, even as upon it I gaze."

"Well, I . . ."

"No! There can be no argument of it!" She opened her eyes wide, then laughed. "I am thinking that you do not know quite what to make of me, young Will."

He flushed a bit, hoping it wasn't noticeable in the dappled sunlight and shadow. "You've got that right enough, I guess. Most of the people I know are pretty simple, when you come down to it. It's plain enough what they're thinking, and why they do what they do. But you and the Doctor—I just can't see how you ever ended up here in Texas. It seems like everything that really matters to you must be back in Europe." When he saw her grave expression, he flushed even more. "I'm sorry. It's none of my business."

She looked at him shrewdly. "You cannot understand. You are of the New World, *are* the New World, even in your cells. Under the microscope my best friend could look at you and see as much!" She shook her head. "All scheming and contrivance was the world we left behind. Nothing real, nothing true. There, for us all dreams were dead. Here is the dream, though not always easy."

"But what *is* the dream?"

"Is it not the same for all? To slide through life in happiness in a singing ever soaring, a soaring ever singing like the lark!" She laughed and paddled her feet in the water. "The dream is this place."

"Liendo? Or this spot here on the creek?"

"Liendo, yes, and here where we are sitting, yes. But the place I mean to say is *Texas!* I tell you truly, more void of patriotism no woman is there than me. A citizen of the world am I and all my life have been. But this place, Texas, has a charm of me, a charm of a peculiar kind, such as nearing it is no other part of the wide earth. To live in a place of such dreaming means more than villas and palaces."

They sat quietly for a while, gazing at the sunlight on the water. In the trees above their heads a jay called out. A breeze wafted up the creek bed, carrying the scent of honeysuckle.

"Even someday again I will sculpt," she said quietly. "Truly sculpt—oh, yes! My good friend Governor Oran Milo Roberts tells me that the new capitol in Austin decorations will be needing—sculpture and monuments to honor the dead. My name he promises to put forward. I ask you, in all of Texas lives there any other sculptor with my qualifications, who has sculpted men of greatness? Surely not! To Austin shall I go, and sculptures fit for Texas shall I make! It shall happen, this."

"I do believe it shall," said Will.

"Only sometimes . . ." She pulled up one leg and rested her chin on her knee. She gazed at the water splashing on the stones. "Sometimes all charms go flitting off, like the lark, and everything seems savagery to me. Fallow are all the seeds that I have tried to sow, and this Texas is a vast, cruel desert that cares not a whit for such as me. So alone and alien do I feel that sometimes I fancy I am shipwrecked and drifted among the Bushmen. But even Bushmen would appreciate me for something, if only for a morsel to fill a Bushman's stomach!"

The way she raised her eyebrows permitted him to laugh. He even ventured a riposte. "Surely, Miss Ney, even the 'hoodlums' of Hempstead are preferable to cannibals."

"Do not be so sure!"

The call of a nearby jay was answered by another. The breeze shivered the treetops, causing the patches of sunlight surrounding them to stir crazily about, skimming over the mossy stones and glinting on the water. In the spot before Miss Ney, the idle paddling of her foot seemed gently to fold light and water into quicksilver.

"Yoo-hoo!" There was a cry from the direction of the house, and a moment later Dave came tramping down the creek bed. "Morning, Miss Ney." He tipped his hat, then waved a bit of paper in the air. "I fear that the time has come for our departure."

"What's happened?" said Will.

"Horace just came back from town. A telegram arrived at the station this morning. Seems I must hurry back to Austin to resume my role as professional alarmist."

"What does it say?"

"See for yourself." Dave handed him the telegram. Will had to squint to make out the letters beneath the bright, shifting spots of sunlight.

> D. SHOEMAKER C/O LIENDO PLANTATION
> RETURN AUSTIN NEXT TRAIN—STOP
> MAYHEM—STOP
> MURDER—STOP
> ANOTHER SERVANT GIRL DONE IN—STOP
> GAINES

The Journey Back:

*S*CANNING the headlines and finding nothing of particular interest, William Sydney Porter peers over the top of his newspaper at Dr. Kringel in the seat opposite. The doctor's nose is buried in a book. The man is not a bad traveling companion, Porter thinks. He talks neither too much nor too little. He does not chew tobacco, and smokes neither cigars nor cigarettes. He does not snore at night. He never refuses a nip from Porter's pocket flask, and dutifully cancels the debt by paying for breakfast or dinner. He is clearly smart as a whip but never shows off, and has a good sense of humor. If he seems a bit vague about his personal history, his evasiveness is balanced by his respect for Porter's own reticence about his past.

Porter nods at the book in Kringel's hands. "I see you've moved on from *Cabbages and Kings.*"

"Ah, yes, I finished your book of stories last night. I found it delightful!"

"One critic compared it to *The Golden Ass.* I wasn't sure if I should be flattered or insulted."

Kringel smiles. "I was most impressed by the atmospheric setting of Anchuria. You must have spent some time in the tropics."

"A little." Porter has no desire to discuss the lonely months he spent in Honduras, fleeing from embezzlement charges. He changes the subject. "My new collection will be called *The Four Million,* and the setting is far more exotic—New York City. But what's that you're reading now?"

Kringel smiles. "Another treasure from my satchel—Dr. Edmund Montgomery's new book, *Philosophical Problems in the Light of Vital Organization.*"

"Has Dr. Montgomery published many books?"

"No. Many articles, yes, but this is his first book."

"May I see it?"

"Of course." Dr. Kringel hands him the volume, which has maroon boards and handsome gold lettering.

"Published by G. P. Putnam's Sons," Porter mutters, impressed. He flips through the book, noting the chapter headings: "Substantiality" . . . "Causation" . . . "The Epistemological Dilemma" . . . "The Sensori-Motor Agent" . . . "Sentiency and Purposive Movements" . . . "Teleology in Nature" . . .

"I'm disappointed," Porter quips.

"Why?"

"No illustrations!"

Kringel laughs. "It's not a novel, Herr Porter."

"But where are the drawings of protozoa with all the little labels? I seem to recall . . ." He suddenly realizes that he dreamed about Liendo, just last night; he had forgotten the dream until this instant, but now it comes back to him in a flash. In the dream, he was in Dr. Montgomery's study, with its crude furnishings. He took book after book from the shelves, only to find them all filled with bizarre letters unlike any he had ever seen. He picked up a manuscript from the table, and saw that it was written in the same indecipherable characters, interspersed with the Doctor's drawings of grotesque organisms seen under the microscope. He, a lover of words and stories, found himself trapped in a room filled with books, unable to read a single word! The dream left him feeling vaguely resentful and intimidated. How amazing that a mere dream, drawn from an experience that took place years ago, can stir such emotions! He seems to be taking two journeys at once, one a rail trip to a place called Texas, and the other a mental excursion into his own past.

He turns his attention to Dr. Montgomery's book. A hefty tome it is—450 pages! He turns to the opening chapter and reads the first sentence:

> Pondering philosophical questions from the standpoint of natural science, the present writer has during a lifetime of research become convinced that some of the principal standing problems which have vexed ancient and modern thinkers may find their more or less complete solution by having recourse in their interpretation to facts of vital organization.

Porter blinks. Really, how many people out of a thousand would bother to read on, after an opening like that? Where is the wit, the sense of mystery or alarm, the tantalizing "hook"?

And yet . . .

His eyes dart over the words again, and he is struck by the reference to finding a "more or less complete solution"—to what, he cannot quite make out, but surely the quest for a "complete solution" is what keeps any reader forging ahead to the end of any book. Indeed, is it not what keeps every man trudging on through life, that promise of finding a solution to life's mysteries? Is it possible that Dr. Montgomery, with his microscope and his pond water specimens down in Texas, can truly know more of life's secrets than William Sydney Porter, the chronicler of the Four Million? Has the Doctor's unique insight pierced a veil drawn over the eyes of other mortals? What could such a man possibly know, possibly tell him of Eula Phillips?

"You may borrow it, if you like," says Dr. Kringel. "I have already read it, of course. And I brought along plenty of other reading to keep me busy." He pats the brown leather satchel beside him.

"Yes, well, thank you. Since I'll be seeing Dr. Montgomery soon, I suppose I ought to acquaint myself with his book." Porter smiles wryly and thumbs through the pages. A sentence catches his eye:

> Qualitative developmental elaboration of extra-conscious, interdependent, and interacting power-endowed existents is the essential fact to be recognized in perceptible nature, not interpretable as the mere necessary and causatively equivalent concatenation of mechanically moved inert masses.

And after all that, the sentence has a footnote appended! Never in a million years would he read such a volume from cover to cover. Who would? He lays the book aside.

"Something puzzles me, Dr. Kringel. You're a philosopher; perhaps you can enlighten me."

"Certainly, if I can."

"I thought philosophy was about 'do this' and 'don't do that'—with a bit more window dressing, of course, and some fancy feats of logic thrown in, but pretty much, in the end, about—well, good versus evil."

"Ah . . ." Dr. Kringel nods pensively. "I think, perhaps, Mr. Porter, you are confusing philosophy with religion. The popular conception of philosophers is rather misinformed; people imagine us as long-bearded hermits whose sage advice, if only other mortals would heed it, would result in a world of perfect bliss."

"And that's not the way it is?"

Dr. Kringel shakes his head. "While the end result may be a consideration of the proper way of living, the 'meat and potatoes' of philosophy, if you will, addresses more abstract considerations. For example, how do we determine what is and is not real in the perceived world? What is the nature of subjective consciousness? In Dr. Montgomery's monistic speculation, a central question arises: what differentiates living and nonliving matter, that which is 'vitally organized' and that which is inanimate?"

"What separates the living and the dead, you mean?"

"Exactly."

Porter nods. "So Dr. Montgomery is asking, what does it mean to be alive, or not alive? Every man wonders about that."

"Yes, but most men ponder the question in direct relation to themselves. Dr. Montgomery's consideration is rather more esoteric—but no less fascinating, I assure you."

Porter hums thoughtfully. "So you're saying that if a man was trying to decide, say, whether or not to kill himself, a philosopher wouldn't necessarily be the best person to advise him."

Dr. Kringel smiles. "Perhaps not, though a philosopher might be able to broaden the man's consideration of what exactly it means to reduce oneself to inanimate matter by an act of will."

"I see. No wonder people still go to priests and bartenders for advice!"

Dr. Kringel shrugs. "Men seek enlightenment wherever they can find it. In your stories, for example."

"People read O. Henry to be entertained."

"Yes, but if the stories and characters were patently false, they would provide no entertainment, would they? They would merely be a waste of time. You must start with a kernel of truth, I think."

Porter smiles. "Sure, the story's got to ring true, or it's just so much bunk. And it doesn't take a philosopher to judge—a bank teller or a shopgirl can tell whether I've pulled off a good story or a dud."

"Enough about philosophy," says Kringel. "Perhaps *you* can enlighten *me* about something."

"Certainly, if I can."

"Who are the most popular writers of today? Whose work will still be read—say, a century from now, in the year 2006?"

"Besides, of course, my own works?"

"That goes without saying!"

"Oh, I suppose about the most popular writer alive nowadays must be Francis Marion Crawford. He's everywhere you look, in every café and streetcar; people would sooner leave home without their keys than without a Crawford novel. It's a pretty sure bet his books will still be around in a hundred years. Folks'll always want to read about sophisticated society ladies and lovelorn European counts, especially the women readers. I'll bet we could walk through this train right now and confiscate a dozen copies of *Katherine Lauderdale*."

"Yes, even *I* know of Crawford. He is ubiquitous. Who else?"

"Well, probably nobody matches Crawford for winning over both the critics and the mass readership, but I suppose there's Mary Tappan Wright . . . Richard Harding Davis . . . Aaron Warren Travis . . . David Graham Phillips—all as famous as the president, and every one a bona fide immortal, if you trust the critics."

"Curious, that all these popular writers use three names, while O. Henry has less than two."

"I never thought of it that way. Do you suppose the editors at the classy rags like *Scribner's* pay by the number of names in the byline? That could explain how David Graham Phillips rates a thousand dollars per short story, and the *World* barely pays for my lunch!"

"Ah, well, I was only curious. As editor of *The Monist*, I know something of the publishing business, though very little of the popular press."

Porter nods. He tries to imagine editing a stack of articles from contributors who all write like Edmund Montgomery. The mind boggles!

Dr. Kringel leans forward. "Another misconception about philosophers, if I may revert to that subject, is that they have, or should have, the means to account for all human behavior. Far from it! There is much that no system of philosophy can adequately explain. These murders in Texas, for example—the work of the Servant Girl Annihilators . . ."

Porter sighs. It is almost amusing, the degree to which Dr. Kringel seems to have become obsessed with the doings of the Servant Girl Annihilators. Scarcely a conversation passes without the man bringing up the subject. Porter regrets now having ever told him the facetious term he coined for the unknown culprits. It grates on him to hear another person use it; it forces him to take a harder look at the lost innocence of his youth that he idealizes in retrospect. Innocence has two faces, he thinks, and one of them is not so pretty—the one that can produce a phrase like "Servant Girl Annihilators," utterly oblivious of the pain and degradation that surrounded those crimes. Only the most callow youth could be so glib! Every time Dr. Kringel parrots the phrase back at him, it rankles.

"It seems astounding," Dr. Kringel says, "that so much blood could have been shed in such a fashion, and that the crimes are not more famous. And equally astounding that a solution should have eluded the authorities."

"Ah, yes, well . . ." Porter has already described the crimes as best he can remember—or most of the crimes, at any rate, excluding certain details which are too personal to touch on. What more is there to say? "You must realize, that sort of crime—repeated again and again over such an extended period, with so many victims—was a new phenomenon. Remember, this was a good three years before Jack the Ripper! We had no precedent for

Steven Saylor

such atrocities. Crimes of passion, a husband killing his wife, even a mother killing her baby—you saw those sorts of things in the newspapers all the time, and they were horrible enough. But the work of this maniac—or maniacs—stunned everyone. No one knew what to make of it."

"And of course, the fact that the initial victims were colored servant girls . . ." Dr. Kringel leaves the thought unfinished.

"The authorities did their best, I suppose. But they were inadequate for the task." Porter looks out the window. A dazzling sunset is in the making; all across the horizon, golden rays of light pierce heaping masses of blood-red clouds. It will be time for dinner soon, then bed, then another morning and another state put behind them while they sleep. Clickety-clack, with every passing minute the train carries them farther from New York and closer to Texas. The reality of going back suddenly unnerves him. So many ghosts . . .

A sudden pain shoots up his spine. His back has not been bothering him all day, but now it begins to stiffen and ache.

"And you must keep in mind," he says, gritting his teeth, "this was also a good two or three years before the invention of Sherlock Holmes! Retired Texas Rangers and Pinkerton snoops, those were our only models of detection. Rangers tracked down outlaws on the frontier; Pinkertons infiltrated labor unions and spied for the bosses. People didn't have the superhuman expectations of investigating detectives that they've since picked up from popular fiction. The closest things we had to a Sherlock Holmes were the bloodhounds!"

"And plenty of blood for the hounds to scent, from the sound of it," says Dr. Kringel wryly.

"Oh, yes, buckets of blood. And bloody handprints at the scene of every crime—but none of these newfangled notions about fingerprints! No one had yet come up with this theory that fingerprints are unique, so no one ever thought to take notice of the bloody handprints all over the place. Of course, even now, some juries still refuse to accept fingerprints as evidence."

"Ah, yes, science is ever ahead of popular acceptance."

"And twenty years ago, the science of criminal forensics was primitive indeed. Evidence pretty much boiled down to who saw what, and when."

"How unfortunate for the victims of the Servant Girl Annihilators," observes Kringel.

"Yes, Herr Doctor—most unfortunate." He winces at the pain shooting through his back. "And not only for the victims. It wasn't just the victims who suffered . . ."

He watches the sun dip below the horizon. The golden rays disperse. The blood-red clouds become flatter and darker, until they resemble a vast bloodstain smearing the sky.

PART THREE

BLOODHOUNDS
UNLEASHED

∽

Austin: May to December 1885

24

⌘

"$\mathcal{A}$PPALLING!" declared William Holland to an empty classroom.

It was the afternoon of Wednesday, the 13th of May. The school day was over, but with the longer days of spring there was plenty of afternoon sunshine left, filling the classroom with long beams of westerly light. The children—all but one—had gone home, as had Holland's assistant, Mr. McKinley. Holland sat alone at his desk.

Glimpsing a movement from the corner of his eye, he looked out the window. The one pupil who remained, Moses, a tiny boy of eight, was climbing in the big oak tree in the schoolyard, the branches of which were hung with ropes and swings. Satisfied that Moses was staying in the schoolyard as he had been told, Holland returned his attention to the newspapers on his desk. The stack consisted of the last week's copies of the *Statesman*. Holland had made up his mind to read, in order, all the stories which had to do with the murder of Eliza Shelley on the night of Wednesday, May 6.

Eliza; Holland's wife was named Eliza. So was the young heroine of Mrs. Stowe's novel. But the fate which had claimed Eliza Shelley was even more awful than that which threatened poor Eliza as she raced across the ice fleeing Simon Legree and his hounds. No novel Holland knew of, not even *Uncle Tom's Cabin*, described horrors of the sort which had befallen Eliza Shelley.

A thirty-year-old woman with three small children—it sickened him to think of it. What sort of monster would deprive those children of their mother? And for what? For a few fleeting moments of pleasure—pleasure of a sort so debased and unnatural that to describe it as bestial would be an insult to beasts. No animal he knew would kill a female of its kind and then copulate with it!

He had purchased each of the newspapers as they came out, scanning them hurriedly as time allowed before shutting them up in his desk drawer. He did not care to take the papers home with him, where the females of his household might read their lurid accounts, nor could he leave them in the open on his desk, where his students might read them. Events of the last week had kept him so busy that only now did he have time to take out the newspapers and carefully read through them. The details they recounted were appalling.

He heard a sharp noise—a scream—from outside. He rose from his desk and peered out the window. It was only little Moses, squealing with excitement as he slid down one of the ropes. A typical boy—though so small for his age! If Moses was not careful, he would burn his hands on the rope; but thus did children learn, by experiences of pain or gratification. Holland returned his attention to the newspapers, and read from the first story reporting the crime:

THE FOUL FIENDS
KEEP UP THEIR WICKED WORK—
ANOTHER WOMAN CRUELLY MURDERED,
At Dead of Night by Some Unknown Assassin.
Another Deed of Deviltry in
the Crimson Catalogue of Crime!

When Dr. L. B. Johnson went to market on Thursday morning about six o'clock, he had no idea of the terrible tragedy that had been enacted on his own premises during the night.

Dr. Johnson lives with his wife and her little niece in a neat cottage on the corner of San Jacinto and Cypress streets, the Central Railway track being immediately in front of the house. Some forty or fifty steps in the rear, behind a fence with a gate, stands a small cabin of one room, with an alley behind it. This cabin was occupied by a colored woman named Eliza Shelley, and her three small children. The woman had been in the service of the Johnson family as a cook for about six weeks.

On returning from market, Dr. Johnson found his wife and little niece in

A STATE OF ALARM,

and heard his wife exclaim, "I believe Eliza has been murdered!" In the doctor's absence, the lady's attention had been directed to shrill, childish screams coming from Eliza's cabin. Thinking it was merely some noisy altercation between Eliza's children, she sent her niece to inquire the cause.

The little girl came back pale and out of breath. She had taken only a brief look into the room, but that glance had revealed so awful a sight that she dared not enter and came running back through the gate. Mrs. Johnson went to have a look, and the sight sent her running back to the house as well, where now, all breathless and alarmed, she conveyed her fear and horror to her husband.

Dr. Johnson steeled himself for the ghastly sight and went to have a look. Stretched out on the floor of the cabin lay the poor cook, quite dead. Her head was disfigured by several wounds, including a deep round hole above one ear and another between the eyes, which may have been inflicted by a sharpened file or an ice pick. More horrible to look at was a gaping wound over her right eye fully two inches long and nearly as wide. A large, sharp blade, probably that of a hatchet or ax, had cleft through her skull to the brain.

The pillows and sheets were

SATURATED WITH BLOOD

and the room was in great disorder. The murderer had dragged his victim from bed and placed her on a pile of quilts and blankets. Her limbs were outstretched and the center of her body elevated, and her night dress displaced in such a manner as to suggest that she may have been outraged after death.

No weapons which might have inflicted the wounds were discovered in the room. The only possible clue discovered by Dr. Johnson himself was the track of a barefooted man leading up from the alley to Eliza's door and returning again to the alley. The soil is sandy and the footprints clearly demarked, revealing the impression of a short, broad foot.

THE MURDERED WOMAN

was about thirty years of age, of medium size, and of un-mixed African blood. She had a husband in the peniten-tiary, to whom she was said to be greatly devoted. The doctor and his wife testified to her excellent character. So far as they knew, she never had company in her cabin.

Eliza had three little boys, all of whom occupied the same bed with her. The eldest is some eight years old, but to the STATESMAN reporter who questioned him, he did not appear to be larger than a boy of five or six. The poor little fellow had a dazed look, which was but natural in view of the circumstances. He was also distracted by the crowds of people (mostly colored) who arrived in a continuous stream beginning early in the morning to visit the site of the atrocity. It required some time and effort to get him to talk, and when he did speak his tale was quite confused. The substance was as follows:

"A man came into the room in the middle of the night. My brothers and my mother kept sleeping but I woke up and got out of the bed. The man seized me. He said to keep quiet or else he would kill me. He pulled me into the corner and made me lie down. He said to stay still and cov-ered me up with a blanket."

The boy at times seemed somewhat bewildered, and his account was rambling. He had no clear idea, for instance, whether the man was colored or white. It may have been quite dark in the room. He also seemed to indicate that the man wore a white rag over his face, though this assertion was unclear.

At some point the boy seems to have fallen asleep again, unaware that anything had happened to his mother until he woke the next morning. One might think that fear would have kept the boy awake and alert, but instead it seems to have acted on him as a soporific.

The other two boys were too young to tell anything about the matter.

Picture these three little unfortunates, quietly sleeping while their mother lay stretched on a pile of blankets on the floor nearby, horribly murdered. The light of day brought to them a terrible revelation.

Late in the afternoon, Marshal Lee

MADE AN ARREST,

namely of one Andrew Williams, said to be a half-witted colored boy about 19 years old. He was barefoot at the time, a slender clue perhaps, but the barefoot tracks spoken of above will be measured and a comparison made.

The murder was the theme of considerable discussion throughout the city yesterday, coming on the heels of the assault on Dr. Stoddard and the fire deliberately set at his dentistry office on the Avenue, and following as it does along the lines of the brutal nocturnal outrage which was committed upon another servant girl, Mollie Smith, last December. Neither of those crimes has yet been solved, nor do they seem likely to be; that is the sober opinion of many in Austin. Some are inclined to lay the blame for this state of affairs on the police, and such expressions as "inefficient" and "no good" are common.

Others think that the police are not to blame, since on any given night only four men are on duty at once, and such a small contingent can scarcely be expected to guard every block, or to anticipate a particular spot where an attack might occur. This class blames the city council for not appointing more men, and some among them are arguing that the citizens themselves should immediately organize a vigilance committee.

Wherever the blame should go and whatever should be done about it, the dissatisfaction is widespread. The colored people seem especially alarmed. One man who came to see the murder site was overheard by the reporter to say that from now on he would never leave his house after dark, for fear that his wife might be murdered.

Governor Ireland should offer a reward in this case, as he has done in the recent arson case. It does not matter that the victim is an obscure colored woman. Her life was as dear to her, and should be held as sacred, as that of the proudest lady in the land.

Shaking his head, Holland put down the paper, then he glanced out the window to ascertain his charge's whereabouts. The boy was still in the oak tree. While Holland watched, Moses climbed squirrel-like into the tallest branches of the oak tree, beyond the highest rope. Holland grunted, a bit fretful for the boy's safety, but decided to let him be. He had climbed tall trees himself when he was a boy, and had managed not to break his neck. Besides, he thought, let the boy keep playing as long as there was daylight; let him tire himself out, and so assure a deep, long sleep tonight, perhaps without nightmares.

He returned his attention to the newspapers. Not the least appalling aspect was the arrest of Andrew Williams, whom Holland had known for years. Andrew Williams was simpleminded from birth, and utterly harmless. He had since been released for lack of evidence, but the arrest must have been terrifying for him!

In the week since, another colored man had been arrested and was still in jail. Ike Plummer was about thirty, and almost as simple as Williams. There was, to be sure, a connection between him and the murdered woman; the *Statesman* reported that they had lived together some weeks back, before Eliza went to work for Dr. Johnson—apparently Eliza was not quite as devoted to her incarcerated husband as the original newspaper story indicated—and they had recently had an argument in front of a witness, who said that Plummer demanded money from Eliza. On the night of the murder, he had been out drinking and had no alibi.

But Holland was unconvinced. If Plummer merely wanted money from Eliza, why should he murder her in such a diabolical fashion? And surely the boy, who had spoken to the killer, would have recognized a man who not long ago resided with him and his mother.

None of these objections seemed to have occurred to Marshal Lee, who appeared content to arrest any colored man on the least shred of suspicion. All too often Holland had encountered men like the marshal in positions of authority, who presumed any colored man to be capable of theft and murder, and just as incapable of honesty or virtue. At such a time, it was unfortunate indeed for the colored people of Austin that a man like Lee was marshal. It was colored women who had been horribly murdered. It was innocent colored men who were being caught up in Marshal Lee's net.

Holland would have to act, as he had acted to help Lem Brooks. There was no one else who could bridge the gap between the colored people of Austin and the men who ran the city. And yet there was so little that he could do; he chafed at his impotence! If he were a white man with his father's name and his education and accomplishments, he would call for Lee's resignation. But if he were a white man, he might be on the city council—or mayor! As it was, the city officials would pay no heed to criticism of one of their own, coming from a colored man. As long as the white folk were happy with him, Grooms Lee would remain marshal.

A thought suddenly occurred to him, too vaguely formed to quite take shape. Something was slightly askew, not quite right . . .

Holland looked out the window, thinking the cause of his anxiety might be the boy; but Moses was all right. He had discovered a natural seat formed by two intertwining branches high up in the oak tree, and was comfortably settled as if in an easy chair, his arms spread out on the branches and his tiny legs dangling in the air, taking in the view to the west. No doubt the tall buildings along the Avenue and the red sun sinking beyond Mount Bonnell made for quite a sight.

He returned his attention to the newspapers and leafed through them, looking for the first report of the murder. There was some reference toward the end of the story, about the dentist who had been attacked . . .

He found the passage: "The murder . . . coming on the heels of the assault on Dr. Stoddard and the fire deliberately set at his dentistry office on the Avenue . . ."

It seemed to Holland that there was some connection that he could not quite put his finger on.

He recalled another passage from farther back in the story, and scanned the columns until he found the word *rag*: "The boy . . . somewhat bewildered . . . seemed to indicate that the man wore a white rag over his face, though this assertion was unclear . . . the boy seems to have fallen asleep again . . . it seems to have acted on him as a soporific."

A soporific . . .

The unformed thought flitted about Holland's brain so teasingly that he stood up and began to pace, slapping the fist of one hand against the palm of the other. "Rag!" he said. "Rag . . ."

He strode to the open window and stuck his head out. "Moses! Moses Shelley! Climb down from that tree and come inside. Be careful, now!"

The boy descended with such speed and agility that Holland smiled in spite of himself, thinking of a squirrel. All the boy needed was a big fluffy tail! A moment later, little Moses came running into the classroom.

"It looks like you were having a good time out there."

"Yes, sir, I s'pose."

"What could you see from up there?"

"Jus' the sun goin' down." The boy was a little out of breath, but otherwise seemed perfectly normal. One would never have guessed that such an awful event had befallen him only a few days before. Eliza Shelley had no relations in Austin, her husband was in the penitentiary, and no one had come forward to claim her children. Pending some more permanent arrangement, the two younger boys had been taken in by a preacher and his family. Holland had agreed to take care of Moses, whom he knew from his attendance at the school for the last few months. The boy was a slow reader, but good at numbers.

"Moses, I want to ask you about something."

"Yes, sir?"

"It's about the bad man who came into the cabin and threatened you. May we talk about that?"

The boy made a nervous shrug and nodded. "I s'pose."

"You said something about him wearing a white rag, didn't you?"

Moses looked momentarily perplexed. "A white rag. Yeah, I remembers."

"And the man was wearing this rag."

"Didn't wear it. Put it. Like this." Moses put his open palm over the bottom half of his face.

"He looked like a bandit, then, with the rag over his face so that all you could see were his eyes?"

Moses shook his head uncertainly. "Didn't *wear* it. *Put* it."

"You mean he held it over his face?"

"No. Did like this." Again the boy repeated the gesture of placing his open hand over his nose and mouth.

"Oh, Moses!" Abruptly, with a start, Holland saw the connection. "He put the white rag over *your* face."

"I s'pose." Now Moses seemed suddenly doubtful.

"And then you fell into a deep sleep."

"I s'pose. Don't rightly recollect. When I waked up . . ." The boy's face gave a twitch and a look came into his eyes that sent a chill through Holland. He reached for the boy and pulled his tiny body against him.

The chain of thoughts in Holland's head seemed to him persuasive. A dentist's office had been broken into. What might be kept in a dentist's office? Chloroform. What was the use of chloroform? To anesthetize patients. Chloroform spread onto a rag and held over a little boy's face could render him unconscious—indeed, might even kill a boy as tiny as Moses. The same thing could have been done to his two younger brothers while they slept, and for that matter, to his mother. Eliza Shelley was repeatedly stabbed and hacked, yet no one heard her cry for help.

It seemed to William Holland more certain than ever that Eliza Shelley had not been killed by a barefooted half-wit who had come to her cabin looking for money.

That same afternoon, at the Harrells' boarding house, Will Porter was writing a letter.

The letter was to David Hall, of the ranching family that had taken Will in when he first came to Texas. Hall was up in Colorado. Will had never been there, but it seemed to him that it must be a far more lively and interesting place than Texas. "Town is fearfully dull," he wrote, "except for the frequent raids of the Servant Girl Annihilators, who make things lively during the dead hours of the night; if it were not for them, items of interest would be very scarce, as you may see by the *Statesman*."

25

⏤❦⏤

$\mathcal{T}$ H E Robertson brothers, as was their custom, had lunch that Friday at a table reserved for them at the Iron Front, located at the back of the big room, well away from the bar.

"Has Gaines lost his mind?" The mayor folded back a copy of the *Statesman* with a snap. "Listen to this: 'Misgovernment! It degrades the capital city. It leads to murder, arson, burglary, and robbery. It costs the taxpayers of Austin enormous sums of money, but leaves defenseless people at the mercy of the lawless. Organized society is for the sake of mutual protection, but here the city government takes in all it can get and dispenses absolutely nothing.' Well, that's utter rubbish! Who does Gaines think regulates the streetcar lines, and sees to the sidewalks—"

"Read on, brother," said the district attorney, sipping from his cup of strong black coffee.

John Robertson muttered an imprecation under his breath and resumed. "'On a cold December night, the stark, stiff form of the servant girl Mollie Smith was laid out upon the ground to become a ghastly, grinning, startling horror of the daylight.' Now, really, a description like that borders on the obscene! 'Since then, there have been a hundred diabolical entries made into private homes in our midst, and numerous attacks upon peaceable men and women, any one of which might have led to a murder equally as gruesome. And yet there is no protection from the fiends and no retribution against them.'" He slapped the paper against the table. "I tell you, this is journalistic excess of the very worst sort!"

James Robertson attacked the steak on his plate with his knife and fork. "He has a point, unfortunately. There *has* been a perceptible rise in crime in recent months. Houses broken into—"

"By vagrants passing through, no doubt."

"More shootings than usual in Guy Town—"

"Prostitutes and gamblers quarreling among themselves!"

"Nevertheless, a rash of crimes have been reported since the new year, and my office has very little to show in the way of prosecutions. People are beginning to feel unsafe in their homes. This arson on the Avenue and the murder of another servant woman have stirred the hornet's nest."

"I'll tell you who's been stirring the hornet's nest! Listen: 'It is humiliating in the extreme to the citizens of Austin that life should be as unsafe now as when savage Indians lurked upon the outskirts of the newborn town and sent their deadly shafts into the hearts of any intrepid inhabitants who ventured outside. The current state of affairs is actually *more* unsafe, for it is those who should be most secure, women and little children in the very heart of the city, who must tremble in fear of the midnight assassin.'"

"Keep reading, brother. Everyone else in town has read it, so there's no point ignoring it."

"It gets worse: 'The woman who will put a bullet through the heart of one of these night prowlers should be honored by the people and presented with a consolation purse.' Is Gaines advocating that everyone should arm their servant girls with shotguns?" He shook his head. "What about the latest arrest, of this Ike Plummer fellow? What are the chances of getting a conviction?"

"I could work up a circumstantial case, I suppose. But the fellow obviously didn't do it."

The mayor grunted with exasperation. "Why in heaven's name does Grooms Lee go about arresting innocent men and wasting everyone's time?"

"The marshal wants to be seen doing *something*." James Robertson noticed a movement at the front of the establishment. "Look who just walked in, half an hour late—our lunch guest. I must say, my predecessor in the district attorney's office looks as dapper as ever."

Taylor Moore, wearing a summer suit of linen duck, stopped at the bar to shake hands with a few constituents, then made his way to the Robertsons' table. "Is this a private wake, gentlemen, or can anyone mourn? I've never seen a pair of gloomier faces."

"You're late, Representative Moore."

"My apologies, Mr. Mayor." Moore did not bother to look at the menu, but ordered his standing special of a bloody steak, mashed potatoes, and a tall glass of Budweiser.

The men exchanged pleasantries, but soon turned to the subject of crime. Taylor Moore had served four terms as district attorney, and James Robertson was not above seeking his advice. "I'm thinking," said Moore, "that perhaps the marshal's whole approach to finding this killer is based on a false premise."

"Go on." The district attorney plunged his fork into his last piece of steak.

"Let's go back to the murder of Mollie Smith. It was taken for granted that whoever killed the poor woman must have done so in a fit of passion. People suspected a spurned lover, or some man with a particular hatred for her."

"The woman was hit in the head with an ax and raped," said James Robertson. "Lust and hatred—what other motives could there be? That would seem to me to describe a spurned lover. The man would have to possess a particularly bestial nature, but we know that such men exist. When you were district attorney, you must have seen the worst dregs of humanity."

"Nothing compared to the specimens I've encountered in the state legislature!" said Moore. "My point is, the marshal's investigation of the previous case resulted in only one arrest, and that of a man who turned out to have an ironclad alibi. Now there's been another murder, in circumstances suspiciously similar. Once again, the marshal is adhering to the 'common knowledge' that it must have been done by someone who already knew the woman, intimately. I predict that the results will be as barren as before."

"What would you have the marshal do differently?"

"First of all, I'd put to him the possibility that the same man who killed Mollie Smith may have killed Eliza Shelley."

"Perhaps. But it doesn't appear that the women even knew each other. If they had a man in common—"

Moore shook his head. "You're still assuming that the killer was someone the victims already knew."

The mayor frowned. "Are you suggesting that some fellow took a sudden whim, on two occasions months apart, to murder and ravish a woman he didn't even know? Do you think we have a maniac who wanders about Austin with an ax on his person and breaks willy-nilly into servant quarters looking for victims?"

"No. I suspect there must have been some degree, perhaps a very high degree, of premeditation. Still, the killer may have scarcely known his victims. He might merely have seen them at a distance. The salient point is the similarity of the crimes. Again, the victim is a colored servant woman. Again, the woman is bludgeoned with a sharp object, probably an ax. And again, she appears to have been outraged—and in a most unnatural fashion, as she was dying or after she was dead."

Moore's lunch arrived. He took a swallow of beer and cut into his steak. It was very rare, as he liked it, and bled profusely onto the skirt of mashed potatoes. "Gentlemen, I suggest that one man committed both crimes. I further suggest that we are dealing with a kind of maniac, a man with a sick hatred, not just of these particular women, but of womankind. His motive is not jealousy or revenge. He's committed these crimes to obtain a kind of gratification, as repulsive as that may seem. If that's the case, gentlemen, I fear he's liable to do it again."

The staff of the *Statesman* were treated that afternoon to coffee by William Pendleton Gaines, who dispatched his printer's devils to the Lundberg bakery on the Avenue to fetch pastries. Gaines stood in the aisle between the desks of Hiram Glass and Dave Shoemaker, a cup of coffee in one hand and a half-eaten Sally Lunn in the other.

"Gentlemen, we can all be proud of the job we've done in the last two weeks. People are snatching up the *Statesman* faster than we can print it! We've all pulled together—and it hasn't all been smooth sailing. There was that hitch when we got word of the Eliza Shelley murder and our crime reporter was out of town. But Hiram Glass stepped in, as he did on the arson story, and did an exemplary job. Not every reporter could obtain an intelligible interview from a distraught eight-year-old boy. All those years of talking to babbling idiots in the legislature must have prepared you for the task."

"The boy seemed considerably more 'eddicated' than Rutabaga Johnson," said Hiram Glass with a wry smile. The fact was, talking to young Moses Shelley had been the easiest part of the job. Looking at the corpse had been considerably harder. But hardest of all had been having to face Marshal Lee. Since the incident at the burned-out dentist's office, Hiram had developed a mortal fear of the man.

"Well, gentlemen, back to work!" A chorus of groans ensued. Gaines raised an eyebrow. "Gentlemen, the vigilance of the press is a covenant with our readers, and this city is in a state of crisis. We must steel ourselves for the task and forge ahead!" He headed for his private office, but not before taking the last Sally Lunn with him.

"Slave driver!" muttered Dave. He turned to the papers on his desk. He had been organizing his notes about Elisabet Ney. In the wake of the latest murder, Gaines had forgotten about the Ney story, but there was no telling when he might suddenly take a renewed interest in it. Dave was trying to remember whether or not Bismarck was spelled with a *c* when he heard Tommy and the new printer's devil tittering nearby. The two boys stood at the big table where advertising copy was laid out for proofreading. Dave got up and walked over.

The new devil was a redhead, like Tommy, and to look at the two of them one might think Gaines had taken them on as bookends. His name was Caleb, but nobody called him that.

"What's so funny, Beelzebub?" said Dave.

The boy covered his mouth and giggled.

"Mephistopheles, perhaps you can enlighten me."

Tommy's face turned even redder than usual. He pointed to a scrap of paper on the table. Dave picked it up and perused it. A sample block of copy was accompanied by an engraved illustration. Dave glanced at the drawing, jerked his head back and wrinkled his brow, then squinted in disbelief. "What in blazes . . . ?" He read the block of copy and burst out laughing. "Don't tell me Gaines is actually going to run this!"

"What are you babbling on about?" asked Hiram.

"Hiram—this is perfect for you! I'll bet you already have one of these doodads, tucked away in that medicine cabinet in your desk."

The printer's devils tittered uncontrollably and then dispersed as Hiram got up from his desk and strode to the table. "What is all this nonsense?"

Dave handed him the piece of paper. "See for yourself. Some fellows will spend their money on just about anything."

The illustration depicted a thin belt, drawn as it would appear when worn around the waist, though no human model was shown. At the back of the belt was a cinch, from which emanated little lightning bolts. Suspended from the front of the belt was a short strap with a loop at the end. Beneath the illustration was a typeset block of copy:

MEN! READ THIS!

Are you debilitated through indiscretions or excesses? WE GUARANTEE A CURE by this new and improved ELECTRO-VOLTAIC BELT AND SUSPENSORY or refund money. Made for the specific cure of generative weakness. Gives continuous, mild, soothing currents of electricity directly through all weak parts, restoring them to health and VIGOROUS STRENGTH. Electric current felt instantly or we forfeit $5,000 in cash. Greatest improvements over all other belts. Worst cases PERMANENTLY CURED in three months. Sealed pamphlet. Send 3-cent stamp to Sanden Electric Co., 219 N. Broadway, St. Louis, Mo.

"Isn't that the same address as the place that makes your hair dye?" asked Dave.

"It most certainly is not! And the product I use isn't a dye. It's a hair restorative."

"Whatever you say, Hiram. But look at that drawing! It's obscene. Gaines can't possibly mean to print it."

"Any obscenity is entirely in your imagination, Shoemaker. All I see is a belt."

"But what do you think that little dangly part in front is for? Do you suppose a fellow's supposed to stick his Johnny Whilliker through that?"

"I suspect so."

"Would you walk around wearing it under your clothes all day? Or just while entertaining a lady?" Dave laughed. "Can you imagine the look on a woman's face if you were to pull down your pants and—"

"The type of women you associate with are likely to have seen stranger things."

"But it can't be safe. Look at those lightning bolts shooting out of it!"

"I imagine the cinching device in back contains a voltaic battery of some sort."

"Good Lord, and the current is supposed to run through the belt and down into the dangly part?"

"Why not? The therapeutic effects of electricity are only now beginning to be understood. Obviously, the manufacturers of this product have discovered that a steady, mild voltaic current can act as a curative for certain . . . masculine malfunctions."

"You kill me, Hiram! I'll bet you *do* own one of these contraptions."

"I most certainly do not. But the principle is sound."

"Well, there's no way you'd ever get me to strap on one of these things and poke my Johnny Whilliker through the bull's-eye."

"You should be thankful that such devices exist. Impairment of the masculine function can strike any man. 'Debilitated through indiscretions or excesses'—does that strike a chord, Shoemaker?"

"When I'm indiscreet, I'm never excessive. And when I'm excessive, I'm always discreet. My masculine functions are just fine, Hiram. I don't need any lightning bolts to wake up my Johnny Whilliker."

"I wish you'd stop using that vulgarism."

"I'd use the Latin, only it sounds dirtier." Dave snatched up the piece of paper from him. "Everyone, look at this!"

Hiram returned to his desk, nose in the air. He looked over his shoulder, then discreetly reached for a notecard, upon which he wrote:

Please send pamphlet to:
Hiram Glass
General Delivery
Austin, Texas

He inserted the card into an envelope, together with a three-cent stamp.

26

$\mathscr{A}$FTER an early dinner, the parents of Miss Emmeline Wilkins withdrew to their room upstairs, leaving their daughter and her two friends to entertain themselves in the parlor. It was a Friday night, the 22nd of May, two weeks and two days after the murder of Eliza Shelley.

The warm afternoon had faded to a clear, mild evening. The young ladies left open the windows that faced onto the large front porch, but the air was so still that no breeze stirred the lace curtains, nor was one needed. It was one of those rare golden hours in Austin when the temperature indoors and out was in absolute equilibrium, and all the world seemed bathed in the soft, sleepy afterglow of a perfect spring day.

Though she had no voice for singing, Emmeline had a considerable talent for the piano and adored the love songs of Stephen Foster. While she played upon the keyboard and silently mouthed the words, her visitors listened in silent appreciation. Emmeline's cousin Delia sat at one end of the long red sofa. Next to Delia was her sister-in-law, Eula, who was down visiting from Williamson County. Eula's feet were on the floor but she reclined sideways so that her head rested upon Delia's lap. Delia languidly wafted a fan of lacquered Chinese wood, while with her other hand she idly fingered a strand of Eula's golden hair.

Little by little the night grew darker. Crickets began to chirrup. A moth flitted against the window screens. The drowsy hour passed. Emmeline played a quicker tune. Eula sat upright and stretched. Delia fanned herself more heartily. Laughter came easily, and with it some friendly teasing.

Eula was married and Delia was a widow, but Emmeline was as yet unattached. "It seems unfair," Delia remarked, "that we staid matrons should be monopolizing a bright young belle such as you on a Friday night, Emmeline. Surely there must be a dance or some other function where you should be showing yourself off to the young men."

"No," said Emmeline coyly.

"No, there is no dance; or no, you should not be showing yourself off?"

"Oh, there is surely a dance somewhere in town tonight," said Emmeline airily. Her fingers tripped across the keyboard, playing a comical little passage of Mozart. "And no doubt all the young ladies in search of a beau are there, competing with one another and showing themselves off."

"So why aren't you there?"

"Perhaps I already have a beau."

"Emmeline! You never said!"

"Look at the smile on her face," Eula said, sighing. "Do we know the young man?"

"I don't think so."

"Why isn't he here?" demanded Delia. "Eula and I would gladly chaperone the two of you."

"He works late on Fridays. Perhaps, in a little while . . ." She glanced expectantly in the direction of the window.

"I see," said Delia. "Then it's a good thing that we *are* here to chaperone you."

"And to keep you amused until he gets here," added Eula.

Her secret revealed, Emmeline became almost giddy. She was at her most attractive and appealing when her nervous energy was stimulated and her natural vivacity outshone her other attributes; Emmeline was not a particularly pretty girl. Next to Delia's dark beauty or Eula's golden radiance, Emmeline had a common face, framed by hair of neutral brown. Her figure was woefully out of keeping with the fashion of the day. Those without an hourglass figure could attempt to attain one through artificial means such as corsets, but Emmeline's natural shape resisted reconfiguration by even the most binding undergarments. She had taken comfort in a recent article in a magazine to which her father subscribed—*Popular Science Monthly*—which compared modern ideas of shapeliness with those of the ancient Greeks, as embodied in statues like the *Venus de Milo*. The article gave measurements which it claimed to represent the classical ideal of womanhood: height, five feet, four and three-quarter inches; bust, thirty-two inches; waist, twenty-four and one-half inches; hips, thirty-four inches.

Emmeline had examined her own body, using a tape measure, and found that she was not too far off the classical model. This gave her some solace on those occasions when her mother could not seem to pull Emmeline's corset tight enough, or when Emmeline found herself in the company of other young females, like Delia and Eula, whose successfully corseted figures would have struck Aristophanes as more suitable to wasps than to women.

Nevertheless, Emmeline was preoccupied with thoughts of how to make herself more attractive to the young man who was courting her, and the pursuit of physical beauty became the topic of conversation as the three women awaited the arrival of Emmeline's suitor.

"Do you remember how thin my arms used to be?" said Emmeline.

"I'm sure I don't know what you mean," said Delia tactfully.

"Oh, but it's true. If I were a tall, slender girl it might have been all right, but as it was they stuck out from me like pins from a cushion."

The image made Eula laugh.

"But look at me now. I venture to say that my arms are as full and shapely as those of any other girl in Austin." Unlike her friends, whose dresses emphasized their figures while concealing their necks and limbs, Emmeline wore an old-fashioned dress with a square neck and short puffed sleeves which left her arms bare.

"I agree," said Delia. "Your arms have filled out very nicely. Nature simply took a little extra time to work out your proportions."

"It wasn't nature, cousin Delia. It was deliberate exercise."

"You built your arms from playing the piano?"

"No. For the past six months I've been taking regular walks and exercising with dumbbells," said Emmeline proudly. It was another secret revealed, and she felt giddier than ever.

"Dumbbells? Wherever did you get them?" asked Delia.

"Papa bought them for me from the ironworks over on Waller Creek. I started with five pounds. Now I use ten pounds."

"Remarkable!" said Delia. "Where on earth did you get such an idea?"

"From that book you gave me last year for my birthday."

"Oh, yes—*What Can a Woman Do?*" Delia had seen two copies at a bookshop on the Avenue, and had bought them both. One she gave to May Tobin, who claimed to read from it every night, as others read from the Bible. The other was a gift for Emmeline, for Delia had begun to worry that Emmeline might never marry, and so might benefit from the book's practical advice. It was filled with true stories about women who had entered the workplace to become all sorts of things—journalists and government clerks, photographers and wood engravers, typesetters and telegraphers, even doctors and lawyers. There were examples of how a woman could earn a livelihood without leaving her home, by taking in boarders or keeping bees or making dresses or raising poultry. (May had wryly noted that nothing in the book dealt with her mode of making a living; Delia had sardonically suggested that May write a chapter and submit it to the publisher in Detroit.)

"But I don't seem to recollect anything in the book about women becoming weightlifters, like strongmen at the fairground," said Delia.

"Don't be silly," said Emmeline. "The book contains nothing of the sort. But that's where I got the idea, nevertheless, from the chapter at the end of the book."

"I don't seem to recall . . ."

"Oh, it's my very favorite chapter, by far. 'Toilet Medicines,' taken from something called *Arts of Beauty* by Lola Montez. Who is Lola Montez, anyway?"

"Only the most famous woman in Europe since Josephine Bonaparte," said Delia. "Beautiful and scandalous, mistress to dukes and counts."

"No wonder mother blushed when I asked her."

"And does Lola Montez lift dumbbells?"

"No, but she once knew a girl who had thin arms, just like me, and that was how the girl solved her problem, so I decided to try it. And it worked! Miss Montez seems to know everything about every sort of toilet concoction. She gives recipes for tooth powders and skin creams, and ways for a lady to get rid of a mustache or keep her hair from turning gray, and she says that sleeping in soft white kid gloves will give you soft white hands. Oh, and, Eula—she gives a recipe for a formula that she says is guaranteed to fade tanned skin."

Eula blinked, a little taken aback. "I always wear a bonnet and gloves in the garden," she said quietly.

"Oh, but living on a farm, being out of doors all the time, a bit of tan is unavoidable, I should think. Here, I shall go and get the book right now."

"Oh, you needn't—"

But Emmeline was off before Eula could say another word, and came back carrying a thick little volume with an ornately embossed cover. "What can a woman do?" She leafed through he pages. "Ah, here it is. 'An excellent wash to remove tan is called *Crême de l'Enclos*,'" she read, pronouncing it *cream-day-la-enclose,* " 'and is thus made: new milk, one-half pint;

lemon juice, one-quarter ounce; white brandy, one-half ounce. Boil the whole and skim off any scum. Use it night and morning.' Oh, and, Delia, look—on the same page there's a formula guaranteed to fade freckles!"

Delia snapped shut her fan and cocked an eyebrow. Eula laughed behind her hand.

At that moment there came from the open porch windows the sound of singing on the still night air. The three women sat and listened as the singing grew closer.

Four male voices sang in perfect harmony. Eula was not even sure what words they were singing, but the music seemed to quicken something within her. She closed her eyes and listened.

Emmeline stepped to the nearest window. She drew the curtain aside, narrowing her eyes and brushing the delicate lace against her cheek as she did so. Delia rose and joined her, and then Eula. The three woman pressed so close together that her friends could feel the warmth of the blush that suffused Emmeline's cheeks and bare arms. Beyond the porch, beneath the oak tree in the front yard, stood four silhouettes, lit from behind by the glow of the half-moon.

Mrs. Wilkins entered the parlor. "Emmeline, is it—?"

"Yes, Mother."

"Wonderful! I must invite them up to the porch right away."

"Not yet, Mother!" Emmeline said with a laugh. Her friends had never seen her so radiant. "Let them finish the song."

The voices from the yard rang clear and sweet, singing an old sea chantey:

> "My ship is rigged and ready and I must be sailing;
> When shall I return, love, I just do not know.
> I shall cross oceans, be guided by the stars' light—
> And the best star of all is the light in your window."

When they were done, Emmeline exhaled a sigh. Mrs. Wilkins, a lamp in hand, proceeded to the foyer. She opened the front door and stepped onto the porch. "Jack Yeager, is that you? Bring your friends up on the porch." She hung the lamp on a hook, suffusing the porch with a cozy glow. "Would you gentlemen care for lemonade and ginger snaps? Emmeline is entertaining friends this evening, but I'm sure she can spare some time to say hello, especially after a song as pretty as that."

Mrs. Wilkins stepped back inside and hurried to the parlor. "Emmeline, come! Delia, Eula, chaperone her, would you? I shall serve the lemonade and then stay out of the way—Emmeline doesn't need me hovering over her." She headed toward the kitchen.

Emmeline proceeded to the foyer. Eula hung back. Delia took her hand. "Come along, sweet. Let's have a look at these serenaders. It's terribly romantic, isn't it?"

Eula lowered her eyes. "I think I'll stay here."

"Nonsense! You heard Mrs. Wilkins. We staid old matrons are to play chaperones. Come along—Emmeline is at the door, and she can hardly go out there alone, can she?"

"But I . . ."

"Eula, what's the matter? It shall be fun! While Emmeline and her beau stutter and blush, we can flirt with the others."

"Delia, that would hardly be proper."

"Why not? I may be a widow, but I'm well past wearing black."

"But what about me? I'm a married woman—and a mother!"

"That needn't be a problem; if we take this off." She reached for Eula's hand and gently pulled at her wedding ring.

"Delia, what are you doing?"

"Shh! Emmeline will hear."

"Emmeline will notice if you take off my ring!"

"Nonsense. Once she's out that door, she shall see nothing but Jack. Here, do you see how easy that was?" Delia tossed the ring in the air and caught it, then turned to Eula with a grin. "Don't worry, I shall keep it safe for you. Now, come!"

"But, Delia—"

"You enjoyed the singing, didn't you? Then come and tell them so."

They joined Emmeline, who was waiting impatiently at the door. After smoothing their skirts and checking themselves in the mirror, the three women stepped onto the porch. After a bit of nervous shuffling, each of the men took off his hat and introduced himself. Delia introduced herself as Delia Campbell, Emmeline's cousin, paying a call with Emmeline's friend, Eula Phillips, neglecting to preface their names with either Mrs. or Miss.

Jack reached for Emmeline's arm and conducted her to the swing at the far side of the porch. The other men held their hats and leaned against the rail. Mrs. Wilkins brought out a tray with a pitcher of lemonade, a bowl of cookies, and glasses. After serving everyone, she withdrew.

Delia leaned close to Eula and spoke in her ear, barely moving her lips. "The one with the ginger mustache—he's positively dazed by you!"

Eula kept her eyes lowered for a moment. She could sense the man's presence before her. She looked at his hands, which seemed to clutch his hat so forcefully that his knuckles blanched. Finally she looked up, into two eyes as blue as her own. They looked at each other steadily for what seemed a long time, until the young man finally spoke.

She shook her head. "I'm sorry. I didn't hear you."

"Eula—it's a beautiful name," he said, still speaking so softly that she had to lean forward to hear him. She glanced about, strangely disoriented. To one side, Jack and Emmeline were on the porch swing, talking quietly, oblivious of everything else. To the other side, Delia had engaged the attention of the other two members of the quartet, and the three of them were laughing heartily at something. Eula returned her gaze to the young man, who had introduced himself as Will Porter.

"A beautiful name," he said again, not sure if she had heard him.

"Thank you," said Eula.

"It's from the Greek word for 'good,'" he said.

She smiled faintly.

"I know, because I looked it up in a book," he said, and then looked vaguely alarmed, as if he had given something away. It was hard to tell for certain, under the reddish glow of the lamp, but he appeared to blush.

He seemed to her so young, so earnest, so helpless that he reminded her of Jimmy back in their courting days. There was an innocence in his eyes that captivated her. He was at least her age if not a bit older, yet she at once felt protective of him.

She studied his face openly, and he did the same. Having been granted permission to look at her by the fact of her looking back, he could not disguise how eager he was simply to stare at her. He was quite handsome, she thought, with his broad jaw and his wavy ginger hair, and in spite of his elaborately coiffed mustache; such an obvious gesture of vanity in the middle of his face only made him seem more vulnerable.

"You're a scholar, then, Mr. Porter?"

"I beg your pardon?"

"Looking up names in books, to find root meanings."

"I suppose I am a bit bookish. And you?"

"I love books," said Eula. "Ever since I was a little girl, and my father read *Ivanhoe* aloud to me."

"Ah, Sir Walter Scott." He seemed stumped for a moment, then brightened. "Where I come from, in North Carolina, when I was a boy, the better sort of people, the people with money, used to hold knightly tournaments, inspired by *Ivanhoe* and all that."

"Really?"

"They wouldn't actually joust and knock each other off horses, but they did have contests of skill on horseback—scooping up rings with lances, slicing through watermelons with cavalry swords. The young knights would decorate themselves with colored crepe and cardboard, and carry the scarves of ladies in the stands."

"It sounds very romantic."

"To tell you the truth, I thought it was a lot of folderol. But I was too young to appreciate it, I suppose."

"Yes, things change as we get older, don't they?" Eula said, and sighed. "Of course, it's not the things which change; it's us. We can never see the world as it truly is, because the way we see it keeps changing. A place you knew as a child seems so different when you go back as an adult—smaller, less magical. It's the same with people, even those closest to you; you think you know them, yet that's only an illusion . . ."

They fell to staring at each other again. It was clear that he would not or could not break the spell, so she finally took it upon herself to do so. It required an act of will to lower her eyes, draw a breath, and try to think of something harmless to say.

Will's friends moved toward them, laughing at some joke from Delia. More lemonade was served. The general conversation moved on to summer dances and rowing parties on the river. Eventually Mrs. Wilkins decided enough time had been spent in courting for one night. She came out to fetch the tray and tactfully bade the serenaders good night by asking them to sing a final song before moving on.

The men replaced their hats and withdrew to the yard. The women sat on the porch, Emmeline and her mother in the rockers, Delia and Eula together in the swing, holding hands. While the men sang "Come Where the Roses Bloom," Delia discreetly replaced the ring on Eula's finger.

Will Porter's speaking voice had been deep, but Eula hadn't realized that he was the bass singer. She listened to him now, supplying the foundation of sound upon which the others built, producing notes as rich and mellow as the rumblings of a violoncello.

The serenading party moved on; two of the others in the group besides Jack Yeager had belles to court that night. Will was the only one who had come along solely to sing and provide moral support.

He spent the rest of that night in a strange mood, between suppressed excitement and a kind of giddy despair. Now he knew her last name. With a few discreet questions to Jack Yeager, who could get the answers from Emmeline, Will could find out more about Eula Phillips—where she lived, who her family was, how often she visited.

About one thing, which he had already suspected, he was now certain. There had been no wedding ring on Eula's finger. That heartened him, at first, until he noticed, quite clearly under the soft glow of the lamp, the marked difference between the tanned skin of her hands and the paler band of flesh around her ring finger. By the mark of the sun there could be no doubt that she usually wore a wedding ring.

Eula Phillips was a married woman—yet her eyes, gazing into his, had given him hope.

27

*T*HE next morning—the 23rd of May—being a Saturday, William
Jesse Swain slept late. The comptroller's office would be open till noon, but
no pending business required his presence as head of the department.
Swain did not believe in overtaxing himself. He was not a workhorse! He
thought of himself as a thoroughbred in training for a long and arduous
race. The goal was the Governor's Mansion. No champion ever won races
by pulling a plow every day! Learning to pace oneself—that was the secret.
Adequate rest and relaxation were every bit as important as hard work, and
so on Saturdays, while Mrs. Swain did her shopping and visiting, William
Swain allowed himself the luxury of sleeping late.

He slept so late, in fact, that he did not bother to eat his usual hearty
breakfast. He had an appointment to meet his young assistant William Shelley for lunch, and so made do with the pot of coffee and a sweet roll
brought up to his room by the serving girl.

While he made his toilet and dressed, his copy of the *Statesman* remained unread on the breakfast table downstairs, and so Swain left his
house without having read the story boldly headlined, "MORE BUTCH-
ERY!"

Swain's house, one of the largest and finest in the city, was situated just a
block north of the capitol grounds. He was to meet young Shelley at
Scholz's Beer Garden, some four blocks to the northwest. The short walk
would serve to stimulate his appetite for some of the excellent roulade
served at Scholz's.

The 1500 block of Congress Avenue, where Swain lived, was a handsome stretch of real estate, beginning with his house on one corner and ending at the other with the splendid edifice of the Swedish Evangelical Lutheran Church. But as Swain walked east, the character of the neighborhood changed dramatically. Turning north onto Brazos Street, only a block from his house, he strolled past humble dwellings hardly better than shanties.

Outside one of these humble houses Swain noticed that some horses had been hitched, and on the broken-down porch were gathered three men in blue serge coats with gold braid, wearing flat-topped caps—city policemen. Knocking forcefully on the door was a tall man whom Swain recognized as Marshal Grooms Lee. Though Swain had no reason to know or care, the house was the home of Cynthia Spencer and, since the death of Mollie Smith, of her son Walter.

An old colored woman answered the door. The marshal demanded something of her in a harsh tone. Swain slowed his gait but did not stop. Once past the house, he pressed on, whistling a gay tune.

Across from the beer garden, he paused for a mule-drawn streetcar passing through the intersection. His attention was drawn to the house across from Scholz's, catty-corner to where he stood. A number of horses and buggies were drawn up around the property. A crowd, including a large number of colored folk, had gathered in the yard. The occasion was not festive, judging from their faces; perhaps someone in the house had died.

Recommencing to whistle, Swain crossed the street, mindful to avoid a number of fresh mule droppings. He was hungry for roulade!

William Shelley awaited him at a table situated near the fountain. Soon Swain was settled in his chair, blowing foam from the top of a beer mug. A peacock strutted by, displaying tail feathers in full array.

"I suppose you saw the commotion across the street, sir?" said Shelley.

"What? Oh, yes. What it's about?"

"This." Shelley put a folded page of the *Statesman* in front of him.

"Haven't seen today's paper yet," muttered Swain. "What's this? 'More Butchery!—Another Colored Woman Brutally Murdered—Unknown Fiend Escapes from the Scene—When Will It End?' This happened in that house across the street?"

"In the servant's cottage out back," said Shelley. "Another murder, almost identical to the last. Somebody broke in during the middle of the night, took an ax to the servant woman, and had his way with her."

"Terrible!" Swain peered at the newspaper. "Irene Cross was her name.

Good God! It says here that the poor woman's right arm was practically severed in two, and a cut to her head extended halfway around her skull. 'She had practically been scalped.' Ugh! And you've shown me this just before my lunch."

"No one in Scholz's is talking of anything else, sir. People keep getting up from their tables to wander over and gawk at the house."

"I certainly shall not! Let the law handle the matter." Swain squinted thoughtfully. "I wonder if those policemen I saw outside that house over on Brazos Street have any connection with this?"

"What's that, sir?"

"Something I saw on the way over. Good man, Marshal Lee. He was a damned fine Ranger. And his father's doing a splendid job running the capitol commission. Ought to be, for thirty-six hundred a year—almost as much as the governor makes! But if Joseph Lee can keep construction on schedule, he's worth every penny. The contractors want to use convict labor to quarry the granite over in Burnet, and bring over Scottish masons to cut the blocks—that's got the labor unionists up in arms! But I didn't come here to talk politics. This is my day off." He cleared his throat. "I take it that my appointment for two o'clock has been taken care of?"

"It has, sir. As before, we'll take a hackney cab together, and I'll let you off around the corner from Mrs. Tobin's house. She'll be expecting you at the rear entrance. I'll be back with another cab at four o'clock, to pick you up at the same spot around the corner."

"Excellent! You're a miracle of efficiency, Shelley. Why don't you drop in at May's yourself this afternoon? You've been working damned hard. You deserve a treat, young man."

"Perhaps I do, sir, but I'll tend to that on my own time." Shelley's lips compressed in a tight smile. He had accompanied Swain on his initial visit to May Tobin's house, so as to make introductions (Swain was "Mr. Compton," easily remembered for its similarity to Comptroller), but thereafter had scheduled his own visits so as not to overlap with those of his boss. He saw no reason to invite an embarrassing situation; he did not care to be seen by Swain in a state of undress or in the afterglow of passion, nor did he care to see Swain in any such state. Also, the two men had similar tastes—they were both currently seeing the same woman, Delia Campbell. Shelley did not mind sharing her with Swain, as long as there was a decent interval between their visits.

Their meals arrived. Swain gazed at his plate of roulade and sauerkraut with delight. The day was turning out splendidly.

* * *

Across town, in Bellevue mansion, William Pendleton Gaines was greeting luncheon guests.

His wife would normally have served as hostess, but Augusta was visibly advanced in her pregnancy and in no condition to be presented to gentleman visitors. Gaines relied greatly upon his wife's skills as a hostess, and for the duration of her indisposition he had withdrawn from formal entertaining. In the case of Dr. Terry and Dr. Fry, however, he had made an exception. After being back in Austin for a few weeks, and making the acquaintance of many of the town's leading businessmen, the doctors had announced their intention to depart again in a matter of days. Before they did so, Gaines made up his mind to invite them to Bellevue for lunch.

Normally, after a bit of conversation in the parlor, Augusta would have offered to show the visitors around the house. But how would Augusta have dealt with the blind phrenologist? It would be rude, Gaines thought, not to offer to show Dr. Terry around, for every visitor to Bellevue was invited to the upstairs gallery to see why the house deserved its name. But should Dr. Fry also be invited, or should Gaines offer the blind man some alternative amusement—and what would that alternative be? He could hardly offer the man a stereoscopic viewer, or a book of epigrams, or even a deck of cards!

The obvious solution appeared when his father came down early for lunch. The elder Gaines was seventy-seven. He eschewed the fashion for beards and was clean-shaven. Outfitted in a pale summer suit with a boutonniere in his lapel, a gold watch chain dangling from his waistcoat pocket, and his fringe of wispy white hair freshly pomaded and combed, he looked very much what he was, a retired Southern planter. To be sure, he was a trifle deaf and not as sharp as he once had been, but surely he and Dr. Fry could find something to talk about for a few minutes while Gaines conducted Dr. Terry to the upper gallery.

The guests arrived, introductions were made, and handshakes exchanged. Unfortunately, Gaines Senior did not seem to grasp the reason for Dr. Fry's dark glasses, and stared at them in consternation; short of shouting, "Papa, the fellow is blind!" into the old man's ear horn, Gaines was at a loss. Nor did Dr. Fry, perhaps because he could not see the horn, seem to appreciate the old man's handicap; he ignored Gaines's example of speaking loudly and addressed the old man in a low monotone.

"He's a bit hard of hearing," Gaines explained quietly. "You'll need to raise your voice."

"Ah, yes!" Dr. Fry nodded, then went on speaking exactly as he had before. Gaines Senior leaned forward, staring at the bespectacled, incomprehensible visitor and looking utterly perplexed.

With some misgivings, Gaines left the two of them alone in the parlor.

The tour took longer than he expected. Dr. Terry expressed an interest in virtually every painting and piece of furniture they passed, and several of the items had interesting histories which Gaines was happy to recount. The doctor was also fascinated by Bellevue itself, which had been built by the previous owner in imitation of a French château out of massive limestone blocks quarried from the very hill upon which the house stood. The structure was an architectural curiosity, built in several levels on a steep slope which fell away to the west; wooden galleries had been attached so as to take advantage of the splendid views. Gaines had been living in the house for only a year, and delighted in showing it off. Out on the upper gallery, they strolled to the southwest corner and leaned on the balustrade, gazing at the distant Colorado sparkling beneath the noonday sun. Talk of Bellevue turned to talk of a dam and the city's future. At last the sounding of the gong for lunch drew them back into the house.

As they approached the parlor, Gaines heard what sounded like shouting. He drew ahead of Dr. Terry and hurried into the room.

His first impression, impossible as it seemed, was that the two men were having a tussle on the rug, wrestling like a couple of schoolboys. Rejecting that notion at once, but still trying to make sense of the strange tableau, Gaines was seized with the horrible idea that his father had fallen ill and collapsed to the floor, and that Dr. Fry was awkwardly, blindly attempting to assist him. But that explanation did not seem to fit the case, either. Gaines watched the two of them in speechless wonder.

Gaines Senior was out of his chair and down on the rug, literally on all fours except for the hand that held his hearing horn to one ear. Facing him and squatting over him in a most uncouth manner, with his hands on the old man's head and his mouth pressed to the ear horn, was Dr. Fry. "Strong character!" declared the doctor, speaking loudly into the horn.

"What?" shouted the elder Gaines.

"I said, *strong character*—that is the predominant feature of your personality, sir. You have the head of a lion! Your head very much resembles that of Daniel Webster, whose death mask I once had the privilege to examine. Such a prominent middle forehead suggests a retaliatory nature; you are sluggish when at rest, but fierce when aroused. Your enemies had best leave you in peace, sir!"

Gaines Senior sought to rise up enough to free the hand on which he was balanced, so as to feel his forehead for himself, but the enthusiastic explorations of the phrenologist's fingers confounded his efforts. "This indentation in your lower lip, sir, and the way the corners of your mouth turn down—signs of a somewhat sarcastic nature. No doubt you have passed that trait on to your son, who employs it to his advantage in the publishing trade."

Gaines Senior seemed to nod agreement, as best he could with the doctor's hands pulling at his lips and moving over his face.

"And your eyes, likewise slanted downward at the corners—"

"I beg your pardon!" Gaines could watch in silence no longer.

"Ah, Mr. Gaines—I didn't hear you come in. Is Dr. Terry with you? How went the tour?"

"Dr. Fry! Please, get up off the floor! And, Papa—what on earth are you doing down there? Let me help you." Gaines shook his head. Such a thing would never have happened if Augusta had been present.

They repaired at once to the dining room, where Gaines Senior put down his hearing horn and resisted all attempts to draw him into conversation; Gaines suspected the old man was sulking because the examination had been interrupted. He queried his guests about their immediate itinerary and future plans. "I do hope that this recent rash of crimes hasn't played a part in your decision to leave the city."

"Oh, no," Dr. Terry assured him. "To be perfectly frank, it's the heat that's frightened us off! We keep hearing such dreadful stories about the Texas summer that we've decided to spend the season tending to business elsewhere."

"Perhaps a wise idea," allowed Gaines. "When shall you return?"

"Around the end of August. Dr. Fry and I have reserved an office on the Avenue and arranged to rent a fine little house nearby. We plan to move the bulk of our assets to Austin over the next six months, and to throw our energies behind construction of a dam. Once that happens, we will be positioned to establish a major patent medicine manufactory here. Austin's future will be our future."

"Hear, hear!" said Gaines. Even the sulking Gaines Senior joined in the toast, holding his head up proudly like an irascible old lion.

The Robertson brothers were also taking lunch, at their usual table at the back of the Iron Front.

"This is a catastrophe," declared the mayor gloomily. "Two murders in two weeks!" He shook his head. "I'm up for reelection in December! For God's sake, James, we've got to put a stop to it."

The district attorney chewed thoughtfully and swallowed. "Perhaps, if Grooms Lee can't produce an arrest, the city should hire outside detectives."

"Pinkertons?"

"Or men from some similar agency, from out of town; New Orleans or Houston, maybe. Something to consider, John. As you say, you're up for reelection. December will be here before you know it."

At the same hour, spirits were at a low ebb inside the Black Elephant.

Lem Brooks had just finished reading aloud the newspaper account of the attack on Irene Cross, for the benefit of a half dozen patrons at the bar who couldn't read, among them Alec Mack.

"If'n this was happenin' to white women, can you imagine the to-do they'd be makin'?" said Alec.

Hugh Hancock scurried over on his bandy legs. "If'n it was white women, Alec Mack, a mob would'a lynched a couple o' po' colored fellow 'fore now!"

"Marshal Lee ain't stayin' home polishin' his gold buttons," observed Lem glumly.

"What you mean?" said Alec.

"Lem means the marshal was in here bright and early," said Hancock, "askin' where Lem was last night, makin' him give account o' hisself. Then the marshal headed up to Walter Spencer's place—damn near 'rested *him*, jus' 'cause his Mammy's place be nearby to where Irene Cross was murdered. I swear, Marshal Lee be like a dog with a bone, thinkin' he can tear hisself off some more meat if'n he jus' gnaws long and hard enough."

Alec grinned. "Jus' pitcher an old hound dog with that fancy little gol' braided marshal's cap on his head!"

Hugh Hancock didn't laugh. "You think it mighty funny, Alec Mack, but you ain't likely to laugh if'n Marshal Lee come after you, askin' where you been las' night. What you tell him then?"

The grin vanished from Alec's face. The fact was, last night he had been right there, in the Black Elephant—with his ladyfriend. Hancock had gone to bed early and Lem had allowed Alec to sneak in the back way. He and Rebecca Ramey had locked themselves in the storage room and spent the better part of the night on the old settee where Hancock took his naps during the day.

Flinching a little, Alec managed to meet Hancock's eyes. There was no accusation in them, just the uneasiness they all felt. The man didn't suspect a thing.

"I tells you this much," said Hancock. "It behooves ever' one of you here, and ever' black man in Austin, to be able to give account of hisself for ever' hour of ever' day and night, from now on—where you goes, who you's with, where you comes to rest at night. There's not a colored man in Austin safe from Marshal Lee. We's all jus' so many bones to be chewed up and buried in that man's back yard!"

Will Porter rose early that morning and spent the day doing the best thing a man could do on a perfect spring day, short of passing the time with the girl of his dreams. He went tramping in the rugged hills and along the shady creeks west of town.

He began at Shoal Creek, where he visited for a while with the crazy Colonel and his crew, and then pressed on to the west, through open fields and woodland. He came to the railroad tracks and stopped to watch a train chug by, headed north to Williamson County and beyond. Beyond the tracks was Johnson Creek, where another band of tramps was camped. Not recognizing any of them, and not in a mood to make new friends, Will pressed on, through shady oak groves and fields strewn with wildflowers, all the way to a bluff overlooking the Colorado, where the river came down from the north and made a great eastward bend to cradle the city like a child in the crook of its mother's arm.

Still restless, he turned and headed north, upriver, going steadily uphill until he found himself ascending Mount Bonnell. He had not expected to come so far. At just under eight hundred feet, Bonnell was hardly a mountain, but the climb was still hard work, especially when he had to scramble over limestone boulders or around clumps of cactus. Eventually he came upon a graded road and the way became easier.

As he approached the summit he saw buggies parked here and there and heard voices through the trees. On such a bright Saturday afternoon, people had flocked to Mount Bonnell with picnic baskets. Will caught a glimpse of two young lovers, their backs to him, sitting side by side on a blanket spread over a limestone ledge. They put their heads together. Their faces drew close. They kissed. Will looked away and walked on.

He came to a vantage point near the summit and turned to have a look. The distant city was a cluster of low buildings beside the river, with few notable landmarks on the skyline. That would change when the new capitol was built. The great dome would tower above everything else, a man-made mountain of dusky pink granite.

He turned around. A few more steps brought him to the sheer western face of the mountain. The green river was directly below, like a gleaming, sinuous snake. Beyond the river, rugged hills rose to peaks even higher than Mount Bonnell. The place where he stood was called Lover's Leap.

He stepped a little farther out on the ledge, curious to see how steeply the face of the mountain fell away. He discovered another, lower ledge, which appeared to lead to yet another, like a steep natural stairway in the broken face of the rock. He took a step down, then another.

He was careless. He was tired from the climb. His legs were more wobbly than he realized. A chunk of brittle limestone gave way under his foot.

It happened in the blink of an eye. His feet slid out from under him and the whole mountain seemed to lurch. His head spun and his stomach flopped upside down. His scrambling heels set off a little avalanche. He flailed his arms and caught a spindly mesquite branch.

His feet found solid ground. He regained his balance. The noisy little avalanche continued for a moment, then ceased. He sucked in a deep breath and clutched the branch with white knuckles. From far below, he heard the splash of stones striking the water, barely audible above the pounding of his heart. He climbed slowly, cautiously onto safer ground.

Above him, peering through leafy branches, stood the two lovers, the man holding the woman, both wearing expressions of concern. Will blushed furiously and hurried past them.

His knees shook. He was tired and thirsty. He started to dust himself off, then realized that his hands were scraped and bleeding. One of his elbows was bleeding, too. He had torn a hole in the sleeve.

He might have cadged a ride back into town, but he was in no mood to talk to anyone. It would be dark by the time he got home, but at least the walk would be downhill.

He took a final look at the distant city, then started back, more restless than when he set out. The whole day long, even when he was scrambling on the rock face, he had thought of nothing but Eula Phillips.

It was not until bedtime that night, as he was disrobing, that William Gaines Senior discovered that something was missing. The old man could not locate his watch, which he always kept in his waistcoat pocket, connected by a gold chain to a button on his trousers. Both watch and chain were missing, though the button was still in place. He alerted his son to the circumstance, and the two of them, along with the servants, set about searching the house.

The watch was a fine piece of workmanship, intrinsically valuable, but its sentimental value was considerably greater. It had been given to the elder Gaines by Mirabeau Buonaparte Lamar, the second president of the Republic of Texas. Engraved inside the cover was a rhyming couplet authored by the poet-president himself:

> These hands sweep 'round in ceaseless flight,
> To note each hour and mark it right.

After a solid hour of searching, the watch was still missing.

The last time the elder Gaines could remember looking at the watch was shortly before coming downstairs for lunch. He had not stirred from the house all day, except to go into the garden after the guests departed, where he sat in a chair beneath the trees and napped for a while. Unless one of the servants had stolen it, which Augusta Gaines declared impossible, the watch had to be somewhere on the property.

William Pendleton Gaines, in reconstructing his father's movements, remembered all too vividly the discovery of his father on the floor with Dr. Fry hovering over him, blindly examining the old man's head. Gaines pushed the image from his thoughts almost at once, for it was not a moment he cared to dwell on. But for an instant—so briefly, in fact, that the thought seemed hardly to have occurred—he entertained a wholly unfounded and, indeed, impossible suspicion.

28

*M*AY passed into June, June into July.

No arrest was made, either for the murder of Eliza Shelley or that of Irene Cross.

For a while, the city of Austin was haunted by an acute dread, an anticipation of more slaughter to come; but days turned to weeks, and weeks to months, and there were no further murders. As it had after the death of Mollie Smith, the wave of public outrage swelled, crested, and then dispersed, leaving behind a residue of uncertainty and mistrust.

Perhaps it was the ungodly heat of that summer, driving men to acts of violence, or perhaps the unpunished murders had unleashed some primal savagery, or perhaps it was simply that people, their nerves frayed, paid closer attention to such things, but it seemed to many in Austin that their city had suddenly become a more dangerous and disorderly place.

Reports of burglaries and assaults were in the paper almost every week. There was the case of the commercial traveler who was shot at through his bedroom window at a boarding house on San Jacinto Street; a chase ensued, but the shooter got clean away. There was the shocking incident of a mother, a white woman, who reported her infant child to be missing; the body of the boy was discovered in a shallow grave amid overwhelming evidence that the mother herself had killed him. A city employee was accused of molesting a flower girl who wandered into Guy Town one night; it was later determined that the girl was not nearly as young or innocent as had been presumed, and the true crime was attempted blackmail by the girl's mother. These incidents had no connection with the murders, but as the mayor fretfully remarked to his brother, they kept the pot simmering.

In response to growing criticism, Marshal Lee complained that a police force of only twelve officers was too small for a city the size of Austin, and requested that the city hire more men.

Will Porter whiled away the summer as he had the winter and spring, residing rent-free at the Harrells' boarding house, working every now and again down at the cigar shop, singing in church choirs to keep up his good reputation with the mothers of Austin, serenading with friends, getting tipsy in Guy Town and declining to visit prostitutes with Dave Shoemaker. The hot weather encouraged boating trips on the Colorado and dips in the swimming hole at Barton Springs.

Some days Will would stir from his room only as far as the front porch, where he would sit and rock for hours, conversing with passersby and reading dime novels about cowboys or detectives. Some days, when the heat was at its worst, he would hardly leave his room at all, but would sit on his bed wearing nothing but his underwear, playing his guitar, writing poems, smoking cigarettes, and dozing.

Sometimes he would wake up stiff between his legs, and pass the whole day in a state of constant arousal. He would close the thin curtains at the window, lock the door to his room, and lie on his bed naked, covered with a sheen of sweat, using his hands to pleasure himself, twice, three times, as many as four times in a row without being sated. He fretted that such excessive self-abuse was an indication of something seriously wrong with him; but Dave Shoemaker, the only person to whom he could confide such a worry, laughingly assured him that priapism was normal for a young man his age—especially an unmarried man too poor or too pure to relieve himself by the means provided in Guy Town. Will did not confide, even to Dave, the name of the person who most often joined him in the fantasies which accompanied these long, languid bouts of sinful pleasure.

By asking discreet questions of several parties and piecing together the answers, Will had learned quite a bit about Eula Phillips. He knew that she had been married for over two years to a man named Jimmy Phillips, who was the son of a fairly prosperous builder and contractor in town. He knew that Jimmy was notorious for drinking, and that Jimmy and Eula had left Austin at the first of the year to live on a farm in Williamson County. He knew that the farm was owned by a man named George McCutcheon, and he speculated that McCutcheon was the man in the farmer's hat who had picked up Eula and Delia after the debate at the legislature. He knew that Delia Campbell was a widow, and was Jimmy's sister, Eula's sister-in-law, and that the two women were "closer than two peas in a pod," as Emmeline Wilkins told Jack Yeager. And he knew that Eula was the mother of a baby boy.

With all that he had discovered about Eula Phillips, he had every reason to push her from his thoughts and forget her.

Toward the end of July, Will fell into a bit of work at a drugstore on the Avenue. The pharmacist's regular assistant was ill, and the man who usually filled in was away from town. The pharmacist queried the other drugstore owners, asking if anyone knew of a trained assistant who could fill in on a strictly temporary basis. Someone at Morley Brothers recommended Will. Will had sworn that he would never be a soda fountain clerk again, but in this case he would be working behind the pharmacist's counter, and he needed the money.

On his second and last day of working at the store, he had a curious experience.

That morning, at about ten o'clock, the pharmacist, an old man with white hair, was tending to some paperwork at his desk at the very back of the store. The clerk at the soda fountain was polishing spoons. Will was busy checking inventory against a stock list, moving along the rows of jars and bottles and boxes on the shelves behind the pharmacy counter. The little bell above the door rang, indicating that someone had come in. Will stepped to the counter. The smile on his face cracked when he saw that it was Delia Campbell.

He cleared his throat. "Mrs. Campbell, isn't it?"

She studied his face. "Yes. You and I met . . . ?"

"On Emmeline Wilkins's porch, ma'am, a couple of months ago. I'm Will Porter. I came along to help serenade that fine lady."

Delia nodded. "Ah, yes. The bass singer."

"I confess and plead guilty. Yet here I am behind a counter instead of behind bars." She laughed so charmingly that Will dared to say, "Is your friend with you?" His heart pounded in his chest.

"My friend?"

"The other young lady who was visiting Miss Wilkins that night—I believe her name is Eula Phillips."

Delia smiled. "No, Mrs. Phillips is not with me today."

"I hope she's well." He felt compelled to say something, anything, so as to keep speaking of her.

"Why, yes, Eula is perfectly well. Had you heard otherwise?" She looked at him quizzically.

"No, not at all. I was only . . ." He noticed the piece of paper in her hand. "Can I help with your list, Mrs. Campbell?"

"My list? Ah, yes." She looked at it. "Yes, I suppose . . . if you happen to have dried chamomile flowers . . ."

"I'm sure we do. Anything else?"

"Only . . . extract of cotton root?" She seemed uncertain whether such a thing existed.

"I believe so." He managed a smile. "They should be pretty close together, both starting with C. Anything farther down the alphabet?"

She looked at the list and seemed to hesitate. "No, that will be all."

"Chamomile is harmless," he said as he filled the order, "but you do realize that cotton root extract can be poisonous? I take it you're getting it for a specific purpose."

"Actually, I'm buying it for someone else."

He nodded. "As it's a poison, I'll need you to sign the purchase register."

She looked at him and blinked. "Certainly."

Will placed the register and a pen before her. He wrapped up the items. She paid with coins from her purse and turned to leave.

Will bit his lip, then blurted out, "Please give my regards to Miss Wilkins, if you should see her before I do."

"Certainly, Mr. Porter." Delia moved toward the door.

"And also—to Mrs. Phillips."

She stopped, turned about, and smiled. "I'll do that, Mr. Porter."

He couldn't seem to stop. "Is Mrs. Phillips . . . in Austin, at present?"

She gave him a shrewd look. "No. Mrs. Phillips is with her husband, at the McCutcheon farm up in Williamson County. But I'll be sure to tell her that you inquired after her well-being."

His encounter with Delia Campbell had a curious sequel, later that day.

The pharmacist was manning the counter. Will was once again checking the inventory. He was squatting down, counting some items on a low shelf, when the bell rang and a man walked up to the counter.

"I'll be needing some ergot," the man said, in a gruff voice.

"Ergot. Right," said the pharmacist. "You stay where you are, Will. I'll fetch it."

Will nodded. He noticed the customer from the corner of his eye, but

didn't look up. Ergot, he recalled, was a fungus that grew on rye. It was powerful stuff, potentially poisonous. Taken internally, it caused blood vessels to
constrict. People took it for megrim headaches, but it could also induce
muscle contractions and abdominal cramps. Consumed in high enough
quantities, it could cause gangrene.

The pharmacist returned with a jar containing a fine purple powder, so
dark it was almost black. "Ergot can be dangerous, you know."

"Yes, I know," said the man.

"Mind if I ask what you want it for?"

There was a pause. "Headaches. What they call the megrims."

"It's for you, then?"

The man nodded.

"You taken it before?"

There was another pause. "Yes."

"So you know the right dose, and about putting it under your tongue.
That's the quickest, safest way to get it into the bloodstream."

"Right. I've got a medical almanac at home that explains all that."

"And you know never to give it to a woman who's in a family way."

"Of course. That's in the almanac, too."

"All right, then. I'll need you to sign the purchase register."

"Why?"

"Just a formality. Anything that could be poisonous, we have you sign the
register. How much do you need today?"

The man looked at a list in his hand and cited an amount. The pharmacist measured out the powder, wrapped it up in wax paper, and rang up the
charge. It was not until the customer was about to leave that Will realized
there was something familiar about him. It was the hat he wore, a farmer's
slouch hat. Will glanced up just as the man was turning away, and caught
the barest glimpse of his face.

Will stood and watched mutely as the man left the store, making the little bell jingle. Will hesitated, then stepped from behind the counter.

The pharmacist called after him. "Where you going, Will?"

"I have to step outside . . . just for a moment. I'll be right back."

Will followed the farmer for half a block, until he saw him step off the
sidewalk and into a buggy where Delia Campbell sat waiting. Will was almost certain it was the same man he had seen outside the state building,
meeting Delia and Eula after the debates.

Delia and the man conversed for a while, both looking very serious. The
man seemed to be upset about something. Delia placed her hand on his

and gave him a quick kiss on the cheek, which seemed to calm him. The man snapped the reins and they headed up the Avenue.

Will went back into the store. When the pharmacist turned his back for a moment, Will opened the purchase register and looked at the last entry. The word *ergot* was entered, with an amount and price. The signature was that of George McCutcheon.

The pharmacist turned back. Will shut the book.

The pharmacist gestured to the jar of ergot, which was still on the counter. "Put that away for me, would you, Will?"

"Certainly." Will reached for the jar. "Do you sell much ergot, sir?"

"Not a lot, but pretty steady. Some folks it helps with headaches, some folks it don't. Lots of folks are afraid to use it, because they've heard it's poisonous, which it can be."

"Did I hear you say something about . . . not giving it to a woman?"

"Not if she's pregnant. Ergot can bring on birth contractions. Sometimes doctors use it to induce an overdue birth. That's why I'm careful when I sell it. Every pharmacist has heard the horror story about the pregnant woman who makes an ergot tea to cure her megrim, and causes herself to abort the baby. Imagine having that on your conscience! Of course, some women use ergot to cause an intentional abortion."

"Really? Straight ergot?"

"Oh, they mix it with other things. There's all sorts of formulas. Stuff tastes foul and it's hard to keep down, so they usually put it in a digestive tea of some sort."

"You mean . . . like chamomile tea?"

"Chamomile, sure. And sometimes they'll mix in other toxins, to make sure they kill the fetus—foxglove, hellebore, mistletoe, cotton root . . ." He saw the look on Will's face and nodded gravely. "You're right to blanch, young man. Abortion's a dangerous business for everyone concerned. A woman can kill herself along with her baby. And in Texas, unless you're a doctor and the mother's life is in danger, helping a woman induce an abortion can get you five years in the penitentiary."

Will stared at the jar in his hands.

"Well, are you going to put that away like I asked you, or are you just going to stand there?" said the pharmacist.

"Right away, sir." Now Will understood why McCutcheon looked so agitated when he climbed into the buggy, and why Delia gave him a kiss on the cheek. Together, they had purchased the formula for an abortion.

He wondered if Eula knew.

29

*C*IGARS all round!" cried William Pendleton Gaines. "It's a girl!"

Beelzebub was dispatched to fetch a bottle of Irish whiskey from Gaines's office. The staff of the *Statesman* gathered around with their cups and the bottle was empty within seconds. The atmosphere became dense with smoke.

"A perfectly healthy baby girl!" boasted Gaines. "Mother and child are both resting comfortably. And let me tell you, gentlemen, Augusta went through the ordeal like a soldier. Like a general! Women are braver than men, that's for sure. You know what she said to me, right in the middle of it? I was out on the gallery, mopping the sweat from my forehead, trying to catch a breath of fresh air, and she called to me from her bed, 'Stop pacing back and forth like that, you're making me nervous!'"

Across the room, Hiram ran his unlit cigar under his nose, sniffing it. "Why do you suppose it is, Shoemaker, that we have this custom of proud fathers handing out cigars to celebrate the proof of their virility?"

"Never thought about it." Dave puffed on his cigar, surrounding himself with smoke.

"Shoemaker, pull that thing out of your mouth. Now take a good look at it! Doesn't it strike you that the shape of a cigar is suggestive of a certain part of the male anatomy?" Hiram held his cigar between thumb and forefinger at a forty-five-degree angle and wagged it at Dave.

Dave looked dubiously at Hiram's cigar, then at his own. "Blast you, Hiram Glass! Now how can I possibly put this thing back into my mouth after the picture you've put in my head?" He glanced across the room, where the other employees were gathered in a circle around Gaines, all puffing away on their cigars. A moment later they turned their heads toward Dave, wondering what he was laughing at.

Jimmy was drinking again.

In the middle of the afternoon he had announced that he was off to Taylor, eight miles up the road, to buy supplies. When Jimmy didn't show up at suppertime, Eula's worst suspicions seemed to be confirmed. There was a saloon in Taylor.

Delia was visiting the farm. She, Eula, and McCutcheon had finished supper, and the colored serving woman had just brought out a tray with coffee, cream, and sugar, when Jimmy arrived home. They knew he was drunk from the noises he made. The front door opened, followed by the sound of stumbling as Jimmy tripped on the threshold. The front door closed with a quiet, stealthy click. Then there was a banging noise and a muffled curse; that was Jimmy bumping against the little table in the foyer.

They heard his heavy tread in the parlor. They heard him make cooing noises as he stopped to look at the baby, sleeping in a crib next to the upright piano. A moment later he appeared in the doorway of the dining room. He had the hoot-owl look he got when he was drunk—his lips puckered in a circle and his eyes unnaturally big. His shirt was stained with sweat at the armpits, and his sweat reeked of whiskey. To see him that way, Eula could hardly remember the handsome boy who had once courted her. She lowered her eyes and twisted her napkin between her fists.

Delia sat upright and stared hard at her brother. McCutcheon leaned back in his chair and crossed his arms. "What the hell have you been up to?" he said.

Jimmy smirked. "Why, George, you oughtn't to say a word like 'hell' in front of two *ladies*." His speech was only a little slurred, but that was no indication of how drunk he was; Jimmy could keep talking in a fairly normal manner long after he couldn't walk a straight line.

"That's not an answer, Jimmy."

"I don't see how it's any of your business what I get up to, George McCutcheon, so long as I do my work around here."

"You left quite a bit of work undone this afternoon."

"So? I'll get to it tomorrow. There's always tomorrow in this godforsaken place. No shortage of tomorrows."

"For heaven's sake," said Delia, "have some coffee and try to sober up."

"Why are you always scolding me, Sister? Why are you always against me?" Jimmy stared blearily at the coffee service on the table. "Did I miss dinner? I suppose I did. But there's no cups! Where's that colored girl? Hiding in the kitchen? Here, I'll set out the china." He stumbled to the cupboard. While the others flinched, he pulled out cups and saucers and placed them haphazardly on the table. The clatter was alarming, but nothing broke.

Jimmy went to his regular chair, pulled it out from the table, sat down heavily, and reached for a cup. He proceeded to pour cream halfway to the top of his cup, then added several spoonfuls of sugar, then pulled a flask from his pocket and topped off the cream with a generous amount of whiskey. He swallowed the concoction in a single draught.

Delia made a face. McCutcheon scowled. Jimmy stared back at them with his hoot-owl expression.

"Jimmy, you look like a fool," said Eula. She crumpled her napkin and threw it to the floor. "Your eyes are that big!" She made two circles with her forefingers and thumbs.

"Say that again." The sudden menace in Jimmy's voice was strangely at odds with his spooked expression.

"I said, your eyes are that big!" Eula leaned across the table, extending her arms so that her hands were inches from Jimmy's face.

He grabbed at her wrist, but she snatched it away. He picked up his empty cup and cocked his arm. Eula ducked. Jimmy threw with a drunk's aim, and the cup came near to hitting Delia as it sailed across the room and shattered against the wall.

Eula let out a little scream. Delia got up and ran from the room.

"I'll kill you!" Jimmy shouted. He grabbed a table knife and tried to get up, but he was clumsy and fell from his chair.

McCutcheon banged the table. "Stop it!"

In the parlor, the baby woke and began to cry.

Jimmy got to his feet. Eula stayed where she was, holding her hands up defensively, staring back at Jimmy defiantly.

"I'll kill you!" he shouted again, brandishing the table knife.

"Stop it!" yelled McCutcheon.

Delia ran back into the room and grabbed Eula's shoulders. Eula refused to take her eyes from Jimmy's. Delia had to pull her from the room. In the parlor, Eula hurriedly picked up the crying baby, then Delia ushered her through the foyer, out of the house and into the yard.

The moment Eula was out of sight, Jimmy seemed to lose steam. He looked at the knife in his hand, then at McCutcheon. "It's none of your business, George. Don't interfere. This is between me and my wife."

"Not when it's under my roof," said McCutcheon. He stayed in his chair, his jaw thrust out and his body stiff with tension. "For God's sake, put that knife down, Jimmy. You're liable to hurt yourself."

Jimmy's lips trembled. "Maybe I should. Maybe that's what I ought to do."

"Don't be stupid, Jimmy. Damn it, if you can't hold your liquor, you ought not to drink at all! You're acting a fool. Now put that knife down."

Jimmy turned the knife this way and that, catching his reflection in the blade. "Maybe I am a fool." He sobbed and started to weep. "I'm a fool for her, George. Eula's made a fool of me. She's seeing another man."

"What? Don't be ridiculous."

"All those trips back to Austin—she spends as much time there as she does here. The two of them are always whispering behind my back—"

"Who?"

"Her and Delia. My own sister, helping her make a fool of me! They think I don't know what's going on, but I do. She's found a lover."

"Jimmy, what are you saying?" McCutcheon kept his eyes on the knife.

"Eula has another man."

"Do you have the least bit of evidence of such a thing?"

"I don't need evidence! I'm her husband. I can tell."

"For Christ's sake, you don't know what you're saying."

"She doesn't love me anymore, George. I don't think she even loves the baby. She's wicked! But I love her. I can't help it."

"You're talking nonsense, Jimmy. Sure, Eula's not happy here. She hasn't been from the start. She likes it better in Austin. That's why she goes there so much. That doesn't mean . . ." McCutcheon shook his head. "She's with Delia all the time she's in Austin, or else visiting her father at the hotel. She sleeps under your parents' roof. How can you imagine she has time to sneak off and see a lover? It's your imagination that's wicked, not Eula. You're drunk and you're letting your imagination run off with you."

Jimmy looked at him pathetically, his face flushed and wet with tears. "I am?"

"You drink yourself into a stupor, and then you come up with these crazy notions. Of course Eula loves you, and the baby. How can you think anything else? It's your drinking she hates. Who can blame her?"

Jimmy put the knife on the table. "You're right, George. You're right, you're right, you're right! I'm a drunken fool, and who can blame her if she doesn't love me anymore?"

"Jimmy, for God's sake—"

"But I'll tell you this!" Jimmy was suddenly belligerent again. "If I ever found out that she was going with another man—if I ever found that out for a fact—do you know what I'd do?"

"Jimmy, stop—"

"I'd kill her, that's what I'd do. I'd kill her. And then I'd kill myself."

"For God's sake, Jimmy," McCutcheon whispered hoarsely, "how can you even think such a thing? You're a better man than that. What would you do, make an orphan of your child? Or would you kill the baby, too?" Jimmy gave a start and drew back, appalled. "There, do you see how crazy this is? Just stop this kind of talk, do you hear? Stop it, before Eula comes back and hears you."

Jimmy quietly wept. He staggered and leaned against the wall.

McCutcheon looked at the shattered cup on the floor. His late wife had inherited the set of china from her mother. "Go wash your face, Jimmy. Then go to bed."

Out in the yard, Delia and Eula stood side by side in the darkness, warily watching the front door. Eula held the baby. He had stopped crying, but he was restless and kept thrashing his limbs. The chirring of crickets rose and fell on the still, warm air.

"You shouldn't have stood up to him like that," said Delia. "When you saw me run, you should have done the same. I can't believe I had to come back after you!"

"I don't want him to think I'm scared of him when he drinks. I'm not."

"Then why are you trembling?"

"Because I'm angry! I despise him when he's like that."

"But what's the sense of taunting him?"

"I didn't!"

"You told him he was a fool to his face."

"I told him the truth. I can't stand the stupid way he looks when he's drunk."

Delia laughed bitterly. "Sweet, sweet Eulalia, you have so much to learn about men!"

"I know a thing or two already."

"I suppose you do." Delia looked at her sidelong. "Eula, I've never seen you like this."

"I've never felt like this. I swear, Delia, I've had enough of it."

"Do you mean to leave him?"

Eula's defiance abruptly deserted her. "I don't see how I could. What would my father think? I don't have any money of my own." She looked at the infant in her arms. "And the baby . . ."

"Jimmy *does* love you. You and the baby both."

"Does he?" Eula watched the door. "What do you think is happening in there?"

"George McCutcheon is doing whatever menfolk do to calm each other down. He'll do a better job than we could."

"Either that, or Jimmy's stabbed him to death and he'll be coming after me next."

"Nonsense! You know as well as I do that Jimmy's all bluster and no backbone."

"Is that why you ran from the room so fast?"

Delia sighed. "I've been fighting with Jimmy a lot longer than you have, ever since we were children. He used to throw rocks at me."

Eula laughed. "It's a good thing his aim is so rotten!"

"When he throws a tantrum, it's best just to get out of his way. Once it burns itself out, he feels stupid and sorry."

Eula swallowed hard. "Delia, he picked up a knife and said he'd kill me."

Delia put her arm around Eula's shoulders. "Oh, Eula—you *are* trembling! Don't even think it, Eula! He'd kill himself first. You know that's the truth."

"Is it?"

"Eula, I'm no fool where my brother's concerned. I see him for what he is."

"But have you ever seen him so crazy? Delia, you ran from the table like you were running for your life."

A shadow moved across the parlor window and a figure appeared at the door. The women stiffened, then relaxed when George McCutcheon stepped onto the porch. "You can come back inside now," he said. "I put him to bed. I'm surprised you can't hear his snoring all the way out here."

The two women walked to the porch, Eula holding the baby and Delia holding Eula. To Eula, everything seemed wrong with the world. The farm was a prison. Her marriage was a failure. The baby in her arms felt as heavy as a block of stone. The only thing that felt good and right to her was the touch of Delia's arm around her shoulders, holding her tight to still her trembling.

3 0

⌘

$\mathcal{I}$N retrospect, it was fitting that they came together on the grounds of the lunatic asylum.

It was a Sunday. After church, Will was supposed to go boating on the river with his serenading pals, but at the last minute the plan fell through. Will had found himself with nothing to do, restlessly pacing the front porch of the boarding house.

It was yet another endless August day. For two weeks there had not even been a thunderstorm to break the monotony. Every day the sky was the same, an endless expanse of blue crowded with puffy white clouds receding to infinity in every direction. Below the sky lay the little city, and all within and around the city was the living earth, rank with greenery, overrun with trees, vines, and weeds all steaming with moisture. The whole world seemed sapped of energy, limp from humidity. Easterners imagined Austin to be in the arid West, but Will had lived in true cattle country and knew better. Austin was in and of the South—the hot and humid, sweaty and sultry South, where the month of August stretched into infinity like the puffy white clouds overhead, and a fellow could pace a hole in a porch on an endless Sunday afternoon with nothing to do.

It was Dave who rescued him. Will looked up at the sound of a passing hackney cab and saw Dave Shoemaker inside. Dave stopped the cab, waved him over, and asked if he cared to accompany him on an excursion to the asylum grounds.

The State Lunatic Asylum was located on the Waco Road, three miles north of town. The isolated complex of buildings dominated the flat, empty landscape, and presented a curiously whimsical aspect to the approaching visitor. The limestone buildings had pitched roofs surmounted by dozens of octagonal, ornately decorated cupolas, each of which rose to a spire capped by a spherical knob. The effect of so many pointed domes on the skyline suggested a sprawling Turkish castle or a Russian kremlin plunked down in the middle of Texas. The haze of a steaming August afternoon smeared the horizon, confounding any sense of distance and lending the asylum an even more fantastical aspect. The shimmering mass of domed rooftops seemed to hover just above the earth.

The asylum's board of directors held a progressive, environmental view of lunacy. They believed that immediate physical surroundings had a tremendous influence on the insane. Sights, sounds, colors, and smells had the power to increase or diminish the unsettled state of the lunatic's mind. Ugliness aggravated insanity; beauty alleviated it. Thus it was good therapy to remove the insane from the noisome hubbub of the city. Pleasant, orderly surroundings were the key to recovery. Accordingly, the board had landscaped the extensive grounds adjacent to the asylum with flower gardens, lawns, shaded pathways, statuary, fountains, a greenhouse with rare tropical plants, a gymnasium, outdoor exercise yards, swings, and tennis courts. On Sundays, the grounds were free and open to the public.

Dave and Will descended from the cab. They walked through the gate and down a sunny gravel pathway scented by towering banks of honeysuckle. The path continued through a grassy area strewn with colorful blankets wherever pecan or oak trees offered shade. Amid wicker picnic baskets, men leaned back on their elbows with shirtsleeves rolled up and collars unbuttoned on account of the heat, and ladies in sunbonnets and white dresses cooled themselves with bamboo fans. Flower beds surrounded a sparkling fountain with a winged cupid. Beyond the fountain was an open grassy area where boys were playing football. From beyond a nearby hedge came the sound of tennis balls being batted.

"You're here to work?" said Will.

"Yes, Superintendent Denton has deigned to give the *Statesman* an hour of his time."

"On a Sunday?"

"This is the day he can show off his best inmates comporting themselves among the visitors."

"Isn't this a story for Hiram Glass? He covers state affairs."

"Yes, it was supposed to be Hiram, but he woke up feeling too poorly to get out of bed."

"What's wrong with him?"

"Severe case of Guy Town influenza, I suspect."

"A hangover?"

"Hiram's suddenly discovered wine, women, and song. At his age! Whatever he got up to last night, he's not up for interviewing Superintendent Denton today, so here I am. But I don't mind filling in for him. Being a crime reporter has been pretty dull lately. Hasn't been a servant girl murder in months."

"I suppose we're due for another one," said Will.

From the band shell at the far end of the grounds came the strains of a Strauss waltz.

"That's my cue," said Dave, looking at his pocket watch. "I'm to meet the superintendent at the band shell in ten minutes. I suppose you can amuse yourself for an hour or so?"

Will strolled down the gravel path. A woman came toward him, pushing a baby carriage.

"Mr. Porter, isn't it?"

"Mrs. Campbell!" He tipped his hat and glanced at the sleeping infant in the carriage. He frowned, momentarily nonplussed. According to Emmeline Wilkins, Delia was a widow and childless—and determined to remain so, if his suspicions were correct. Whose baby was this?

As quickly as the question formed in his mind, so did the answer. His pulse quickened. He saw her from the corner of his eye, standing beside Delia. He felt a sudden panic.

"Mr. Porter."

He looked up. As soon as his eyes met hers, his anxiety vanished. He felt as a spooked horse must feel, calmed by its rider. He felt at once as he had felt that night on Emmeline's porch, held by her gaze, enclosed within it, safe and warm. To look into her eyes was to feel his soul come to rest.

Delia took a sidelong look at each of them, and then, without a word, pushed the baby carriage down the path and left the two of them alone.

Will glanced about. No one was watching. No one could hear. "Eula! I think about you all the time."

"I think about you, too, Will." Another woman might have lowered her eyes demurely, but her gaze was steady.

He stepped back, so that he could see all of her. Her dress was white, finished with a layer of some loose gossamer stuff; where the sun broke though the canopy of leaves above them, the material shimmered with dazzling spots of light. The sleeves were modestly long, but made only of the gossamer stuff, loose and puffy, through which he could plainly see the sleek flesh of her shoulders and limbs. Her hair was pulled up beneath a white hat made of the same gossamer stuff, with a broad, round brim to shield her from the sun. Strands of golden hair escaped from the hat to float in wisps about her face. The neckline of the dress left her throat bare; for a necklace she wore a blue ribbon with a porcelain locket. He lowered his eyes. "You're wearing your wedding ring today."

Her face hardened. "My husband's name is Jimmy. He's Delia's brother. And I have a baby, as you've seen. I should have told you at Emmeline's."

"I knew you were married when I met you. It doesn't matter."

She lowered her eyes. He felt her slipping away from him. He could hardly keep from touching her.

"This place—all these people. We can't—"

"My sister-in-law is here to chaperone me. I don't see how it could be improper for us to stand here and talk, Will."

"But I don't want to just stand here and talk."

She looked at him steadily. "I understand." She bit her lower lip. "I'll be in town tomorrow. During the day, I could—but I suppose you must work."

"No." He shook his head and laughed. "I'm a wastrel, a good-for-nothing. My days are my own. I'm free as a millionaire."

"Do you know a place called Swenson's Ruin?"

"I've been there." He frowned. "But it's like this place, isn't it? People go there to picnic—"

"Not on a Monday at three in the afternoon. There won't be a soul there, except us." She reached out and boldly touched his arm, then turned and walked away.

The streetcar carried him east on Pecan Street, past stores and saloons and into a part of town he seldom visited. The streetcar passed the parklike tract of land containing the old French Legation, turned north up Navasota Street for a few blocks, and then headed east again, skirting the State Cemetery. At the stop for Tillotson Normal and Collegiate Institute he disembarked. He walked across the grounds feeling out of place among so many colored faces. The main building was a four-story structure with a mansard roof, like something on a Parisian boulevard. From an open window he heard a lecturer expounding on a problem in geometry.

Beyond the college grounds, where the land sloped down toward Boggy Creek, the landscape became wilder. A grid of streets had been laid out, but the houses were few and far apart. The dirt road came to an abrupt dead-end amid a mass of scraggly undergrowth, including a daunting array of prickly pears. He began to think that he had lost his way, until he spied a horse and buggy hidden within a coppice of oak saplings. He had arrived early, but she had arrived ahead of him. She was as eager for their meeting as he was.

After a bit of searching, he located a pathway and entered the thicket. The atmosphere was stifling and utterly still, until the sudden clacking of a cicada gave him a start. The insect's monotonous droning rose and fell behind him as he penetrated farther into the thicket.

The narrow, stony path veered this way and that, and finally opened into a large, gloomy clearing shadowed by ivy-covered trees. The place was like the interior of a cathedral, with a sense of enclosure and lofty space, illuminated by a uniform gray light except where a few sunbeams filtered through, muted and colored by the leaves. He was on a bluff above Boggy Creek where the land had once been cleared and then reclaimed by nature.

In the middle of the clearing stood a ruin of stone walls marking the cruciform plan of a mansion with four wings. The weathered walls were two stories high and traced with clinging vines. There was no roof.

Scattered about the clearing, amid weeds and prickly pears, were big blocks of stone spotted with green and yellow lichen. Some were carefully stacked, while others lay tumbled about. A horned toad sat atop a fragment of an ornamental cornice. It puffed up its body at Will's approach, peered at him defiantly, then scurried into the underbrush.

The ruin had been built by a Swedish immigrant named Swenson who made a fortune ranching. But Swenson had been a staunch Unionist, and when Texas seceded he sold his properties at a loss, fled to New York, and never came back. The grand villa he had begun on the outskirts of town was left unfinished and allowed to fall into ruins.

"This would have been the ballroom."

Will looked up. She stood within the ruins at one of the bay windows. A ray of sunlight penetrated the leafy canopy and transformed her unpinned hair into a golden aureole.

"I've been coming here since I was a little girl. I love to come into this room and imagine it with Persian carpets and fine wallpaper, paintings in gilded frames and crystal chandeliers. And filled with people—men in evening dress and women in fancy gowns. I think it would have been the grandest house in Texas."

Will stood below the window with his hat in his hands. "You're like me," he said quietly. "You like to imagine things."

Her smile was melancholy. "Sometimes it doesn't take much imagination to see the way things should have been. Come see for yourself. Be careful of the places where the floor's fallen through."

Will circled the ruins until he found the porch, which lay tilted and broken. He passed through the open portal and went to the place where she was waiting for him.

31

S H E said she would come that night. She never did. Still, Alec waited. He saved himself for her.

He waited in the little storage room at the Black Elephant; *their* room, as he had come to think of it. He reclined on the old settee, a pillow behind his head and his legs slightly bent; the settee was big, but not so big that a man of his height could stretch out head to toe without having to bend a bit. He had taken off his shirt and balled it up behind his head, to add a bit more fluff to the old, broken-in pillow. His pants were loosely gathered at his waist by a thin rope belt, but his fly was undone. The opened flaps formed a snug cinch for his genitals, which were exposed to the warm, humid night air. At the moment, he was only partially aroused. He had not touched himself for several minutes and was deliberately trying to think of something, anything, other than Rebecca.

It was early Sunday morning, in the wee hours before dawn of the next to last day of August. Alec Mack, for one, was ready for the month to be over. The weather had been beastly hot, hotter than any summer he could remember . . .

His body was covered with sweat. The lamp that burned low in the corner lit up the little beads of moisture that clung to the fine whorls of hair across his chest and belly. Rebecca liked to run her palms over the nappy fur that covered the hard ridges of his belly and the broad planes of his chest, especially when he was slick with fresh sweat. The thought of her touch made him reach down and grip himself, the way she sometimes did, to make a fuss over him, to guide him into her. He was fully hard in an instant, ready for her. Where was she?

While out doing Saturday shopping for the Weed family, Rebecca had dropped by his mother's place. Sallie Mack didn't approve of her son receiving a female visitor, even in the middle of the day. Mr. Phillips had been kind enough to allow Alec to sleep in Sallie's little house and had even given Alec a bit of work now and then; Sallie didn't want him to rile things up. But it wasn't the first time Rebecca had dropped by, and as she never stayed for more than a minute or two, and was always polite and respectful to Sallie, and appeared to be the only woman in Alec's life, Sallie grudgingly received her. Rebecca seemed too old for Alec—the woman had an eleven-year-old daughter!—but she was certainly pretty. Sallie gave the two of them a minute alone on the stoop of the little house while she stepped around the corner to water her tomato vines.

Rebecca told Alec that she could slip out for an hour or two late that night, as long as her little girl was sleeping soundly. As usual, Alec had to ask Lem Brooks for permission to use the storage room, but over the course of the summer that had become little more than a formality; with the onset of the hot weather, Hugh Hancock went to bed early and trusted Lem to count the till and close up the Elephant. The storage room was available for Alec just about any night he needed it.

So there he was on the settee, waiting for Rebecca long after the hour when she should have come, saving himself for her, thinking of their last time together . . .

His pulled his hand away, not an instant too soon.

He lay still except for the rise and fall of his chest, savoring the sweet ache of frustration. He turned his head and nuzzled the pillow, smelling her scent on it—not a perfume, because she never wore such a thing, but the scent of her body where she had touched the pillow, placed beneath her hips, or behind her shoulders, or under the dense black jungle of her hair.

Alec tossed the pillow aside. He couldn't stand to be in the stuffy little room a moment longer. He got to his feet, gathered himself inside his pants and closed his fly. He picked up the lamp and stepped into the barroom. The tall windows facing Pecan Street were shuttered after closing time, and the big, long room was pitch-dark. Alec tiptoed to the back door and tested it; sure enough, Lem had left it unlocked. Rebecca could have come in with no problem.

He blew out the lamp, set it aside, and stepped into the alley. He expected the soft glare of the near-full moon, but the moon had set already. It was the vague, uncertain hour before dawn. The world was dimly lit by a glow that seemed to have no source and to cast no shadows.

He walked up the alley, past the little house where Hugh Hancock lived, and circled around to the front of the Elephant. Not a soul was stirring. The whole length of Pecan Street was as quiet as a graveyard.

He decided to walk by the house where Rebecca lived. The place was nearby, only a couple of blocks south and a couple of blocks west. To be sure, Rebecca had told him never, ever to come calling. Rebecca's employer, Mr. Valentine Weed, owner of the Globe Livery Stable, considered her a model of colored womanhood and took personal pride in her apparent chastity; no man had ever been known to call on Rebecca and her little Mary. But Alec had no intention of paying a call. He would merely stroll by the place, just to see what he might see.

That was his intention, anyway.

His course took him across open ground, for behind the buildings on the south side of Pecan Street the whole back half of the block was a parking lot, and empty at night. The next block south had been left empty by the city planners, who intended someday to make it into a park. It was while crossing this open, barren patch of weeds that Alec first heard the ghostly howling.

In that wide-open space, beneath the pale, predawn sky, the howling seemed to echo from several places at once. It was impossible to tell how many dogs produced it. When Alec stopped and stood still to listen, the howling vanished altogether, and all he heard was his own breath and the beating of his heart.

He thought at once of the creatures Lem Brooks had been warning him about, ever since Lem got out of jail. But what did a pack of howling dogs have to do with Lem's dog ghosts? Nothing at all, Alec told himself. So what if a few harmless, hungry mutts were prowling the alleys downtown, looking for scraps of food? There was no cause to feel afraid of such wretched creatures. A fellow ought to pity them.

Still, when the barking and howling recommenced, Alec gave a start and hurried on, feeling suddenly exposed and vulnerable standing in the middle of the open patch. He reached the far corner and headed down Cedar Street. The Weed house was just a block away.

It occurred to him that his path was also taking him very close to a certain other house. It was only a block south of the Weeds that the murder of Eliza Shelley had taken place.

Alec shivered, though the air was warm. First, around the new year, Mol-

lie Smith had been horribly murdered and molested. Come May, Eliza
Shelley had been killed and ravished on her bedroom floor, in the presence
of her three little children, a crime almost impossible to imagine. Only a
couple of weeks later, the same thing happened to Irene Cross across from
Scholz's Beer Garden. Since then, three months had passed, and there had
been no more murders. Maybe the summer had just been too damned hot
for the killer to stir himself!

The baying of the hounds recommenced. They were definitely coming
closer, and now he could hear three distinct howls. Three women had been
murdered—and now three dogs were running through the streets of Austin,
howling and barking, coming closer and closer . . .

He knew what Lem would say: *Cain't you hear them dog ghosts, come to
warn you off? Run, you crazy fool!*

The Weed residence was just ahead. There were lights inside the house.
Why should that be, at such an early hour, when everyone in Austin was
asleep? Unless something was wrong . . .

Alec's heart was in his throat. He tried to swallow it back. Why was he letting himself get spooked? Just because some dogs were howling, and the
house was lit up, and Rebecca had promised to come but never showed up . . .

The Weed residence was situated on a little hill above the intersection of
San Jacinto and Cedar streets. There was no easy way to tiptoe up, peek in
a window, and tiptoe off; the retaining wall that shored up the hill restricted
access to a flight of steps that went directly up to the front porch, or else to
the driveway, which entered the back yard through a break in the wall.
There was no question of Alec going to the front door and knocking. He
sneaked into the back yard.

Behind the main house was a little cottage, but from what Rebecca had
told him Alec knew that it was used only as a wash house. Rebecca and her
daughter, Mary, slept in the big house, in a little room off the kitchen. Yet the
door to the little wash house was open and emitted a shifting light, as from a
lamp held by someone moving about inside. Two men's voices came from
the little house, as well. Alec stayed back amid the shrubbery and listened.

"Awful! How could anyone—"

"She's no more than a child! It's unspeakable. Where's her mother?"

"Inside. Unconscious when we found her. Still not in her right mind—
has no idea what happened. I think she must have been hit in the head,
sandbagged maybe—there's no blood in the house that I could see. The
fiend must have knocked the child unconscious, too, before he dragged her
back here, and did this to her."

"The mother doesn't know yet?"

"No. Oh, God, she mustn't see this! It would surely kill her."

"Have you sent for—"

"Marshal Lee's in the house now, and the doctor's been called for. The marshal sent for a tracker right away—ought to be here any minute. We'll hunt the monster down like the animal he is. Holy Mary! Did you see that?"

"What? What?"

"I swear, I saw the child twitch! I think she may still be alive! Oh, Jesus, I'm sick . . ."

The light within the wash house swayed and pitched, then a man emerged from the door. In one hand he held the lamp, in the other a shotgun. He ran jerkily into the yard, his body stooped. He put down the lamp and clutched his stomach. Not ten feet from where Alec stood, the man proceeded to vomit.

Quickly, while the man was still bent over, Alec bolted down the driveway into the street. He ran blindly, not sure what direction he was going. He rounded a corner and suddenly saw them emerging around the far corner of the block—the dog ghosts!

There were three of them, as he had thought, three of the biggest and meanest-looking hounds he had ever seen, all barking and snarling, leaping wildly in the air, their eyes flashing with green fire. The sight was so uncanny that Alec nearly fainted from terror.

He turned to run. The first rays of the rising sun struck his eyes, dazzling him. The terrible glint in the hounds' eyes had not been hellfire, but flashes of sunlight. When he glanced over his shoulder, he saw why they seemed to leap so strangely in midair—they were restrained on leashes held by the man who rounded the corner after them. The man shouted:

"Stop, nigger! Stop where you are!"

But Alec didn't stop. He ran as fast as he could.

32

⌘

S AND BAGGED, they say. Mother and child both hit in the head—rendered unconscious—then the little girl was dragged out of the house to an outbuilding . . ."

John Robertson looked across the table at William Pendleton Gaines, who was waving his fork and speaking with a mouth full of mincemeat pie. The mayor had been dreading this lunch at the Iron Front ever since he scheduled it the previous week. Relations between himself and Gaines were strained at best, given the *Statesman's* relentless editorializing against the city government. But Gaines had requested this meeting as a member of the Board of Trade, and Robertson could hardly have refused. There was always a slim hope that he might yet secure the paper's endorsement in the upcoming mayoral election.

The purpose of their Monday lunch was for Gaines to introduce the mayor to two prominent newcomers to Austin, Dr. Fry and Dr. Terry. The ostensible agenda was a discussion of the business climate, in particular the pros and cons of constructing a dam, but the horrifying events of Sunday overshadowed all else.

"According to the *Statesman*, the monster ravished the child in a most brutal manner," said Dr. Terry, "and drove something long and sharp, like an iron pin, into each of the girl's ears. You might think such a thing would have killed her instantly . . ."

"Yet she was still alive when Mr. Weed found her later," noted Dr. Fry, "though not for long. There was no way to stop the copious bleeding from her ears."

"They say the mother should survive, at least," offered Gaines. "But she has no recollection of her assailant. Either she never saw the man, or the blow dislodged her memory. An arrest was made—but this morning the police released the fellow!"

"There was no evidence against him, except that he happened to be in the vicinity," noted the mayor glumly. "No blood on him, no weapons."

"No evidence?" said Gaines. "The man ran from the bloodhounds, didn't he?"

"Most people do." The mayor cleared his throat. "Anyway, the district attorney is not much impressed with the reliability of bloodhounds. The only thing more unreliable, according to him, is an eyewitness."

The blind phrenologist laughed. "I'm obliged to agree with you there, Mayor Robertson. But they say those hounds chased the Negro for hours, all over town. The fellow must have strong legs—but not much sense! Somehow he acquired some asafoetida powder—broke into a druggist's shop, perhaps—which he sprinkled all over his feet. When the officers finally cornered him, they had to pinch their noses, the stuff stinks so. He told them he thought it would throw the hounds off the scent. Imagine! The foul odor of asafoetida is so strong that a man with a head cold could have tracked him down. I say a fellow that stupid must be guilty of something. What is his name?"

"Alec Mack," said Dr. Terry.

"Oh, how I should like to examine the head of this Mack fellow!" declared Fry. "The expert testimony of a phrenologist, pertaining to criminal characteristics of the accused, should be admissible in court! If it were so, I would offer my services at once, free of charge. The fellow who ravished little Mary Ramey will almost certainly display a misshapen amatory bulge at the back of his head, a clear sign of depravity. His forehead will slope back sharply above his eyes, betraying an absence of moral character. And I would not be surprised if his head flares outward behind the ears, where the traits of destructiveness and secretiveness are situated. Give me clay, and I believe I could mold the head of this fiend who ravished little Mary Ramey, sight unseen—relying solely on the science of phrenology!"

"Fascinating!" said Gaines. "You might revolutionize the science of criminal detection!"

Mayor Robertson impatiently waved to the waiter and called for the check.

Swenson's Ruin lingered in Will's memory.

In the shell of the unfinished ballroom they had drawn close, embraced and kissed. They explored each other with their hands, at first tentatively, then feverishly, tearing at each other's clothing in a kind of delirium, exposing just enough of themselves to become joined. They remained upright, Eula's back against the wall, the sun beaming down through swirling motes of dust.

Then they heard voices in the clearing.

They paused, still joined, looking into each other's eyes, trembling with pleasure, listening. There were two voices—a colored couple. Will and Eula never stopped, but continued more slowly and deliberately, the constraint of keeping silent adding an exquisite, excruciating delicacy to the act. They looked into each other's eyes the whole time.

She clutched him and convulsed. He thought, incongruously, of holding on for dear life to a bolting horse. There was the same sense of striving to contain something wild and willful, the struggle of flesh against flesh.

He felt his own crisis begin. He tried to withdraw from her. She clutched him so tightly that he lacked the strength to escape her. He thought his very essence must be melting and pouring into her, leaving him an empty shell, like the ruin around them.

Swenson's Ruin had been too public, after all. But where could they meet? "I know of a place," Eula told him. It would cost money, she said. He told her he had none. She said it didn't matter; she would pay. She would take care of everything. He would merely have to meet her there, the next time she came to town.

The place was a house on Congress Avenue, close to the river, owned by a widow named May Tobin.

Days passed, then weeks, and Will did not hear from her. She had given him no way to contact her. All he could do was remember Swenson's Ruin, and wait.

September was half over when she finally sent word. He saw the postmark when he pulled the letter from the box on the Harrells' front porch, and tore it open at once.

> Mr. Jones,
> Our hostess will be expecting us at 3 p.m. on Wednesday.
> The house number is 103.
>
> E.

"But that's today!" he said out loud. He looked at his pocket watch; it was only ten o'clock. But what if he had gone out tramping before the post came, and had come back after dark to find her letter? The thought tied his stomach into knots. At the same time, the prospect of seeing her again, after so long, on such short notice, made him light-headed.

Through the window above his desk, the clerk who manned the front office at Zimpelman & Son's ice factory had a clear view of the unassuming house catty-corner across the street at 103 Congress Avenue.

"Look at that one," said the clerk to a delivery driver, shortly before three o'clock that afternoon. "If Mr. Webster's dictionary had an entry for Nervous Ned, they could use a picture of that fellow to go with it! Have you ever seen one so green?"

"Nervous Ned" was the clerk's name for a particular kind of caller at 103. Most visitors strode directly to the door, rapped the knocker, and stepped inside without ever turning around, inviting as little scrutiny as possible. Then there were the Nervous Neds.

The clerk and the delivery driver watched the light-framed young man of slightly less than medium height, with wavy ginger hair and a well-waxed mustache, who paced to and fro in front of the house across the street.

"First I seed him comin' this way, down the Avenue," said the clerk. "Passed by Widow Tobin's house and barely broke stride; glanced at the place and kept walkin'. Looked like he might be headed for the lumberyard, but didn't stop there. Got to the toll bridge, then turned around. Crossed over to this side, but wasn't lookin' for ice. Headed back up the Avenue, stopped across the street from Tobin's house and just stood there, starin'. I had to help a customer, probably took me a good five minutes, and when I came back here and looked out the window—there Nervous Ned still was, eyeballin' that house like a cat watchin' a bird! Finally crossed the street again, zigzaggin' back and forth. Now he's in front of the house, pacin'. Probably take him another five minutes 'fore he gets up his courage to knock on the door."

"I'll bet he never does," said the delivery man with a laugh.

"I'd take you up on that bet, but it'd be stealin' your money. I've seen many a feller out there callin' at the Tobin house, ever'thing from Brazen Bob to Nervous Ned, and they *always* knock, ever' one of 'em. Just takes some longer than others to screw up the courage. See! Looky there!"

Sure enough, the young man, looking fretfully at his pocket watch, made his way to the porch and reached for the knocker.

"How I envy the young buck," said the clerk ruefully. He was a married man with four children, and it seemed to him that the young caller at May Tobin's house must have a life of infinitely greater pleasures and infinitely fewer complications. The clerk turned back to his paperwork.

Across the street, the door to 103 Congress Avenue opened. The young man on the threshold managed to say, "I believe you're expecting me. My name is . . . Mr. Jones."

The woman who answered the door gave him an appraising look. She smiled, and had to stifle a laugh. The pursuit of female company brought out the comical in most men, she had discovered, but few had ever struck her as being so awkwardly equipped for the chase as this one. She seldom had callers so young. Was he blushing because of the situation, or because he had just told a lie? "Ah, yes, Mr. Jones! I am indeed expecting you! I'm Mrs. Tobin, but you must call me May. I'm pleased to meet you."

May Tobin shook his hand with a grip as firm as any man's. She was not quite what Will had expected; she looked like someone's grandmother. He stepped into the foyer and she closed the door behind him.

"Normally, when a man visits my house for the first time, I like to show him a little hospitality—get to know him a bit, perhaps over a glass of sherry in the parlor. But I've heard such glowing accounts of your character, Mr. Jones, that I feel I know you already. And Miss Harmon arrived ahead of you. I know she's quite eager to see you. I'll take you straight to her room. Perhaps later, if you care to relax in the parlor, I can play something on the piano for you."

He noticed random details as they passed through the house—the piano in the elegant parlor, the tasteful wallpaper in the hallway, the plush carpet underfoot. It seemed to be a respectable household owned by a widow of comfortable means. He took a deep breath and began to relax. May knocked on one of the doors, then smiled at him and headed back to the parlor.

Eula opened the door. Without a word she took his hand and gently pulled him inside. They had only to touch again, to look into each other's eyes, and the link between them was reestablished in the instant.

The room was dim and cool. The bed was soft and smelled of rosewater. Her clothes made a rustling sound as they fell to the floor. For the first time they were naked together. There had been something fitful, almost cloying about their lovemaking at the ruins; here, they were like children playing. It reminded him of the joy he felt singing, of producing something beautiful with his body and blending in harmony with another. Where did his body stop and hers begin?

Later, they had the luxury of lying in bed together for an hour or so. A colored servant girl knocked on the door, and at Eula's request brought them a pitcher of iced tea and bowls of lemon sherbet. He felt like a Roman emperor, to have his senses indulged with so much pleasure.

"So I'm to be Mr. Jones," he said.

"In this house, you are," Eula said. "Think of it as a custom—like a writer taking a pseudonym."

"If I were ever to take a pseudonym, I hope I'd come up with something more imaginative than 'Mr. Jones.' You must have mulled over that one for all of two seconds."

"Which was all the time I had, if I was to get the letter in the post to you."

"I'll bet half the men who come here are Mr. Jones."

"Maybe, but not many would fit the description I gave to May of *my* Mr. Jones."

"And what was that?"

"I told her that he was young but manly, with the handsomest mustache and the bluest eyes in Austin."

"Your eyes are bluer," he said, and reached for her. She drew back.

"We can't."

"Why not?"

"We don't have time. We have the room for only another ten minutes."

He gave her a stricken look.

"I'm sorry. I should have told you before."

"But only ten more minutes—"

"And then the room is promised to someone else. That's how it works here."

He looked about the cozy, simply furnished little room, cool and dim in the heat of the afternoon. It was no less precarious, in the end, than Swenson's Ruin.

He reached for her hand and pressed it to his sex, as if to prove how strong was the case for making love again. With a sigh and a laugh, she acquiesced.

When they were done, they silently washed the sweat from each other's bodies, using towels and a basin of cool water. Eula wrapped herself in the bedsheet and watched him dress.

"When will I see you again?" he asked.

"I'm not sure. I think we may be moving back to Austin soon. Things on the farm aren't going well . . . between my husband and Mr. McCutcheon."

"Can I write to you?"

She bit her lip.

"Perhaps Delia would be willing to pass letters between us."

Eula laughed. "I'm sure she'd love to! Which doesn't mean that we should let her."

He smiled wanly. "You've made a pun. Letter; let her."

"What a strange fellow you are, Will Porter."

"Mr. Jones!" he reminded her, then covered her mouth with a kiss.

"Go now," she whispered.

In the hallway, as he walked toward the parlor, he heard voices from another bedroom. He recognized the man's voice at once—it was Dave's colleague, Hiram Glass!

"No, I won't take it off!" Hiram said in a snappish tone, then lowered his voice so that Will heard only fragments: "I need it, that's why!—nothing to fear—electricity—perfectly natural—vital force—not uncommon—"

The woman kept laughing as if she couldn't help it. Will had a sudden wild notion that it was Delia, and as quickly dismissed the idea. Delia was in his thoughts because of Eula; surely he only imagined that it was her voice. A liaison between Hiram Glass and Delia Campbell was too bizarre to contemplate!

He stepped into the parlor, and encountered another surprise. Sitting on the sofa with a cigar and a glass of whiskey was William Shelley. The two had not spoken since the day Shelley knocked Will down in the lobby after the Senate debates—the first day Will saw Eula.

Shelley laughed. "If it ain't the whelp! Don't tell me May thinks you're old enough to play with the grown-ups. Shouldn't you be at choir practice?"

Will stared back at him dumbly, until May Tobin gently but firmly took his arm. She smiled at him sweetly as she steered him toward the foyer. "You've kept so busy, we've hardly had a chance to speak. You must come again, Mr. Jones."

"Jones!" said Shelley with a snort. He puffed on his cigar, producing a cloud of smoke, and threw his head back, laughing.

3 3

$\mathscr{T}$H E dengue fever, which had been spreading through Texas all summer, struck Austin in September.

William Pendleton Gaines was among the first sufferers. His symptoms included headache, a high fever, a rash over much of his body, and severe pains in his joints and back. From his sickbed at Bellevue, he dispatched an editorial on the epidemic:

> The word "dengue"—pronounced as two syllables—is of Spanish origin, derived from a Swahili swear word. It is sometimes corrupted as *dandy,* which we assure you it is not, or given the nickname "breakbone fever." We propose to drop the superfluous last syllable of "dengue" and make the spelling phonetic for English speakers, thereby giving the malady its proper name: the "dang" fever. Lay in a choice selection of swear words against the time when you get it, for you will need them!

Lucinda Boddy cooked and cleaned for Mr. J. B. Taylor, whose house was on Guadalupe Street, catty-corner from the new university grounds. When she fell to the dengue, far from being able to take care of Mr. Taylor and his household, she was unable to take care of herself. In her thirty-odd years, Lucinda had never experienced anything like it. She was burning up one minute, shivering the next. Every joint in her body creaked like a rusty hinge. Her back ached so that she could hardly sit or stand upright. Lucinda felt like she had been broken on a rack, tossed in a frying pan, and then doused with ice water.

On the morning of Sunday, the 27th of September, after a day and night of lying mostly unattended and utterly miserable in her little room at Mr. Taylor's, Lucinda managed to drag herself up the block to Major Dunham's house. Major Dunham was an attorney and editor of the *Texas Court Reporter*. Lucinda's friend Gracie Vance worked for Major Dunham and lived in the cabin in back of the Dunham house along with her man, Orange Washington. Gracie was a Christian soul; Gracie would take care of her.

Lucinda walked to the back of the Dunham house. She knocked on the cabin door, but got no answer, so she knocked on the kitchen door. Gracie stepped out, wearing a calico apron dusted with flour from the apple cobbler she was making.

"Lawdy, Lucinda, you are a sight! You's as scraggly as a wet kitten. Po' thing, you come down with the dandy, ain't you?"

"I reckon so," answered Lucinda weakly. "Oh, Gracie, somebody gots to take care of me for a while. I cain't hardly stand up. I feel like I's been sewed up in a burlap bag full of rocks and rolled down a hill." Lucinda hugged herself and shivered.

Gracie pressed her palm to Lucinda's forehead, leaving a flour handprint. "You's hot as blazes, chile! Let's get you into the cabin. I'll fix up the cot. Orange done gone out for the day, so there won't be nobody to disturb you. I'll nurse you best I can, honey chile, but they say there ain't nothin' you can do but just let that dang fever burn itself out."

Gracie put Lucinda to bed and brought her a pitcher of ice water and some cool rags for her forehead, then headed back to the kitchen. Sundays were busy days for Gracie. The Major and his wife, after attending church in the morning, usually had company over for lunch. Gracie had to spend the morning cleaning and cooking and laying the dining room table, then had to serve lunch, then had to clean up afterward.

On this day, the Major's guests were two doctors—an odd-looking pair, Gracie thought as she carried dishes to and from the table. One of them was blind and wore dark little spectacles. The conversation started with comments about how sparse the congregation had been that morning, due no doubt to the dengue—Gracie gathered that the two doctors had attended church as guests of the Dunhams—then touched on doctoring and lawyering, then settled on the subject of building a dam. It sounded like the doctors were trying to talk the Major into pitching in money for such a thing. Obviously, they didn't know how tightfisted the Major was!

Gracie took a shine to the blind fellow after he made a fuss over her apple cobbler. Gracie was used to being flattered on her appearance, for she was a very attractive woman, but the true way to her heart was to praise her cooking. If the Lord had made her beautiful, she had nothing to do with that, but her apple cobbler was her own doing and something she was justly proud of.

After lunch, the Major and his guests withdrew from the dining room to smoke and continue their conversation in the parlor. Mrs. Dunham withdrew to her sewing room. Gracie cleared the table and washed dishes, working as fast as she could. As soon as she was done, she would be free for the day and could commence getting ready for church. Like most of the colored denominations in town, Reverend Massey's First Baptist Church held no morning worship service. The first Sunday service was at three in the afternoon. Most white folks attended morning services and then came home to eat; colored folks like Gracie worked the first part of Sunday fixing and serving the white folks' lunch and then took off to worship afterward. Sometimes Gracie had to work late and missed the three o'clock service, but she always attended the later one at eight. Whenever she could, she preferred to attend both services. Once the white folks were fed and the kitchen was cleaned up, all the rest of Sunday was for singing and testifying, with a bit of socializing between.

That Sunday, with Lucinda to look after, Gracie missed the three o'clock service. She figured that succoring the sick was a Christian act, and reasoned that the Lord would forgive her for missing Reverend Massey's sermon that afternoon. Lucinda was a picture of suffering as she shivered and groaned on the cot. Gracie knew what she would be praying for at the evening service—to be spared from the ravages of the dandy fever!

As the day wore on toward evening, Gracie realized that Lucinda would be needing fresh clothes and some of her personal things if she was going to spend the night. It was while Gracie was down the street, fetching Lucinda's things from Mr. Taylor's house, that her man, Orange Washington, arrived home.

Orange liked to spend the better part of a Sunday down at the Black Elephant, gabbing with friends and sitting in the morning sunshine on the corner bench outside, then stepping inside in the afternoon to have a sandwich and a beer and maybe play a game of cards upstairs. After a hard week of working at the brickyard, Orange figured it was hardly sinning if a man wanted to relax with a beer and a few hands of monte on a Sabbath afternoon. He never got too drunk or lost too much money, and always headed home in time to change into his church clothes and attend the eight o'clock service with Gracie.

Gracie disapproved of the time Orange spent down at the Elephant, but putting up with it was a small price to pay to have a man who was a regular churchgoer, even if he sometimes entered the sanctuary with beer on his breath. Her last man, Dock Woods, had never once gone to church with her, which she should have taken as a sign. Dock had turned out to be no good; he thieved from her and probably would have thieved from Major Dunham if Gracie hadn't kept a close watch on him. Dock drank hard, and when he was drunk he could turn mean. When he took up with Oliver Townsend, who had served time in the county jail for stealing chickens, Gracie had had enough and kicked him out. That had been months ago, but Dock still came by occasionally, asking for favors. Sometimes, if he was drunk, he made threats. Orange had warned him to stay away, and so had Major Dunham, but he kept coming back.

The sky was darkening and Gracie was still down the block fetching Lucinda's things when Orange arrived back at the cottage that evening, after a very satisfying afternoon of cards at the Elephant. It was dim inside. He struck a match and lit a lamp, then saw the figure on the cot. He held up the lamp and stepped closer.

"Lucinda Boddy, is that you?"

Lucinda's fever had begun to climb. She peered back at the man standing over her and cringed. "Don't hit me, Dock!" Lucinda had been with Gracie once when Dock Woods came by and made threats. She was deathly afraid of him.

Orange laughed. "Lucinda, it's me, Orange. Damn, I ain't half as ugly as Dock Woods, and you knows it!"

The figure hovering over her, lit up like a demon by the lamp's harsh light, drew closer. Lucinda was too weak to rise. "I'm warning you, Dock Woods . . ." was all she could manage to say.

"Dang it, Lucinda, I ain't Dock!" Orange shook his head. "You come down with that dengue fever, ain't you?"

At that moment, Gracie stepped into the cabin. She put down Lucinda's things and went to her.

"I think Lucinda be 'lucinatin'," said Orange. "She keep callin' me Dock."

After a bit, Lucinda's fever seemed to break. When Gracie told her she had mistaken Orange for Dock, Lucinda had no recollection of it and thought Gracie was making it up to tease her. She managed to sit up and swallow some chicken broth.

Gracie was late for church and eager to get going, but hesitated to leave.

Lucinda saw her fretting. "You and Orange git along to church," she said. "I be all right—pro'ly sleep the whole time. Now git! No sense missin' a whole day of church on account of me."

In the end, Gracie and Orange went to church, leaving Lucinda alone. As she had predicted, Lucinda fell asleep almost at once, and slept so soundly that she did not wake when Gracie and Orange came back later that night. She did not wake even when the two of them had an argument and raised their voices—Orange had fallen asleep during the sermon, and Gracie blamed it on the beer—and Major Dunham yelled at them from his bedroom window to be quiet. Lucinda continued to sleep while Orange and Gracie made up to each other in the bed only a few feet away from her; Gracie insisted that they do it very quietly, and Orange contained his bleats of ecstasy as best he could.

By midnight, everyone in the cabin was asleep. All was peaceful for an hour or so.

So soundly did Lucinda sleep that she only wrinkled her nose a bit when Gracie screamed into the handkerchief soaked in chloroform that covered her face. When Orange, bolting to his feet, was sent sprawling to the floor by the blow of an ax against his head, Lucinda merely frowned and pulled at the covers.

She had just begun to stir, disturbed by all the movement in the room, when the butt of the ax struck her forehead.

The blow was not as powerful as the one which felled Orange, a mere tap by comparison. Nevertheless it fractured her skull and pressed a sliver of bone against her brain. Lucinda's mind would never be the same afterward.

She never consciously realized what had happened. The blow registered in her mind as a stunning cataclysm, cosmic in scale, like the earth cracking in two or the sky exploding into flames. She slipped into a nightmare in which cymbals crashed and a high-pitched whistle broke her head wide open. Then her body was split open, like a wishbone being pulled apart, her legs wrenched in opposite directions.

"I'll take this one," a voice said. Was it God taking her up to heaven, or the devil fetching her to hell?

Something penetrated her between the legs and moved inside her. She was opened up at both ends and skewered clean through, like a pig on a spit. Icy cold flames licked up and down her body.

She vaguely thought she heard Gracie scream.

* * *

Lucinda woke with a headache as big as creation. She shivered with fever. By all rights she should have been too weak and wounded to move, but she got to her feet. She swayed crazily, like a tree lashed by wind. The room tilted. Bright moonlight poured in through the open window. She took a step and tripped over something.

There was a lamp on a table near the door, burning so low that it cast only a tiny glow. She reached for it and raised the wick. A tall flame leaped up, blackening the inside of the glass chimney. The thing she had stumbled against was Orange, lying on the floor. The blood on his head glistened beneath the light of the lamp. She heard him moan.

Something blocked the moonlight at the window. There was a man standing outside, looking in.

"Don't look at me! Put out that light, god damn you!" said the man. Flickers of light danced weirdly across his face. He looked like a demon from hell.

"Dock?" she said. "Oh, God! Don't kill me, Dock!"

"Put out that light, I said!"

Lucinda blew out the lamp, then threw it at him. It struck the raised sash and shattered the glass. The noise was like the heavens crashing. The room was filled with the stench of kerosene.

She ran out of the cabin screaming, then up the side yard. The earth pitched and swayed beneath her. She staggered up the front steps. Major Dunham stepped onto the porch clutching a pistol.

"What on earth is it, woman? There's blood all over you!"

"Oh, Major, we's all dead!"

"Stay here," said the Major. "Don't go in the house, all bloody like that! Lie on the steps."

For Lucinda, the world flickered and spun down into darkness.

The Major stepped into the cabin and saw Orange sprawled on the floor. An ax lay nearby. He saw no sign of Gracie. The kerosene fumes stung his eyes. He retreated back to the yard and peered about in the bright moonlight.

Just north of his property was a vacant lot, and north of that a two-story house with some outbuildings. From an upstairs window a woman in a nightdress leaned out. "Major Dunham, is that you? I think there's some-body behind my stable. I heard some noises from down there."

Pistol in hand, his heart thumping, the Major walked across the vacant lot toward the stable. Something was lying on the ground beside the building, partly illuminated by the bright moonlight and partly hidden in the black shadows.

The woman called down to him. "Can you see anything? What is it, Major?"

Major Dunham looked at the body at his feet and felt his gorge rise. Had it not been Gracie he was looking for, he would never have known it was her, for her head had been beaten to a gory pulp. In the grass nearby lay a brick, glistening all over with blood.

Something gold and glittering caught his eye—a slender chain clutched in one of Gracie's hands. The Major knelt down and saw that the chain was attached to a pocket watch. Gracie owned no such thing, of that he was certain. Where on earth had the watch come from? The Major decided to leave everything as it was. Perhaps the marshal would be able to make sense of it.

34

*W*HY bother to write a whole new story?" said Hiram Glass. "These murders are all the same! Might as well run the last one again. Just change the names."

"I could say the same about your coverage of politics," snapped Dave. He was in no mood for banter. Justice Von Rosenberg had kept him out of the inquest. Marshal Lee refused to talk. Gaines was demanding a two-column report for the next edition, and all Dave had to show was a desk covered with scraps of paper.

Hiram tapped his chin. "Let me guess: a colored servant girl, living in back of her employer's house, has been horribly ravished and murdered. Marshal Lee, after an investigation lasting at least ten minutes, has arrested the last colored man known to have passed within a hundred yards of the property. In the next story, it will be revealed that the black man has been released due to lack of evidence, and that the police have no other suspects. End of case—until next time. There, I've written it for you."

"Hiram, I swear to God I'm going to strangle you."

" 'White Man Murdered'—now *that* would be news!"

Dave smiled in spite of himself. "And I'll bet Grooms Lee *still* couldn't solve it."

The office door swung open. Hiram craned his neck. "Here comes Nemesis. Fully recovered from the dengue fever, it appears."

William Pendleton Gaines held up a sheet of paper. "Gentlemen, I give you my masterpiece: 'To Your Tents, O Israel!' What do you think of the title? Not too melodramatic, is it?"

"I suppose we should hear the text." Hiram leaned back in his chair and crossed his hands behind his head. Dave fiddled with a pencil and tapped his foot. Gaines cleared his throat and commenced.

"'Yet another bloody tragedy has blackened the fame of Austin! On a brilliant moonlit night, on one of the principal avenues of the city, less than a hundred yards from the university grounds, wholesale murder has been committed. And not one murder, but two!

"'This latest butchery follows the same grisly pattern perpetrated in this city over the last months. In every instance, the attack has been made on a servant girl living on the premises of her employers. In every instance, the guilty parties have escaped scot-free.

"'The thing has gone far enough! It must be stopped at any cost! The attacks heretofore have been made on Negro servant girls, and so far as can be determined, by Negro men. These people are as entitled to protection as anybody else. And if these murders go unpunished, their perpetrators will only become more emboldened. We will be startled one morning by the announcement that some gentleman's family have been murdered in their very beds!

"'The officers of the law have failed to give us protection. Assassins with hatchets in hand lurk undetected upon our streets. Mere panes of glass stand between these murderous ravishers and our smooth and fair-skinned wives and daughters!

"'Let us organize at once into a vigilance committee to keep watch over the city, day and night! This is a public duty, as imperative as if a band of Comanche Indians were threatening the city. Make every doubtful individual explain his presence. Send every suspicious character out of town at once, never to return. We do not counsel hasty action or any violation of the law, only a temporary assumption of power by the people, who may act more swiftly and surely than the slow process of warrants and all the paraphernalia of the law. Austin must be made too hot for any but honest citizens who have nothing to fear from scrutiny. Strike fear into the hearts of the evildoers!

"'The men of Austin are brave men, proud veterans of battle and sons of veterans, capable of protecting their families! Any man who shirks the task is a poltroon! To your tents, O Israel!'"

Gaines clutched the paper and raised his fist, to a round of applause from the staff.

"Well, gentlemen, what do you think?"

Dave frowned. "Are you sure you want to editorialize for forming a vigilance committee?"

"I mean every word I say. The time has come for citizen action! If you had a wife and daughter yourself, as I have, you'd understand just how serious this situation is. This manifesto is going in tomorrow's paper, along with a full account of the murders—which brings me to you, Dave Shoemaker. The printer says you haven't given him a single line of copy! What are you waiting for?"

Before Dave could answer, there was a commotion in the hallway and the office door swung open. Marshal Grooms Lee strode into the room dressed in his gold-brimmed cap and gold-embroidered blue jacket, followed by two burly men in black hats and long black coats. One of the men had a red beard; the other's was black. These two were followed by a lanky black man wearing a coat too small for him, and a teenaged girl with a large bosom and hair so blond it was almost white.

The marshal looked particularly cocky. The two men in black had stony expressions. The Negro and the blond girl both looked nervous.

"Now there's a motley crew," muttered Hiram.

Marshal Lee shouted across the room. "Mr. Gaines! I'd like to see you in your private office."

"What's this about, Marshal?"

"You'll see. Oh, and you might want to bring Shoemaker along. I hope he hasn't written his story about the Gracie Vance murder yet."

Gaines took a seat behind his big desk, with Dave nearby. The marshal and the others sat across from them. Grooms Lee was as smug as a cat with a canary in its mouth.

"Well, Marshal," said Gaines, "who are these folks and what is this all about?"

Lee gestured to the men in black, who sat to either side of him. "Mr. Gaines, may I present to you Officers Hennessey and Hanna, of the Noble Detective Agency of Houston." Hennessey had the red beard, Hanna the black.

"So the city finally brought in outside detectives!" said Dave.

"Not *finally*, Shoemaker." Lee smirked at him. "Officers Hennessey and Hanna have been in town for over two weeks."

"Nobody told me about this," said Gaines.

"We thought it best if they arrived without fanfare," said Lee. "No sense tipping off every pickpocket and petty criminal by announcing it in the *Statesman*."

Gaines raised an eyebrow. "And who are these others in your party, Marshal?"

"Material witnesses to the murders of Gracie Vance and Orange Washington. This young lady is Miss Inga Olafson, who's in the service of Professor Tallichet, who teaches languages at the university. The colored fellow here is Johnson Trigg. He's about as shiftless a fellow as you'll ever meet, but he's got a keen pair of ears. Ain't that right, Johnson?"

"Oh, sure enough, yes sir!" Trigg grinned and nodded.

Lee shot a look at Dave. "Neither of those names is for publication yet, mind you. Now I should tell you first of all that Hennessey and Hanna were already making substantial progress into solving one of the previous murder cases—I can't yet divulge specific details—when this latest outrage occurred. Having 'em ready on the spot made all the difference. The men who murdered Gracie Vance and Orange Washington are behind bars this very minute."

Dave took a good look at Hennessey and Hanna. Noble, he thought—what a name for a detective agency! What were detectives anyway, but strong-armers and snitches for hire? Rich men in the industrial cities up north hired them to spy on labor unions; bankers and merchants hired them to infiltrate gangs and track down stolen goods; politicians hired them as bodyguards when they went canvassing in hostile precincts. In such a dangerous line of work, nobody expected them to stick to the letter of the law. When people thought of private detectives, they pictured brass knuckles, not a magnifying glass. Hennessey and Hanna were as expressionless as a pair of wooden Indians. Occasionally one of them would work his jaw back and forth and look about the room suspiciously.

"It was a couple of colored fellows who did the murders," said the marshal. "Dock Woods was implicated right off by Lucinda Boddy. His accomplice was his good friend Oliver Townsend."

Dave snorted. "The notorious chicken thief?"

"Chicken thief?" said Gaines.

"Oliver Townsend's claim to fame is the fact that he never steals anything valued over twenty dollars," explained Dave. "That way, he never commits a felony, and the worst he ever gets is county jail on misdemeanor charges. 'Always count your chickens' is his rule. If he thinks the value of his loot exceeds twenty dollars, he puts one back. One time he got caught with $19.75 worth of chickens in his bag!" Dave shook his head incredulously. "It's quite a step from chicken thief to ax murderer." He would have added *rapist*, but for the presence of the girl.

"Just sit quiet for a while and listen, Shoemaker," said the marshal. "Lu-cinda saw Dock Woods outside the cabin window, during or shortly after the murders. Major Dunham informed us that Dock came by every now and then to harass Gracie. The Major had warned Dock to stay away, but the nigger kept coming back. Early this morning we rode out to where Dock lives and works, on a farm about five miles from town. I brought him back in handcuffs. Among his things we found a shirt with a substantial amount of blood on it."

"What does Dock Woods say?" asked Dave.

"He says he's innocent, of course! What coon isn't, when you catch him red-handed? But the real case against Dock comes from this fellow here. Stand up, Johnson Trigg! One of the first things Officers Hennessey and Hanna did when they arrived in town was to make inquiries among the col-ored population, with the aim of establishing a network of informants. John-son here has proved to be a gold mine. Teacher's pet, you might say. That's because you're as curious as a cat, aren't you, Johnson?"

"Yes, sir, I reckon I is!"

Marshal Lee grinned and nodded, mimicking him. "Go ahead and give these gentlemen the gist of your story, Johnson. Tell it just like you did to Officers Hennessey and Hanna."

Johnson Trigg fingered the buttons on his coat nervously, but looked Gaines straight in the eye. He seemed eager to tell his story. "Well, sir, it was like this. Sunday night, pro'ly round nine o'clock, I seen Oliver Townsend right outside this very building, sitting on the steps. He was talkin' to some other colored fellow I didn't know, sayin' to this fellow, 'I is gonna kill Gra-cie Vance!' That's what he said. And this other fellow says back to him, 'You do that and they'll catch up with you, sure as molasses.' And Oliver Townsend says back at him, 'I been killing 'em as I please, and they ain't caught up with me yet.' I swear, them's the very words he said."

"But this is fantastic!" said Gaines. "Do you mean that all the murders—"

"Let the man finish, Mr. Gaines." The marshal crossed his arms and nod-ded to Trigg, who went on excitedly. "Well, sir, th'other fellow shook his head and went off, and then after a while Oliver Townsend took off, too. He started north up Colorado Street, and I took it in my head to follow him. The moon was shinin' bright and he just kinda sauntered this way and that, so it wasn't no trouble to follow him. I never lost sight of him the whole time, till finally he come up outside that house where Gracie Vance live, and he met up with another man. I couldn't see the other man good 'nough so's to make out his face—"

"Dock Woods," said the marshal. "We know from Lucinda Boddy that Dock was there, and we know that he and Townsend were confederates. Go on, Johnson."

"Well, I cain't say it was Dock Woods as I never seen the fellow's face, but this other fellow, he say to Townsend, 'We best not go in there tonight. They's got somebody stayin' in there with 'em,' and Townsend, he say, 'We gots to do it tonight! We gots to kill Gracie Vance! Now come on!' And they snuck alongside the house toward the cabin out back. I stayed in the shadows, wonderin' what was to transpire. I heard a bunch of funny noises, but I couldn't tell what none of 'em was. I reckon it was ten minutes later there come a crashin' and a screamin' and I decides to git myself out of there 'fore I gits into trouble. The next mornin' I come to learn that Gracie Vance been murdered jus' like I heard Oliver Townsend say he was gonna do, and so was her man, Orange. Since I's already on speakin' terms with Officer Hen'sy and Officer Hanna, I figured I ought to tell 'em what I seen."

Having finished his tale, Johnson Trigg sat down.

"Dave, I hope you took all that down," said Gaines.

"Don't worry," said the marshal. "It's all in the sworn statement."

Dave nodded slowly. "Of course, there's not a single detail of the crime that Mr. Trigg couldn't have picked up from hearsay."

"Are you impugning the witness, Shoemaker?"

"Now, sir, I'd never make up such a story!" Trigg rose to his feet again. "And I wouldn't be talkin' now, if it wasn't for what else I know about Oliver Townsend."

"What's that?" said Dave.

"Sit down, Johnson," said the marshal.

"But, sir, like you say, he be 'pugning me! Which the gentleman surely wouldn't do if he knowed about the time at the Black Elephant when I heard Oliver Townsend say he was gonna kill Rebecca Ramey, and then sure enough that very night she was murdered."

Dave scoffed. "Your facts are mixed up. Rebecca Ramey wasn't killed; her little girl, Mary, was."

Trigg shook his head. "Well, I reckon I'm a mite confused. But I'm not lyin'! Oliver Townsend went after Rebecca Ramey and her little girl, and I heard him talkin' 'bout it 'forehand."

"If you knew Townsend killed Mary Ramey, and you heard him say he was planning to kill Gracie Vance, why didn't you warn her, or go to the police?" said Dave.

"Well . . ." Trigg shrugged. "I didn't know for *certain* that he killed that

Ramey chile, I just 'spected him. That's why I followed him Sunday night, after I heard him say he was aimin' to kill Gracie, to see if he was really gonna do it. There wasn't no way I could stop him without him knowin' I was followin'."

Dave looked at Hennessey and Hanna, who remained as expressionless as ever. "Tell me, Trigg, did either of these detectives coerce you into coming up with this story? Did they threaten you?"

"Why, no, sir!"

"Did they offer you anything? Whiskey? Money?"

"Well . . ."

"This is ridiculous! You call this man a witness?" Dave shook his head. "I think you might want to put a shorter leash on your two bloodhounds, Marshal. For one thing, Dock Woods has an alibi. I've talked to the farmer he works for. The man saw Dock go to bed at ten o'clock, and he woke him up at four the next morning to do some plowing."

"The murder took place at one in the morning," Marshal Lee said. "Plenty of time for Dock to ride into town and back again."

"Without waking the farmer?"

"What about the blood on his shirt?"

"It's Dock's own blood. The farmer told me Dock cut himself last week and got blood on the shirt."

Gaines rose from his desk. "Now, Dave, enough of that! I think Mr. Trigg's story is terrific. We'll run his whole statement, verbatim."

"But, Mr. Gaines—"

"And I think we should work the name of the detective agency into the headline. 'The Noble Detectives Do Their Part!' What do you think?"

Dave sat back in his chair, shaking his head.

"You better go now, Johnson," said the marshal, glaring at him. Trigg obediently left the room.

Gaines turned his attention to the girl, who was shifting in her chair uneasily. He smiled at her. "What about your other witness, Marshal?"

The marshal sat back in his chair with the look of a man who had regained his footing after momentarily losing it. "Miss Olafson here can explain the gold chain and pocket watch found in Gracie Vance's hand. It's her watch."

Miss Olafson spoke with a Swedish accent. "It was my father's watch," she said. "It came to me when he died."

"And how did it come to be in Gracie's hand?" said Gaines

The marshal answered. "We figure that Gracie must have pulled it off the man who murdered her, in the struggle."

"And how did that man come to have it?" said Dave.

"All I can think is that he must have stolen it from my room," said the girl, touching her bosom. "Almost always I wear it on the chain around my neck. But I must have left it in my room one day last week, for suddenly I could not find it. The window is usually open. If I left it on my dresser, anyone could have climbed in and taken it. When I saw in the newspaper that they had found a gold watch on a chain, I went to the police at once and asked to see it. It was my watch!"

"Here's the thing itself." The marshal produced an ornately worked gold watch on a slender chain. "We figure it must be as Miss Olafson says—the killer of Gracie Vance at some previous time stole the watch from the Tallichet house and had it on his person when he attacked Gracie. Gracie pulled it off him. She was grasping it when the Major found her. No one in this office, I'm sure, wants to imagine what might have resulted if Miss Olafson had been in her room when the fiends came in and stole her watch . . ."

"Did the thief take anything else?" said Dave.

"Only the watch was missing," said the girl. "But I have nothing else of such value. The watch is very precious to me. I wear it almost always, even when I sleep." She shook her head. "But I must have been careless and left it in my room. How could anyone have stolen it from around my neck?"

"How indeed?" said Gaines, who took the opportunity to look openly at her bosom. The discussion was reminding him of something, though he could not quite put his finger on it. "May I see the watch, Marshal?"

"Certainly."

It was a lovely thing, to be sure, but not truly of the finest craftsmanship. His father's missing gold watch had been considerably more valuable. He blinked. That was what the conversation had reminded him of—the elder Gaines's lost watch! It, too, had gone missing, and no one knew quite when or how. Surely it couldn't have been stolen off his father's person, any more than Miss Olafson's watch could have been taken, without her knowledge, from around her neck. It was a curious coincidence, this matter of watches gone missing. Gaines thought of the magpie, the bird who purloins shiny objects to decorate her nest. Some people were said to be human magpies, drawn to glittering objects . . .

An old suspicion flashed through his thoughts, so briefly that it registered in his mind only as a fleeting, nonsensical notion: could there be such a thing as a *blind* magpie attracted to glittering trinkets?

Gaines might have asked the Swedish girl a very simple question, and the answer might have set into motion a complicated series of ideas; but the question never quite took shape in his head, and evaporated before it could reach his lips.

He might have asked Inga Olafson if she was acquainted with a certain Dr. Fry, the Blind Phrenologist.

And she would have answered: yes, for that very person had dined with her employer only last week, and afterward had volunteered to give her an examination, free of charge. Simply by feeling her head, he had been able to tell her many curious and interesting things about herself.

35

*E*ULA Phillips moved back to Austin on Friday, the 2nd of October.

Will knew the day it happened, for he had been discreetly perusing the Phillips residence whenever he walked by. A few times he had spied Delia Campbell through the windows, and because they liked to sit on the porch in the afternoons he knew Mr. and Mrs. Phillips, Eula's in-laws, by sight.

One day he struck up a conversation with the colored woman who lived with her son in the little house at the back of the property. She was hanging washing out to dry, and it seemed perfectly innocent that Will should stop and exchange a few words with her. Her name was Sallie Mack, he learned, and her son's name was Alec.

"I suppose you do all the washing for the Phillips family?" Will remarked.

"Yes, sir. That I does."

"I suppose you'll have more work to do soon. I hear that Jimmy Phillips and his wife are coming back to Austin." It was a harmless remark, but his heart pounded in his chest.

"That's right, sir. You a friend of young Mr. Phillips?"

"An acquaintance. Do you know when they're moving back?"

"I reckon they's 'spected on Friday, sir. Comin' in on the afternoon train from Hutto."

Will tipped his hat and walked on. As soon as his back was turned to Sallie Mack, he broke out smiling.

That Friday, he walked by the Phillips residence several times. He noticed no activity until late in the afternoon, when he saw that a large trunk had been deposited on the verandah between the main house and one of the annexes. The screen door of the annex was propped open by a brick. Mrs. Phillips came bustling out of the main house, crossed the verandah carrying a pile of folded bedding, and disappeared into the annex.

A moment later, a young man stepped out of the annex and onto the verandah. His sleeves were rolled up. His wavy black hair was mussed. He leaned against a post, smoking a cigarette. He looked like Delia. Jimmy Phillips was handsome, Will had to admit, though even from across the street Will could see signs of dissipation in his young face.

Will heard a baby cry. A moment later Eula stepped onto the verandah with the child in her arms. Her hair was disheveled and her face drawn. Still, the sight of her made Will's heart leap. She walked across the verandah and said something to Jimmy, who seemed to ignore her.

Suddenly Jimmy's gaze fell on Will. The fact of being noticed startled him into movement. Rather than turn and walk away, he began to cross the street at an oblique angle, keeping his face turned toward the Phillips residence. Every time he glanced at the verandah, Jimmy was staring back at him. Will kept his face expressionless and looked straight at Eula. Their eyes met. He saw a glimmer of recognition and surprise, but no other reaction. He tipped his hat to the two of them and walked on. It was a perfectly innocent gesture, he told himself; a neighborly gesture.

As he rounded the corner, he heard Jimmy demand of her, in a loud voice, "Who the hell's that fellow? How do you know him?"

Will's face turned hot. He walked quickly on.

"Damned stonecutters! Damned unions! Damned politicians! Damned contractors!" Joseph Lee pushed himself away from the dinner table, scowling.

"You shouldn't let them bother you so, Father," said Grooms Lee. He had changed out of his marshal's uniform and put on a tie. His father appreciated formality at the dinner table.

"Bother me?" said the old man. "Ha! Not a one of 'em bothers me—I despise 'em, that's all. I'm seventy-five years old, son, and that's too old to be losing sleep over other people's foolishness. Let 'em bicker among themselves all they want! Whoever thought that putting up a building could cause so much commotion?"

Joseph Lee was of the same generation as the elder William Gaines. He had lived in Austin for fifty years. His appointment to the Capitol Building Commission was a plum delivered at the end of a long career of public and party service. His handsome salary was one of the highest in the state government, but the job did entail riding shotgun on an endless train of chiselers, schemers, and scoundrels.

"Do you want to hear the latest?" he barked.

His son had a great deal on his mind, but dutifully nodded.

"The word is that one of the major contractors was embezzled out of five thousand dollars in state funds by one of his employees. And do you know how the fellow found out about it? That's the real scandal! Both the contractor and the employee, unbeknownst to one another, happened to pay a visit to the widow May Tobin's house on the same day. After tending to what he came for, the embezzler started bragging to his ladyfriend about the five thousand he'd siphoned off from his employer—but the contractor happened to be passing in the hall and heard every word. An uproar followed, and the contractor chased the embezzler up Congress Avenue, both of 'em in their underwear! The upshot was, the embezzler paid back the money and got out of town, and the contractor's keeping his mouth shut." Joseph Lee scowled. "I ask you, what are two such fellows doing in a house like that in the first place? The vice in this town has gotten out of hand. Something ought to be done about it. You're the marshal, son."

"At the moment, Father, my hands are full."

"With these murders, you mean. But don't you see, it's all connected. When vice is allowed to flourish, it brings on worse things. It's Pandora's box. Clean up Guy Town! The only way to stop the spawn is to shut down the breeding grounds."

"I wouldn't mind shutting down the Black Elephant." The Elephant was just two blocks south of the elegant house on Hickory Street where the Lees lived; it galled Grooms Lee to lie in bed at night and think of all the crimes that must have been conceived over a shot of whiskey in that den of darkies, only a few steps from his own home.

"Putting Hugh Hancock out of business would be a start," agreed his father.

"But shutting down May Tobin's house would be another kettle of fish. Likely to catch a few whales too big for the net."

Joseph Lee shook his head. "Something's got to be done about these murders. Six bodies so far, going back to that girl at New Year's, and not a single conviction, nor a single thing done to clean up the vice in town. People are talking, and not just the local folk. 'The shame of Austin,' they're calling it. If you're to launch a successful career in politics, especially at the state level—"

"The detectives from Houston are on the job, Father. I made two arrests within twenty-four hours of Gracie Vance's murder."

"But you told me yourself that those arrests aren't likely to hold up. Did you see Gaines's editorial the other day? 'To Your Tents, O Israel!' The man is calling for vigilantes! He outright says that the police can't be relied on to protect women in their beds at night."

"We'll see what he says in a few days—after I make an arrest for the murder of Mary Ramey."

"Ah, the little colored girl who was dragged from her mother's arms and ravished in Mr. Weed's wash house. Well, there's a start! People will be relieved to see such a monster brought to justice. Colored fellow, I suppose?"

"Of course. One I've had my eye on for quite some time."

Joseph Lee smiled at his son, who at that moment looked like a little boy to him. Ever since he was a child, Grooms had never been one to back down; he was never so defiant as when he was unsure of himself. His mother had been the same. Sarah had died giving birth to him; Grooms had always been special, because he was all that was left of his mother. His service in the Rangers had made his father very proud.

Now his son was being sorely tried. The mayor, the district attorney, the *Statesman*—the whole citizenry of Austin!—were looking to his little boy to restore law and order. The task seemed to have run away from him; the elder Lee doubted sometimes that Grooms could master it. He would never utter such a doubt aloud, but it communicated itself to his son nevertheless. If Grooms Lee had been a different man, the desire to please his father might have been a spur to some satisfactory resolution; but Grooms Lee was like the horse who bolts when spurred, and someone was likely to be trampled.

Grooms Lee had not been completely forthright when he told his father that an arrest for the murder of Mary Ramey was imminent. He was still not ready to charge Alec Mack, but he was ready to bring him in for questioning again. The detectives from Houston had been investigating Alec since the day they arrived. They had come up with no new evidence and no witnesses against him, but they suggested that the marshal take him into custody anyway, on trumped-up charges if necessary. Once Alec was behind bars, Hennessey and Hanna would be able to extract a confession from him. The two detectives assured the marshal that they had done the same thing many times before, in similar circumstances. They knew how to make a man confess.

Alec Mack was known to be living with his mother. Lee might have apprehended him there, but the detectives advised against it. Sallie Mack's little house was situated immediately behind the family residence of Mr. James Phillips, and just across an alley from the Hirshfeld estate; there was no reason to disturb the peace of those respectable members of the community. Instead, Hennessey and Hanna advised the marshal to call Mack out of the Black Elephant, where he could almost certainly be found on a Saturday night, using some pretext to put him off his guard. They also advised the marshal to wait until after midnight, so as to catch Mack at his most inebriated. A strong man who was a little drunk was hard to handle; a strong man who was fall-down drunk was easy. The marshal would also need a legal pretext for locking Mack up, and a charge of drunk and disorderly conduct would do nicely.

The lateness of the hour would also serve to shield the officers from prying eyes as they escorted the prisoner several blocks north to the jail. Hennessey and Hanna intended to make the short trip one that Alec Mack would never forget.

The marshal put aside any misgivings he might have felt about the methods which the detectives proposed. As Gaines had pontificated in his editorial, the time had come to put aside some of the cumbersome "paraphernalia" of the law. The crisis demanded more effective measures.

It was almost two in the morning when Marshal Lee stepped into the Black Elephant, alone. He stood in the open doorway with his arms crossed, scanning the noisy crowd until he caught sight of Alec Mack, who was sitting at the bar. Alec looked back at him with glazed eyes and then averted his face. Marshal Lee called his name. Alec didn't respond, even when Lem Brooks nudged him from the other side of the bar.

Hugh Hancock scurried in from the back room. "There a problem, Marshal?"

"No. I just have a little business with one of your customers. Only he seems a mite deaf tonight. Alec Mack! Come over here, you dog! See what I mean? He won't even look up."

Hancock walked to the bar. After some whispered encouragement from Lem Brooks and some pokes from Hancock, Alec slid off his stool and trudged toward the door. The marshal thought it was rather comical, the way the little black man pushed the big one ahead of him. The noise in the bar had fallen to a sullen murmur.

"What's the matter with you, Alec Mack? You got cotton in your ears?"

"What you want with me?" Alec's speech was slurred. Ever since Mary Ramey's murder, he had been drinking heavily. The terror of being pursued by the bloodhounds haunted his nightmares. Rebecca was in such a state that she refused to see him. "What you want?" he repeated. His voice trembled.

It amused Marshal Lee to see a man as big as Alec look so scared. Colored men were all cowards, as far as he was concerned. He had never met one yet who wasn't frightened of him. "Nothing for you to be worried about, Alec. We had some trouble with a couple of niggers just down the street, and I need you to identify 'em for me. You can do that, can't you? It might behoove you to give the police a bit of help. Count in your favor one of these days."

"Lawd's sake, go with him," said Hugh Hancock, giving Alec another shove.

Alec frowned and stepped past the marshal, out the door. Lee took his arm and the two of them stepped off the sidewalk, heading east.

A more direct approach to the city jail would have been due north, up Neches Street, but Lee had his reasons to go a block out of the way. Heading out in a direction away from the jail would keep Alec off his guard. There would be fewer houses along the route he had in mind, and thus fewer people who might be disturbed by noises in the dead of night. If they had headed directly up Neches Street, after a couple of blocks they would have passed directly by the marshal's own house, where his father was sleeping soundly.

"Where you takin' me, Marshal?" Alec looked blearily up and down Pecan Street. A few saloons were still open, but not many men were out on the sidewalks.

"Just one block down, to Red River Street," said the marshal. "See, just a few more steps—careful, don't trip. And now we turn left. Just keep going a ways. You see that alley, this side of the lumberyard? There's a couple of men down there I want you to have a look at."

They stepped into the alley. Alec peered drunkenly into the darkness. "Don't see nobody," he said. Something dropped over his head and cinched tight around his neck.

They swarmed over him. Alec couldn't tell how many there were. The noose tightened around his neck. They dragged him to the ground and started kicking him.

"A while back, I said I was going to keep an eye on you. You remember me saying that, Alec Mack?" The marshal grunted. "You ran from those bloodhounds, after you killed Mary Ramey—thought you could get away by putting stink powder on your feet. You run from me, you stupid coon, and I'll shoot you dead!"

The beating continued until Alec lay completely still. Then they pulled him to his feet by the noose around his neck. Someone whipped him across the face with a pistol. Another pistol was jabbed into his back. After that, it wasn't the marshal who spoke, but a couple of other men, both with Irish brogues.

"March, nigger!"

"Where you takin' me?" Alec pleaded.

"Where do you think? To the nearest tree. We're gonna hang you by the neck for raping that little girl."

They marched him up Red River Street. The scattered houses were all dark. At Ash Street they turned left and kept on until they reached the square block of overgrown parkland across from the Wesley Chapel.

"Plenty of trees here."

"Sure, plenty of stout limbs for hanging. What do you say we do it right across from the nigger church?"

"Capital idea! We'll leave his corpse hanging, so his nigger friends can spit on it before they go in to say their Sunday prayers!"

Alec clutched at the rope around his neck. He managed to wedge his fingertips between the rope and his throat. "Oh, Lawd, please, don't hang me!"

One of the men struck his face. "If you're gonna talk, nigger, it'll be about your sins. Tell us how you raped that little girl. What was it like, poking your thing into a tiny hole like that? They say you tore her wide open."

They knocked him to his knees and tightened the rope again. "Ready to confess? Nod your head and we'll let you talk. Otherwise, we're gonna throw this rope over the nearest branch, then haul you up till your toes don't touch the ground."

Alec struggled to loosen the rope. He heard a whooshing noise. He rolled his eyes up and saw the other end of the rope fly through the air and loop over a branch above his head. In a panic he sprang to his feet and started running. The rope pulled free. He ran through the high grass and underbrush, tripped on a tree root and fell, then scrambled to his feet. The men ran after him, whooping with excitement. It was like being chased by the bloodhounds, but much worse. The dogs had fangs, they could bite and make him bleed—but the men meant to hang him!

Above the pounding of his heart, the cracking of branches, and the whooping of the men, Alec heard a distant, ghostly barking. The dog ghosts! The dead women! Now little Mary Ramey and Gracie Vance were among them, and probably Orange Washington, too. It was not like the barking of bloodhounds, all in a pack; their voices came from all over, from every direction. Alec imagined that each one must be outside the house where she died, and altogether they were singing a mournful song and howling at the moon. But why were they barking now? Why had they not warned him, earlier tonight? It was as if they were mocking him . . .

Then he realized the truth: the dog ghosts weren't barking out a warning. They were howling a lament. It was their way of welcoming him. Alec would be among them soon. The men would catch him—he couldn't possibly outrun them all, any more than he had been able to outrun the bloodhounds—and when they caught him, they would hang him, for a crime he never committed. He would die as innocent as little Mary Ramey. He would leave the living and join the dead . . .

As they reached the edge of the park, one of the pursuers got hold of the loose rope flailing behind Alec and dropped to the ground with it. Alec was wrenched backward. Had he not been clutching the noose frantically with his fingertips, the rope would have snapped his neck. Instead he flipped into the air and fell flat on his back. The wind was knocked out of him. As he lay paralyzed on the hard, cold ground, he heard the clamor of the dog ghosts echoing among the stars overhead.

The men swarmed around him, kicking and yelling.

"You're gonna die now, nigger!"

"We're gonna hang you for sure!"

He rolled onto his belly, trying to escape the blows. One of the men stepped on his neck, grinding his face into the dirt. Two others twisted his arms behind his back. "Where are those nippers?" said the marshal. A moment later, cold metal slipped over Alec's wrists and clicked shut.

The foot lifted off his neck. Alec struggled against the handcuffs. He was powerless now. There was nothing he could do to stop them. He spat out a mouthful of blood and dirt and tried to scream. The sound that came out was a hoarse croak that made the marshal laugh.

Across the street, a light flashed. A man stood on a front porch holding a lamp in one hand and a pistol in the other. "What the devil's going on?" he called.

Grooms Lee peered at the man for a moment, then yelled back. "Police business!"

"Is that the marshal?"

"It is. Now go back inside!"

"What's happening there? You woke my wife with all that racket. She's scared out of her wits."

"We've got a man here resisting arrest—drunk and disorderly—headed for the calaboose. It's under control now."

They pulled Alec to his feet. He began to sob uncontrollably. The men wrinkled their noses. Alec had emptied his bowels in his pants.

The city jail was only a couple of blocks away. Marshal Lee, Hennessey, Hanna, and two uniformed officers hauled Alec through the streets, making unsteady progress. Alec would go along meekly for a while, then start bucking like a mustang. Despite the noose and the handcuffs, he put up a good fight. They were all exhausted by the time they reached the jail and dragged him upstairs.

They left the handcuffs on him. They took off the noose and clamped an iron collar around his neck, then left him. The collar was connected to an iron ring in the floor by a chain so short that Alec couldn't stand upright. He had to lie on the cold stones or stand stooped over. He was drunk and exhausted and covered with cuts and bruises. He stank of his own piss and shit. He was afraid to fall asleep. What if they tried to hang him while he slept?

But Alec Mack need not have worried about sleeping for several hours yet. A few minutes later the two big Irishmen in black coats came back. Hennessey and Hanna looked at him as if he were a cockroach to be crushed, and put on their brass knuckles.

3 6

~⚡~

$\mathcal{W}$ILL Porter at last had that elusive thing which all the world thought that a young man should have: a job. Not a part-time, on-again, off-again wisp of a job like his work at Harrell's cigar store; no, this was a bona fide, respectable, shine-your-shoes-and-wear-a-tie *job*.

Like most things in his life, for good or ill, this one pretty much fell out of the sky and into his lap. Will had usually done a bit of bookkeeping wherever he worked, whether at drugstores or at Harrell's, and that apparently qualified him to be taken on as an apprentice bookkeeper by the estimable firm of Maddox Bros. & Anderson, general land agents. Anderson was Charles Anderson, the father of a serenading friend and Will's latest patron.

The labor was neither difficult nor demanding, the atmosphere of the office was congenial, and the pay—a hundred dollars a month—was downright generous. There was the added advantage that the office was located in the same building as the *Statesman*. Will could invite Dave Shoemaker to lunch anytime he wanted, and could even pick up the tab.

Still, Will chafed at the change in his fortunes. He was used to his time being entirely his own, even if he mostly wasted it. He had the idler's conception of time as a placid ocean extending to infinity in all directions—boring, perhaps, but roomy. A man with a job suddenly found himself stranded on dry, rocky earth, staring forlornly at the mere puddle of free time at his feet.

There was an unsettling irrevocability about accepting genuine employment. Once the all-consuming maw of a real job opened up and swallowed a man, there was no way out of the whale's belly short of committing suicide or becoming a hopeless drunk. Will was bound to become respectable now. Next would come advancements and raises in pay, then marriage, then a comfortable little cottage, then a family . . . and it all started because a fellow got tired of always coming up short when everybody else pitched in a nickel for a pitcher of beer.

The job gave him something to think about other then Eula Phillips. It also meant that he was no longer free to come to her at any given moment, should she chance to summon him. But the hard fact was, since that one blissful afternoon at May Tobin's house, Eula had not contacted him again.

He checked his mail every day; she sent no message. Of course, since she was now back in Austin and lived only three blocks from him, she could deliver a note herself, or have Delia do it, or pay some boy on the street a penny. But there had been no note.

Why did she not contact him? He told himself that she must be busy, setting up house after the move from the farm. But how many days could it take to unpack a trunk? Perhaps her husband's suspicions had been aroused, and he was watching her every move; perhaps her baby had been sick and needed constant care; perhaps Eula herself had come down with dengue fever. Even so, could she not at least send him a note to say that she couldn't see him for a while? It would need to say no more than that, it would not even need to be addressed or signed, and he would understand. A simple scrap of paper pushed under his door with the words *I cannot see you for a while* and his mind would be at rest. Instead, she was silent. Will went through every excuse he could think of, except the possibility that she had simply lost interest in him.

Over and over again, he tried to recall the exact look on her face on the day she moved back, when he saw her on the verandah and their eyes met. She had recognized him; she had looked surprised. Had her face expressed anything else—regret, longing, distaste, hatred, hope? No: only recognition and surprise. There had been no time for anything else; the moment passed too quickly. He might as well have exchanged a fleeting glance with the Sphinx.

The look Jimmy Phillips had given him that day had been less ambiguous. Considering that, Will was hesitant to stroll by the Phillips residence too openly or too often. Still, it was a public street, and now that Will had a job it was reasonable—indeed, necessary—that he should pass by the house at least twice a day, going to the office and coming back again. He occasionally caught glimpses of Mr. and Mrs. Phillips, and Sallie Mack the washerwoman, and Delia, and even Jimmy, but never Eula. With the cooler days of October, the door to her room off the verandah was always shut; he couldn't even hope to hear her voice. Will imagined her inside, sitting in a rocking chair perhaps, holding the baby in her arms and singing to it, and he felt absurdly jealous of the child.

At night, alone in his room, he wrote to her. He composed pithy, clever letters, like those to his male friends, but when he read them over, his jokes seemed pathetic and his puns puerile, and he tore them up. He wrote long, romantic letters that laid his heart bare, but when he read those he blushed with embarrassment; had any lover in the history of the world ever spouted such drivel? His best efforts were like something from the novels women read on trains and then threw away before meeting their husbands at the station. And to think he fancied he would someday be a writer!

Will could have written a novel with all the paper he went through, attempting to write a letter to Eula Phillips.

At last, one afternoon at work, when he had a spare moment and couldn't keep his thoughts off her, he scribbled the simplest possible message on a scrap of ledger paper:

> *E.,*
> *When will I see you again?*
>   W.

He slipped the note into an envelope and sealed it. On the envelope he wrote *Delia*. That evening, on his way home from work, he dared to step into the Phillipses' yard, stole up to the bedroom window he knew to be Delia's, and dropped the envelope inside. His heart pounding, he retreated back to the street. As he passed the alley in back of the property, he saw Sallie Mack taking clothes from the line. Suddenly ebullient, he tipped his hat and said hello to her, but Sallie kept her head lowered and didn't speak.

The next day, passing the Phillips residence on his way to work, from the corner of his eye he saw Delia emerge onto the front porch and walk briskly down the steps. She appeared not to notice him, but as he crossed the street she caught up and began to walk alongside him, as if by chance.

Delia gave him a sidelong look. "You've been very indiscreet, Mr. Porter."

"You got the note, then?"

"I found it on the floor under my bedroom window, yes."

"Did you give it to Eula?"

"I showed it to her."

"What did she say?"

Delia pursed her lips. "You must understand something. This is a very hard time for Eula. She was unhappy at the farm. So was Jimmy. They both wanted to come back to Austin, and now they have. They have a baby, you know. They're trying very hard to make something of their marriage."

Will nodded. "Then she doesn't want to see me again," he said bitterly.

Delia sighed. "I don't know what Eula wants. I don't think she knows, either."

He shook his head. "I can't believe she feels nothing for me. That day at the widow's house—"

"She may care for you a great deal, Will."

"But I can't see her?"

"Not now."

"But someday?"

"I don't know. Eula isn't a free woman. You knew that from the start."

The memory of a precise moment at May Tobin's suddenly claimed all his senses. He could hear Eula's sigh, feel again the touch of her naked flesh, smell her hair. The memory was so powerful that it seemed more vivid than the present moment. He clutched Delia's arm. "I have to see her again!"

"You can't. Not now."

"Can I write to her, at least?"

Delia shook her head. "If anything should change, Eula can write to you."

"But what harm can there be, if I give the letters to you? After she reads them, she can burn them if she must, or give them to you for safekeeping. If I can't see her, she must at least let me write to her."

Delia looked at him. He reminded her of her brother, pleading to be given another chance. In Delia's experience, all men were like that, desperate for whatever they happened to want at a given moment. Men were like babies, always crying for attention; but if crying didn't get them what they wanted, they could resort to brute force. "They pretend to be helpless," May told her once, "they even think it's true, but don't ever forget that they're physically stronger." In every man there was a degree of menace. Jimmy had a good measure of it, and even poor Will Porter must have his share, as harmless as he seemed. Delia decided to placate him.

"If you insist on writing to her—"

"Yes?"

"I can't stop you. Do it just as you did yesterday: put my name on the envelope and drop it into my window. I'll see that Eula gets it. But you mustn't expect her to write back to you."

"I understand."

They parted. As he headed toward the office, Will was already composing a letter in his head. This would be *the* letter, he told himself, the one that would melt her heart.

Feeling flush with wealth and optimistic about the future, Will treated Dave Shoemaker to lunch that day at the Iron Front. Every so often Will would pull a scrap of paper from his coat pocket and jot down a phrase, so as not to forget it. Dave assumed he was writing a short story or a poem, and didn't pry.

At their usual table at the back of the establishment, the Robertson brothers were also having lunch. Either the steaks were unusually tough, or their knives were unusually dull; the meal was almost more work than it was worth.

"The city elections are practically upon us," said the mayor gloomily. "If the vote were today—"

"But it's not," said the district attorney. "The 7th of December is still two months hence. A lot can happen between now and then. Getting elected is like getting away with murder—it's all a matter of timing."

"If one more murderer gets away with it between now and election day, it shall be the end of me as mayor!"

James Robertson sat back, took a deep breath, and smiled. "I was saving the good news for dessert, big brother, but your mood's so sour I shall give it to you now."

"What good news?"

"It looks like hiring those Houston detectives is finally going to pay off. Marshal Grooms Lee assures me that within hours he shall have a full confession for the rape and murder of little Mary Ramey."

"Hallelujah for that," said the mayor quietly. "Who is the monster?"

"The marshal's original suspect, the fellow the hounds tracked down: Alec Mack."

"He's confessed?"

"Not yet. But the marshal assures me that the man will do so presently. Mack's in custody now."

"In custody? On what charge?"

"That's the beauty of it! Mack wasn't brought in on the murder charge. Lee arrested him for drunk and disorderly conduct, compounded by resisting arrest. But now that he's in the calaboose, Lee is confident that Mack will crack any minute."

The mayor blotted his lips with his napkin. "I see. This explains why William Holland wants to have another meeting."

"I got a note from him this morning, too. Well, if Holland wants to complain about Alec Mack's arrest, he won't get far with me. Being colored is no excuse for creating a disturbance at two o'clock on a Sunday morning; Mack will have to take his licks for that. And if Holland means to complain again about the lack of progress in solving the murders, I shall ask him what *he's* done to dissuade his colored brethren from slaughtering their own womenfolk."

"James! That's not worthy of you. William Holland is a decent fellow, and half-white, to boot."

"Well, my patience has worn a bit thin, too. I only hope that when I obtain a conviction against Alec Mack for the murder of Mary Ramey, our friend Holland will be as eager to thank me as he has been to complain." The district attorney smiled. "There's more good news. Thanks to the men from the Noble Detective Agency, we may also have an arrest soon for the very first of these murders, that of Mollie Smith. You may remember that suspicion fell on the dim-witted fellow who lived with her, and received a wound to the head himself, name of Walter Spencer. Hennessey and Hanna tell me that they've subjected Spencer to fresh scrutiny and are certain they'll obtain evidence enough for an arrest quite soon, perhaps even another confession." He leaned across the table toward his brother. "Once charges are brought against these fellows, I'll do some juggling with the dockets and see if I can't schedule the trials so as to coincide with the election. What do you say to that, big brother? Surely nothing would do more to help your reelection than a couple of timely convictions to show that something's being done about these awful murders."

"Amen to that," said the mayor.

"You see, John, I'm doing what I can to make both you *and* Mr. Holland happy. These murderers shall get their comeuppance. The law will not be mocked!"

37

$\mathscr{A}$LEC Mack did not confess to the murder of Mary Ramey. After nine days and nights, he was released from the city jail and allowed to go home. When his mother saw what they had done to him, she wept.

The story of what happened to Alec Mack was first reported not in the *Statesman*, but in the evening *Dispatch*, a small Republican daily notoriously sympathetic to the colored population. The story in the *Dispatch* was based on interviews with Hugh Hancock, who had seen the arrest; with Sallie Mack, who tearfully described her son's scars; and with Alec Mack himself, who claimed to have been kept chained like an animal and to have been repeatedly beaten and tortured while he was incarcerated. The bruises and abrasions around his neck gave credence to Mack's assertion that he had been repeatedly strangled by a noose until he lost consciousness, then revived by buckets of water thrown in his face.

The *Dispatch* story also contained comments by a white man, Mr. Press Hopkins, a respectable carpenter living at 908 Trinity Street. On the night of the arrest, the commotion in the little park across from the Wesley Chapel had awakened his wife, who had subsequently awakened Hopkins, telling him, "There's a lynching going on!" Hopkins ventured onto his porch with a lamp and a gun, and claimed to have seen Marshal Grooms Lee, along with two uniformed policemen and two other men, kicking and beating a prisoner who was lying on the ground, apparently in convulsions. It was Hopkins's belief, based on utterances overheard by himself and his wife, that the men intended to lynch the prisoner, and refrained from doing so only because he called out and questioned them.

William Pendleton Gaines strode into the *Statesman* offices that after-noon, clutching a copy of the *Dispatch*. "This is an outrage!"

"You mean the torture of Alec Mack?" asked Hiram Glass.

"Hell, no! It's outrageous that we were scooped by this Republican rag! Where's *our* story, damn it?"

"We should give Marshal Lee a chance to defend himself," suggested Dave. He grinned across the aisle at Hiram, who flashed a thin smile in re-turn. The idea of the marshal being called on to give an account of his be-havior, like an errant schoolboy, strongly appealed to them both.

And so the Alec Mack affair began. Under different circumstances, the mis-treatment of a colored prisoner in the calaboose might have attracted little notice, much less outrage. But a growing number of responsible citizens had begun to lose patience with Marshal Grooms Lee. They blamed his inability to make a solid arrest on laziness or incompetence; they ques-tioned his judgment in hiring private detectives from another city, and endowing those detectives with extraordinary powers; they suspected him of having gone well beyond the law in his interrogation of Alec Mack. Even a colored man was innocent until proven guilty.

Some had never liked Grooms Lee from the start. His father's political connections counted for him in some circles, against him in others. Some wanted Lee out of the way because they coveted the job of marshal for themselves or an associate. These various foes of the marshal were not all natural allies. It was the Alec Mack affair, occurring after nine months of unsolved murders and two months before the city elections, that acted as the catalyst. A faction dedicated to the end of Grooms Lee's career coa-lesced within the body politic and on the city council—which, after the elections in December, would have the duty of either reappointing the mar-shal or hiring a new one.

Marshal Lee declined an informal interview with the *Statesman*. Instead, he delivered a written statement, which the paper published verbatim. He began with an attack on the story in the *Dispatch*, and proceeded to give his version of the arrest:

> About two o'clock on Sunday morning, October 4th, call-ing officers Johnson and Connors and detectives Hen-nessey and Hanna to my aid, I proceeded to the Black Elephant saloon, where I expected to find Alec Mack.

Upon reaching the saloon, I halted in front, while those with me proceeded some distance beyond. Seeing Alec inside, I called to him to come to the door and to go with me. I saw he was very drunk and expected to have trouble with him, knowing his vicious disposition when under the influence of liquor.

Upon arriving at the place where my aides were standing, I informed him that I wished to question him in the murder of Mary Ramey, and proposed holding him in the city jail for that purpose until such time as he was sober enough.

Anxious to conduct all my movements as quietly as possible, I directed that we proceed to our destination through as many unfrequented streets as possible. While on our way to the jail, and particularly while passing Press Hopkins's residence, Mack was very boisterous, at times violent, struggling with all his might to get away from us. His screams and yells were enough to frighten any lady. I have not learned that anyone was thrown into convulsions. We had several severe tussles with him. We did manage to put a pair of nippers on him, but he was not maltreated in any way. Only such force was used as was absolutely necessary to conquer him.

Upon reaching the calaboose, Mack became furious and commenced to fight vigorously, viciously, and well nigh successfully. I never saw such resistance by any prisoner before. We finally got him into the corridor and a cell was opened, at sight of which he renewed his struggle. In order to restrain him, he was shackled and chained to a ring in the floor, else he would have bolted before we could turn the key on him.

If Mack has any bruises or scars on his person, they are the result of his own desperate efforts to resist arrest and incarceration. He is one of the most desperate and vicious men I have dealt with in my tenure as marshal. He will bear close watching.

The statement spread oil upon the waters. Even the marshal's staunchest opponents conceded that he deserved an impartial hearing of the facts.

* * *

At first, Will's letters to Eula were mere notes, short, discreet, and restrained. Many consisted of a single question: *When may I see you again? Are you well? Do you remember?*

She did not reply.

His letters to her became longer and less restrained. Instead of making a fool of himself with cosmic declarations of love, his sense of humor took over. Thus he wrote to her, around the middle of October:

> *Dearest E.,*
>
> *Since you were evidently put off by my previous suggestion that you introduce me as your cousin Louis from St. Louis (though I still think that would be a fine ruse), how's this for an idea: I will buy a putty nose and false eyebrows for a disguise and knock on your door under pretext of being a commercial traveler. What does the family need? Liver tonic, sheet music, garden shears? I can supply the finest products at a loss, thereby insuring that the family will invite me back and be glad to see me when I come. All this, just to get a glimpse of your smile on a regular basis, say once a week. Write back at once to express your opinion of this scheme. If I do not hear from you, I shall assume you approve, and will commence shopping for the nose tomorrow.*
>
> *Will-ingly yours,*
> *W.*

What did she think when she received such a letter? Did she laugh? Sigh? Think him sweet, or mad, or hopelessly childish? Could she not read between the lines and see how he was suffering? Did she feel nothing for him, not even the empathy one feels for a wounded stranger?

Did she live in fear of her husband? The fellow certainly looked mean enough. Was she dominated and watched over by her mother-in-law? Had she decided for the sake of her child to give up all hopes of happiness? Perhaps she longed for Will as dearly as he longed for her, and resisted flying to his side only by an enormous act of courage and self-sacrifice; perhaps she was noble rather than cruel, and he was wicked to tempt her. Perhaps his letters caused her to suffer exquisitely, and in silence. Who could know? Even Delia claimed to be unable to tell what Eula wanted.

Perhaps money was the problem. Could it be as simple as that? Eula had paid for the room at May Tobin's when he couldn't. Perhaps she had run out of money. Will's circumstances had changed; he had a job now and could pay for the room. He wrote to let her know:

Enchanted Vowel,
   Did I tell you, I have honest employment now and am flush with legally gotten gains? Is lucre a problem? I can pay. What day shall I tell the widow to expect us? Shall I wear the putty nose, so as to be discreet, or shall you?

Will-fully yours,
W.

There was no response.

Perhaps Eula was not receiving his letters. Was it possible that Delia was a faithless go-between, that she had gone over to her brother's side, that she was reading Will's letters for a laugh and then tossing them away? One Saturday he chanced to see Delia in front of the display window of a dressmaker's shop on Pecan Street. He sidled up next to her.

"Have you received my letters?" he asked.

"Yes, Mr. Porter."

"Have you passed them on?"

"I have."

"But she sends no reply."

"I don't know what to tell you, Mr. Porter. My sister-in-law is . . . *busy* these days. For the time being, you must rein in your feelings. You must play the stoic."

"I'd rather hear that from Eula herself."

"I'll tell her." Delia headed into the dressmaker's shop. She paused in the doorway and smiled over her shoulder. "Oh, and Will—whatever else you may do, do *not* come to the house wearing a false nose. What with all these crimes in town, Jimmy might shoot you dead before you could say a word!"

October gave way to November. Autumn hardened into winter. The days grew shorter. The dengue fever subsided. There were days of Indian summer, when golden sunlight shone through the naked trees, but on other days, cold winds swept down from the north, mantling the sky with iron-gray clouds.

With the change of seasons, Delia shut her bedroom window and locked it. Not to be thwarted, Will discovered that there was a very thin gap where the upper and lower sash met. The gap was just wide enough to admit his final letter to Eula Phillips:

Favorite Letter of the Alphabet,
    The days are cold, the skies are dark. How I need your smile to warm me!
    I will trouble you no more. Does this relieve you? Do you care at all?
    Walk with me down the Avenue, past the widow's place and onto the bridge. See there, far below, the dark, turbid stream? Rushing and whirling and eddying under the dark pillars with ghostly murmur and siren whisper. What shall I find in those depths? Rest?—Peace?—Catfish? 'Tis but a moment. A leap! A plunge! And then—oblivion? They say a man once disappeared into those depths and returned to the land of the living with a horse collar and a hoopskirt. What do we know of the beyond? We return no more to this world of trouble and care—but where do we go? Are there lands where no living traveler has been, where no mortal foot has trod? A chaos, a void—perhaps Bastrop—perhaps New Jersey! Will we fare worse there? We could not be given worse fare. To get there we pay the worst fare.
    Hark, a cry from the ice factory! A man orders us off the bridge. Does he fear we will jump? No, we forgot to pay the toll.
                                    Lacking will to go on,
                                          W.

The evening after he delivered the letter, Will took a long walk down the Avenue. He lingered for a while across the street from May Tobin's. In the space of half an hour he saw several hackney cabs come and go, depositing and picking up passengers. The men wore turned-up collars and hats with turned-down brims. The women wore veils. Such disguises hardly seemed necessary, given the darkness.

On the day of their tryst, had Eula arrived and departed thus, hiding her face behind sequins and tulle, like some truant beauty from a sultan's harem? Will smiled, remembering the room, the bed, the lemon sherbet. He cringed, remembering his unexpected encounter with William Shelley in the parlor.

Eventually, someone in the house noticed him. An enormous colored man stepped onto the porch and gave him such a look that he moved on.

He walked past the lumberyard and the ice factory, paid the toll, and stepped onto the bridge. It was perfectly normal and acceptable to loiter on the span for a bit, taking in the stars above, watching mysterious bits of drift-wood float by below, wondering at the eddies glimmering silver and green beneath the moonlight; a bridge was as much an amusement as a means of passage. But the toll taker did not like the way Will looked at the water, and told him to either cross or come back.

Will returned to the northern terminus, walked again past the ice factory and the lumberyard, and passed directly in front of the Widow Tobin's.

A hackney cab pulled up and let out two gentlemen, who stepped directly in front of Will in order to cross the yard. One of the men tipped his hat; he was a big fellow with pince-nez spectacles and a bristling mustache. He seemed to be guiding his friend, a tall, thin man who carried a cane and wore the cobalt-blue spectacles of a blind man.

"What an odd pair!" Will thought, walking on. He tried to recall where he had seen them before.

THE meetings of the Austin city council were as stormy as the weather. The December election loomed like a thunderhead.

At the meeting of October 19, Alderman R. J. Hill, a partisan of Marshal Lee, proposed an ordinance to increase the number of policemen. There followed an acrimonious debate, during which it became clear that Alderman Hill was in the minority. The consensus held that the marshal, having accomplished nothing with the force at his disposal, would do no better with twice the men. "Double-naught still amounts to naught," as Alderman Radcliff Platt succinctly put it.

Platt owned a livery stable on East Pecan Street. At fifty, with his white hair and bushy white mustache, he looked a bit like the famous author Mark Twain. He was no less intolerant of humbug, and just as irascible when it came to castigating fools. He was also an implacable foe of the marshal, during whose tenure Platt believed the police force had become degraded, demoralized, and debauched. "There's men on the force ain't fit to be there. They don't think twice about dragging innocent fellows into the courts, and then braggin' about it. No sir, you won't see me votin' to increase the force until this council discharges ever' man who's on it now, and hires some decent fellows to take their places!"

The council voted down the ordinance proposed by Alderman Hill. It was a stinging vote of no confidence in Marshal Lee.

The controversial detectives from the Noble Agency of Houston, Mr. Hanna and Mr. Hennessey, had been discharged by Marshal Lee. Alderman Hill proposed that the council hire other detectives.

"If you ask me," said Alderman Platt, "bringing in them damned detectives did a lot more harm than good. I wouldn't touch either one of those rats with a ten-foot pole! Maybe we ought to hire *two* sets of detectives—one to do the detecting, and the second set to keep an eye on the first!"

Alderman Hill withdrew the proposal rather than put it to a vote.

Worse was to come for the marshal and his partisans. Following a proposal by Alderman J. W. "Bud" Driskill, the wealthy cattle baron (and soon to become the city's premier hotelier), the council formed a special committee "to fully investigate the conduct of the special detectives while in the employ of the city of Austin, and further, to investigate the alleged outrages upon the colored man Alec Mack by the said detectives and by certain city officers."

The investigating committee took statements from Hugh Hancock, Sallie Mack, Alec Mack, and Press Hopkins. Subpoenas were issued to Detectives Hennessey and Hanna, who could not be located. Subpoenas were also issued to Marshal Lee and police officers Johnson and Connors, who were ordered to appear before the committee on Tuesday, the 10th of November.

The marshal and his men showed up at the council chambers accompanied by their lawyer. Dudley Goodall Wooten, son of a prominent Austin surgeon, was only twenty-seven, but he was a Princeton graduate and had a cosmopolitan air. Wooten was tall and thin and wore a black frock coat. He was clean-shaven and kept his hair quite short, except for a forelock twisted into a curl on his forehead. He had the look of a dandy, which often disarmed opponents in the courtroom, to their regret.

The committee informed the marshal and his men that they intended to question each of them individually and alone.

Mr. Wooten replied that he would have to be present if any of his clients were to be questioned.

The committee informed the marshal and his men that neither they nor their attorney would dictate rules of procedure to the committee.

Mr. Wooten objected that his clients had the right to be represented by counsel during all phases of any investigation. He demanded that his clients be allowed to confront and cross-examine any witnesses who made allegations against them. He further demanded that his clients be allowed to call their own witnesses.

The committee again reminded Marshal Lee and the officers that their attorney was not to dictate rules to the committee.

Mr. Wooten objected that his clients had no legal obligation to relinquish their right to counsel at the behest of an ex parte, Star Chamber committee which intended to conduct its affairs in secret.

The committee instructed the marshal and the officers to withdraw into the anteroom, from which they would be summoned singly, without Mr. Wooten.

After a whispered exchange, Marshal Lee, Officers Johnson and Connors, and Mr. Wooten rose and left the chamber.

The committee conferred briefly, then sent a clerk to summon Marshal Lee. The clerk returned alone. The anteroom was empty.

Later that same day, at the regular Tuesday night meeting of the city council, the committee members delivered their report, together with a strong denunciation of what they deemed deliberate attempts by Marshal Lee to thwart their efforts to give the matter a full, free, and fair investigation. The committee referred the matter back to the council and asked to be discharged.

Marshal Lee and Officers Johnson and Connors delivered their own statements to the council, denouncing as false any allegations that they had abused a prisoner in their custody, and denouncing the committee's illegal attempts to conduct its business in secret and to intimidate witnesses.

A motion was made to refer the matter to the city attorney. In effect, the investigation into the alleged abuses against Alec Mack came to an end.

The city election was less than a month away.

"Hiring Dudley Wooten was a good idea, Father," remarked Grooms Lee at the dinner table that night, sliding his forefinger under his collar to loosen it a bit. The hour was late, and the collar was chafing him. "I didn't think much of his baby face at first—that stupid curl in the middle of his forehead! But he's sharp as a tack and stubborn as a bulldog. We've got 'em on the run now."

Joseph Lee pondered his soup glumly. On the face of it, the situation was absurd! Some colored women of no account had been murdered, by one or more colored men. It was a distasteful and messy business, but what else could one expect when a race of savages were cut free from their rightful masters and left to their own moral devices? A colored man had been questioned by the police, who were only doing their job, and who might or might not have been a bit rough with him—and such a hue and cry had resulted that it was liable to be the end of his boy's career!

It all came down to politics and jealousy. Joseph Lee was too old to care what others thought of him—but it pained him to see his son brought down by the animosity of small-minded men. He had such hopes for the boy!

If only the books could be closed on one of the murders . . .

"What's happening with that other colored fellow you intended to arrest a while back—the one involved in the first murder?"

Grooms Lee put down his spoon. "It so happens that the district attorney and I were discussing Walter Spencer this afternoon. I think I've finally talked Robertson around to seeking an indictment—especially as it seems there'll be no case against Alec Mack. He thinks he can expedite the process and schedule a trial before the city elections."

"Still, it may be a hard case to prove," observed his father. "Wasn't Spencer hit in the head and knocked senseless by the same ax that killed Mollie Smith?"

"So it appeared. But what better way to divert suspicion from himself? If you ask me, the blow to his head was never that serious. How hard can it be for a darkie to pretend he's in a daze?"

"I assume, then, that those detectives found new evidence against Spencer?"

Grooms Lee did not answer at once. "It's not really a question of new evidence. I've figured all along that it had to be Spencer who killed Mollie Smith. It was the district attorney who disagreed, but now he's seen the light. Just you watch, Father. Once we send Spencer up to be hanged, folks will forget all this fuss over Alec Mack."

"I hope so, son," said Joseph Lee. Still, he was fretful. In his long years of experience, he had seen many a fine fellow—men as brave and upright as his own son—brought down by the machinations of lesser men. The hard truth was that much of the world was run by unscrupulous careerists, men who wouldn't hesitate for a heartbeat if they thought that by ruining some other poor fellow they could further their own advancement.

On Friday, the 20th of November, the district clerk filed an indictment against Walter Spencer.

The next morning, Marshall Lee and several of his men arrived at the house of Cynthia Spencer on Brazos Street. The marshal asked for her son.

When Walter appeared, the marshal told him that he was under arrest for the murder of Mollie Smith.

Walter trembled. Cynthia Spencer wailed and tore her hair. Every colored person in Austin knew the story of Alec Mack.

They need not have worried. The arrest was carried out in broad daylight, and not a finger was laid on Walter as he was marched to the calaboose, where he was locked up in a clean, dry cell to await his trial.

39

FANNIE Whipple's house on Red River Street was not nearly so elegant as May Tobin's place on the Avenue. The roof leaked in places. The front porch was overdue for a fresh coat of paint. There was no fancy brass knocker on the door. Inside, the hall carpet was worn and the wallpaper in the parlor was peeling. Still, Fannie prided herself on maintaining an establishment where her visitors could feel comfortable. Every bed had a good mattress, the pillows were stuffed with goose down, and the sheets were kept crisp and clean. No one ever complained of the beds in Fannie's house.

Fannie Whipple and May Tobin, each working independently, had arrived at similar ideas of how to run their households. If they had been men openly engaged in what the world deemed legitimate commerce, their operations might have been discussed in the business columns of the *Statesmen*. But the covert ways of women such as Fannie and May were known only to the immediate circle of those who sought them out. The two women had not even known of each other's existence until a mutual client happened to remark to each of them on certain similarities shared by his two favorite establishments in Austin.

All the men and women who came to May's house were white. "Fannie's girls" were all, like herself, colored, or of mixed race, as were many of her male visitors, but there were also white men who frequented Fannie's house, and among those white men, quite a few had been known to pay an occasional visit to May, too. Both women perceived that it made no sense for them to regard one another as rivals, given that male visitors came to their different establishments seeking different things, or at least different shades of the same thing. The women met and formed a cordial bond based on mutual regard, as any two businessmen in the same field might do, and thereafter they engaged in friendly give-and-take. If a fellow at May's happened to express an appreciation for colored beauty, May would refer him to Fannie. Likewise, if one of Fannie's white visitors should inquire about establishments with women of his own color, and if he should appear to be of the proper caliber—Fannie, too, was patronized by the occasional cattle baron, politician, or university professor—she would refer him to May. The women kept one another apprised of visitors who had proven to be difficult or dangerous, and met every so often to discuss the temperament of the city's law enforcers.

And so, Fannie was not entirely taken aback when, one November evening, a note arrived from May Tobin, saying that she would be obliged if Fannie would put up a couple of white women, both fine young ladies and friends of May's, at her house on Red River for a day or two; the ladies would pay for their rooms, of course.

It was all quite mysterious. "Now why do you reckon these girls need some place to lay their heads in the first place?" she asked herself. "And if they's such good friends of May's, why ain't they stayin' with her? And what are some of my fellows likely to think if they catch a glimpse of a blond head and a pair of blue eyes in this house? I don't want nobody gettin' the wrong idea about the color of this establishment, it'll only lead to confusion and trouble! And where am I gonna put up a pair of fine white ladies, anyway? I s'pose I best clear out the two bedrooms upstairs to make a suitable place for 'em!"

The young ladies arrived an hour later. Fannie ushered them into the parlor. It was not as elegant as May's parlor—there was no chandelier or piano—but the rug was new and there was a roaring blaze in the fireplace. The brunette introduced herself as Delia and her friend as Eula. They were both strikingly beautiful and carried themselves like true ladies of quality, though they were both highly agitated. Fannie offered them tea and dispatched her servant girl to fetch it.

"Lawdy, you both look like you seen a ghost!" said Fannie.

"Oh, Miss Whipple," said Delia, "you have no idea."

"There's a fellow back of this," said Fannie sagely.

"My husband," said Eula quietly.

"Who also happens to be my brother," added Delia.

"Oh, dear!"

"He drinks," said Eula.

Fannie nodded. "Don't they all? One of these days they'll make liquor 'gainst the law, and I won't be half-sad."

"There was a terrible fight," said Delia. "I'm ashamed of my own part in it. Honestly, you'd think we were both still ten years old, the way Jimmy and I carry on sometimes."

"Brothers and sisters!" said Fannie. "They's nobody can carry on a fiercer fight, 'cept husband and wife. Pullin' hair and th'owin' rocks—brothers and sisters jus' be practicin' for marriage when they's little. A woman gots to learn to defend herself, and the earlier the better."

Delia sighed. "I can't say that I'm proud I swung the shovel at him."

"You *what?*"

"I swung a shovel at him."

"She didn't just swing it," said Eula. "She hit him smack in the face."

Fannie covered her mouth and shrieked with laughter. Delia and Eula looked at each other, flustered, then couldn't help joining her.

"I don't see nothin' to be 'shamed of," declared Fannie. "Ain't been the man born yet who couldn't use a mite more sense knocked into his head. If it take a woman with a shovel to do it, then 'So Mote It Be,' as them Masons say. What happened then? You knock him cold?"

"Hardly," said Delia. "I think he was too drunk to feel much pain. It only made him madder. I ran into my room and locked the door. Jimmy kept yelling and banging on the door, but I wasn't about to open it—"

"Open it?" said Eula. "How could you, with him yelling like that? 'I'll kill you! I'll kill you, God damn you!' That's what he kept yelling. Blood streaming down his face—"

"Lawdy!" Fannie shook her head.

"Then he kicked in one of the door panels," said Delia.

"Lawd o' mercy!"

"Then Mother and Father somehow pulled him away from the door. I slipped past them and ran into the yard with Eula. Jimmy came after us, but I picked up the shovel again and Eula stood behind me, and we screamed for the police. It was so humiliating! All the neighbors were watching. Poor Mother, it just about killed her." Delia's eyes shone with tears.

"Did the police come?"

"No, thank goodness," said Eula. "Jimmy was running out of steam. He started babbling and crying and let his parents put him to bed. Delia and I packed a few things and got out of there as fast as we could. I told Mr. and Mrs. Phillips that we were going to Manchaca to stay with my sister. We headed straight for May Tobin's. But May doesn't have room for us tonight. She said we could stay with you for a while. Jimmy would never find us here. Is it really all right, Miss Whipple?"

"Lawd, chile, a woman gots to have someplace to go when her man's on the rampage."

"Bless you, Miss Whipple! Thank God for you and May Tobin."

"Call me Fannie, chile."

Eula stared at the fire. She began to weep. Delia put her arm around her. "It's the baby," explained Eula.

"Baby!" exclaimed Fannie. "Lawd, chile, a slip of a thing like you has a baby?"

"A little boy. I left him with Mrs. Phillips. It seemed like the only thing to do. I didn't know for sure where we'd end up. He'll be all right, won't he, Delia? Jimmy loves the baby. Jimmy would never hurt him."

"Of course not," said Delia. "Don't cry."

"But—I miss him. I miss the baby!"

"Of course you do. Cry, then, if you need to, dearest—"

Eula laughed through her tears. "But you don't understand. *I miss him.*"

Delia wrinkled her brow.

"Don't you see? I wasn't sure I *could* miss him. But I do. I miss my baby! I'm not so unnatural, then, am I? I'm not such a monster, after all!"

Eula burst into fresh tears. Delia embraced her and cooed and stroked her hair. Fannie Whipple stared at the two of them, trying not to judge. White folk could be mighty peculiar!

Delia and Eula spent that night at Fannie's house. Late the next night, a young white gentleman came to call on them.

It was none of Fannie's business who the fellow was or which of the women he came to see, as long as someone paid for the rooms, but one of her regular girls, who had a talent for overhearing things, told her that the fellow was a government clerk named William Shelley, and that he was the right-hand man of the next governor of Texas and practically ran a whole state department by himself. Fannie thought he looked too young to be all that important, but his manner was awfully cocky. "And he's mighty good-looking," the girl noted.

Late that night, Eula and Delia left Fannie's house, escorted by William Shelley. Some rooms had opened up at May Tobin's.

A few days later, while Jimmy was out, Delia returned home. She took the baby and met Eula at the station, and saw the two of them off on the southbound train to Manchaca, where Eula's sister lived.

Eula was only taking her mother-in-law's advice. Ever since his return to Austin, Jimmy had been drinking more than ever, and Mrs. Phillips had suggested to Eula several times that she ought to go stay with relatives for a while. If Jimmy could be made to think that Eula might actually leave him for good, Mrs. Phillips reasoned, perhaps he would finally straighten up. It was what they all wanted—for Jimmy to stop drinking, get a job, and become a good husband and father.

The trial of Walter Spencer, accused of murdering Mollie Smith "by striking and cutting her with an ax," commenced on the very day that city elections were held, the 7th of December.

Many in Austin were glad to see some legal action at last being taken in the first of the servant girl murders, and looked forward to a successful prosecution and hanging. Others found the timing of the trial suspicious, and believed it merely served to point up the woeful inability of the city to solve the crime problem. It was difficult to determine exactly how much the commencement of Walter's trial helped the incumbents and how much it hurt them, or to construe a mandate either for or against Marshal Grooms Lee.

In the mayoral contest, John Robertson's opponent was Joseph Nalle, a successful businessman known for his explosive temper. Nalle had dabbled in politics before. During his last term on the city council, an argument with a fellow alderman had turned into a street brawl that ended with Nalle stabbing the man twice in the heart. Nalle, a tiny fellow weighing less than 120 pounds, successfully pleaded self-defense. His aggressive style attracted admirers, especially when compared to John Robertson's plodding earnestness, but some reflected that Nalle might be the wrong man to lead the city out of the current crime rampage. The results reported in the *Statesman* the next day showed Mayor Robertson retaining his office by the slim majority of 1,327 votes to 1,293.

In the opinion of many voters, the city elections left matters in Austin more muddled than ever.

The trial of Walter Spencer lasted three days.

District Attorney Robertson had little to present that was not already common knowledge from newspaper reports and word of mouth. Nevertheless, he called a number of witnesses, among them young Tom Chalmers, whom Walter had awakened on the night of the murder; Nancy Brown, the nurse who lived in the house and tended to Mrs. Hall, and could testify to Mollie's regular tongue-lashing of the accused; the doctors who examined Mollie Smith and treated Walter's wounds; and Lem Brooks, whose testimony verified the victim's loose morals.

The jury consisted of a cross section of the male citizenry, from J. M. Day, the wealthy and well-known cattleman, to Wesley Edwards, a colored porter at the Avenue Hotel. They deliberated only briefly before returning their unanimous verdict.

Walter Spencer was found not guilty of the murder of Mollie Smith.

The new city council deliberated equally briefly on a motion put forward to the effect that Mr. Grooms Lee should not be reappointed to the post of city marshal. The motion passed. Grooms Lee was never fired; he was simply not rehired.

Will Porter spent much of his free time during the month of December rehearsing for *The Mikado.*

The traveling Emma Abbott Grand Opera Company, which had performed previous engagements at Millett's Opera House, was returning at the end of the month. Their matinee performance, as announced on the printed handbill, would be "The First Production by a Grand Opera Co. with THREE PRIMA DONNAS, Full Chorus and Orchestra and an enormous cast, of the Japanese Craze, THE MIKADO, by Gilbert & Sullivan." A representative from the company had come to town early to recruit singers for the chorus. Will and his serenading partners successfully tried out, and rehearsed with the other local chorus members as often as they could, gathering around a piano and sharing the sheet music. No payment was offered, but Will was promised several free tickets, and not for the cheap, fifty-cent gallery seats, but for reserved seats in the orchestra, which cost a dollar. The tickets would make excellent Christmas gifts.

The distraction offered by the rehearsals was something he sorely needed, for certain events occurring just down the street from his boarding house were impossible to ignore. The shouting match which had taken place in the front yard of the Phillips house was the talk of the neighborhood for days; Will did not witness it himself, but heard several versions of it. Jimmy Phillips's behavior was shameful, people said. He and his sister both had been coddled too much when they were children. The sight of them having it out in public—Delia brandishing a shovel, Jimmy being pulled away by his parents—scandalized the neighborhood.

Regarding Jimmy's wife, people were mostly sympathetic. She was such a pretty thing, and made a sweet sight when she walked down the street pushing her baby carriage. How could she have known the trouble she was marrying into? She had gone off to stay with her sister in Manchaca, people said—who could blame her?—and rumor had it that she might not be coming back.

Hearing such gossip, Will could not help but feel a thrill of unspeakable hope. To hear Jimmy Phillips so thoroughly upbraided gave him comfort, and to know that Eula must be even more miserable than himself gave him a perverse satisfaction. The path to happiness remained as murky as ever, but out of such volatile elements, who could say what might result?

It was profoundly disheartening, then, when early one morning toward the middle of December Will noticed a Booth & Son wagon pulled up in front of the Phillips house. A crew was unloading several large crates.

"What are you delivering?" Will asked one of the men, who was an acquaintance.

"A suite of bedroom furniture."

"For old man Phillips and his wife?"

"No, for Jimmy. A surprise for his wife, I reckon—early Christmas present. Jimmy's stopped drinking, they say. Got himself a job working construction on the new fireman's hall."

"A spur-of-the-moment reformation, I suppose?" Will raised a skeptical eyebrow.

"All I know is that Mr. Booth is willing to give the fellow credit. He's letting Jimmy buy this stuff on the installment plan. We're supposed to uncrate it and put it together right away so's it'll be ready when his wife comes home this afternoon."

"Comes . . . home?" said Will dully.

"I reckon she'll be impressed. It's secondhand, not brand-new, but it's handsome furniture, solid pine."

Passing the Phillips house on his way to the office the next morning, Will chanced to see Jimmy Phillips leaving for work. Jimmy paused in the doorway to receive a farewell kiss on the cheek from Eula, who held her baby in one arm. She looked well rested after a night in her new bed, Will thought, and not so desperately miserable after all.

* * *

"What the devil has got into Gaines?" exclaimed Dave Shoemaker.

"Other than a lot of expensive whiskey and cigars and culinary delights beyond my lowly means, I can't imagine," replied Hiram Glass. "But I assume you refer to something specific."

"Have you seen this? This item he put in today's edition? This is what happens when the owner of a newspaper makes himself the editor—there's no one to edit *him!*" Dave passed the freshly printed edition across the aisle, jabbing his finger at the item in question. "Honestly! Does he think the city's gone too long without a murder?"

"Murders sell newspapers," noted Hiram, breathing in the smell of fresh ink.

"He's like the little boy who throws salt in the holiday punch. Imagine running such an item only a few days before Christmas!"

Hiram cleared his throat. "I presume you refer to this item headlined, 'The Assassinations: The Time of the Moon When They Occurred.' It sounds very scientific."

Dave snorted.

Hiram read aloud: "'Do sane men calmly plot and carry into effect horrible murders by the glaring light of the moon? Does the moon, as some assert, affect certain maniacs and intensify their disease? One thing is certain: virtually all the terrible assassinations of servant girls during the last year were committed within seven days of the full moon and under its baleful glare.' Fascinating!"

"Keep reading."

"'Soon, a full year will have elapsed upon the murder of Mollie Smith, marking a grim anniversary. And soon, the waxing moon will be full again. Will it shine down upon yet another bloody scene of cruel and ghastly death?'"

Dave shook his head. "Gaines is practically inviting the killer to strike again! It's madness."

Hiram arched his eyebrows. "Moon madness!"

4 0

⚜

$\mathscr{A}$s she lay down to sleep that Christmas Eve, Mrs. James Phillips, Sr., decided that she had much for which to be grateful. Eula was back with Jimmy. Jimmy had stopped drinking—he swore it was for good this time. Come January, the couple would celebrate their third anniversary. And Delia—headstrong, willful Delia—seemed to have made a genuine peace with her brother. Their public shouting match had embarrassed Delia as much as the rest of them, and hitting Jimmy in the head with a shovel seemed to have knocked as much sense into her as him.

It occurred to Mrs. Phillips that she should also give thanks that Sallie Mack's boy Alec was still among the living. No one could ask for a better tenant and washerwoman than Sallie. The poor woman had suffered greatly while her son was in the jail, and afterward had been heartbroken at the awful things done to him. No matter how hard her own lot sometimes seemed, Mrs. Phillips had only to think of Sallie Mack to be reminded of how truly blessed she was.

The house had been quiet all day long. Delia was out of town, visiting friends in Rosenberg Junction. Mr. Phillips was not feeling well, and spent most of the day in the spare bedroom, sleeping and reading. Mrs. Phillips kept busy in the kitchen, making holiday candy and watching the baby.

Around five o'clock, to be sure, there had been a particularly unpleasant quarter-hour. Mrs. Phillips had stepped into the parlor to find Jimmy and Eula on the sofa. Jimmy was reading the newspaper, Eula a novel. Eula lay on her side with her head in Jimmy's lap. It was such a pleasing picture that Mrs. Phillips stood quietly and watched them for a moment. Truly, they were a beautiful couple! Presently Jimmy noticed her standing there. He stirred. Eula sat up. Jimmy folded the newspaper and began to pace the room in his usual listless manner, then out of thin air proposed to go down to Booth & Son to pay an installment on the bedroom furniture. Eula frowned and bit her lip.

"But it's already five o'clock," Mrs. Phillips said.

"They'll be open late tonight, Mother, for the last-minute Christmas buyers."

This was the time of day, Mrs. Phillips knew, when her son was most sorely tempted to take a drink. And on this particular day, when so many people left work early, and even nondrinkers indulged in a bit of rum or hard cider, temptation was likely to come looking for Jimmy.

"If you go out now, Jimmy, you'll be out until midnight."

"Nonsense, Mother."

"It's Christmas Eve, Jimmy. Lots of folks are out. What if someone invites you to have a drink—"

"I'll go straight to Booth & Son and then come straight back," Jimmy insisted. "I just need to stretch my legs and get some fresh air. I won't be gone more than a quarter of an hour."

"I'll bet you the price of a cigar that you're not back in fifteen minutes," said Mrs. Phillips, trying to make light of her fear.

"You're on!" Jimmy grabbed his coat and was off.

Mrs. Phillips and Eula sat and talked about nothing in particular, each looking at the mantel clock from time to time. It was already growing dark outside. Mrs. Phillips had never passed such a dreadful quarter-hour. She asked Eula what she was reading.

"Oh, something by Francis Marion Crawford—*An American Politician.* It's about an Englishwoman who falls in love with a Boston Democrat."

"*Are* there Democrats in Boston?" asked Mrs. Phillips.

"I suppose it's meant to be whimsical. The people in the novel are all very rich and sophisticated, and they've all been to London and Paris." Eula sighed. "I don't think Austin is very much like Boston."

"I can't see why you should want to read a novel about a politician, anyway. This town is full of them, and they're all full of themselves!"

"Oh, I think politicians aren't all that different from other men," observed Eula with a faint smile.

Mrs. Phillips heard the sound of Jimmy's footsteps on the porch. It was a quarter-hour to the minute after his departure. She could have wept with relief.

After dinner, Eula let her hair down and sat on the floor in the parlor. While the baby crawled about on the rug, Mrs. Phillips sat behind Eula on the couch and helped her arrange her front hair in curl papers. Jimmy picked up Eula's copy of *An American Politician* and read quietly for a while, then fell into a glum mood.

"What's wrong, Jimmy?" his mother asked.

"Oh, I've got the blues. About money, mostly." Jimmy's job on the fireman's hall had just ended.

"Don't fret too much, son. No one's hiring now because it's the holiday season. Come the new year, you're bound to find another job."

Around ten o'clock, Eula and Jimmy and the baby retired to their room across the verandah. Eula said she had a craving for something sweet. Mrs. Phillips smiled and told her she couldn't have a bite of Christmas candy until Christmas Day, but said she would bring them some nuts and apples in a bit.

Mrs. Phillips looked in on her ailing husband, tidied up the kitchen, then cracked and roasted some nuts and sliced some apples. She crossed the verandah, feeling a sharp nip in the air, and entered the room to find Jimmy and Eula lying together on their new bed, facing each other, with the baby between them. Jimmy's arm was outstretched, so that the crook of his elbow made a pillow for the baby's head and his hand was on Eula's head, gently stroking her hair. The two of them were laughing and talking in low voices as they played with the baby's hands and feet.

Mrs. Phillips put the tray on the bureau, next to the lamp. She went back to the main house, thinking again what a beautiful couple they made. The bitterness between them seemed to be a thing of the past.

Mrs. Phillips prepared for bed. As she would be up and down all night tending to her sick husband in the next room, she did not undress entirely, but kept on her basque and stockings. She threw a shawl about her shoulders and lay back on her bed. The mantel clock in the parlor chimed eleven times. Soon she drifted into a light slumber, thinking of the many things she had to be grateful for that Christmas Eve.

It was perhaps an hour and a half later, after midnight, in the wee hours of Christmas Day, when she was awakened. She sat upright and listened. The cry came from the direction of Jimmy and Eula's room.

She hurried to the verandah. The cold air nipped at her ears. Perhaps she had only imagined the cry, she thought. Then she heard it again. It was Jimmy's voice, so strangely pitched that she barely recognized it.

"Oh, Mama!" he cried. "Oh, Eula!"

Mrs. Phillips crossed the verandah and opened the door.

The lamp was still burning on the bureau, though the flame was very low. Jimmy lay on the bed, waving his arms frantically in the air as if fending off an invisible attacker. "Oh, Mama! Eula, darling!" he cried, in a strange voice that turned the back of her neck to gooseflesh. The baby sat upright among the pillows against the headboard, sucking on a sliver of apple in his little fist.

For years to come, this was the scene that would haunt her nightmares. This was the image which her conscious memory would picture again and again, compulsively, against her will: the sight of her son's arms flailing in the air like monstrous snakes, and the baby sitting upright and staring at her dumbly with innocent, wide-open eyes, clutching that little piece of apple.

The lamp flickered. She blinked. As if a red lens had dropped before the projected image of a magic lantern, everything in the room seemed all at once to become saturated with the color of that shiny red apple. Jimmy and the baby were both covered with blood. The pillows were soaked with blood. A bloody ax lay in the middle of the floor.

Eula was nowhere to be seen.

As was his custom on Christmas Eve, William Pendleton Gaines hosted a party in his penthouse office. It began around suppertime and would last until midnight. All the *Statesman* employees were invited, as was anyone else who worked in the building, including the staff of Maddox Bros. & Anderson, for whom Will Porter worked.

The night staff of the *Statesman* had to work their regular hours that evening, putting together the Christmas morning edition, but much of their work had been done in advance and the workers moved freely back and forth between Gaines's office and their own, ink stains on their fingers and pens tucked behind their ears, carrying plates of food and cups of punch or eggnog. The holiday spread was a veritable banquet, with roasted chickens, warm and cold salads, platters heaping with Malaga grapes and roasted nuts and sliced oranges, sumptuous fruit cakes and bowls of fresh whipped cream.

A storm had passed through earlier in the week, but on this night the sky was clear. The door that led onto the penthouse balcony was left unlatched so that people might step outside to get a breath of cold, fresh air and enjoy the view of Pecan Street and the Congress Avenue skyline beneath the moonlight. It was on the balcony that Dave Shoemaker found Will, who had disappeared some time before. He was alone, gazing abstractedly over the stone rail at a streetcar passing below.

"It's cold out here, Will!"

"Is it?"

"I don't suppose you want to talk about it?"

"About what?"

"Whatever's been eating at you lately."

"Me? I'm happy as a lark."

"You're miserable as a mud puppy! Luckily for you, I know a medicine for melancholy."

"Are you a doctor?"

"Be patient and see."

Dave escorted Will inside and proceeded to medicate him. After several cups of strong eggnog, Will's mood altered dramatically. "Do you know what's missing from this party?" he asked Dave. "Music!"

"We've already sung every carol in the book," said Dave.

"Then it's time for some Gilbert and Sullivan!"

Will proceeded to entertain anyone in earshot with a highly abbreviated version of *The Mikado*. He had learned not just the choruses but many of the solos by heart, and along with his natural bass could eke out an excruciating falsetto. His one-man show soon attracted a large audience. It helped that most of his listeners were as medicated as he was.

He plunged into the song of the clownish Ko-Ko, the reluctant Lord High Executioner:

"As someday it may happen that a victim must be found,
I've got a little list—I've got a little list
Of society offenders who might well be underground,
And never would be missed—who never would be missed!
There's the nigger serenader, and the others of his race,
And the piano organist—I've got him on the list!
And the people who eat peppermint and puff it in your face . . ."

Dave withdrew to another corner with a heaping plate of food. Hiram Glass joined him.

"Your young friend's quite an entertainer," observed Hiram.

"He's just drunk. And in love, I suspect."

"That's no excuse."

"Surely it's the only excuse that's worth a damn."

"You, Dave Shoemaker—sentimental?"

"It's the eggnog, I reckon."

Across the room, Will was dashing through the convoluted plot. "So Ko-Ko says, 'By the Mikado's law, when a married man is beheaded his wife is buried alive.' And Nanki-Poo and Yum-Yum both gasp, 'Buried alive!' And Ko-Ko says, 'It's a *most* unpleasant death.'" William Pendleton Gaines, who was on his fifth cup of punch, cackled with laughter.

"So, Hiram, what are your plans for Christmas?" asked Dave.

"I plan to sleep all day long, maybe all week—go into hibernation and not come out until 1886."

"Does that mean you'll be staying up late tonight?"

Hiram flashed a thin smile. "As a matter of fact, I *do* have a reservation for a quarter past eleven at a certain widow's house later this evening."

"A reservation?"

"According to Mrs. Tobin, Christmas Eve is her busiest night of the year. All her rooms are booked well in advance."

"Who would have thought!"

From across the room came the sound of Will trilling in falsetto:

"Here's a how-to-do!
If I marry you,
When your time has come to perish,
Then the maiden whom you cherish
Must be slaughtered, too!
Here's a how-to-do!"

"I don't much care for Gilbert and Sullivan," said Hiram dryly. "Their sense of humor is entirely too morbid for my delicate sensibilities. What time is it getting to be, anyway?"

Dave pulled out his pocket watch. "Close on eleven."

Will, as the pompous bureaucrat Pooh-Bah, cried out, "'Chop it off! Chop it off!'" Gaines roared with laughter.

Hiram and Dave, having cleaned their plates, accompanied one another back to the table to forage for seconds. Hiram went first. He picked out a pair of drumsticks and piled his plate with macaroni and bean salad.

Will launched into the Mikado's big number. It fell in his natural range, and he boomed out the song with gusto:

"My object all sublime
I shall achieve in time.
To let the punishment fit the crime—
The punishment fit the crime!"

As Hiram moved toward the beverage table, he tripped. He managed to keep his plate upright but struck the table hard with his hip, upsetting the punch bowl, which sloshed its blood-red contents all over his groin.

There was a peculiar crackling, popping noise. Hiram let out a scream. His plate went flying through the air, scattering beans and bits of macaroni. The plate struck the floor and shattered into pieces.

Oblivious of the interruption, Will kept singing,

"To let the punishment fit the crime—
The punishment fit the crime!"

Dave lunged forward. He grabbed Hiram's shoulder to steady him—and received a shock such as he had never felt before!

Dave let out a yelp and bolted back. Hiram began to thrash about like a madman, clutching at his midsection. "Get it off me! Get it off me!" he screamed. Across the room, Will began to lose the attention of his listeners, until even he realized that something was seriously amiss.

Hiram tumbled to the floor, kicking and writhing, his teeth clenched in a maniacal grin, his face the color of ashes. Every time Dave tried to touch him, he recoiled from the shock. Suddenly Hiram clutched his chest and went stiff. His legs and toes extended in a rigid line. His body convulsed like a plucked bowstring—once, twice, three times—and then he went limp.

His mouth was set in a grimace. His eyes were wide open.

"What in blazes?" said Gaines.

"Oh, Jesus—I think I know!" Very cautiously, fearing a shock, Dave reached out to touch Hiram's forehead. It was covered with clammy sweat.

"Beelzebub! Mephistopheles! Get a doctor!" Gaines bellowed. The printer's devils went scurrying from the room. "Everybody else, except Dave, clear out! Out of here, now, all of you!"

When they were alone, Dave undid Hiram's pants. "I knew it! He's wearing that damned suspensory."

"What?" Gaines was aghast.

"A voltaic suspensory. You should know what the thing is. They run mail order advertisements for them in the *Statesman*."

"Well, yes, but I never thought to actually see one. Good God, you mean it wraps around his waist and then goes down to circle his . . ."

"That's exactly what it does."

"But what powers the thing?"

"There's some sort of battery in the back. I'm afraid to touch it!"

"Surely it's safe. Electricity is good for people."

"Maybe he put in too strong a battery, or maybe—look here, how badly frayed this section is. You can see naked wire! And when the punch got him wet—oh, Hiram. Hiram!"

"It must have been his heart, don't you think?" said Gaines. "For God's sake, close his eyes, Dave!"

His hand trembling, Dave reached out with two fingers and gently shut Hiram's eyelids.

The door opened. Gaines looked up and saw Will standing meekly in the doorway. "Damn it, unless you're the doctor, stay out of here!"

"But I—it's only—there's a man asking for Dave out here."

"For heaven's sake, tell the fellow to wait," said Gaines. "Show some respect for the dead, sir!"

"But he says Dave ought to come right away. He says there's been another murder."

Will went along with Dave. He couldn't stay at the *Statesman* offices after what had happened, and he was too excited to go home. The night was like a tamed horse suddenly gone wild, bucking this way and that.

The man who had come for Dave led them south down Congress Avenue, toward the river.

"Where the hell are we going?" asked Dave.

"It's a house on the south side of Water Street, a block east of the Avenue."

"Who lives there?"

"An old geezer named Moses Hancock and his wife. He's some kind of mechanic, I think."

As they passed May Tobin's house, both Dave and Will looked fleetingly at the lamp in the front window. Will thought of Eula. Dave thought of Hiram, who would never appear to claim his room that night. At the next intersection, they turned left.

"On the south side? This is all lumberyard," said Dave.

"There's houses on the next block," said the man.

They pressed on and came to a row of four little houses, all alike. It was obviously the second house they wanted; there were several horses hitched and a small crowd already gathered in the yard and on the porch. Dave pushed his way through. Will followed. A hubbub of voices surrounded them.

"—hit in the head a couple of times, at least. I heard one of the doctors say her skull's fractured in two places and there was—"

"Hit with what?"

"What do you think? An ax!"

"—husband found her in the backyard. His neighbor saw him carry her back into the house. That's how he got so much blood all over him—"

"—says he saw two men jumping over the back fence—"

"—after they raped her. Susan Hancock—Moses Hancock's wife! A white woman! Dragged out of her house and raped! It's come to this—"

"Listen! You can hear 'em comin'—bloodhounds!" The fevered conversation grew hushed as the baying of the hounds echoed across the cold, crisp air.

A uniformed policeman stood at the open front door. Dave tipped his hat. The man begrudgingly allowed him to step past, but blocked Will. Dave jerked his thumb and said, "He's with me." The policemen moved aside.

In the parlor, two men with doctor's bags were on their knees, bending over a figure on the floor. Nearby were two basins with several blood-soaked rags scattered about. The water in one of the basins was red and opaque; the water in the other was only slightly pink. A large man with a grizzled beard and a stunned look on his face sat in a wooden chair nearby, the front of his shirt covered with blood—Moses Hancock. Next to Hancock, warming his backside at the fireplace, was the newly appointed marshal, James Lucy. It was true, what people said—the fellow was hardly bigger than a boy. He must have had his uniform specially tailored to fit him, Will thought. Grooms Lee's old uniform would have swallowed him up.

Dave pulled out a pad and pencil. "Is she still alive, Dr. Burt?"

Dr. Burt scowled at them over his shoulder. "Oh, it's you, Shoemaker." He turned back to the patient without answering. "What do you think, Dr. Graves? Is there any way to stop the bleeding from her ears?"

"I'm afraid not. And look here, above her left ear, where the bone's been shattered—you can see clear through to the brain. Good God, she's convulsing again!"

The two doctors drew back, allowing Will a clear view of the woman on the floor. Her hair was densely matted with blood, as was the bosom of her dress, but they had cleaned her face, enough to show that she was considerably younger than her husband. Her eyes were wide open but showed no trace of white; it was as if the sockets had filled with blood, upon which her hugely dilated pupils floated like two pools of blackness. Blood streamed from her ears. Her arms flailed. The doctors held them down. Her chest heaved and her throat quivered. Thick, dark blood welled up between her lips, pouring over her cheeks and chin.

Will covered his mouth and turned away. He staggered out of the room, through the foyer, past the policeman and onto the porch. He was just in time to see the arrival of the bloodhounds. The moonlight gleamed on their shiny coats.

The policeman at the door pointed to a gate at the side of the house and shouted to the man with the leash, "Take 'em around back. I'll tell Marshal Lucy you're here."

As the baying of the hounds diminished, a man on horseback rounded the corner from the Avenue and galloped toward the house. He rode into the yard and right up to the porch. "Is Marshal Lucy here?"

"He's inside," someone said.

The man dismounted and ran to the front door. The policeman stopped him. The man said something in a low voice and the policeman at once drew back and let him pass. Will thought he overheard what the man said, but it scarcely seemed possible; surely he imagined it. But then a man in the crowd whispered, "Did he say there's been another murder? I swear that's what I heard him say!"

The hubbub swelled. The crowd rushed up to the policeman at the door. He raised his baton and told everyone to move back.

A little later, Dave emerged from the house, walking quickly and keeping his eyes straight ahead. He walked past Will as if he didn't see him. Will ran after him.

"Where are you going?"

"To catch a hackney cab in front of the widow's place," said Dave. "Hurry up, if you want to come!" He broke into a run.

Will was still feeling nauseous and lagged behind. Dave disappeared around the corner onto Congress Avenue. By the time Will caught up, a cab in front of May Tobin's house was pulling away. Will sprinted and leaped onto the sideboard as the cab gained speed. He climbed in beside Dave, who was shouting at the driver to go faster.

Will sat back, breathless and queasy. The jostling of the cab made him feel worse. "Where are we going?"

"There's been another murder!" shouted Dave.

"I know that. But where—"

"Wait—be quiet. I have to do this while my memory's fresh." Dave held his notepad in a patch of moonlight, squinting at the notes he had taken at the Hancock house and adding more scribbles. He muttered and cursed every time the pitch and sway of the cab sent his pencil skittering off the pad.

Will sat back and clutched his stomach.

The cab raced north along the Avenue until it came to Hickory Street. "Here, driver! Turn left!" Dave shouted. The driver made the turn so sharply that one side of the cab lifted clear off the ground. Will thought he would throw up for sure. Dave lost his pencil, which went flying through the window.

"God damn it!" Dave yelled. He looked helpless for a moment, then snapped his notepad shut and stuffed it into his breast pocket. "Go faster!"

The cab sped through the intersection with Colorado Street, almost running down two late-night revelers who scurried in opposite directions. One of them dropped a whiskey bottle, which shattered with a loud explosion.

"Faster!" Dave yelled. Will had never seen him in such a state.

"Throw cold water on it!" the driver shouted over his shoulder. "We're almost there—one more block—the corner of Hickory and Lavaca, right?"

The queasiness in the pit of Will's stomach intensified. "Where are we going?" he said.

The cab lurched to a halt. Dave pressed a coin into the driver's hand and leaped out. Trembling, breathless, queasy, Will sat motionless and watched Dave run across the yard, up to where a small crowd had already gathered before the verandah that connected the main part of the Phillips house with the annex where Jimmy and Eula lived. The verandah itself was brightly lit with lanterns.

The driver peered at the scene. "What the hell? Murder, did he say?" The man jumped down from his seat and went to join the crowd.

Will sat for a while, reluctant to leave the quiet darkness of the cab. A strange numbness seeped through him. At last he stirred and stepped out of the cab, moving like a man in a dream. The sounds of the crowd were muffled. The light from the verandah was oddly glaring, almost blinding. The cold night air seemed thick and heavy.

As he crossed the yard, all he could think was that he was stepping onto forbidden ground. This property was off-limits. This was the last place on earth where he was welcome. He was not allowed here. And yet, here he was, walking across the Phillipses' yard and up the short flight of steps . . .

Suddenly a policeman blocked his way. "Off the verandah, mister. Back in the yard."

A voice Will scarcely realized as his own said, "I'm with Dave Shoemaker. From the *Statesman*."

The policeman backed off. "Well, don't touch anything. And don't step on that footprint."

Will looked where the man was pointing. There was a blotch on the wooden floor of the verandah. For a moment he couldn't make it out, then realized it was a footprint. Beneath the harshly glaring lanterns, the blood still looked wet.

The door to the little annex stood open. Will moved toward it, again with the prickling sensation of entering a forbidden place. As he stepped inside, Dave brushed past, stepping out. Dave was scribbling in his notebook and didn't notice him.

The room was brightly lit, though not as brightly as the verandah. The first thing Will noticed was the basin of water on the floor, its surface reflecting shiny points of light; there had been basins of water in the Hancock parlor, too, he thought dully. A colored woman—Sallie Mack—was stooped over the basin, wringing out a rag, staining the rose-pink water a deeper red. She unstooped herself, went to the bed in the corner, and handed the rag to a white woman—Mrs. Phillips, who was tending to a man on the bed. Will couldn't see the man's face, because Mrs. Phillips blocked his view, but he knew it must be Jimmy. The bed and the pillows had been strewn with towels; here and there blood penetrated the towels with circles of red, like wounds seeping through a dressing.

He was standing in their bedroom.

He was standing in *their* bedroom. That was the full measure of how great the catastrophe must be, that he, of all people, should be standing there, unchallenged, virtually unnoticed. The room was like a vanquished city: the walls had been breached and the guards had scattered; the mother wept over her son; the sanctuary stood open for any stranger to violate. A sense of doom hung so thick in the air that it choked him.

He looked about the room. Details etched themselves indiscriminately into his mind. Nearby, atop the bureau, he noticed a book with a green bookmark inserted halfway through; the spine read *An American Politician* by F. Marion Crawford. This detail registered with the same weight as the fact that an ax was lying near the foot of the bed, the blade and handle smeared with blood.

He found himself distracted by the bureau, and the little vanity, and the bed itself. This was the bedroom suite he had heard about, Jimmy's gift to Eula, the proof of his reformation, the reaffirmation of their marriage. How he hated these inanimate pieces of wood! Hated them so much that he gleefully would have taken an ax and chopped them all to bits, and burned every plank and knob until nothing but ashes remained. He had imagined the bedroom suite to be infuriatingly beautiful, the most beautiful bed and bureau and vanity that ever existed, smooth and polished and gleaming, furnishings of perfect delight, obscenely seductive. By the light of the glaring lanterns the pieces looked pathetically shoddy and secondhand, stained and scarred and crudely made. He felt ashamed of himself for having hated them so much. Mrs. Phillips chanced to look at him with a stricken, befuddled expression on her face, and his shame drove him from the room.

The lanterns on the verandah dazzled him. Rather than move toward the murmuring crowd in the yard, he moved in the opposite direction, not thinking where he was headed.

"Don't step on the footprint!" the policeman yelled, but Will heard only a vague nattering. He stepped down into the back yard, so deep into forbidden territory that it was beyond imagining. He might as well be on the moon!

There were lanterns at the back of the yard, where several people were gathered in a circle. It was like a garden party. He felt giddy and oddly disconnected from his body, the way he sometimes felt when he had a fever. He moved toward the little group to see what they were all staring at.

The men were talking among themselves, their voices strangely devoid of emotion.

"They did her just like they did all those colored girls—smashed her skull in, then dragged her outside to finish it."

"Must have raped her. You know they must have."

"The doctors'll be able to tell."

"Must have been two of 'em. One to hold down her arms with that plank of wood, while the other—"

The group was so tightly huddled that he couldn't see much. Some of the men glanced over their shoulders and saw him, then drew apart to make room, as if it were only polite to allow the newcomer to have a look.

Eula lay on her back. She was naked. Her legs were spread apart and her arms extended over her head, so that her body formed an X. A long piece of planking had been laid across her upper arms. There was no expression, no hint of human personality to be read on her face. Her head had been smashed in.

From far away, carried across the cold, still air, came the distant baying of bloodhounds. The sound of the dogs was joined by another—the lonely, moaning whistle of a railroad train somewhere on the Missouri-Pacific line, steaming through the night.

The Journey Back:

*N*OTHING frees the intellect and stimulates the mind like a train journey, thinks William Sydney Porter. Even a short trip on an elevated train in New York is conducive to a rarefied state of contemplation, from which plots and characters spring full-blown like Athena from the brow of Zeus; many an O. Henry story has been conceived while clattering above the streets of Manhattan, catching glimpses of faces in windows and watching the throngs of humanity below.

The long journey from New York to Texas has been many times more stimulating. He has gazed for hours at the ever-changing scene outside the window, lulled by the rhythmic clickety-clack of the wheels, nestled safe as a baby in his comfortable seat and yet exhilarated by the constant sense of motion and speed. In this bemused mental state, not just stories but whole anthologies have passed through his head. At night he sleeps without dreams, for the dreams all visit him during the day.

He feels as if a cool, bracing wind has swept through the cluttered attic of his mind, clearing away cobwebs and cleaning dust-choked corners, bringing to light memories stored far back in the recesses of his mind.

Until he was under way, he had no idea how much he needed this trip. Bless Dr. Kringel, best of all traveling companions, for appearing out of nowhere and whisking him away! Bless Dr. Edmund Montgomery down in Texas, for sending the mysterious summons that set the trip into motion.

In these last stages, as Texas looms nearer—they shall arrive tomorrow— Porter has found himself contemplating the figure of Dr. Montgomery with considerable curiosity. What secret can the philosopher possibly know about the fate of Eula Phillips twenty years ago? What conceivable connection could exist between Eula and Montgomery?

He continues to dip occasionally into his traveling companion's copy of Montgomery's *Philosophical Problems in the Light of Vital Organization.* Porter still cannot make hide nor hair of it, but from the text and from his own scant memory, he has drawn a mental picture of the author. He imagines the aged Dr. Montgomery with white hair and great white sideburns and a Scottish burr. It amuses him to think of the man as a philosopher-hermit-sleuth, contemplating old crimes from his shady retreat at Liendo and coming up with solutions based on pure logic and philosophical insight. What a lucrative series of stories one might milk out of a character like that! Alas, Porter has no talent for detective stories. Like those of Mark Twain, his occasional forays into detective fiction inevitably turn into parody; no one but the English can write with a straight face about "clews" and lost heirs and hidden trapdoors. Still, he might have a bit of fun with a philosopher-hermit-sleuth; if ever a book deserved a bit of lampooning, it is surely *Philosophical Problems in the Light of Vital Organization.*

Of more immediate interest to Porter is a volume he picked up in a secondhand stall at the station in St. Louis, an old copy of a novel called *An American Politician,* by F. Marion Crawford; the dealer insisted on being paid a nickel for it. Porter bought it without knowing quite why, except that he recalled mentioning Crawford to Kringel as the exemplar of the popular American author. But just now, picking up the book, a vivid memory comes back to him: *An American Politician* was the book he saw on the bureau in Eula Phillips's room, on the night of her murder. He closes his eyes. He can see the book exactly as he saw it then, lying on the bureau in the glaring lantern light, with a green bookmark sticking out from somewhere in the middle, marking the point where Eula had laid the volume aside, never to return to it. How curious that such a memory should have stayed in his mind after all these years! He would forget that night entirely if he could, every moment of it, and yet he cannot forget even a detail as insignificant as this.

Smiling at Dr. Kringel in the seat opposite, he opens the novel and begins to read. A few pages in, he comes upon a passage which so strikes him that he reads it several times. It is a sentimental description of the novel's heroine, a typical paean to maidenhood, and yet the words haunt him:

Fresh young roses of each opening year, fresh with the dew of heaven and the blush of innocence, coming up in this wild garden of a world, what would the gardener do without you? Where would all beauty and sweetness be found among the thorny bushes and the withering old shrubs and the rotting weeds, were it not for you? Maidens with clean hands and pure hearts, in whose touch there is something that heals the ills and soothes the pains of mortality, roses whose petals are yet unspoiled by dust and rain, and whose divine perfume the hot south wind has not scorched, nor the east wind nipped and frozen— you are the protest, set every year among us, against the rottenness of the world's doings, the protest of the angelic life against the earthly, of the eternal good against the eternal bad.

He thinks of Eula. Reading that passage twenty years ago, did she see herself in it? Did Jimmy Phillips read those words and picture his wife? Certainly, if Porter had read those words at the time, he would have thought of Eula. This was just how he had pictured her, even knowing that by giving herself to him she was an adulteress. He put her on a pedestal. She did not deserve it. But what did she deserve?

He suddenly feels foolish, to have paid a nickel for such rubbish. He feels an impulse to toss the book out the window. But what would Dr. Kringel think?

He reads on. The margins are airy. The type is easy on the eye. He flies through the pages. Crawford, he must admit, is a smooth stylist, and his wealthy, sophisticated characters are quaintly agreeable—indeed, the whole enterprise is entirely too smooth and too agreeable for Porter's taste. Where is the action, the surprising turnabout, the homely touch, the spice? To be sure, there is a villain of sorts (absurdly named Pocock Vancouver!), and some nonsense about the country being run by a trilateral conspiracy. The thing that keeps him reading is not the plot but the morbid fascination of knowing that Eula Phillips must have read these same words, twenty years ago, in the very hours before her death. At some point, he thinks grimly, he must reach the place where her reading was interrupted. He will be able to finish the novel, as she was not.

His thoughts wander. He reads distractedly, scanning the words but only barely apprehending them, turning the pages by rote until he is halfway through the book.

He turns another page. Something falls out of the book and flits into his lap. It is a rectangle of thin green cardboard.

Dr. Kringel, noting the movement, peers over his newspaper. He sees the look on Porter's face. "What's wrong?"

"What? Nothing at all." Porter picks up the green bookmark and fingers its smooth edges. Such bookmarks must be as common as—as common as novels by Francis Marion Crawford! It means nothing that he came upon this particular marker in this particular copy; it merely signifies that the last reader grew weary of the bland story and the bland characters and never finished. To entertain any other notion—to imagine that the very copy he saw in Eula's room that night might somehow have ended up years later in a secondhand bookstall in St. Louis, and that he of all people should have spotted it—the likelihood of that is so infinitesimal as to border on the impossible, surely. It suggests a degree of coincidence at which even O. Henry would balk!

He carefully slips the bookmark into his breast pocket. He resumes reading, but the words run together. He clears his throat, which has suddenly gone tight, and perseveres, but now the whole page melts before his eyes. Blinking is inadequate to dispel the tears that blind him.

"Mr. Porter!" Dr. Kringel puts his newspaper aside and leans toward him, his brow wrinkled with concern. "Are you not well, Mr. Porter?"

To be sure, Porter's back is aching again, and he feels the need for a drink of whiskey. A uniformed Negro looks into the compartment with a quizzical expression; having heard the word "porter" cried out, he thinks he has been summoned. "May I help you gentlemen?"

Porter averts his tear-streaked face. Kringel shoos the attendant away.

"Mr. Porter, what on earth is the matter?"

Porter wipes his eyes with his handkerchief. "Eula Phillips," he says quietly.

"Ah, that name, which Dr. Montgomery cited in his letter. What does it signify, Mr. Porter?"

Badgered for details about the Servant Girl Annihilators, Porter has already told Dr. Kringel everything he can remember about the slayings of the colored women; it has surprised him, just how much he recalls, though some of the details are jumbled. He also told him how the year of killings ended, with the murders of two white women on the night of Christmas Eve, 1885. But until now Porter has avoided mentioning the name of Eula Phillips.

Now Porter unburdens himself. He explains, clearly and bluntly, without excuse or apology, who Eula Phillips was and how he came to know her. He tells Kringel of the horrible way she died, and of the terrible secrets that came out after her death—the scandal that ensued—the trial—the terrible, lingering doubts . . .

Dr. Kringel listens intently. Occasionally he nods to express sympathy or to show he understands. Dear Dr. Kringel, best of all traveling companions!

Afterward, Porter feels greatly relieved. The sensation is not of having shrugged off a heavy stone, but of having sloughed off a cumbersome skin, like a snake. What is the past, he thinks, but a series of skins we have worn and abandoned? Discarded identities litter a man's past, the lifeless shells of the people he once was.

That night, while he sleeps without dreams, the train crosses from Arkansas into Texas.

It is preposterous, as he knows full well, but Porter imagines he can tell by his first breath upon waking that he is back in Texas. The air is richer, freer, more expansive somehow. The horizon is closely hemmed in by tall shaggy pines, but whenever he glimpses a clear patch of sky he could swear it looks bluer than it did the day before. Once they leave the piney woods of East Texas, the sky will open up, bigger than anywhere else on earth.

They eat breakfast just past the town of Palestine. Austin is only hours away.

Dr. Kringel consults his timetables and unfolds a map on his lap. "You know, there is no need to go all the way to Austin. We could change to a connecting line before we reach Austin—here, at Hearne—and cut directly down to Hempstead. Or do you wish to visit Austin first?"

The question poses a dilemma. The whole point of the trip has been to visit Dr. Montgomery and to discover whatever information he has to impart regarding the murders of twenty years ago. Memory has opened an ancient wound, and Montgomery promises to heal it.

On the other hand, can he really come so close to Austin and not pay a visit? He has not set foot in the town since he left for Ohio to serve his prison term for embezzlement, eight years ago. He never thought he would return. He still can hardly believe that such an odd chain of circumstance has brought him back to Texas.

"Do you know," he says to Dr. Kringel, "I think I just might prefer to go on to Austin and spend the night there, then go to Hempstead tomorrow, or the day after. There are some places I should very much like to see again . . ."

"And people to visit?"

Porter gazes out the window. "I think not. O. Henry doesn't know anyone in Austin, you see, and I doubt that many people in Austin know of O. Henry."

"Surely you are wrong about that, Mr. Porter. O. Henry is famous, and not only in New York. Even in Austin I think he must be a little famous."

"Perhaps. But to be famous and to be known are two different things. Incognito I began this journey, and incognito I shall remain, especially in Austin."

"But what name shall you use there? You will have to register if you stay in a hotel."

Porter thinks for a moment. "Jones," he says. "I shall be Mr. Henry O. Jones."

Kringel smiles. "Very well. But I think that I myself would prefer to press on to Hempstead today. After so many years of correspondence, I am most eager to finally meet Dr. Montgomery face-to-face. Would you mind terribly if I go ahead of you to Liendo, and leave you to your own devices in Austin?"

"Not at all. Actually, I think I'd prefer to be on my own in Austin. It'll be like old times, when I first lived there—footloose and unfettered, free to go tramping as I wish."

The train pulls into the little town of Hearne. Porter joins Dr. Kringel on the platform to say farewell.

"Better to say *au revoir*," Dr. Kringel notes with a smile. "I shall await you at Liendo. You know, I have a bit of time before my train comes through. I believe I shall send a telegram to Dr. Montgomery and Miss Ney, to let them know when I shall arrive. *Au revoir*, then, Mr. Porter."

"*Au revoir*, Herr Doctor Kringel."

The last thing Porter sees before reboarding the train is the tall, narrow figure of Dr. Kringel stepping into the telegraph office, carrying his ever-present brown leather satchel. What on earth is in that satchel, to stuff it so full?

His journey recommences. He feels a bit lonely, but also relieved; his confessions to Kringel regarding Eula Phillips made him feel closer to the man, but a bit self-conscious. It will be good to be alone with his memories for a while.

As the train gathers speed, he begins to feel a curious exhilaration. A bit of whiskey heightens the feeling nicely. Only ninety-one miles to Austin! The train passes through Gause and Milano Junction, Rockdale and Watson, Thorndale and Taylor, then Hutto and Round Rock. Past the Duval station the countryside takes on suburban trappings; farms give way to orderly blocks of houses and little general stores.

Above the treetops he catches sight of the pink granite edifice of the

Capitol. If he squints, he can make out the Goddess of Liberty perched atop the dome. What does she hold in her upraised hand—a star, a scythe, a torch? Was that not the quest he jokingly assigned himself, when he decided to make this journey, to determine what the goddess holds? But he cannot tell. The distance is too great.

As the train pulls into the station off Congress Avenue, he takes a deep breath and feels a thrill of homecoming. But on the platform, waiting for his baggage, he experiences the let-down of the traveler arriving with no one to greet him and the tedious task of finding a hotel room for one. Smiling faces welcome his fellow passengers; he envies them. There might have been a face or two to welcome him, had he arranged it; it was his own choice to arrive without notice. He left this town in shame. He returns in secret.

The feeling of homecoming was only an illusion, after all. He has no home here. He has shed the skin of his past. His life is elsewhere. Here he is a ghost, and shall move among ghosts.

PART FOUR

"TO BE ALIVE, WHAT IS IT?"

⚜

Austin: December 1885 and After

41

$\mathcal{J}$T was a grim business to be tending to on a Christmas evening, thought William Holland as he strode up Congress Avenue in the darkening twilight with the cold north wind in his face.

Holland was in the company of several dozen other colored men. Despite the gravity of their collective purpose, Holland smiled to think that he should find himself literally situated between the sacred and the profane. On one side of him were Hugh Hancock, Lem Brooks, Alec Mack, Walter Spencer, and a number of other regulars of the Black Elephant. On the other side were the Reverends Anderson, Massey, Grant, Swan, and Smith, pastors of the five colored churches in town, with members of their congregations.

They were headed for the state office building. The mayor had called a meeting of concerned citizens. The subject was to be the atrocities of the previous night, and what to do about them.

The day had dawned cold but clear, a perfect Christmas morning, with freshly cut cedar boughs scenting the Holland home. This would be little Moses Shelley's first Christmas without his mother. Holland had bought his ward a top, and not just any top, but the most beautiful top ever made, machine-carved out of oak and painted green, with a fine steel tip. Holland himself tried it out on Christmas Eve after Moses was asleep. His best throw kept the top spinning for five minutes. He would have tried for six, but his wife confiscated the top, decorated it with a red ribbon, and hid it behind the mantel clock.

Holland's chief task as he saw it that Christmas morning was to bring boy and top together. That done, he could look forward to a meal of turkey and dressing and cranberry sauce, to be followed by the afternoon service at his church.

While Moses was still abed, Holland drank his first cup of coffee and opened the *Statesman*. Turning to the page for local news, the first thing he saw was an advertisement in large type for *The Mikado* at Millett's Opera House. Next to that, in considerably smaller type, was a headline:

BLOOD! BLOOD! BLOOD!
LAST NIGHT'S HORRIBLE BUTCHERY.
The Demons Have Transferred Their
Thirst for Blood to White People!

Holland hurriedly read the account, his stomach turning at the lurid descriptions of the victims—blood gushing like a fountain from Susan Hancock's mouth, the body of Eula Phillips discovered "entirely nude" and spread-eagled, her arms held down by a wooden plank, her head smashed in. Despite the speedy arrival of officers at the scenes of the crimes and the use of bloodhounds, there had been no arrests.

A knot tightened in the pit of Holland's stomach. After the erroneous arrest of Lem Brooks, after the long, hot summer of one killing after another, after the torture of Alec Mack, after the needless trial of half-witted Walter Spencer, after a year of colored women living in nightly terror of murder and rape, this was the worst possible thing that could happen. It was enough to shake a man's faith in God.

Everyone—every white person, at least—assumed without question that the killer or killers must be black. As long as the victims were black as well, the white citizenry and their elected officials were outraged—to a point. Now that point had been crossed. Now the victims were white women—two of them in a single night, and on Christmas Eve! Now the city of Austin was likely to vent true rage, and the end result, Holland feared, would very likely be the body of a colored man hanging from a rope.

He was reading the story a second time when a messenger arrived at his door bearing a cream-colored envelope. Holland tore it open and extracted a handwritten note:

Dear Mr. Holland,
    As mayor, I am calling a meeting of concerned citizenry to

convene this evening at 7 p.m. at the state office building. I expect a large attendance and some short tempers, but I am optimistic that cool heads will prevail. I think it would be good to see the gallery filled with your people. Perhaps you should consider speaking up tonight, on behalf of the colored population.

John W. Robertson

There followed for William Holland a busy day.

That afternoon, he managed to drop in at services at all five colored churches, and convinced all five pastors to give him a few moments to speak.

He urged everyone to attend the meeting that night. Though he saw expressions of doubt and fear on many faces, he was given a respectful hearing everywhere he went, except at the Wesley Chapel, where the doors were open and the service was letting out when he arrived. After a desperate plea from Holland, the pastor called the congregation back. Most returned to their seats. Holland explained his purpose. When he told them that the colored people must show the rest of Austin that they were as outraged by these newest crimes as anyone else, a little man in the back row spoke up.

"You mean, like they been so outraged over the killin' of colored women—lettin' it go on for a whole year?" The man's tone was scornful. He was short, and the woman in the pew in front of him wore a formidable bonnet, so that Holland could not see the man's face.

"It's up to us to show them that there's no difference between the killing of a white woman and a black woman, or ought not to be," declared Holland.

"First colored man that show up at that meetin', they's like as not to haul to the nearest tree!" said the little man. "Pro'ly haul him right out here across from this chapel, where they come close to hangin' Alec Mack."

"If one colored man were to show up, yes, I'll grant you that he might attract the anger of the crowd like a lightning rod," said Holland. "That's why we must show up in numbers. The important thing is to show our faces. To show that the colored people of Austin have nothing to be ashamed of, or to hide, or to feel guilty for. Who has suffered more than we have from these fiendish crimes? We have lost mothers and daughters and wives. Little boys and girls have been turned into orphans. I grant you, they think it's one of us. They've made up their minds that these killings are the work of colored men—"

"Well, ain't they?" cracked the little man.

"I don't know. No one does," said Holland grimly. "But I do know this: there's been too much killing and suffering already, and there's likely to be more killing yet, unless we show that we expect and deserve the rule of law. We must stand together. We must hold our heads high."

"Holdin' your head up jus' make it a better target for a noose," said the man. "Stay stooped and keep your head down, that's what I say!"

"Is that how you walk through life, sir, not looking where you're headed?" snapped Holland. "You must have run headfirst into quite a few brick walls. No wonder you're so addlebrained!"

A round of laughter and foot-stomping announced that Holland had won the argument.

Outside the chapel, Holland lingered for a while, talking with the pastor and some of the aldermen. Presently the wag who had heckled him came walking boldly up. Reverend Swan crossed his arms and raised an eyebrow. Some of the aldermen pointedly walked away. Now that Holland saw his face, he recognized the man.

"Well, Mr. Hugh Hancock," said Holland, "I take it that you'll be serving liquor in the Black Elephant tonight instead of attending the meeting."

"On the contrary, Mr. Holland!"

"I don't understand."

"I attends church once a year, Mr. Holland, on Christmas Day. I reckon you preached the best sermon I's heard in many a year—no offense to you, Reverend Swan. You know what I's gonna do? I's gonna close the Elephant tonight, and I's gonna tell all those worthless Negroes to get theirselves down to this meetin'. What time should we meet up with you?"

The meeting took place in the assembly hall where some months before the House of Representatives had debated the question of women clerks. The atmosphere in the room made Holland think of a nest of yellow jackets that had been hit with a stick. A loud, angry buzz filled the air. The acoustics in the gallery, where Holland and the colored contingent sat, made it seem that the buzzing emanated from all directions, surrounding them. The crowded room was warm and stuffy, despite the cold wind blowing outside.

Mayor Robertson ascended to the podium, banged the gavel, and called the meeting to order. As the crowd quieted down, there were a few boos and catcalls directed at him, along with yells at the catcallers to shut up. Robertson stared steadily from face to face. "Hear me out! We'll get nowhere if we resort to shouting and sniping at each other. You all know why we're here, and I don't doubt that you're all in a fine temper at being called to a meeting like this on Christmas Day. I won't try your patience, reciting the details of the crimes that have plagued this city for a year. Murder after murder, and now these latest outrages—these damnable, cowardly, inexplicable assaults on the two ladies last night! We're all angry. We've all had enough of it—every man in this room, white and black." Robertson glanced at the gallery and looked Holland straight in the eye.

There were cries of "Hear, hear!" and "What do we do now?"

Robertson went on at a louder pitch. "After every one of these horrible crimes, the authorities have done everything in their power to find the guilty parties and put a stop to more crimes—hear me out! Hear me out now!" He banged the gavel. "Plaster casts have been made of suspicious footprints. Bloodhounds have been dispatched to track every scent. Detectives have been employed to ferret out every clue. Any man with the least suspicion attached to him has been questioned. One man has been subjected to a trial by jury. But all these efforts have ended in failure. The criminals have not been captured. The crimes continue.

"I look to you, the men of Austin, to put an end to this bloodshed. We must stop this rampage of killing. We must rescue the fair name of Austin. We are men, protectors of our households, and we must act as men. Otherwise we might as well put on petticoats! But we are also citizens, and must act within the law. Mob rule will solve nothing. A mob demands instant justice and hangs men on mere suspicion. Judge Lynch is worse than no law at all. We must not turn against one another. White and colored together must unite to hunt down these fiends and bring them to punishment!"

Robertson won a round of applause and the meeting proceeded in a noisy but orderly fashion. Those with something to say lined up at the podium. Some were applauded, some were booed, some were laughed at.

An old veteran suggested a military solution: surround the city with armed men, let no one leave, and arrest any man unable to account for his whereabouts at the time of the murders. Catcalls denounced the solution; what if the killers had already left town? Another speaker suggested that the city enlist a hundred citizens in a covert auxiliary force, the membership of which would be known only to the marshal and the mayor. The idea of secret police was roundly rejected.

A number of speakers blamed the plague of murders on the loose moral climate encouraged by the saloons, gambling dens, and bawdy houses in Guy Town. The mildest remedy proposed was that saloons should be forced to close at ten o'clock. Others called for a complete suppression of vice in

Austin, along the lines of recent efforts to clean up Dallas. "Why do we allow this never-ending Saturnalia of dissipation in the city?" asked one speaker, with rhetorical relish. "Why are not the White Elephant and the Black Elephant suppressed?" A following speaker suggested, as there was no White Elephant saloon in Austin, that the moralist should put a rein on his metaphorical pachyderms.

There was much discussion regarding the formation of a vigilance committee empowered to act independently of the police force. William Pendleton Gaines spoke in favor. "As a newspaperman, I feel I can speak of such committees in a national context, and I would point out that in Baltimore and San Francisco such groups have done exemplary work. They capture and dispose of known killers. Their mere presence drives bad men out of town. To the folks in those cities, 'vigilante' is a term of honor!"

Gaines's comments received loud applause and cries of support.

A heated debate ensued. Various motions were put forward. The more moderate speakers, like the mayor, were also the most skilled parliamentarians. By means invisible to the more truculent members of the crowd the moderates managed to have their way. What began as a call for a hundred armed vigilantes was watered down until it became an advisory committee of forty men, made up of representatives (three white, one black) from each of the ten wards, to act in cooperation with the mayor and the marshal and to raise reward money. There were grumbles of dissatisfaction, but a great deal of hostility and frustration had been vented, which was precisely what the mayor had hoped for.

William Holland was among the committee members. He was called on by Mayor Robertson to say some words on behalf of the colored population.

As he stepped up to the podium, Holland felt at once relieved and anxious. Things had gone far better than he expected. Catastrophe had been averted, at least for now. The room was like a bomb successfully defused, but there was still a great deal of powder packed into that bomb. As he looked out at the sea of white faces staring back at him, Holland had never felt more conscious of his color. He had learned to deal with powerful white men on an individual basis. He had attended two Republican national conventions. He had served a term in the Texas legislature. But he had never faced a crowd such as this one.

A phrase from the morning's headline kept echoing through his head: *The Demons Have Transferred Their Thirst for Blood to White People!* How many white men in that crowd looked at him and saw not William Holland, the accomplished educator and son of a Texas statesman, but a creature only barely human standing upright at the podium, more closely related to devils and monkeys, just another darkie with a taste for white women and white blood?

Holland was frozen by sudden panic. It was stupid and inexplicable, but no less paralyzing for that. He had not experienced such embarrassment since his first public speaking class at Oberlin College. His tongue turned to lead. The top of his head seemed to disembark and float away, like the hot air ascension balloons at Scholz's Garden.

Then he heard a voice from the gallery. "What's the matter, Brother Holland? Cat got your tongue? You didn't have no trouble puttin' me in my place this afternoon, in front of God and Reverend Swan!"

Good-natured laughter filled the gallery and spilled to the main floor. The tension broke.

"Thank you, Brother Hancock," Holland said, finding his voice, "for reminding me of my purpose." The little man folded his arms over the railing of the gallery and grinned at him.

William Holland said what he had come to say. "It seems to me that I should scarcely have to speak the plain truth, but I will. The colored people of Austin are as law-abiding as the white people. That is a plain fact. And the colored people of this city are just as anxious as anyone else to see guilty men punished, whatever their color may be." By subtle emphasis, Holland asserted that the killer or killers might be black—or white.

"Why should the colored people of Austin not crave justice, and an end to these murders? Terrible suffering has been visited upon us in the last year, inflicted by the perpetrators of these horrible crimes. Colored women have been unspeakably molested and murdered. Their friends and loved ones have had to live afterward not just with the normal pains and regrets of ties severed by death, but with nightmares of how those deaths occurred.

"Children have been orphaned. One of them I've taken into my own home, Eliza Shelley's little boy Moses. When his mother was outraged and slaughtered, that little boy lay in his bed not ten feet away. One of the victims was no more than a child herself. In her last moments of life, little Mary Ramey faced horrors that no man or woman should ever have to endure.

"Others have suffered. Innocent colored men have been falsely accused and thrown into prison. They have been chased by dogs, been put in chains and brutally mistreated. The only one to actually stand trial was quickly and unanimously acquitted. If the lynch law reigned in Austin as it does in all too many places these days, every one of those men would be dead now—

and the murders would still be going on. I was heartened tonight to hear so many responsible leaders of this community denounce any impulse to resort to vigilance committees. 'Vigilante justice' is a handsome name put upon the very worst excesses of injustice. No good ever came of hanging an innocent man."

"That's where you're wrong, mister!" a man in the crowd yelled. "Hang the wrong man, and you still set an example to others. A body swinging from a rope sends a message, loud and clear. Sometimes all it takes to set things right in a town is a single lynching—don't matter if the hung fellow was personally guilty or not. Towns all over the South have figured that out, and they're happier for it. Fear is the only thing that'll keep some people in line. Them colored fellows you say was falsely accused—if one of them *had* been hanged, right on the spot, who's to say that wouldn't have stopped these murders right then and there, by puttin' the fear into the real killer?" The man looked at Holland with an expression of contempt, and smiled smugly when there were scattered cries of agreement from the crowd.

Holland looked steadily at the man. If the mayor could retain his composure in the face of such hostility, then so could he. "I'm not much impressed with your argument, sir. Hang the wrong man, and the message you send is that you didn't have the wits to catch the right one. You only encourage the true culprit, because you show him that he's smarter than you are. You're like the farmer who strings up the cat because something's been killing his chickens. All he does is lose himself a good mouse-catcher. Meanwhile, the fox watches from the woods and grins."

There were hoots of laughter, especially from the gallery. Holland might have stepped down from the podium then and there, but he felt emboldened to say something he had been unsure of saying before.

"The fact is, I'm glad this meeting was called. I'm glad to see the people of Austin stirred up and ready to take action. I only wish this had happened sooner. I wish you all had been this angry when Gracie Vance and Orange Washington were killed three months ago, or when little Mary Ramey was outraged in August, or in May when Irene Cross was murdered and Eliza Shelley's children were orphaned. I wish we had held this meeting a year ago, when Mollie Smith was murdered. Where was the outrage then? Where was the call for citizen action and vigilance committees?"

From the gallery came the sound of weeping; Walter Spencer, sitting between Lem Brooks and Alec Mack, had broken into tears and was hiding his face in his hands. Holland looked out at the sea of white faces and could tell that he had pushed the matter as far as he dared to. Any more, and they would bridle at having something bitter forced down their throats. Better to let them go home and chew on it by and by.

"But as my blessed mother would say, there's no point dwelling on when bygones was used-to-be's. The mayor has brought us all together, and together we must see that these killings stop."

42

⟳

*F*EAR gripped the city, as cold and bitter and relentless as the endless northers blowing down from Oklahoma.

The *Statesman* advised all citizens to arm themselves and be constantly on watch: "If you see or hear anyone tinkering at your window or door latches, 'aim low and let 'em have it,' as the saying goes. Ask questions later."

One mistaken arrest after another was made around Austin, including that of a man seen washing what was believed to be a bloody shirt in the Colorado River. It turned out that the brown spots on the shirt were pecan stains, and the red effluence was the cheap dye from a new pair of red socks.

Will Porter spent the better part of the next few days at Millett's Opera House, rehearsing for *The Mikado*. A man from the Emma Abbott company arrived in town early to fit the chorus in costumes and drill them in stage directions. Will learned his entrances and exits and the cues to flutter his Japanese fan or snap it shut. At the sold-out Monday matinee he performed flawlessly.

He began rehearsing at once for another play, an amateur production of *The Black Mantles*, scheduled for late January.

The old year gave way to the new. Will worked hard at his bookkeeping job. He kept so busy that he seldom had time to cross the hall to say hello to Dave in the *Statesman* office, much less go to lunch with him. In the evenings he rehearsed. More touring productions and amateur theatricals were booked at Millett's; Will signed up to sing in the choruses. On Sundays he sang in church.

All his friends seemed to be engaged in serious courtships. Will made a new year's resolution to do likewise. The previous March, at a ball to celebrate laying the cornerstone for the new capitol building, he had met and danced with a charming girl named Athol Estes. He had seen her since at dances and church socials. She was only seventeen and still in high school, and one of the Zimpelman boys (of ice house fame) was courting her, but she always welcomed Will's attentions and laughed at his jokes. Athol was not especially pretty—not in the showy, blinding fashion of certain women—but there was an innocence about her that appealed to him powerfully. Her freshness and simplicity made him feel mature and sure of himself.

In short, in the weeks after Christmas Will did everything possible to avoid thinking about the one thing that would otherwise have dominated his mind to the exclusion of all else. He filled his days with work, his nights with singing, and his notions of romance with sweet, innocent Athol. These preoccupations were like so many bricks laid in a wall and sealed with mortar, made fast against the sea of dark thoughts that lay beyond.

Nevertheless, rumors and speculations about the Christmas Eve murders reached his ears. There was so much talk and so many reports in the *Statesman* that it was impossible not to follow some of it.

He knew, for instance, that for several days after the murder, Jimmy Phillips remained insensible and unable to speak, gripped by a terrible brain fever due to the ax wounds to his head. For a while, the doctors were uncertain whether Jimmy would live or die. In the end he pulled through, but was unable to give any coherent account of what had occurred on Christmas Eve.

It seemed clear enough to everyone that the killing of Eula Phillips was of a series with those that had come before. The pattern was the same: the killer struck whatever man or woman was in the room, rendering them dead or unconscious, then dragged the victim of his lust out of the house to sate his desires by moonlight. No one doubted, at first, that this was exactly what had happened to Jimmy and Eula.

The other murder of Christmas Eve seemed to follow much the same pattern. Susan Hancock and her husband, Moses, a much older couple than the Phillipses, had been alone in their little house; their teenaged daughters were at a party. Susan Hancock was in bed. Moses Hancock dozed in a rocking chair in the parlor, next to the fireplace, having consumed a considerable amount of alcohol. A noise woke him. He went to the bedroom. His wife was gone; the sheets were twisted and bloody. A trail of blood led him out of the house. In the back yard he saw two shadowy figures who fled at his approach. He found his wife lying on the ground, groaning and terribly wounded. He carried her back into the house, trailing blood. Later, a bloody ax was found in the back yard, just as a bloody ax had been found next to Jimmy and Eula's bed.

If Moses Hancock had been in bed with his wife, rather than dozing in the parlor, who could doubt that he would have ended as Jimmy Phillips, Walter Spencer, Orange Washington, and Rebecca Ramey did, struck in the head and knocked insensible or dead while the fiends dragged Mrs. Hancock outside to ravish her? But Moses Hancock had been in the parlor, and so had escaped the ax. Hancock was lucky to be alive and unharmed, people said.

Too lucky, said some.

Hancock was known to be violent when he drank. Susan Hancock had expressed a fear that her husband would murder her; she had told her preacher so, and had written as much in a letter to her sister in Waco. Some claimed to have seen the letter, and said it had a bloody fingerprint on it, the mark of a previous attempt on her life. There was also the matter of the bloodhounds brought to the scene. The dogs had scented nothing at the point where Hancock claimed to have seen the two men jump the fence, and failed to picked up a single trail leading away from the premises. If no one had left the site, then who murdered Susan Hancock?

People began to raise questions about Jimmy Phillips, as well. Neighbors recalled the incident in November when Jimmy, screaming "God damn you, I'll kill you," chased his wife and sister into the front yard and had to be fended off with a shovel. Jimmy Phillips was a dangerous drunkard, his marriage a shambles, his brain fever a sham; such rumors became so widespread that James Phillips, Sr., felt obliged to grant an interview to the *Statesman* in order to defend his son's character. "Jimmy and Eula were as happily mated as any young couple I know of, and always got along smoothly," he insisted.

But the rumors persisted. It was said that on the night of the murders, bloodhounds had picked up a scent from the piece of wood used to pin down Eula Phillips's arms. The dogs followed the trail only a short way toward the fence, then doubled back toward the verandah, rushed into the bedroom in a barking mass and surrounded Jimmy, rearing up on the bed and frightening his poor mother almost to death. One rumor had it that Jimmy confessed to the murder then and there, delirious as he was.

Rumors began to circulate regarding Eula Phillips. At the Tin Cup in Guy Town, a group of hackney cab drivers were overheard talking about the murders. Several of them claimed to have driven a woman from the Phillips house to a notorious location on the Avenue, on more than one occasion. Speculation arose as to what sort of wife Eula Phillips had been. There were whispers about behavior that could drive any husband to drink, and maybe to murder.

Of this whirlwind of rumor and innuendo, Will was only dully aware. He knew and yet managed to ignore every step of the events that transpired in the wake of the Christmas Eve murders. When, toward the end of January, Moses Hancock was arrested for the murder of his wife, Susan, Will's waking thoughts were preoccupied with his imminent appearance as Sampson in *The Black Mantles.*

A few days later, Jimmy Phillips, still appearing haggard and shaken, was arrested by Marshal Lucy and charged with the murder of his wife.

The arrest was the talk of the town, discussed in boarding houses and banks, millinery shops and vegetable markets, church pews and saloons. It was talked about in the house at 103 Congress Avenue, where Fannie Whipple responded to an urgent invitation to take tea with May Tobin; and at the state office building, where a nervous Comptroller Swain called a nervous William Shelley into his office for a private meeting; and at the *Statesman,* where Dave Shoemaker listened to the telephone with one ear and to Gaines with the other and jotted down details, gazing all the while at the empty desk of Hiram Glass; and across the hall at the offices of Maddox Bros. & Anderson, where Will Porter diligently added columns of figures and hummed Gilbert and Sullivan tunes to himself, trying not to listen to the other clerks and their gossip.

That night Will awoke in a cold sweat, having dreamed not of fluttering Japanese fans or Athol or ledgers filled with numbers, but of *her,* as he had first seen her in the gallery during the debates, and as he had last seen her in the back yard of the house down the street—and he wondered, as he forced those images from his mind, what had become of the letters he wrote to her, the sweet, sad, foolish letters, which Delia had agreed to hold for safekeeping.

Taylor Moore thought and thought, until his head ached from thinking. His thoughts were like a dog chasing its own tail around and around, wearing a circle in the dirt. The tail was too short to get hold of.

The tail was too damned short!

But the good citizens of Austin were paying Taylor Moore to think the thing through; to consider every possibility; to solve the puzzle; to nip the tip of the too-short tail and hold on tight. And so Taylor Moore sat in his upper-story law office on Congress Avenue and pondered the matter until his head ached. The lives of at least two men depended on it.

The citizens committee formed in the wake of the Christmas Eve murders voted to expend a portion of the reward fund to hire a special prosecutor. Who better for the post than the people's representative from the Seventy-fifth District, the Honorable Taylor Moore? He had been a dogged prosecutor during his four terms as district attorney. His stirring defense of Senate Bill No. 79 had established his reputation as a champion of women, and the women of Austin were especially eager to see justice done in the murders of Susan Hancock and Eula Phillips.

But there was a problem: Taylor Moore was not convinced beyond a reasonable doubt that either Moses Hancock or Jimmy Phillips was guilty. Moore was not the sort of man to send a fellow to the gallows merely to further his own career. He genuinely cared about punishing the guilty and putting an end to the atrocious murders plaguing the city. He was far from certain that convicting Hancock or Phillips would serve either purpose.

It had been Moore's belief for some time that the killings of the colored servant girls must be the work not of some jealous, vengeful lover, but of a singular maniac, a man with a peculiar hatred of women and a revolting sexual appetite. When Grooms Lee set about hounding various colored fellows because they were romantically linked to the victims, Moore had shaken his head at the marshal's simplemindedness. When his friend James Robertson decided to prosecute Walter Spencer for the murder of Mollie Smith, Moore had advised strongly against it, and tried not to be smug when the prosecution failed miserably. The killer of the servant girls, Moore argued, didn't murder in a drunken rage or a jealous fit, like the common sort of killer; he murdered in a premeditated, methodical manner, with the express intention of gratifying a necrophiliac desire. The monster was obviously able to move freely in society, and so his nature must not be evident on the surface, yet there could be little doubt that he belonged in a lunatic asylum.

What, then, was Moore to make of these latest atrocities? Were the murders of Susan Hancock and Eula Phillips of a series with those of the colored servant girls, or entirely separate, both from those murders and from each other?

It had been Marshal Lucy's decision to pursue the husbands. Lucy, another former Texas Ranger, was a hundred times better lawman than Grooms Lee. The pint-sized Lucy was diligent, clever, and dogged—a human bloodhound, as the *Statesman* called him. Lucy quickly sniffed out the unhappy states of the Hancock and Phillips households and began collecting evidence against the husbands. It was the marshal's opinion that Moses Hancock and Jimmy Phillips killed their wives, perhaps with premeditation, more likely on impulse, and then, to escape suspicion, deliberately made the crimes look like those of the servant girl killer.

Moore's thoughts began their whirling chase again, nipping at the elusive tail of conviction. Could Jimmy's wounds have been self-inflicted? What were the chances that not one but *two* men, hardly a mile apart and acting independently, would kill their wives within the space of an hour—and on Christmas Eve? What were the further chances that *both* husbands would then try to make the crime look like the work of the servant girl killer? What were the chances that one of the women was murdered by her husband, and the other by the servant girl killer—almost simultaneously? If both Christmas Eve murders were the work of the previous killer, why was there a change of pattern, with two in one night, and with white women as victims, not colored servants?

Moore spun about in his swivel chair and gazed out his office window. Two streetcars passed each other, clanging their bells. Pedestrians scurried along the sidewalks, wrapped in heavy coats and scarves. A stiff wind gusted from the direction of the capitol grounds, stirring dust and mule droppings.

At some point, he would have to decide whether to protest a prosecution he could not countenance, or go along with it wholeheartedly. If Hancock and Phillips were guilty, he would do everything in his power to hang the wretches. But if they were not, where did that leave the eight victims murdered and outraged over the previous year? Where was their killer? When might he strike again?

When all the depositions were taken and the evidence sorted, the district attorney dropped the charges against Moses Hancock. The case was simply not strong enough, and James Robertson was still stinging from his unsuccessful prosecution against Walter Spencer. He did not care to repeat the experience with a white defendant.

The case against Jimmy Phillips was another matter. Evidence kept accumulating, including some intriguing information about the victim,

Eula Phillips. Both Robertson and Taylor Moore became increasingly convinced that Jimmy was the murderer of his wife.

The wheels of justice moved slowly. Jimmy was released on a bond of $2,500 paid by his father, while the grand jury proceeded with its business. Their hearings were kept secret. The *Statesman* complained in its headlines of a "Colossal Star Chamber" at work, but had to make do with rumors.

January gave way to February, February to March. The dreary rainy season came to Austin. The adage "It never rains but it pours" would soon apply to more than the weather.

4 3

⚉

$\mathcal{M}$ AY Tobin sat on a hard metal bunk in a cell at the county jail.

She tapped her foot impatiently. She pulled at the fingers of her black lace gloves. What the place needed—besides a thorough scrubbing and some cheerful curtains to hide the bars in the windows—was an upright piano, to keep a body's fingers occupied and cheer the place up, at least during the day. Nighttime would be another matter. May imagined the *Moonlight Sonata* reverberating off the cold stone walls in the middle of the night, with the constant rain as a backdrop, and decided the effect would be entirely too gloomy.

What she *really* needed was a good cigar . . .

There were footsteps on the stairs. A moment later Marshal Lucy appeared before her cell. In other circumstances, May would have found him a rather attractive fellow. She had a fondness for diminutive men. How precious he looked in his marshal's uniform, like a boy playing grown-up. It was hard to believe he had taken part in the manhunt that put an end to the outlaw Sam Bass, and had once stared down the notorious gunfighter Ben Thompson. Did the Texas Rangers have no height requirement? Such small, delicate hands the man had, and what little feet! His boots, gleaming wet from the rain, were hardly bigger than a child's. May thought how darling they would look, sitting alongside a lady's slippers at the foot of a bed in one of her rooms to let.

May had heard that James Lucy was a recent widower. Many a widower came to May Tobin's for solace, but not Lucy. His first visit had been early that morning. When he knocked at her door, May was still in dishabille.

Bleary-eyed, she peered out the door, past the chain, and thought it was a boy standing on her doorstep. But what store in town dressed its delivery boys in uniforms? She put on her spectacles and saw the unmistakable gold brocade of the marshal's hat.

He had to tilt his face up to look at her, but his expression was not boyish. "May Tobin?" he said.

"Yes?"

"I have come to arrest you on a charge of keeping a disorderly house."

May swallowed hard. "You've caught me not quite up and about yet, Marshal. I'm not ready to receive visitors. Will you allow me to get properly dressed, sir?"

"Certainly, ma'am. I shall wait here on the porch. I should let you know there's another officer at your rear door."

Flanked by the marshal and his deputy, May was forced to walk all the way up the Avenue to the courthouse. She was thankful for the drizzle; there were not many people on the sidewalks. She hid as best she could behind her umbrella.

The judge set her bail at two hundred dollars. She complained that the amount was exorbitant; how could a widow of limited means be expected to raise so much money? The judge scoffed at her objection, and May found herself in a cell at the calaboose, awaiting the reply to a message she had hoped never to have to send.

She sprang up from the bunk, trying to read the marshal's face for some sign of the response. "Well?" she said.

Lucy produced a small envelope. May's heart sank. What did it mean, that her own envelope was being returned to her? Lucy pressed it between the bars, into her gloved fingers. The name of the addressee was written in May's fussy script: *The Honorable Benjamin M. Baker, Superintendent of Public Instruction, State Office Building.*

One end of the envelope had been slit open neatly; May could imagine the fancy sort of letter opener its recipient would have used. She reached inside, extracted a piece of paper, and unfolded it. It was her own letter.

"Did he read it?" she asked.

"Saw the gentleman open it myself."

"But did he actually read it?"

"Suppose so. Stared at it long enough. Considering his post in the state government, I presume he reads very well."

"And there was no reply?"

Lucy cleared his throat. "The gentleman said he doesn't know you, ma'am."

"What!"

"Said he was certain that he had never met you in his life."

May muttered a curse. The marshal's eyebrows lifted. He considered himself a man of the world, but he had never heard a female utter that particular word.

May reread what she had written.

Dear Friend,

I find myself in a most embarrassing situation. I am pressed into financial straits due to the pecuniary demands of an unreasonable judge. I need $200. I should be glad to sign a promissory note in return for your loan of that amount. Will you not assist a widow in need? You know you can trust my discretion.

Your friend,
Mrs. Tobin

The marshal touched the brim of his hat. "If that'll be all, ma'am, I'll let you get back to whatever you were doing before I came in."

"Wait, Marshal! Please, I must get out of here as soon as possible. If Mr. Baker . . . can't remember me . . . I'm sure there are others who can. Won't you take another message for me?"

There was no need to write another letter. With its vague salutation, the message could be sent to any number of gentlemen in the city. Lucy brought pen and ink and supplied another envelope.

She paused, pen in hand, then decided it should go to a certain professor at the university and addressed it accordingly.

The marshal departed with the sealed envelope. In half an hour he was back, and once again returned her own envelope.

"No reply?" said May anxiously.

"I suppose a fellow must have a large store of knowledge to be a professor," said Lucy, "but this one's knowledge does not extend to yourself, ma'am."

The word which Lucy had never before that day heard uttered by a woman was uttered a second time.

May sent out the message again, this time to a certain wealthy cattleman. The recipient not only denied any knowledge of the widow Tobin, but in doing so, resorted to the same curse word that May had uttered.

May asked to send out the message again.

"Ma'am, I've already delivered it for you three times."

"Marshal Lucy, you can't deny me the opportunity to post bail."

"If you can obtain the money. If not . . ."

"Wait! I know whom to ask! I should have gone to him in the first place. Another envelope, please, Marshal? Thank you." She addressed it hurriedly. "He's a true gentleman. He won't deny me. He wouldn't dare. And if he does, if he tells you he doesn't know who May Tobin is, then—then tell him that I shall—I shall—"

"It's not my job to pass on threats, ma'am."

May sealed the envelope and managed a smile. "I was only going to say that if he says he doesn't remember me, I shall be heartbroken. I'm just a woman, after all, Marshal Lucy." She pushed the envelope between the bars.

"So far, ma'am, the list of important fellows in this town who swear they've never met you is pretty impressive. I suppose that's a compliment to you, in a backhanded sort of way." Lucy took the envelope and looked at it. His eyebrows lifted and he let out a low whistle. He read aloud: "'The Honorable William J. Swain, State Comptroller, State Office Building.' Now from what I hear, if this fellow has his way, in a year's time that's likely to read: 'William J. Swain, Governor's Mansion.'"

"Maybe—or maybe not," said May dryly. "Tell *that* to Mr. Swain when he reads the letter."

Marshal Lucy departed. While he was gone, May had another visitor. She knew who Taylor Moore was, though their paths had never crossed. He was the man who had spoken so eloquently in favor of female clerks. In the right circumstances, May would have been quite pleased to make his acquaintance. At present, unfortunately, he was in cahoots with the district attorney. Once a prosecutor, always a prosecutor, May thought. As Moore stepped up to the bars, she retreated to her bunk.

"You appear to be in a spot of trouble, Mrs. Tobin."

"Only temporarily, Mr. Moore."

"Do you think so?"

"A woman in business for herself must expect a bit of harassment from time to time. This episode will pass, just as this March deluge will pass."

"Perhaps. But it appears to me that the people of Austin have experienced a profound change of attitude. Up till now they've been lenient about certain things. They've looked the other way when it came to matters of, shall we say, social intercourse. They're not so lenient now. They're in a mood to clean house. Running an establishment such as yours will become decidedly more difficult in the future, perhaps impossible."

May snorted. "This is Austin, Mr. Moore! The state capital, home of the university, crossroads of Texas, full of visitors, cattlemen, and college boys. Not to mention the seasonal influx of your esteemed but not entirely virtuous colleagues in the state legislature. Visitors from Twohig and Tuna expect to find something a bit more exciting than church socials and society germans. Houses like mine shall always exist in Austin."

"Perhaps. But that doesn't mean that your particular house will stay in business much longer."

May stared at him.

"I see that I have your attention, Mrs. Tobin. Good. Listen to me carefully. The people of Austin are demanding action. They want to see Guy Town cleaned up. They want to see Congress Avenue turned into a respectable street from one end to the other. The district attorney has decided to inaugurate a clean-up campaign, starting down at your end of the Avenue."

"He'd do better to start up at his end, with all the hypocrites in the state office building!"

"You may have a point. But he shall start with you."

"I know powerful men," said May bluntly.

"Ah, but do *they* know *you?* I understand you're having a hard time finding a friend to post your bail."

"If I'm dragged through the mud, I'll drag quite a few others along with me." May stared at the cold stone wall and listened to the rain. "Certain men in this town will see that it never comes to that. Men with wives and reputations to protect. Men with ambition. They'll see that I never stand trial."

"Do you seriously imagine that your so-called friends, who won't even post your bail, will tamper with the judicial system to help you?"

"Once they see the sharks in the press and the pulpits coming after them, they'll climb in the boat with me."

"Where you're all likely to sink together!"

May leaned forward on her bunk and peered up at him. "Why are you doing this to me, Mr. Moore? This isn't about cleaning up Austin, is it?"

"Of course it is. The citizens are up in arms. They want to see people like you run out of town. The district attorney must comply with the people's demands. Of course . . ."

"Yes?"

"There are only so many cases which the courts can pursue with diligence. Some cases take precedence over others. Prosecutions for vice and immorality are hardly as important as a prosecution for murder, for instance."

May leaned back and crossed her arms. "What do you want from me?"

"I believe that you possess valuable information regarding the murder of Eula Phillips."

May bit her lips. "I want nothing to do with that."

"I understand. But you must understand that we are determined to see you prosecuted for running a disorderly house. Unless, of course, your cooperation as a friendly witness is needed in the prosecution of a more important case—the case against Jimmy Phillips."

They looked at each other for a long moment, until they were distracted by footsteps on the stairs. Marshal Lucy tipped his hat to Taylor Moore, who nodded back.

May stepped to the bars. "The message I sent, Marshal? What answer—"

"Never saw Mr. Swain himself," Lucy said. "Had to wait in the anteroom while his assistant, Mr. Shelley, carried it in to him. They conferred for quite some time."

"And?"

There were more footsteps. A figure stepped beside Lucy. It was William Shelley, looking as tightly wound as a bedspring. Without looking May in the eye, he pressed an unmarked envelope into her hand. He turned and descended the stairs without a word.

"Quiet fellow," remarked Taylor Moore.

"Comptroller's pet dog," said Lucy. "Don't seem to have much of a bark."

May tore open the envelope. It was full of crisp currency. She counted it. It was all there, all two hundred dollars. There was no promissory note and no reply. Swain had kept her letter.

A little later, May stepped out the jailhouse door and took a deep breath. She scanned the sky. The rain had stopped for the moment, but dark clouds still loomed. As she debated whether or not to open her umbrella, she heard a familiar voice, and saw a familiar face in the midst of a group of police officers on the sidewalk, heading toward her.

"This be nonsense! This be crazy! I ain't runnin' no house of ill repute— my repute be ever' bit as good as the next landlady! How on earth a poor colored woman like me s'posed to come up with two hun'red dollars?"

The group moved into the jailhouse. For an instant May's eyes met those of Fannie Whipple. Despite her combative tone, Fannie's eyes were wide with panic. Poor Fannie, caught in the same net! What man would be bold enough to post *her* bond?

May hurried on. The sky abruptly opened and poured down a fresh deluge. She opened her umbrella just in time.

A month later, on April 20, the Travis County grand jury indicted Jimmy Phillips, charging that he "did with malice aforethought kill Eula Phillips by striking, cutting, and finishing her with an ax."

Police officers called at the Phillips residence. Jimmy was not there. His parents swore they had no knowledge of his whereabouts.

For a whole week, Jimmy Phillips eluded arrest. The *Statesman* speculated daily on his location and asked, editorially, why an innocent man should hide from the law.

On the 26th of April, Jimmy reappeared in Austin and gave himself up. Some believed his claim that he had been away on personal business when the indictment came down, and headed back as soon as he learned of it. Others, less charitable, speculated that six days was a reasonable amount of time for a man accused of murder to work up the courage to turn himself in.

Jimmy's trial was scheduled to begin on Monday, the 24th of May.

Three times from February to May, Will Porter encountered Delia Campbell on Congress Avenue.

The first time, he barely summoned the nerve to speak to her. The situation was awkward, to say the least, and it was impossible to read Delia's expression behind the black veil she wore. They exchanged a few halting words. At the last moment, as they were about to part, he asked about the letters he had written to Eula, which Delia had agreed to hold in safekeeping.

"I'd like to have them back, please. It's only—if anyone else should ever read them—they could be misconstrued."

Delia nodded. "Of course. I understand, Mr. Porter. I shall return them to you."

The second time he saw her, some weeks later, he asked again about the letters. Delia apologized for not having returned them, and promised again to do so.

The third time, only two weeks before the trial, he asked her quite pointedly about the letters. Delia's veiled face remained unreadable, but her tone was chilly. "I'm sorry, Mr. Porter. I can't speak to you. I expect to be called as a witness at my brother's trial. I can't discuss anything having to do with Eula, with anyone."

"But the letters—"

"I must be off."

"But you said you'd give them back—"

"Really, this is impossible, Mr. Porter. Good day." She hurried down the Avenue, in the direction of May Tobin's house.

44

W ᴴ ᴬ ᵀ did that thermometer in the lobby read?" Dave Shoemaker
tugged at his collar and fanned himself with a folded *Statesman.*

"Ninety-five degrees," said Will, likewise fanning himself. All around the
packed courtroom, manufactured and makeshift fans stirred the warm, humid air. A number of the ladies used colorful folding fans made of bamboo,
or stiff, round fans made of varnished palm leaves. In the stifling atmosphere
of the courtroom the multitude of fans flitted like swarms of butterflies.

Will had not planned to attend the trial, but shortly after lunch, Dave
popped into Will's office and invited him to come along to the courthouse,
saying he could get him a seat. Will begged off, explaining that he couldn't
leave work. His boss overheard.

"Hell, if Dave can get you a front row seat, take the day off," Mr. Anderson said. "There's not a lick of work likely to get done around here, anyway,
what with people popping in every two minutes with the latest word from
the courthouse."

"I can get him a front row seat *every* day," bragged Dave.

"Then it's all right with me if Will takes the whole week off, so long as he
comes in here at lunch and quitting time and tells us what happened. That
way we can get the word straight from the horse's mouth!"

And so Will found himself, practically against his will, sitting in the press
gallery, surrounded by reporters from every newspaper in Texas. There were
correspondents from outside the state as well, including a man from the
New York *World* and another from the Chicago *Tribune.*

Jimmy Phillips entered the room surrounded by his four lawyers. His face was expressionless. He was still damnably handsome, Will thought, despite the raw, ugly scar across his left temple.

Chief among Jimmy's lawyers was John Hancock, one of the best-known defense attorneys in Austin. At sixty-one, Hancock looked harmless enough, rather like a walrus standing upright, with an enormous, shaggy, silver mustache. He was legendary for independent thinking. When the Civil War broke out, he had vigorously opposed secession in the state legislature and fled to Mexico rather than serve the Confederacy. There had been people ever since who referred to him as Hancock the Traitor. Nonetheless, after the war he successfully reentered the political arena and established a brilliant career as a lawyer. In March, Hancock had finished his second term in the U.S. House of Representatives. The Phillips case marked his return to the courts.

Hancock also happened to be the law partner of Nathan Shelley, the father of William Shelley; the connection crossed Dave's mind as he scribbled notes. "Odd—our friend William Shelley doesn't seem to be here," he whispered to Will.

"Should he be?" The last time Will had seen Shelley had been in May Tobin's parlor.

"No reason. But isn't Shelley always in the middle of everything?"

The reporter from the New York *World* shushed Dave. Hancock was beginning the opening statement for the defense.

"Gentlemen of the jury: Jimmy Phillips, the defendant in this case, is a local man, twenty-four years old, born and raised here in Austin. Like his father, a respected builder, Jimmy is a skilled carpenter. His latest job was helping to put up the new fireman's hall. With money earned from that job, as we will show, Jimmy Phillips purchased a suite of bedroom furniture for himself and his young wife and their little baby boy. It was partly a Christmas gift, we may suppose, and partly an anniversary gift—for in January of this year, Jimmy and Eula Phillips would have celebrated their third anniversary.

"You will hear how, on the very night of the tragedy, last Christmas Eve, Jimmy went out specifically to make a payment on that bedroom suite—the act of a conscientious, responsible, forward-thinking young man. It was hardly the act of a man set on killing his spouse that very night and determined to bring down scandal and ruin on his family and child.

"You will hear from the prosecution, I imagine, that there was trouble in Jimmy's marriage. You will hear the character of Eula Phillips besmirched, along with the character of her husband." Hancock thoughtfully pulled at his unkempt mustache. "I would ask you to consider the source of such charges, and to evaluate their importance and credibility accordingly. What marriage exists without the occasional harsh word, the angry spat, the meaningless, empty threat so easily magnified in hindsight? What marriage exists without jealous friends and in-laws all too ready to imagine or even fabricate scandal? Yes, there were bad patches in the marriage of Jimmy and Eula Phillips, due largely to the fact that they had passed through a year of financial hardship and uncertainty. But their marriage had survived that bad patch and was all the stronger for it. On Christmas Eve, peace and reconciliation reigned in the Phillips household. Man, woman, and child were together and content. A happy and prosperous new year beckoned.

"Then fate—terrible and unforeseen—intervened. An unspeakable tragedy occurred; unspeakable, I say, but not unheard of in these parlous times. An unknown assailant or assailants violated the sanctuary of Jimmy's happy home. His wife was dragged from his side, molested, and brutally murdered. Jimmy himself was struck a blow so severe that to this day his mind and memory haven't fully recovered, and may never do so. Was he struck down in a vain, valiant attempt to protect his wife? It would appear so. We might expect that the same husband and father who worked so conscientiously to provide a good home and furnishings for his family would rise to the occasion when the need arose to preserve their safety.

"Imagine this young man's suffering! Imagine his despair! And yet, irony of ironies, today we are assembled here for the express purpose of heaping more suffering and shame upon him. Jimmy Phillips stands accused by the state of murdering his wife—this poor youth who was very nearly murdered himself!

"The prosecution will attempt to convince you that Jimmy was a bad fellow indeed, not only violent and dangerous, but an outright monster—for who but a monster could murder his wife right in front of their baby boy? Such an act goes so completely against nature, is so entirely unlikely in the great balance of things, that I believe the esteemed men of the prosecution, for all their good intentions and their celebrated oratorical skills, will be hard-pressed to convince anyone of it. They will even attempt to convince you—because their whole argument makes no sense without this crowning absurdity!—that the terrible wound which Jimmy Phillips received was self-inflicted, administered by his own hand. A man would have to be superhuman to be able to do such a thing!

"When all the evidence has been presented, all the witnesses called to the stand—and it will be up to you to determine just how reliable or unreliable each of those witnesses may be—when all has been sifted and sorted out, I am certain that you, the gentlemen of the jury, will find that my client is not guilty of this horrible crime. By your wise verdict you will duly release him, so that this poor, grieving widower may continue to recover from his loss and from his wounds as best he can."

Returning to his chair, Hancock paused to touch Jimmy's shoulder with the tenderness of a father comforting a child.

The opening statement for the prosecution was delivered by Taylor Moore, whose lean, sartorial elegance made a sharp contrast to Hancock's shambling walrus gait. His delivery was brisk as he strode back and forth before the jury box with hands on hips and elbows akimbo.

"Gentlemen of the jury, Mr. Hancock is absolutely right when he says that the prosecution must prove its case to you beyond a reasonable doubt. But I don't think that shall be nearly so hard as he makes out, for the facts in this case are glaringly clear.

"In the next few days, we will show that the marriage of Jimmy and Eula Phillips was not mildly troubled by the normal spats of day-to-day living, as Mr. Hancock suggests, but riven with deep and irreconcilable animosities. On the night of last Christmas Eve, Jimmy and Eula were anything but reconciled, as Mr. Hancock asserts. In fact, they were farther apart than ever, and the crisis of their broken marriage reached such a pitch, rose to such a raging boil, that Jimmy Phillips resorted to bloody murder.

"How did he do this? With an ax. Think about the harsh reality of that, gentlemen! We will show you the very ax he used; you will see it for yourselves. This ax was already on the Phillips property on the night of the murder, and so was readily at hand. It was not brought there by some imaginary assailant from the outside.

"Was the crime committed on the spur of the moment, on a wild, unpremeditated impulse? We will show that Jimmy Phillips had behaved violently toward his wife before. Indeed, we know of at least one incident when he brandished a knife at her. More than once, as we will show, Jimmy Phillips told others that he would kill his wife, if he knew her to be unfaithful.

"And was Eula Phillips unfaithful?" As Moore paused for effect, strolling slowly before the jury box, Will felt the skin prickle on the back of his neck. "Sadly, we will show that she was. As a wife, Eula Phillips was not what she should have been. She shared her favors with men other than her husband, and not only once, but numerous times; not only with one lover, but with several; not just for love or simple carnal pleasure, but in all likelihood for monetary gain. Eula Phillips, as we will show, even became pregnant by one of her lovers, and to hide the fact from her husband, she aborted the child. As we will show, she met these multiple lovers at a notorious assignation house on Congress Avenue. Her last rendezvous but one at that house was on the night of the 23rd of December, the day before her death."

The prickling spread across Will's shoulders and down his spine. His face flushed hotly. He was suffocating; the room was like an oven. What on earth was the lawyer talking about? Moore had to be lying; all lawyers lied. Nothing the man was saying made sense . . .

Moore prattled on, in such a glib tone that Will wanted to strangle him before he could pile on more slanders.

"We cannot know every detail of the night of Eula Phillips's death," Moore was saying, "because there are certain facts which only Eula Phillips could tell us, but we can surmise the outline of that fateful evening. By the physical evidence we will present and the testimony of our witnesses, the story will become clear. Eula Phillips went to bed with her husband and child on Christmas Eve, and Mr. Hancock would leave the story there, with husband and wife and baby together in a picture of peaceful contentment. But Eula Phillips did not stay in bed. No doubt, she waited first for her husband to fall asleep. Then she rose, put on a wrap, left the house, and took a hackney cab to the residence of one May Tobin, where Eula Phillips was accustomed to meet her lovers.

"But her assignation fell through. The man who was to meet her that night did not appear, and the room reserved for them was rented to others. May Tobin turned Eula Phillips away, as if in blasphemous parody of the ancient hosteler who pleaded, on the first Christmas Eve, 'There is no room at the inn.' Disappointed, Eula Phillips returned home by the same hackney cab.

"What happened next? We cannot know the precise sequence of events, unless Jimmy Phillips himself will tell us, but we know the fatal outcome. One scenario might run thus: Eula herself fetched the household ax, fearing that her husband might be awake and angry and thinking to defend herself with it. It was she who struck the first blow, and Jimmy Phillips, wounded and enraged, seized the ax from her and returned the blow in kind. If that was the case, Jimmy Phillips's lawyers would do well to tell us the truth here and now, so that they might make a case for self-defense.

"But the true scenario, I fear, was even uglier than that. Jimmy awoke and found his wife absent. He knew or at least suspected the reason for her absence. He brooded in the darkness and nursed his spite, and made up his mind to do something about it. He fetched the household ax, then lay in wait. When his wife appeared, Jimmy Phillips did, with malice afore-thought, strike and cut and kill her with it.

"Did he then cry out, 'Have mercy on me, Lord, I have murdered my wife!' No. For Jimmy Phillips had no intention of taking responsibility for his terrible act. He had thought out ahead of time what he would do next. He picked up the expiring body of his wife and carried her to the back yard, and laid her out in an obscene fashion, in such a way as to divert suspicion from himself—the craven act of a cowardly murderer! Then, his nerves wrought up to an unnatural pitch by the ferocity of his crime, and with a hellish determination to cover his tracks, Jimmy Phillips returned to his bedroom and inflicted a blow to his own head. The ax fell to the floor. Jimmy staggered to his bed. He collapsed beside his dazed child—the baby he himself made motherless!—and like the coward he was he began to cry out for his mother. Pity the child of Eula Phillips, who shall cry out for his mother in vain!

"This is a sordid story, gentlemen of the jury. It sickens me to recount it to you. It is as ugly and vile a crime as one can imagine.

"You may feel tempted, when hearing some of the testimony, to feel sym-pathy for Jimmy Phillips. You may say to yourself, 'His wife was a shameless harlot; she deserved what she got.' But you have not been assembled here to judge Eula Phillips. She was very young; she was weak and foolish. But for those failings she did not deserve to die, and no man had the right to kill her. Whatever sins she committed are between her and her maker now, and she will be judged by a higher law. Your duty is to administer the law of the living. A man who plots bloody murder and reaches for an ax to commit it, a man who orphans his own child and then covers his tracks and cowers be-hind his bandages—such a man may or may not be, as Mr. Hancock would have it, a monster. But he certainly cannot be allowed to escape the judg-ment of the law."

Moore returned to his seat. Will was stunned. All around him the room was alive with movement. The judge banged his gavel, the reporters scrib-bled furiously, the ladies flitted their fans and whispered in each other's ears, the lawyers stacked and sorted bits of paper. But Will sat utterly still. The only other person in the room who sat so still was Jimmy Phillips, as if the two of them had been turned to stone.

The state called its first witness, Mrs. James Phillips. She looked haggard and careworn. She answered the questions put to her in a dull voice, and glanced at her son from time to time with a stricken look. If John Hancock had instructed her ahead of time to tug at the jurors' heartstrings, she could not have done a better job.

She explained that Jimmy and Eula spent most of the previous year at the McCutcheon farm in Williamson County, but returned to Austin in October. She described the layout of the Phillips house. She recounted the events of the fateful night—how Jimmy went out to make a payment on the furniture and returned within fifteen minutes, on a bet; how the evening passed quietly and uneventfully; how Jimmy and Eula retired to their room with the baby; how she brought them apples and nuts, and found all three cuddled together; how she last saw them at some time before eleven and then went to bed; how she was awakened after midnight by the sound of her son crying out, "Oh, Mama!" and "Eula, darling!"; how she went to Jimmy and Eula's room across the verandah and found Jimmy lying beside the baby on the bed, dazed and bloody, with blood spattered on the carpet and a bloody ax lying on the floor; how she noticed a bloody pile of Eula's clothes lying near the bed, but saw no sign of Eula; how she ran to awaken her sick husband, crying, "Jimmy's been murdered! Someone's murdered Jimmy!"; how she then returned to Jimmy, who muttered and raved and slipped in and out of consciousness; how a great many people soon arrived. The rest of the night beyond that point, including the discovery of Eula's body in the back yard, was so confused in her mind that she could not speak with any certainty.

Taylor Moore inquired about her son's drinking. She admitted that from time to time he drank heavily. Moore asked about a specific incident when Jimmy fought with his sister and kicked out a door panel; Mrs. Phillips acknowledged that Jimmy had been drinking when the incident occurred, and that afterward Delia and Eula left the premises, and Eula stayed away for weeks.

"And on the morning after the murder, Mrs. Phillips, on Christmas Day, while you were nursing your son—I believe this was in the presence of a colored woman named Sallie Mack, who works for you—is it not true, Mrs. Phillips, that your son regained consciousness and asked you, 'Ma, where is Eula?'"

Mrs. Phillips looked at her son and then away. She took a long time to answer. "Yes, that's true."

"How did you answer him?"

"I said, 'Eula's dead.'"

"What was his response?"

Mrs. Phillips lowered her face.

"What was Jimmy's response, Mrs. Phillips?" said Moore gently.

"He said—" She swallowed hard. "He said, 'Then I shall surely go to hell!' "

The courtroom reacted. The reporters scribbled madly. Moore backed away from the witness stand, looking pleased with himself. Will decided that he hated the man.

Mrs. Phillips was dismissed. The court adjourned for the day.

There was a mad scurry among the reporters, except for Dave, who had no need to rush to a telegraph office. The men from the Chicago *Tribune* and the New York *World* seemed to know each other. They shoved by Will, stepping on his toes.

"Great stuff, eh?" said the *Tribune* man. He drew his brows together and drawled plaintively, " 'Then I'll surely go to hell, Mama!' "

"Ah, but the real show will commence when they call the defendant's sister, and this woman May Tobin," said the *World* man. "My informant in the DA's office promises me there'll be fireworks."

"Not just sparklers?"

"Roman candles and rockets, my good man!"

At length, Dave shook his wrist to get out the kinks and looked up from his notepad. "You've hardly said a word since we got here, Will. If the trial's boring you, there's plenty of other fellows who'd like to occupy that seat."

"No!" Will gripped Dave's arm. "I have to come tomorrow."

"All right, all right!" Dave laughed. "Will, let go of my arm—you're hurting me!"

45

*T*HE second day of the trial commenced with more witnesses for the state.

Mrs. S. M. Dyer, who lived next door to the Phillips residence, testified to having witnessed the quarrel in November when Jimmy chased Eula and Delia into the yard. She had been alerted to the quarrel by a crash of breaking wood coming from the Phillips house and the sound of Jimmy yelling, "God damn you, I'll kill you!"

R. B. Eanes, Eula's uncle, testified that when Eula left Jimmy for a while in November, after the fight in the yard, Jimmy came to his house looking for her and brandished a knife, saying that he would kill anyone who was hiding her.

Albert Highsmith, a friend of George McCutcheon, testified that he visited McCutcheon's farm several times while Jimmy and Eula were living there, and on one occasion he overhead Jimmy say, in the presence of McCutcheon and others, that if he ever found out that Eula was unfaithful to him, he would kill Eula and then himself. Highsmith thought that Jimmy was drunk at the time.

Alma Burdett of Manchaca, Eula's sister, testified that Jimmy had a suspicious and jealous nature. She could remember several occasions when Eula mentioned a man's name in passing, or merely seemed to recognize a man on the street, whereupon Jimmy grabbed Eula's arm and demanded of her, "How the devil do you know that fellow?"

Sallie Mack testified that she was present when Jimmy Phillips woke on Christmas Day and asked his mother about Eula. When Mrs. Phillips answered that Eula was dead, Sallie clearly heard Jimmy exclaim, "Then I shall surely go to hell!"

"And earlier," said Taylor Moore, "in the nighttime hours after the murder of Eula Phillips was discovered, you assisted Mrs. Phillips in nursing her son, did you not?"

"I stayed up with her, and went and fetched for her, if that's what you mean," said Sallie.

"You fetched for her. Was one of the things you fetched for her a basin of water?"

"Yes, sir."

"And did you see what she did with that basin of water?"

"She used it for washin' Jimmy."

"What particular portion of the defendant's anatomy did she bathe?"

"I begs yo' pardon?"

"What part of Jimmy's body did Mrs. Phillips wash?"

"She washed his feet, sir."

"Did you see the basin afterward?"

"Yes, sir."

"What was the color of the water?"

"A reddish color, like it had blood in it."

Moore introduced a basin into evidence. Sallie identified it as the one she had seen that night.

G. R. Thompson, the police sergeant in charge of the bloodhounds used to track escaped convicts, testified that he and his two best hounds arrived at the Phillips house that night after a number of people had already congregated, but before Eula's body had been found.

"As an experienced tracker, what was the first thing you noticed?" asked Moore.

"Well, sir, I saw splotches of blood and what looked to be some bloody footprints on the floorboards of the verandah, leading to the back-yard steps."

"What did you do then?"

"Well, I let my hounds—these was my best two hounds in the squad, mind you—I let 'em sniff at the bloody spots, and they up and led me straight to the back of the yard, oh, about a hundred and forty feet or so from the verandah."

"What did you discover there?"

"The body of that poor woman. The hounds and me was the first to find her."

"What did the hounds do then?"

"Well, sir, they both up and tried to head back toward the house, which I

thought was mighty peculiar at the time, on account of they know better
than that. They know what their job is."

"And what is that?"

"Well, to strike a trail and lead you *away* from the place. Now the moon
was real bright that night, and I saw some spots on the alley fence that I took
to be spots of blood, and it so happened they was. So I held up the hounds
and put their noses to the spots on the fence, and then I got Justice of the
Peace Von Rosenberg to help me lift the dogs up and over into the alley.
The hounds headed off west in the direction of Shoal Creek, then up Castle Hill toward Nathan Shelley's place, and then south. Von Rosenberg and
I followed 'em all the way to Clarksville and back, but they never did strike
a sure trail."

"Why do you say that?"

"When they strike a trail, they let out a certain kind of howl, sort of like
this—" Thompson cupped his hands and produced a low, mournful howl
that echoed off the high ceiling.

The sound was unearthly, Will thought; it chilled his blood. But behind
him, the reporters from the New York *World* and the Chicago *Tribune* broke
out laughing. The judge banged his gavel and gave them a harsh look.

"Continue, Mr. Thompson," said the judge.

"Well, like I say, those hounds led us a merry chase and we didn't find a
thing, so we finally headed back to the Phillips house. Now, at the time we
left, there was such a crowd and so much noise that the hounds was pretty
distracted, but by the time we got back, things had quieted down, so I
thought I'd give 'em another chance."

"Would the trail have been cold by then?" asked Taylor Moore.

"Well, there's cold and there's cold. These was my best two dogs, mind
you, and the older one is about the best cold tracker I've ever come across.
That dog can track a trail six, maybe even eight hours old. Depends on temperature and dew on the grass and such. Anyway, I let 'em sniff the place
where they'd found the body—somebody had moved her inside by then—
and just like before they headed straight back toward the house, only this
time I let 'em."

"What did the dogs do?"

"They went to the verandah, stopped to smell those bloody footprints,
and then they headed into the bedroom where Jimmy Phillips and his
Mama was. Then they both reared up on the bed, howling to bring down
the moon, just like this—" Thompson threw back his head and cupped his
hands and produced the mournful howl again. The effect was so uncanny
that even the big-city reporters remained silent. "Jimmy Phillips started

moaning for his Mama, and his Mama gave out a yell. I'm afraid the dogs gave 'em both quite a scare before I had a chance to call 'em off."

"What did the dogs do then?"

"Well, there was a bundle of bloody clothes lying close by the bed—a woman's clothes—and the hounds sniffed at that and showed quite a bit of interest. Then they went over to a basin of bloody water on the floor, and they was *mighty* interested in smelling of that."

Moore showed him the basin which Sallie Mack had identified as the one which Mrs. Phillips used to clean Jimmy's feet. "Is this the basin they sniffed at?"

"Sure looks like it," said Thompson.

The reporters in the gallery scribbled furiously. The judge called a recess for lunch.

In all, four doctors had been called to the Phillips house on the night of the murder. That afternoon, all four were called to testify.

Dr. Litten, the family physician for the Phillips household, was the first to arrive at the house, along with his partner, Dr. Cummings, at about one o'clock in the morning. The doctor found Jimmy unconscious, lying on the bed surrounded by a considerable amount of blood. Taylor Moore asked Dr. Litten to describe the defendant's wound.

"Part of the front cuticle of the ear was knocked off, as by a glancing blow. The most serious wound was above the ear, here at the left temple." Dr. Litten tapped his own head. "The wound cut inward and downward and was deepest at the top, more shallow as it went down. That would be consistent with a cut made by the blade of an ax. The edges of the wound were irregular and lacerated. It went to a depth of half an inch, all the way to the periosteum, which was abraded and bruised."

"For the laymen among us, Doctor, what is the periosteum?"

"It's a membrane of tough, fibrous connective tissue which covers the bones, including the skull."

"Was the skull itself damaged?"

"I saw no evidence that the skull was fractured."

"You also examined the body of Eula Phillips, did you not?"

"Yes. Her body was discovered not long after I arrived, while I was dressing Jimmy's wounds."

"Can you describe how you found the dead woman?"

"She was lying on her back, nude. Her forehead had been broken in by some instrument. The wound extended pretty much straight up from the base of her nose." By way of illustration, Dr. Litten pressed the outside edge of his hand perpendicular to his forehead. "The wound was more sunken toward the top of her head, perhaps an inch and a half deep, and an inch and a quarter wide. It could have been caused by a blow from an ax. It was surely the cause of her death, as there were no other wounds on her body. I imagine such a blow killed her instantly."

"She was a petite woman, was she not?"

"Quite small. I doubt she weighed more than a hundred pounds."

"Were there signs of sexual intercourse?"

Dr. Litten looked thoughtful. The men in the press gallery leaned forward in unison.

"I couldn't conclusively say yes or no to that. Given the circumstances, I felt obliged to consider the possibility that she had been raped, either before or after her death, and so I examined her accordingly. Her legs were spread apart, and her private parts were somewhat distended. There was no bleeding. The vagina contained about a teaspoon of white, opaque fluid that resembled male semen, though in my estimation a little darker in color. I later examined it microscopically, and found it to contain no vital or life-imparting germs, such as usually inhabit the semen. However, such germs are not always found in semen; in sterile men they may not be present at all, and even in normal semen they may expire shortly after being deposited. If not semen, it could have been a fluid naturally excreted by the vagina. So, as to sexual intercourse proximate to her death, I cannot say with certainly one way or the other."

On cross examination, John Hancock asked Dr. Litten to describe Jimmy Phillips's condition resulting from the blow to his head.

"The blow produced a great nervous shock and considerable physical disability. Mr. Phillips was under my care for two months after that night, and during that time he suffered nervousness, feverishness, sleeplessness, poverty of circulation, and impaired action of the heart. He continues to suffer those symptoms to a reduced extent to this day."

"When you first examined the defendant, did you consider that his wound might have been self-inflicted?" asked Hancock.

"No, I didn't. Given the circumstances, the thought didn't cross my mind."

"It wasn't glaringly obvious, then, something you might point to and say, 'Looky there, here's another fool gone and brained himself with an ax'?"

Dr. Litten smiled. "No."

"And yet, since that time, the question of whether it could have been a self-inflicted wound has been seriously put forward, at least by the district attorney," noted Hancock. "What is your expert opinion as a medical man on that question? Was the wound self-inflicted?"

"I can't say for certain yes or no."

"Might it have been?"

Dr. Litten drew a deep breath. "I would have to say that it seems to me highly improbable. Not impossible, medically speaking, but highly improbable."

Litten's partner, Dr. Cummings, was called to the stand. He generally agreed with Dr. Litten's description of Jimmy's wound, but expressed the opinion that it was probably caused by two or more blows. "A man may steel his nerves to give himself one stunning blow, but two or three — that seems to me virtually impossible. Natural reflex will not allow it."

Dr. Fisher, who was also summoned that night but did not arrive until three or four o'clock, disagreed with Dr. Cummings about the number of blows, asserting that a single powerful blow had caused the wound to Jimmy's head, but he was equally skeptical of the possibility that the wound was self-inflicted. "After careful study of the wound, it is my opinion that the blow was struck with great force by someone standing *behind* the defendant."

"It was physically impossible, then, for the defendant to have done it himself?" said Hancock.

"In this age of medical miracles you'll be hard-pressed to find a doctor who'll use the word *impossible*," Dr. Fisher replied, "but in this case I'd say next to impossible."

Dr. Bragg, who accompanied Dr. Fisher to the Phillips residence, disagreed with all three of his colleagues. "It wasn't two blows, but one, and it wasn't struck from the back, but from the front. And if you compare it to the blow which instantly killed the defendant's wife, you can see at once why it caused so much less damage. It was delivered with much less force, as evidenced by the fact that it did not fracture the bone, and instead of being delivered head-on, so to speak, it was a glancing blow to the side of the head. I see no reason why a person couldn't inflict such a wound upon himself."

"Then you think it's possible that the defendant's wound was self-inflicted?" asked Taylor Moore.

"I think it is not only possible, sir, but probable." His words produced a hubbub in the courtroom.

Following Dr. Bragg's testimony, the judge adjourned the court. The trial would resume at nine the next morning.

＊ ＊ ＊

It was too hot to sleep that night. Even stripped naked, Will tossed and turned beneath the sheet.

A vision of Eula appeared whenever he shut his eyes; not the beautiful woman whose face had stolen his heart the first time he saw her, but Eula as he had seen her last, her forehead caved in, her face broken. She had been naked. Had he looked between her legs? He couldn't remember, but he kept hearing the doctor's words: *legs spread apart . . . private parts distended . . .*

In his dream he drew closer and closer to the dark, glistening, woundlike place between her legs . . .

Bloodhounds howled in the distance. Behind him, the reporters from New York and Chicago laughed. Dr. Litten was on the witness stand, holding up a glass phial containing an opaque white fluid. "I could find no life-imparting germs in the semen I took from her vagina," the doctor said. Then he pointed an accusing finger at Will. "My medical evidence indicates that the male semen came from that young man in the press gallery!"

The doctor on the stand held up a large drawing of what he had seen under the microscope. It was no longer Dr. Litten but Dr. Edmund Montgomery, and the courtroom was Montgomery's rustic study at Liendo. The drawing showed a protoplasmic specimen shaped like a crumpled sombrero with a fringe of stubby tentacles. The caption read: *To Be Alive, What Is It?*

The judge called Will to the front of the room. He made Will sit at Montgomery's cluttered desk. "If you look through that microscope, young man, you can see Eula Phillips again." Will's heart knotted in his chest. He put his eye to the tube and saw a horrifying red mass of writhing, viscous matter, like a heap of bloody maggots.

Will looked back to the judge, who gazed down at him sternly. "Your punishment, young man, is to write a thousand pages on the subject, 'To Be Alive, What Is It?'"

Will stared at the towering stack of blank paper before him. "But I can't!"

"Then you'll have to do what Jimmy did." Amid the clutter on the desk, Will saw an ax. He picked it up. The handle was slippery and warm. The shiny blade was smeared with blood.

Will woke with a start. Sunlight streamed through the open windows. He had slept the whole night away, yet felt utterly exhausted.

This was the day that May and Delia would testify.

46

⤣

$\mathcal{T}$HE third day of the trial began with Fannie Whipple on the stand.

She was dressed in her Sunday best, a purple dress and a purple hat upon which a yellow bird perched, like a songbird amid heather. She carried herself stiffly and her eyes were wary. She never looked directly at the judge or at either of the lawyers who questioned her.

It was established at the beginning of her testimony that Fannie had been known to run a house of assignation, and was testifying under promise of exemption from prosecution.

Fannie testified that in November, Eula Phillips came to her house on Red River Street, along with Delia Campbell. Fannie knew neither of the women, except as friends of May Tobin. They told her they had fled from home to get away from Eula's husband, who was on a drinking rampage and had threatened Delia's life. While at Fannie's house, they paid for their room and board. They stayed there for one full night, all the next day and into a second night, until about two in the morning, when they both left in the company of a white man.

"Who was this man?" asked Taylor Moore.

The reporters in the press gallery stirred in anticipation.

"I couldn't say," Fannie answered. "I didn't know him from Adam, and he never told me his name."

"But Mrs. Campbell and Mrs. Phillips knew him?"

"He wasn't no stranger to 'em."

May Tobin was called to the stand. She wore a dress of dark blue and black, suitable to a widow. Her expression was almost scornful as she scanned the courtroom through her rimless glasses. Her gaze seemed to pause on certain of the spectators, on whom she bestowed faint nods of recognition. Will lowered his face. The reporters stood up in their seats and jostled each other, trying to follow her gaze. The judge banged his gavel and ordered them to sit down.

As with Fannie Whipple, it was established that May had been known to run a house of assignation, and was testifying under promise of exemption from prosecution.

She was asked about the night in November when Eula and Delia came to her house from Fannie Whipple's.

"Yes, I remember that night," said May.

"Do you remember who accompanied them?"

"I do."

Seats squeaked and groaned. Notepads fluttered in the press gallery.

"Who was this man?"

"His name was Mr. Shelley. A young fellow. I believe he works for a state department."

Dave stiffened. "My God, William Shelley! No wonder he's not here."

The *Tribune* man leaned over from the seat behind. "Is that Shelley with two *e's*?"

Dave nodded. "And John Hancock over there, the defense attorney, is law partners with Shelley's father."

"The old fellow looks fit to be tied," the *Tribune* man whispered back.

Taylor Moore let the hubbub in the courtroom die down before proceeding. "This Mr. Shelley brought Mrs. Campbell and Mrs. Phillips to your house at two o'clock in the morning?"

"Thereabouts."

"Are you used to receiving visitors at such an hour, Mrs. Tobin?"

"Sometimes a room happens to open up at two in the morning. That was the case in this instance, as I recall."

"I see. Did Mrs. Campbell and Mrs. Phillips stay in separate rooms?"

"They did."

"Did Mr. Shelley also stay the night?"

"He did. And the next two nights as well."

"Did he spend those nights with one of the two women?"

"Mr. Shelley spent each of those three nights with Eula Phillips," said May. Will felt as if the seat had been pulled from under him and he was dangling in space.

"I see," said Moore. "Can you say with certainty that Mr. Shelley slept in the same bed with Mrs. Phillips?"

"I can say for certain that there was only one bed in the room. I can't say for sure how much sleep either one of them got."

Laughter erupted in the courtroom, harsh and ugly to Will's ears. All the time that Eula had refused to see him again, refused even to answer his letters, those letters which cost him such pain to write—William Shelley . . . three nights in a row . . .

"After the third night, did Mrs. Phillips remain at your house?" said Moore.

"No."

"Do you know where she went?"

"To the best of my knowledge, she went to stay with her sister down in Manchaca for a while."

"During that particular three-day period in November, did any man other than Mr. Shelley call on Mrs. Phillips?"

"No."

"Previous to that stay in November, had Mrs. Phillips ever visited your house?"

"Yes."

"Would it be correct to say that she came to your house for the purpose of meeting men other than her husband?"

May's eyes flashed. "Sometimes Eula simply came to visit. We were friends, you see."

"Yes, but most times she came to meet with men, in a private room—is that correct?"

"Most times, yes."

"When did these visits begin?"

"I first met Mrs. Phillips in October."

"That was when she began availing herself of your vacant rooms?"

"Yes."

"This was shortly after Mrs. Phillips and her husband moved back to Austin from Williamson County?"

"I believe so."

"Then almost as soon as she was back in Austin, she began meeting men at your house?"

"Yes."

"Can you name these men?"

May scanned the room, amused at the rapt attention of the reporters in the press gallery. Will averted his eyes. "Some of them."

Moore turned to the judge. "Your Honor, in order to establish that such meetings actually did take place, and to establish them as specific events rather than vague generalities, I intend to ask Mrs. Tobin to name those men whom she can."

The judge nodded. "Proceed."

"With whom did Eula Phillips meet at your house, Mrs. Tobin?"

"She met with Mr. Shelley, prior to those three days in November."

"Yes, one might assume that they were already acquainted." There was a scattering of laughter in the courtroom. Some of the reporters made shushing sounds. "But who else, Mrs. Tobin?"

May's face took on a hard, cold expression. "In general, I knew only last names, you understand. I recall that there was a certain Mr. Dickinson. I recall hearing him say once that he worked for a Mr. Joseph Lee."

Dave hissed. The *Tribune* man peered over Dave's shoulder. Will watched him scribble: *John T. Dickinson—Sec'y, State Cap. Bldg. Comm.!*

"Mrs. Phillips met with Mr. Dickinson a number of times, always in the afternoon," May went on. "I did wonder how a man with such an important post was able to find so much free time in the afternoons. It makes one wonder about the dedication of our state employees."

"Yes. Who else, Mrs. Tobin?"

"There was a very handsome young fellow, with the neatest little beard and beautiful curls in his hair. He also came in the afternoon. Very polite. Rather like a schoolteacher. What was his name? Ah, yes, Mr. Baker!"

Dave worked his jaw excitedly. The *Tribune* man was practically crawling over the seat. Will had to squint to read Dave's scrawl: *Benjamin M. Baker— State Supt. Pub. Instruction!—age 35—fastest rising star in Texas politics . . .*

"Were there yet others, Mrs. Tobin?"

"Oh, yes. Mrs. Phillips was a very lovely woman, you know."

"Can you name these other men, Mrs. Tobin?"

May shrugged. "In some cases, when the room was let to Mrs. Phillips, her male visitor didn't give me a name."

"Are you saying that there were others who met with Mrs. Phillips in your house, but that you cannot identify them?"

"That would be correct. Though now that I come to think of it, there was one other who gave me his name . . ."

The press gallery seethed with anticipation. There had been a rumor for days that May Tobin would name a very big name, bigger even than Benjamin Baker—the head of another state department, a man with ambitions for the Governor's Mansion. She had come tantalizingly close already, by naming his young protégé, William Shelley. Would she dare to name Comptroller Swain himself?

"The fellow I'm thinking of, as I recall, was the very first fellow to visit Mrs. Phillips in my house," said May.

"Yes? Well, then, what was his name?"

"Jones. That was it, Mr. Jones. I don't know what he did for a living. I'm not even sure the young fellow had a job; Mrs. Phillips paid for the room herself. Of course it's an awfully common name. Half the fellows who come to my house are named Jones. Imagine that!"

May looked straight at Will. He thought his heart would stop beating. But there was nothing malignant in the secret smile she gave him; it seemed to him rather sad. He lowered his eyes, and his gaze fell on Dave's notepad, where the name *Jones* was followed by a row of question marks.

"After Mrs. Phillips came back from Manchaca and returned to her husband," Moore went on, "did she continue to meet with men at your house?"

"Not for a while. She said she was trying to patch things up with Jimmy. He had stopped drinking, or claimed he had, and she felt obliged to try to make another go of it. But I think there was something else, too. I think she was too afraid of him to come back to my house for a while."

Mr. Hancock objected that the witness was speculating. The offending remarks were stricken.

"But Mrs. Phillips did eventually resume her trysts at your house?" said Moore.

"Yes. She met with a man on the night of December 23rd."

"Who was that man?"

May pursed her lips. "I'm afraid he was one of those fellows whose name I never knew." So many of the reporters mouthed the name *Swain* that it was barely audible.

"When did she next come to your house, after the 23rd?"

"The next night, Christmas Eve."

"The night she was killed?"

The scorn vanished from May's face. The rouge on her cheeks was supplanted by a genuine flush. "Yes. I think I was one of the last people to see her alive."

"What time was this?"

"Between half past eleven and midnight."

"How can you be sure of the time?"

"Eula had an appointment to meet a certain gentleman that night, at a quarter past eleven. I had told the gentleman that he must be punctual, you see, that I would hold the room for him and Eula no later than half past eleven. Christmas Eve is a very busy night. There were others willing to pay very well for that room. But the gentleman didn't arrive on time; he never came at all. When the hackney cab brought Eula, I told her that her friend hadn't come. I told her I had given the room to others. I turned her away, you see. I sent her back to her husband. I wish I hadn't."

"Mrs. Tobin, what was the name of the man whom Eula was supposed to meet on Christmas Eve?"

The reporters held their breaths. May shook her head. "I can't tell you."

"Do you mean that you never knew his name?"

"That would be correct," said May, but without conviction.

Will looked at Dave, who bit his lower lip and slowly shook his head. He seemed distracted and hardly conscious of what he was doing as he wrote on his notepad, *Hiram Glass*, then went over each letter, scratching it out. The *Tribune* reporter leaned forward to have a look. Dave tore the page from his notepad and crumpled it in his fist.

The court recessed for lunch. Dave invited Will to come along to the Iron Front, where all the reporters were headed, but Will declined. He had no desire to be in a saloon full of beer-guzzling reporters laughing and joking about Eula Phillips. He hurried past the other eateries on the Avenue; the conversation would be the same in all of them. He ended up at the Rodriguez tamale house by Shoal Creek, where at least the conversation would be in Spanish. Even there he overheard laughter and the words *puta gringa*.

When had he first made love to Eula? It must have been August; he remembered their tryst at Swenson's Ruin, the rampant foliage, the choking heat. Then Eula moved back to Austin. They met at May Tobin's, and he was Mr. Jones. *The very first fellow to visit Mrs. Phillips in my house*, May had said.

After that, what had become of Eula? All the while he thought she must be suffering a misery equal to his, struggling to remain faithful to her useless husband, all that time she was going back to May Tobin's house, not once but again and again—and never with him. Why not? Because he couldn't pay? Was that why she saw Shelley, and Dickinson, and Baker, and—

Hiram Glass! He could hardly believe it.

Mixed with his jealousy and hurt was a pang of guilt. He had been the first—May Tobin said so. The first! He had opened Pandora's box. Women were weak; it was up to men to be strong. He had known she was married from the start, and yet he had pursued her, tempted her, wooed her, willed her to stray. What could he have been thinking? She had a husband. She had a baby! Whenever a woman fell, there was a man behind it. In all the melodramas and the tragic novels the seducer was a selfish cad, a man without morals, without a soul. Was he that man?

He had no appetite for tamales. He drank one beer after another, then made his way back to the courthouse.

The testimony resumed with Delia Campbell called to the witness stand. She wore a dress of midnight blue, and a small feathery hat with a black veil. Will was struck again by her resemblance to Jimmy. Their eyes and cheekbones were almost identical, and their hair had the same blue-black luster. But their demeanors were entirely different. Jimmy looked haggard and stricken. Delia was so composed as to seem aloof.

"Mrs. Campbell, you are the sister of the defendant, I believe," said Taylor Moore.

"I am."

"Eula Phillips was your sister-in-law."

"Yes."

"You're a widow, are you not?"

"I am."

"And in December of last year, and for some time previous to that, you were residing at the home of your parents?"

"Yes."

"But you were away at the time of the murder."

"I was at Rosenberg Junction, visiting friends. I came back on Christmas Day."

"Last summer, you spent several weeks visiting your brother and sister-in-law when they were living at the McCutcheon farm in Williamson County, I believe."

"Yes."

"Were you present on an occasion when your brother threw a teacup at Eula and threatened her with a table knife?"

"Yes."

"Can you describe that occasion?"

"Jimmy came home late for dinner. He was drunk. Eula . . . taunted him. She was bad about that."

"What do you mean?"

"Eula hated it when Jimmy drank. When he came in that night, and started messing about at the dinner table, she told him he looked like a fool. That was when he threw the teacup at her. Then Jimmy grabbed a knife off the table and waved it at her. Eula and I ran out of the house. That was the end of it. George put Jimmy to bed, and we went back inside."

"By George you mean George McCutcheon?"

"Yes. The next morning Jimmy was as blue as a hound dog, all shame and remorse—as usual."

Moore consulted some papers at his table. "Mrs. Campbell, were you close to your sister-in-law?"

There was a ripple in Delia's composure, like a wind flaw on flat water. "We were friends."

"Did you ever have reasons to believe that she was unfaithful to her marriage vows?"

Delia paused. "Yes."

"What reasons did you have to believe such a thing?"

"Eula and I had no secrets from each other."

"She told you of her infidelities?"

"Yes."

"Even though she was married to your brother?"

"Yes."

"Did she name her lovers?"

"Some of them."

"But this was all a matter of hearsay. Is that correct?"

"I'm not sure what you mean."

"Did you ever actually see her in bed with another man, with your own eyes?"

Delia paused. "Yes. During those days we both spent at May Tobin's house in November, I saw her in bed with Mr. Shelley."

"And did you ever see her in bed with other men?"

"No, I did not."

Moore returned to his table and again consulted some papers. "A few moments ago, Mrs. Campbell, you described an incident at the dinner table of George McCutcheon. Your brother and sister-in-law lived on Mr. McCutcheon's farm—in his house, in fact—for most of last year. From January to September, wasn't it?"

"That would be correct."

"Did you ever have reason to believe that Mr. McCutcheon was among the men with whom Eula Phillips was intimate?"

Delia hesitated. "I imagine you should ask Mr. McCutcheon that question."

"I intend to, Mrs. Campbell," said Moore. "But now I'm asking you."

"Then the answer is yes."

"You believed them to be intimate?"

"I knew them to be so."

"How was that?"

Delia maintained her composure, but not her aloofness; her demeanor became rigid. She didn't answer.

"Mrs. Campbell, is it not true that last July, you and Mr. McCutcheon, in separate visits to a drugstore here in Austin, acquired certain substances which together constitute a common formula to induce abortion?"

There was a commotion in the press gallery. Will sat immobilized, burning with humiliation. George McCutcheon had been there before him. He had not been the first—not even that! Even his guilt was pointless, a grandiose delusion. He had imagined himself a seducer, the agent of Eula's ruin. More likely it was Eula who seduced him! Were none of his memories of her real? Had there been no love at all between them? Was this his punishment, to sit in silence, petrified that his name might be spoken at any moment, while one witness after another lashed him with the truth?

And now, the abortion—he had misunderstood that, as well!

"I refer, Mrs. Campbell, to these ingredients." Taylor Moore read from a list. "Extract of cotton root, chamomile flowers, ergot."

Delia's face drew taut. "George was a lonely man when Eula and Jimmy moved in. His wife had just died. Eula was unhappy, too. I think the two of them—I won't try to explain it. Last summer she told me she was pregnant. She said the baby wasn't Jimmy's. It was George McCutcheon's. She asked me to help her."

"To help her in what way?"

"To obtain . . . those ingredients."

"And you did so?"

"With Mr. McCutcheon's help. It was Mr. McCutcheon who actually gave them to Eula."

Jimmy Phillips put his face in his hands and sobbed. Delia looked at him for an instant, then averted her eyes.

George McCutcheon was called to the witness stand. He was dressed in an old suit that fit him badly, and he wore a tie. His shoes were covered with stains and crusted with mud. He carried his slouch hat in his hand.

Will shook his head. The man was old enough to be Eula's father!

"Mr. McCutcheon," Moore began, "were you present on an occasion when the defendant expressed an intention to kill his wife and then himself, if he should discover that she was unfaithful to him?"

McCutcheon was nervous. He fiddled with the brim of his hat. His voice quavered. "Jimmy said that kind of thing more than once."

"Is that so? I'm referring now to an incident when your friend Mr. Highsmith, who testified previously, was present."

"Yeah, I remember that. A bunch of us was drinking out at the farm. Jimmy was drunk, of course. But that's what he said."

"And there were other times when he expressed such feelings?"

"It preyed on his mind, I reckon. The last time I heard him say such a thing was here in Austin, after he and Eula moved back."

"When was this?"

"Around the first of December, during the time Eula was down in Manchaca. I was in town on some business, and Jimmy walked me to the depot. He was fretting about Eula leaving him. I told him he had to stop drinking, because he was making everybody around him miserable. Then he asked me if I thought that Eula was too fast."

"Those were his words?"

"Yes. I said, 'Well, that's a pretty question to go and ask me! Eula's a good and virtuous woman.' Jimmy said he thought so, too, but his mother thought Eula was too fast. Then he said that if he ever found out Eula wasn't virtuous, he'd kill her, then kill himself."

"The same thing he'd said before, in the presence of yourself and Mr. Highsmith?"

"More or less."

"And on those occasions, did you take the defendant's words to be a veiled threat to yourself?"

"Well, I don't see how." McCutcheon's face reddened. "He wasn't threatening to kill *me*, was he?"

There was scattered laughter among the spectators, which seemed to confuse McCutcheon.

Moore asked him about the incident of the thrown teacup and the brandished table knife. "What happened after Mrs. Campbell and Mrs. Phillips fled the room?"

"Jimmy made to run after 'em with the knife. I yelled at him to stop. He waved the knife at me and said, 'Don't interfere in my family affairs.' I said he was making a fool of himself. I told him to go wash his face and lie down. He fell right asleep."

Moore nodded. "Mr. McCutcheon, is it not true that you were in the habit of having carnal intercourse with Eula Phillips while she lived at your house in Williamson County?"

The judge cautioned McCutcheon. "I should warn you, sir, that habitual carnal intercourse with another person's spouse is legally defined as adultery, and punishable by a fine of up to one thousand dollars. You need not answer the question unless you please to do so."

McCutcheon blanched and squeezed the brim of his hat. "I decline to answer the question."

Moore shrugged. "Did you not, on a day last July, and together with Delia Campbell, buy—" He consulted his list. "Chamomile flowers, extract of cotton root, and ergot?"

"I reckon I bought some ergot."

"And didn't you and Mrs. Campbell buy these drugs for Eula, to aid her in producing an abortion on herself?"

McCutcheon swallowed hard. "I bought the ergot because Delia asked me to, and I gave it to Delia. I never gave those things direct to Eula."

Will, who had been sitting there hating the man, suddenly felt pity for him—the lonely widower, the lover who assisted in his own baby's abortion, the adulterer squirming on the witness stand. And to think that Will had fancied himself the most miserable man on earth, because Eula had turned her back on him!

47

E next day, newspapers across the state carried a notice which read:

> Testifying in the trial of the Phillips case, Mrs. Tobin stated
> that I went to her house one afternoon to meet the unfor-
> tunate Mrs. Phillips. The statement was not true. I had no
> acquaintance with Mrs. Phillips and never met her any-
> where, and never spoke to her in my life. Friends advise
> me that my position as an official demands that I dignify
> the statement with a public denial, otherwise I would not
> feel called on to notice the cruel slander.
>
> Benjamin M. Baker,
State Superintendent of Public Instruction

The other state employees named by May Tobin remained silent.

Except to print Baker's refutation, no newspaper in Texas published the names of the men cited by May Tobin. Reports alluded to their high positions of public trust, and expressed outrage at their alleged behavior, but no one named names. The *Statesman* cited high-minded journalistic principles: "No good can come of catering to a morbid appetite for scandal for scandal's sake." In the last few weeks, William Pendleton Gaines had attended a volunteer firemen's fund-raising dinner with Benjamin Baker, inspected convict labor gangs at the Burnet granite quarries with John Dickinson, and discussed personal legal matters with William Shelley's father.

Speculation was rife that a number of leading citizens had paid dearly for the widow's silence. Some thought a grudging respect was due to the men who had seen their names blackened rather than give in to blackmail. Some asserted that the men were victims of a political smear campaign of which May Tobin was merely an instrument.

In a gesture of journalistic largesse to a man whose ambitions for the Governor's Mansion Gaines had steadfastly opposed, the *Statesman* did mention one name, but only to clear it of suspicion. "In this connection it is due to Mr. Swain, whom reckless rumors have besmirched of late, to state that his name has *not* been mentioned in any way whatsoever in connection with the case." By way of clearing Swain's name, Gaines linked it inextricably to the scandal.

On Thursday, the defense made its case.

John Hancock called several witnesses who testified to having seen bloody handprints on both sides of the alley fence, and footprints in the alley behind the Phillips residence; the implication was that an intruder or intruders had entered the property from the alley on the night of the murder and then fled by the same route. In questioning the witnesses about that night, Hancock managed to allude several times to the other, very similar murder which had taken place only blocks away and minutes before the same fate overcame Eula Phillips.

Ham Riley, a friend of Jimmy's who sat with him during the week after the murder, testified that Jimmy was unconscious most of the time, but occasionally revived and was relatively lucid, asking for water or something to kill his pain, or calling for his mother. On one such occasion Jimmy awoke and said, "Them fellows hit me a hell of a lick!" When Riley asked whom he meant by "them fellows," Jimmy relapsed into a fever and talked gibberish.

Walter Booth of Booth & Son was called to testify that Jimmy had come into his store between half past five and six o'clock on Christmas Eve to make a payment on the bedroom furniture. Booth said that Jimmy was sober at the time.

Hancock recalled George McCutcheon, and questioned him about his relationship with Eula Phillips. "Were you not in the habit," Hancock asked, "after she moved back to Austin with her husband, of coming to Austin and seeing her for the specific purpose of having carnal intercourse with her?"

"No! Not in Austin. Not once in Austin."

"After she moved back to Austin, then, Eula Phillips refused to continue her carnal relationship with you? Did that anger you, Mr. McCutcheon?"

The judge ordered the question stricken from the record, as the witness had not admitted to a carnal relationship.

Hancock pressed on. "Where were you on the night of Eula Phillips's murder?"

"Up in Williamson County, at a party."

"What sort of party?"

"A stag party, at Fred Mitchell's ranch."

"And how many old stags were in attendance?"

"Maybe a dozen."

"Was there much drinking?"

"That's pretty much the point of a stag party, ain't it? So fellows can get drunk without any women fussing at 'em."

"When did the drinking commence?"

"Around sundown."

"Sundown comes early in December. By eleven o'clock you all had been drinking for, what, five or six hours?"

"Maybe."

"So, then: the men who might be able to give you an alibi at the time of the murder were dead drunk?"

McCutcheon ground his jaw and looked at him coldly. "I was home by midnight. Tom Burdett was staying at my house, and I woke him up when I came in. Do you know who that is? Eula's father! He can tell you where I was at the time of the murder—a good twenty-five miles from Austin. Tom and I heard about the murder the next day; I saw his face when he heard it. We took the evening train to Austin together. Call him to the stand and ask him where I was, if you want!"

Hancock, any trace of chagrin hidden behind his walrus mustache, excused the witness.

The centerpiece of the defense was a demonstration which took place that afternoon. The bloody footprints on the verandah connecting the main part of the Phillips house with the annex had been mentioned numerous times by witnesses. Marshal Lucy had preserved a specimen of both right and left footprints by having two portions of the planking, each about a foot square, sawed out and removed from the floor of the verandah. The planks with the bloody footprints were introduced into evidence.

Hancock held up the two pieces of wood, one in each hand, and walked slowly before the jury to give them a good look. The prints had dried to a dark brown but still stood out vividly against the weathered gray wood. They were evidently the bare prints of a man with large feet.

Hancock stooped over and put the boards on the ground, shoulder-width apart. "There he stands!" Hancock announced. "There's your murderer, standing right before you, just as invisible and hard to get hold of as he has been for the last year and a half—all we can see are the bottoms of his feet! Must be a pretty big fellow, to make those prints. You know, if I squint, I can practically see him standing there—right there in front of us—all bloody and holding the body of poor Eula Phillips in his arms." The stifling heat of the courtroom was conducive to apparitions; the image Hancock conjured up was so vivid that one of the jurors let out a little gasp.

"But are these the footprints of the *defendant?*" Hancock asked. "Gentlemen of the jury, I think we must find out."

Hancock's assistant entered the courtroom with his arms full. He spread a drop cloth on the floor in front of the jury, then laid down a smooth pine ironing board. Next to the ironing board he put down a wide, shallow paint dish, into which he poured just enough black ink to cover the bottom. He also produced a measuring tape.

"Jimmy, you will need to bare your feet," Hancock said. Jimmy took off his shoes and socks, then got up and walked barefoot to where Hancock stood before the jury. The reporters and spectators rose to their feet, the ones in back straining on tiptoe to get a better look. The judge leaned over his bench to get a clear view.

Taylor Moore broke from a hushed conference with the district attorney. "Your Honor! If the defense intends to somehow compare the bloody footprints in evidence with ink impressions made from the defendant's feet, I must object. Human blood and ink are not equivalent. There must be differences in the consistency, rate of evaporation, and tendency to spread, differences which only a highly specialized expert could account for."

The judge considered this, then shook his head. "I think we should see what Mr. Hancock's demonstration produces, so long as the measurements are taken by the court's notary."

Hancock nodded to the judge and gave Moore a sardonic glance. "Now, Jimmy, I shall ask you to place each of your feet in the dish of ink, and then stand upon the pine board."

Jimmy did so. Some of the reporters at the back of the press gallery stood on their seats. The jurors looked on, fascinated.

Jimmy stepped off the pine board and wiped his feet on the drop cloth.

The ink footprints looked smaller than the bloody ones. The notary took two measurements of each print, one across the ball of the foot at the widest part, the other lengthwise from the tip of the big toe to the hollow of the foot. The ink footprints measured three and three-eighths inches wide by four and three-eighths inches long. The bloody footprints measured four and one-eighth inches wide by five and one-quarter inches long.

Hancock held up the bloody specimens while his assistant held up the ironing board to give the jurors a closer look. "The difference is appreciable, is it not, gentlemen of the jury? The defendant's inked footprint is three-fourths of an inch shorter in width, and seven-eighths of an inch shorter in length. A discrepancy in each case of nearly twenty percent!"

Moore and Robertson held another hushed conference. "Your Honor!" said Moore. "The state would like to point out that the maker of the bloody footprints, as Mr. Hancock himself has said, may well have been carrying the body of Eula Phillips when he made those prints. We would like to request that the defendant pick up an equivalent weight—"

"Balderdash!" exclaimed Hancock.

"—and produce another set of footprints."

The judge considered for a moment, then nodded. "I don't see why not. It's possible that the added weight might spread his feet a bit."

Hancock raised a bushy eyebrow and snorted. "Very well! What did Mrs. Phillips weigh? I believe Dr. Litten estimated a hundred pounds or so. All right then, let Jimmy pick *me* up. I weigh a hundred and seventy-five!"

There was a roar of laughter from the press gallery. The man from the Chicago *Tribune* pressed his palms together. "Lord, have I died and gone to newspaper heaven?"

The judge banged his gavel for order. Jimmy looked dubious, but with Hancock coaching him, he managed to pick up the man in his outstretched arms and stand upright. Grunting and staggering, he stepped to the dish of ink and wet his feet. He stepped onto a clear spot on the ironing board, stood there while Hancock counted to three, then stepped back onto the drop cloth.

Jimmy lowered Hancock to the floor, then pulled out a handkerchief and wiped his forehead. The afternoon heat was stifling.

The notary stepped forward with the tape measure. The spectators drew a breath.

The notary dropped to one knee, took the new measurements, then double-checked them. He stood and turned to the judge. "There's no difference, Your Honor. Same as before."

John Hancock smiled behind his mustache and patted Jimmy on the back.

The next day, Friday, the two sides made their closing arguments. District Attorney Robertson spoke for an hour. Taylor Moore spoke for two. In the afternoon, the attorneys for the defense made equally lengthy speeches.

The prosecution pointed out Jimmy's violent and jealous nature and his long history of threats against his wife, and the powerful motive for murder provided by her infidelities; the presence of the ax on the property had given him the means. His attempt to deceive the police was clever on the surface, but easily seen through. Who but a guilty man would have cried to his own mother, "Then I shall surely go to hell"? As for the evidence of the footprints, the district attorney darkly suggested that the defense had experimented with the demonstration beforehand to find ways to skew it to their advantage.

The defense portrayed a reformed, responsible husband overtaken and all but destroyed by tragedy. The state, they argued, had done nothing to prove that Jimmy knew of his wife's alleged infidelities; indeed, there was every reason to presume that he remained naively ignorant of her activities to the very end. The defense had shown conclusively that Jimmy's feet did not fit the bloody footprints, and three out of four medical experts had testified that it was virtually impossible that his wounds could be self-inflicted. There was bloody evidence of the murderer leaving the premises via the alley, and the state had done nothing to rule out the likelihood that someone other than Jimmy had perpetrated the crime; indeed, if even half of the behavior attributed to Eula Phillips was true, then there were any number of immoral men in Austin who might have desired to silence her, or take revenge on her for some slight. The state had failed to prove beyond a reasonable doubt and to a moral certainty that Jimmy was the killer; many other hypotheses remained which were just as plausible, if not more so.

The jury was sent to deliberate.

That night Will and Dave and Dave's new friend from Chicago went to Guy Town to get drunk. The *Tribune* man kept up with them for the first few saloons, then went off to his hotel to get some sleep.

"Why are you so friendly with that fellow?" asked Will. "I thought reporters were all rivals."

"I'm hardly a rival to a man from the *Tribune*," said Dave. "All I did was explain to him about the men May Tobin named. Why not? Gaines wouldn't even print the names! I wouldn't share secrets with other Texas reporters, but it can't hurt to have a friend in Chicago. I don't plan to stay in Austin forever."

Will shook his head. "You're making too much sense! We need more whiskey."

A few saloons and several rounds later they arrived at the Tin Cup. "Better enjoy Guy Town while we can," Dave said.

"What do you mean? Guy Town will always be here."

"I don't know about that, Will. There's change in the wind. Husbands killing wives, politicians caught with their pants down, prohibitionists on the march—the powers that be are in a mood to come down on all sorts of vice. Once the verdict is in and the trial's over, you know what Gaines wants me to do? He wants me to go to one of the Chinese laundries on the Avenue, to see if I can't sneak into an opium den and see what it's all about. Some folks want to make opium illegal, so he wants me to try the stuff."

"Let me know if it kills the pain better than whiskey." Will stared morosely at his empty shot glass.

Dave looked at him sidelong. "You know, Will, I didn't tell the *Tribune* fellow everything I figured out."

"No?"

"No. But I'll tell you, Will, because you're a true friend."

"I'm listening."

"Only, I want you to tell me a secret, too. I tell you a secret, you tell me one. Quid pro quo, as Gaines would say. All right?"

"Sure."

Dave lowered his voice. "I know who Eula Phillips was supposed to meet at May Tobin's house on Christmas Eve."

Will grimaced. "So do I. Hiram Glass."

"But how—?"

"I saw you write it on your notepad, before you crumpled the page."

"Poor Hiram," said Dave. "But you have to tell me your secret, anyway."

"What secret?"

"You were Mr. Jones, weren't you?"

Will was so numb that the question hardly stung. "How did you know?"

"I knew there was something odd, from the way you've acted all along. The way you fretted that first day at the trial . . . and when May said 'Mr. Jones,' she looked straight at you, Will—and the look on your face! This thing must have been hell for you."

Will nodded. "You wouldn't ever—you know, in the newspaper?"

"Never! You're a friend, Will. I wouldn't throw you to the lions. Gaines would eat you up and shit you out in one edition!"

They drank another round.

"What was she like?" said Dave.

Will blinked and shook his head. "I don't know."

"You've got to know something! How many times did you see her?"

"You really want to hear?"

"Everything."

"Then I think we'll need another round."

They talked late into the night, until even the Tin Cup closed its doors.

The first faint glow of dawn was lighting the streets when Will knocked on the door to the Phillips residence. He felt oddly clearheaded. The whiskey seemed to have gone out of him in the tears he shed talking to Dave Shoemaker.

Someone was already stirring, for almost at once a hand parted the lace curtains. A moment later the door opened. Delia stood before him in a flannel nightgown, her undressed black hair cascading over her shoulders.

"What do you want, Will Porter?"

"The letters. You said you'd give them back to me."

She wrinkled her nose at his breath. "Lower your voice! Mother and Father are asleep. They're in a terrible state, Mother especially. This thing has just about killed her."

He hung his head. "The letters . . ."

She pursed her lips. "I wish you'd stop asking me. I must have lost them somehow."

"Lost them!"

"There were so many people in the house, so much confusion. I mislaid them."

Will shook his head. "But if anyone should ever see those letters—"

"You didn't sign them, did you?"

"No, but they're in my handwriting."

"Is that what you've been thinking about during the trial? Worrying that your dirty little secret might be dragged out for everyone to gawk at?"

"Of course not! Well—some of the time." He shook his head. "All those things that came out, about the abortion, and the other men, and McCutcheon—was it all true?"

"Yes."

"Eula—she never cared for me at all, did she?"

He heard her inhale, then slowly exhale. By the dim light her face was sphinxlike. "How can I say what Eula felt for you?"

"But you knew her better than anyone."

"I suppose I did. But what she felt for you—not everything fits into words."

"She was wicked. She was cruel."

"Was she?" Delia seemed puzzled by the idea. "Is that what people think? Is that what they're saying?" She shook her head. "I can't see her that way. Eula was Eula. I don't think you loved her at all, Will Porter, not even a little. You only loved something you imagined, a woman you made up out of thin air. You couldn't have known Eula at all if you think she was wicked and cruel."

"I didn't know her—you're right about that!" He trembled with anger. "Then you won't let me have the letters?"

"No." Her voice sent a chill through him.

He started to go, then turned back. "Do you think they'll find him guilty?"

She drew a sharp breath. "I don't know. For Mother's sake, I hope not."

"Do you think he did it? Did Jimmy kill Eula?"

Delia looked at him for a long moment. The growing light illuminated her face, but he still could not read her expression. Quietly, slowly, she shut the door.

48

⌒⤳

$\mathcal{T}$ H E reporters who attended the trial of Jimmy Phillips were of various opinions regarding what the verdict would be. Some thought the prosecution had established a powerful case. Others thought the state had failed to establish anything close to proof beyond a reasonable doubt. All agreed that the trial had produced a spectacular scandal. The Dallas *Morning News* summed up its position: "The trial of Mr. Phillips has demonstrated three things: that Mrs. Phillips was not what she should have been, that several attachés of the government are not what they should be, and that no one can possibly know who committed the murder."

Among those who expected a conviction, the debate was whether the jury would find murder in the first or second degree. First degree pertained to what the law called "express malice," or cold-blooded intent. Second degree pertained to "implied malice, under circumstances tending to excuse, justify, or extenuate." If the jury believed that Jimmy had lain in wait for Eula, had struck her with the ax, and then coolly gone about arranging her corpse and inflicting a wound on himself to divert suspicion, then the sheer brutality and audacity of the crime demanded a verdict of first-degree murder, and hanging. But the jury might deliver a verdict of second-degree murder if they believed that Eula had attacked Jimmy with the ax and that he struck back at her in self-defense—or if they believed that Jimmy was to some degree justified, and that Eula, to some degree, deserved what she got.

The jury deliberated all day Saturday. Late in the afternoon they reached a verdict.

The sweltering courtroom was jammed. The judge called on the foreman. "Have you reached a verdict?"

"We have, Your Honor."

"And what is your verdict?"

The foreman looked at Jimmy, then at the judge. "We the jury find the defendant guilty of murder in the second degree, and assess his punishment at seven years in the penitentiary."

Jimmy's mother fainted. Sallie Mack fanned her while Delia gave her smelling salts. Jimmy bowed his head, wept and clutched at the scars on his temple. Will Porter shut his bloodshot eyes and whispered, "Now it's all over."

A year passed.

By the summer of 1887, much had changed in Austin.

Texas had a new governor. It was not William Jesse Swain. The political machine Swain created as comptroller failed him, and rumors pertaining to his personal vices refused to subside. The famous Indian killer, Sul Ross, defeated him at the Democratic convention. Swain's failed bid for the Governor's Mansion marked the end of his political career.

Among Governor Ross's appointments was that of William Holland to be the first superintendent of the new Deaf, Dumb, and Blind Institute for Colored Youth, which had been established due to Holland's tireless lobbying in the legislature. Holland would continue to serve as superintendent until his death twenty years later.

Will Porter had a new job, working as a draftsman in the General Land Office adjacent to the capitol grounds, where, from his upper-story window, he could watch the construction of the massive new capitol building and the erection of the Goddess of Liberty atop its dome. He continued to sing in church choirs and in the choruses of traveling shows. He worked diligently at his new job, and dreamed, while he drafted, of starting his own newspaper, which he would fill with raucous stories and caricatures—a town like Austin offered no end of things to make fun of! As for his love life, he threw all the charm he could muster into his courtship of young Athol Estes, whose innocence and simplicity grew more appealing to him day by day. Athol's parents did not entirely approve of him, and he was seriously considering eloping with her.

As for Jimmy Phillips, he was again a free man. John Hancock successfully argued before the Texas Court of Appeals for a new trial. The basis of his argument was that the state had introduced conditional threats made by Jimmy ("If I knew that Eula was unfaithful, I would kill her and then kill myself") without subsequently establishing that Jimmy did in fact know of his wife's unfaithfulness; all testimony regarding Eula's infidelity, including that of May Tobin, Delia Campbell, and George McCutcheon, was deemed inadmissible, and the Court of Appeals ordered a new trial. District Attorney Robertson, frustrated but ready to cut his losses, stated in an official memorandum that it would be impossible for the state to obtain a conviction without the use of testimony deemed inadmissible, and declined to prosecute. His reputation forever tainted by the original guilty verdict, Jimmy was nonetheless a free man, safe from the threat of further prosecution.

There were no other suspects. The murder of Eula Phillips, killed on Christmas Eve, 1885, for which a guilty verdict against her husband, Jimmy, was obtained but subsequently overturned, remained unsolved.

The murder of Susan Hancock, killed on Christmas Eve, 1885, remained unsolved.

The murders of Orange Washington and Gracie Vance, killed the night of September 27, 1885, remained unsolved.

The murder of eleven-year-old Mary Ramey, killed the night of August 29, 1885, remained unsolved.

The murder of Irene Cross, killed the night of May 22, 1885, remained unsolved.

The murder of Eliza Shelley, killed the night of May 6, 1885, remained unsolved.

The murder of Mollie Smith, killed in the early hours of December 31, 1884, for which Walter Spencer was tried and found not guilty, remained unsolved.

There was one consolation amid this lack of resolution: the murders had come to an end. After the deaths of Susan Hancock and Eula Phillips, there were no more such outrages in Austin.

The murders became the stuff of legend in Austin and beyond. For many years, whenever any similar, unsolved crime took place in a Texas city or as far afield as New Orleans or Oklahoma City, the press and police would speculate that it was the work of the Austin slayer.

Also by the summer of 1887, the move to construct a dam on the Colorado River had gained such momentum as to be unstoppable, despite the fact that two of the most vociferous early proponents of the scheme, Dr. Ephraim Ebenezer Terry (of Dr. Terry's Liver Tonic and Ginger Aperient) and Dr. Frederick Augustus Fry (the famous blind phrenologist), had mysteriously vanished from the scene. No one knew what had become of them. Early in 1886, William Pendleton Gaines lost more than a hundred dollars in outstanding orders when he received notice that the tonic manufactory in New Jersey had gone out of business. Gaines was as puzzled as everyone else over the disappearance of the two men, who for a while cut such a colorful figure in the business community of the city.

The Journey Back:

AUSTIN — FORMOSA —
THE VIEW FROM MOUNT BONNELL, 1906

1

*T*HE thing in her hand is definitely a star, he decides, gazing up at the Goddess of Liberty atop the capitol dome. She is every bit as ugly as he remembered. Her homeliness is larger than life, a landmark visible for miles.

William Sydney Porter stands at the head of Congress Avenue, at the entrance to the capitol grounds, his head tilted back and his eyes narrowed. He could swear that when the goddess first went up, he could see her clearly without squinting. His eyes are getting old. Like his back and his bowels. Like his soul.

Being back in Austin, he finds himself continually wrenched between exuberance and melancholy, homecoming and alienation. One moment he feels twenty-five again; a moment later, he is a ghost from the ancient past. The sight of some familiar trifle—a cornice on a building, or long-ago lovers' initials impressed in the sidewalk—makes him chuckle and then choke back a sob. He once carved Athol's name in the windowsill of a house on Peach Street; when he stole across the yard to have a look, he discovered that the letters are still there!

There is no single Austin in his recollection, no uniform landscape of nostalgia. He lived there for a dozen years and passed from footloose youth to married man to widower, from singer in church choirs to convicted felon, from green innocence to blackened shame. His nostalgia is like a river, deep here, shallow there, turbulent where the channel is stony, placid where it runs broad and free. The current is freshened by springs of unexpected joy that well up beneath the surface, and in other places constricted in sluggish backwaters of memories best forgotten. He has plunged naked into that river and has forgotten how to swim. He is at the mercy of remembrance.

Thanks to Dr. Kringel's repeated inquiries about the year of the servant girl murders, thanks to the spell cast over him by the rekindled memory of Eula Phillips, the Austin uppermost in his mind upon his arrival was the Austin of the most distant past, the city he came to straight from the ranch. He remembers how charmed he was to find a town where the streets were named for rivers and trees. The river streets remain, but the tree streets have all been cut down, so to speak, the green grid of his youth deforested and rechristened with numbers. Hickory Street, where Eula Phillips lived and died, is 8th Street now. Pecan Street, where he has booked himself into the Driskill Hotel (incognito, as Henry O. Jones), is now 6th Street. Gone are Live Oak and Cypress, gone Willow and Cedar, gone Pine, Ash, Mulberry, and Mesquite, gone Peach, Walnut, Cherry, Chestnut, and Linden, gone Magnolia, Elm, Palmetto, Orange, Maple, and Willow, gone the euphonious Bois de Arc. Now the street signs show numbers, numbers, numbers, from the banks of the Colorado all the way to the lunatic asylum and beyond.

Congress Avenue is paved now; no more winter muck or summer dust devils. Bicycles are everywhere, and the children roller-skate to school. The streetcars are electric — gone the stolid, faithful mules and the dung left in their wake — but still vulnerable to college pranks. From his hotel room window this morning he saw a group of college boys board a streetcar, jump up and down until it came off the rails, then run away whooping with the conductor chasing after them — a fraternity rite of initiation dating from the first days of the university.

Another change he noticed, when he went for a stroll last night, are the so-called moonlight towers that cast a pale radiance over the city in lieu of street lamps. By day the metal towers poking up all over Austin give the city a boldly modern look he finds disconcerting.

There seem not to be many tramps left, even along Shoal Creek. All the Civil War veterans are dead by now, or shut away in the veterans home. The younger generation disapproves of tramping as a livelihood. There is no place for vagrancy in a progressive, prosperous city like Austin.

The streetcars are segregated, he has noticed. The last few rows of seats are turned backward and marked "For Colored." Jim Crow laws are all over the South now. Apparently the local streetcar law just went into effect, for he overheard a hotel maid and porter, apparently husband and wife, talking about a failed boycott by the black people of Austin.

"We shoulda held firm, Alec Mack!" said the woman.

"Folks got to git to work, Rebecca. Look at Lem Brooks, or Moses Shelley—how's they s'posed to git all the way out to Mr. Holland's school without takin' the streetcar? Jim Crow's bigger than we is. I pray it'll be diff'rent for the chil'ren!"

Through discreet inquiries—bartenders are such founts of information!—he has caught up with some of the people who passed through his thoughts during the journey. The pint-sized James Lucy is still marshal. The whereabouts of Fannie Whipple and May Tobin are a mystery, but Guy Town legend has it that the two of them moved to San Francisco together, set up a bordello, and became filthy rich. Taylor Moore is still active in the legal profession. The Robertson brothers are still on the scene; James, the former district attorney, is in the Texas House of Representatives. Mr. and Mrs. Phillips both died before Porter left Austin; according to the bartender at the Driskill, Jimmy died just last year.

Porter gazes up at the Goddess of Liberty. Was he ever perfectly happy here? Perhaps, when he eloped with Athol, back in '87; but oh, how short-lived was that perfect joy! A year later Athol bore him a son—and the baby died the same day. There could be no joy without a shadow after that.

A year and a half later, their second child was born. Athol was terrified that baby, too, would die, but Margaret came into the world healthy and whole. The three of them settled into domestic tranquillity. Will left the land office for a job at the First National Bank, working in a teller's cage. He used to joke: *Here I am, behind bars, when I'd rather be drinking whiskey in front of one.*

By then, the *Statesman* had new ownership and Dave Shoemaker had left Austin for Chicago; his reporter friend at the *Tribune* became an editor and offered him a job. Will began to feel that time was slipping away from him. He was past thirty, and what had he been? Part-time druggist, bookkeeper, draftsman, bank teller—anything and everything but a writer. He saved up some money behind Athol's back and finally had enough to launch his little weekly newspaper, *The Rolling Stone*, which he wrote and edited in his own time away from the bank. When he saw a stranger reading a copy at Scholz's Beer Garden, laughing out loud and poking at his drinking buddies to share the joke, Will knew he wanted to do nothing else for the rest of his life but write stories—stories so clever and droll that people would make their friends stop and read them.

But *The Rolling Stone* lost money from the start. Will managed to keep it going for a year, from spring of '94 to spring of '95, then had to let it die. That was when everything began to go wrong. Athol showed the first signs of consumption; she was always coughing, always tired. Then the examiners reviewed the books at the bank. Will was arrested and charged with embezzlement.

The missing sum totaled $5,654. He would always maintain his innocence. Most of his friends believed him, at least at first. Good old Will Porter! How could such a thing be true? But people who knew how much heart and soul he put into *The Rolling Stone* wondered where he had found the money to launch it in the first place, and how he had kept it going so long. Then, too, the First National Bank was notorious for loose accounting; rumor had it that the officers dipped into the till whenever they wanted, writing chits and repaying the loans at their leisure. If the bank examiners chose to make an example of some hapless clerk who took the same liberty, how sad that the scapegoat turned out to be Will Porter, people thought— even as they accepted that he was probably guilty of something, after all.

If people had known the full truth of the matter—where the money went and why—would they have thought better of him, or worse? But the truth is something he never revealed to anyone, and never intends to . . .

Rather than face trial, he disappeared from Austin. A failure of nerve, his friends said sheepishly; a man can be cowardly without being crooked. But what sort of coward could abandon little Margaret, and leave Athol behind, growing sicker day by day? What kind of man, if he wasn't crooked, ran from the chance to clear himself?

Will fled to New Orleans, then all the way to Honduras, which had no extradition treaty with the United States. There he met and mingled with the charlatans, fugitives, and failed dreamers who would later populate the mythical banana republic of Anchuria in *Cabbages and Kings*.

He was gone for eight months, until word reached him that Athol was dying. He steeled his nerves and made his way back to Austin. The authorities felt sorry for him and bent the rules; blind justice tactfully waited until Athol was in the ground before Will was made to stand trial.

Figures couldn't lie. Will was found guilty and sent to a prison in Ohio. Margaret went off to live with relatives in Pennsylvania. Austin was like a place where a twister had struck. Everything he had built there was devastated, all his dreams razed, the remnants of his life scattered to the far corners of the earth.

Now he has retraced the path of the cyclone to its center. He turns his back on the capitol, blinking away tears.

A group of men comes toward him down the broad sidewalk. The men are well dressed, well fed, silver-haired. Porter does not give them much thought, until he recognizes the man at the center to whom the others defer. He hears the man addressed as "Mr. Mayor." Could it be? Impossible!

But there can be no mistake, for next he hears the man addressed as "Mayor Shelley." Twenty years after the trial of Jimmy Phillips, when political careers were destroyed like clay ducks tossed in the air and shot to pieces, William Shelley is mayor of Austin! He looks as arrogant as ever, though his swagger has become a saunter, thanks to his girth. His cheeks have grown plumper and his eyes beadier—he resembles his old mentor, Comptroller Swain. Mayor Shelley—impossible! But why not? Some men are victims, some are survivors. Porter himself has been both, so why not William Shelley?

As the group passes by, Porter looks Shelley straight in the eye. Shelley looks back, nods and smiles, but shows no sign of recognition; his smile is that of a politician bestowing one upon a presumed constituent.

Eula Phillips was the secret link between them. Did Shelley suffer as Porter did? Did Shelley also love Eula, and imagine he was loved in return? Even now, Porter feels a sting of jealousy. He chides himself; William Shelley had to bear the humiliation of having his secret made public from the witness stand. Still, that was not as terrible as the price that Will eventually had to pay . . .

I need the money, Delia had said. *Mother and Father are dead. There's no one else I can go to. Think of it as a purchase. All these years, you must have wondered what happened to those letters. Well—just the other day I happened to find them. I mean to leave Austin, and Texas, for good—once I get enough money together—and I've been doing some packing, you see, and I found those letters in an old trunk, and it occurred to me, 'Will Porter would probably like to have these back.' Well, you can. And you'll help me, won't you—with some money . . . ?*

He told her he had no money to give her. He was only a bank clerk, with a wife and child to care for.

But you just started publishing your own weekly—that thing called The Rolling Stone. *Silly name for a newspaper, but there must be money from it . . .*

He explained that the newspaper was costing money, not making it, but she wouldn't listen. She wanted money from him—or else, who knew into whose hands those letters to Eula might fall?

He tried to remember what the letters contained. Bits and pieces came back to him. What he recalled most clearly was the reckless passion he felt when he wrote them. The idea that anyone might read them made him break out in a cold sweat. Will was beginning to make a name for himself in Austin; he was a respected family man, worked for a prestigious bank, was a newspaper publisher and a writer. What would people think if they discovered he had written love letters to a married woman, had visited May Tobin's house, had been another of the notorious Eula Phillips's lovers?

Fear worked on his memory. He seemed to recall that his final letters to Eula had struck a desperate note. What had he said? What had he threatened? Lying awake beside Athol in the middle of the night, he imagined that the letters might be literally incriminating, that certain phrases could convey the idea that *he* had had a motive for killing Eula Phillips! The crime had never been solved; nine years later, people still speculated about it. If his name should ever be linked to such a notion, the scandal could ruin him.

He told Delia again that he had no money for her.

But you work at a bank, don't you? she had said, as if the solution to both their problems was so simple that a child could see it. *You handle all that money, every day . . .*

He protested that such an idea was impossible. He vowed that he would never do it. But in the end he did.

He gave her the sum requested. Delia lived up to her side of the bargain. She returned all the letters to him in a bundle tied with packing string. True to her word, she left Texas, and never returned.

That night, while Athol thought he was working on the final issue of *The Rolling Stone*, he read the letters one by one. Were they worth the price he paid? If Delia had made them public, they would have caused him great humiliation, but they were not as incriminating as he had feared. Reading them in private, he found them magical. They brought the dead to life again. They recalled to him the lovesick youth he had been, with a vividness that was overpowering. For that alone, the letters were almost worth the price he paid.

After he read them, he burned them.

Then came the greater price. He had been clever in obtaining the money—a matter of entering a line in this ledger and a line in that—and he fully intended to replace every penny before the loan (for so he thought of it) could be detected. Everything would be as before, only better, because he had been relieved of an old, nagging worry. Then the bank examiners came.

The truth could not help him. If he explained that he was the victim of blackmail and pleaded for mercy, they would demand to know the facts; but he had no way to prove the blackmail had ever taken place, for Delia and the money were gone and so were the letters—if only he hadn't burned them! If he confessed to the embezzlement, unable to use blackmail as an excuse, everyone would think he stole the money out of greed, that he was a common thief. So he lied, and fled in a panic, and came back to watch his wife die and to hear himself called a coward and a crook. He took his punishment in silence. With time off for good behavior, he served thirty-nine months. He made up his mind to start the new century in a new city and never to look back.

Yet here he is, back in the town where everything had been possible, and where everything went wrong.

Porter strolls up the broad walkway that bisects the capitol grounds. It is truly a grand building; even after living among skyscrapers, he is impressed. He mounts the steps and enters the front lobby, intending to proceed to the center of the building and peer up at the inside of the massive dome. But two statues flanking the entrance to the rotunda claim his attention. They were never there when he lived in Austin. He would have noticed such fine pieces of sculpture.

The statues are of white marble, life-sized, with names inscribed on the bases. On the left is Sam Houston; on the right, Stephen F. Austin. Both are clad in buckskin. Houston, the taller and more rugged of the two, holds his right hand to his chest and gazes pensively toward the distance; his left hand rests upon the hilt of a sword. A Mexican blanket is thrown over his shoulders, falling to the ground in folds suggestive of a Roman toga. Austin stands before a tree stump, a map in his hands, a hunting rifle in the crook of his arm.

"Extraordinary work!" Porter mutters. Public sculpture is the great art form of the day—crowds gather whenever a new statue is unveiled—and these two examples are among the finest Porter has ever seen. He calls to a passing attendant, "Excuse me! How long have these been here?"

The man rubs his chin "Oh, I reckon goin' on two, three years—that's right, they went up in '03, jus' 'bout the time I started workin' here. Oh, they was the awfulest fight, 'cause Governor Sayers wanted to stick 'em upstairs facin' each other 'cross the rotunda, and Miss Ney—"

"Ney? Elisabet Ney?"

"That's right, sir. Miss Ney jus' 'bout th'owed a fit. She say to him, 'No, sir! I don't care if'n you *are* the governor, Mr. Houston and Mr. Austin gots to go down in the lobby on either side of the entryway, 'cause that's the way I planned 'em to go, and if you puts 'em any other place, you's no better than a Philistine!' She got her way, too."

"Elisabet Ney! What an amazing coincidence . . ."

"Does you know the lady, sir?"

"Not exactly. But I expect to be seeing her soon."

"You headin' up to Formosa, then?"

"Formosa?"

"The castle she built herself, north of the university."

"Castle? I thought Miss Ney still lived on a plantation called Liendo, near Hempstead."

"Some o' the time, maybe, but her castle where she do her sculptin' be here in Austin. You can go there on the streetcar."

"Is that a fact?" Porter studies the two statues, and ponders the strange, rich fabric of coincidence.

2

Just past 40th Street, the streetcar comes to an unexpected halt. The conductor fiddles with his levers, but the car refuses to move.

"Oh, not again!" complains an old woman across from Porter.

"Second time this week," says the woman's husband. "I declare, the service was a sight more reliable back when they had mules to draw the cars! No mule was ever as stubborn as a 'lectric line when it gives out. Well, Mother, there's nothing to do but walk!"

Porter exits the stalled streetcar. His destination is only a few blocks farther. He strolls through a lovely new suburb with wide streets and big houses set on spacious lots, interspersed with orchards and pastures.

Formosa turns out to be not a castle, exactly, but a massive building of rough-hewn limestone blocks, set in a rustic parklike estate. The architecture is eccentric, to say the least; a classical pediment over a porch with votive niches on either side suggests a Roman temple, while the quaint tower with its crenellated top might be a vision from the Brothers Grimm. The streetcar conductor warned him that the estate was inhabited by "a strange old lady from Germany," in a tone to suggest that Porter should beware of poisoned apples and sleeping spells.

He follows the winding walkway to the porch. He knocks at the double wooden doors. There is no answer. He notices another door, at the base of the square tower, standing wide open. He walks over. "Miss Ney!" he calls. He takes off his hat and pokes his head into the foyer. The inner walls are also made of rough-hewn limestone. The woodwork and stair rails are of unmilled cedar. No wonder people think the place is a witch's cottage! He cannot resist stepping inside.

Beyond the foyer is a large studio with a high ceiling, flooded with light from huge windows in the northern wall. The room is littered everywhere with bits and pieces of plaster and clay molds, boxes full of chisels, files, pincers, hammers, and metal shims, buckets full of rags and brushes, stacks of drawing paper, albums stuffed with magazine and newspaper clippings, and piles of open picture books. The few pieces of furniture are wild and rustic; chairs and settees for Valhalla, he thinks, suitable for Teutonic warlords and Valkyries.

Plaster busts mounted on stands line one wall. He instantly recognizes William Jennings Bryan, the perennial presidential aspirant. Most of the others seem to be Texas statesmen.

One of the busts is of a woman. Her face is vaguely familiar. Her hair is short, parted in the middle and brushed back. The shapeless collar of her smock rests loosely upon her shoulders. Her expression is calm and intelligent. Her features are idealized and ageless, yet so lifelike that he can imagine the lips opening to speak. She would speak with a German accent, he thinks. The bust is a self-portrait. He stands face-to-face with Elisabet Ney.

He imagines a glint of rebuke in her eyes, a reminder that he is trespassing. Porter turns, thinking to leave at once, and is transfixed by a life-size statue that looms over him.

The statue is of a woman, clad in a loose garment like a sleeping gown with one shoulder bare. Her hands are clutched together fitfully to one side. Her head is tilted back, elongating her neck and thrusting her chin forward. Her mouth is grim. Her eyes are barely open. Her face is defiant, but suffering. She might be a sleepwalker, or she might be a murderess.

"Lady Macbeth," announces a voice behind him.

He turns. The speaker is an old lady wearing a large bonnet and spectacles, dressed in loose pantaloons and a smock.

"I beg your pardon!" he says, meaning to apologize for trespassing, but she takes the words to signify that he misunderstands, and so repeats herself.

"Lady Macbeth. My masterpiece she is."

Porter looks at the woman dumbly. Ney looks older than he expected; he would not have recognized her.

"What do you think of her?" Ney gestures to the statue.

"Ah, Lady Macbeth!" he mutters. "Yes, I see now. Wringing her hands—sleepwalking—seeing blood that isn't there. No wonder she looks so fretful. All those . . . murders."

"Murder, yes! Murderings must the dramatists all have, to make their stories. But they are slaves to the chronological, no? First this, then that, one thing after another always following to show the how and the why, the cause and the effect. But a statue not a story is. The sculptor captures only the quintessential, the moment most exemplary of Lady Macbeth. No before, no after, *now* only. This attitude, this suffering, this guilt. Time stops! And there she is, in marble captured."

Porter gazes at the statue. "It's magnificent—like the ones in the capitol."

Ney smiles. "Ah, Mr. Houston and Mr. Austin. They, too, I captured. Free of the flesh are they—ashes to ashes. But in stone, forever stand they. The face of Cicero still we know, into the eyes of Caesar still can we look. The art of the sculptor this is, to honor the dead. As old as the pharaohs, this is."

Porter scans the busts along the wall. "What if one should die, and no one should honor his memory—her memory—after death?"

"Ah, that must be to die forever," says Ney quietly.

Porter nods. "You've made quite a mark hereabouts since I was last in Texas."

Ney looks at him quizzically. "Do I know you, sir?"

"Ah! Well, as a matter of fact, I believe you're expecting me—not here, but down at Liendo. At least, your husband is expecting me."

"Is that so?" Ney narrows her eyes.

"Yes. I shall go down to Liendo tomorrow, I suppose. But as I'm here in Austin, and I happened to learn of the existence of this place, I thought, why not pop up and have a look? I've never seen a sculptor's studio. Not on this scale, anyway. It's quite impressive."

"Built to my exact specifications stone by stone it was," says Ney. "And at no little cost, of money and exasperation, let me tell you!" She squints. "But your name I am still trying to think of . . ."

"Forgive me—I haven't introduced myself. William Sydney Porter. When we met twenty years ago, I was just plain Will, Dave Shoemaker's friend."

Her face is blank for a long moment. She draws a deep breath and nods. Puzzlement furrows her brow again. "How curious! What a small world is it! Yes, Dave's friend—the writer you must be, who lives in New York City now, yes? And your book of stories, what is the title? *Carbuncles . . .*"

Porter winces. "*Cabbages and Kings.*"

"Yes! A copy Dave brought us for a gift, when down from Chicago he came to visit us at Liendo, a few months back. So very proud he was of you, that his old friend should such a handsome book publish, even if you use a *nom de plume*. In return, we gave him a copy of Dr. Montgomery's new book." She nods thoughtfully. "Dave reminded us of that time he brought you with him, to visit Liendo. Twenty years ago, was it really? And yet I remember, yes. Hard times those were for me, waiting and wasting, not knowing what the future was, or if the future ever would be. Like Lady Macbeth I was, trapped in a sleepwalker's trance, and who knew if it should be forever?" She shakes her head, then looks at him steadily. "I remember. Even then, a writer you wished to be, yes? Down by the creek, a talk we had."

"You remember that?"

She smiles. "It was not so often even when I was a girl back in Germany that I had the company of such a striking blue-eyed fellow in a sylvan glen; rarer still at Liendo. Light and air, I remember, and water rippling . . ." Her thoughts wander. "You and Dave, great friends you must have been before he left Texas."

"I suppose we were. I haven't seen him in years and years, though. We kept in touch for a while after he went up to Chicago. Then we lost touch." Porter remembers sending Dave a copy of the first issue of *The Rolling Stone*. Dave never replied; perhaps he was busy, or traveling on assignment, but Will's feelings were hurt. Then came Will's troubles, and like so much else, Dave was lost in the dead past. "Dave Shoemaker! How on earth did he know I'd published a book? How did he figure out I was O. Henry?"

"Dave is a reporter, and reporters are bloodhounds, yes? He comes to Texas on a trip, he hears a rumor about his old friend Will who lives now in New York and a famous writer is. He tracks down the rumor, and next you know, to his old friends Dr. Montgomery and Miss Ney at Liendo he gives a copy of *Carbuncles and Kin* by Henry O., for a souvenir of old times."

He resists the impulse to correct her. "Did you read any of the stories in the book?"

She looks at him uncertainly. "To answer that, I myself would have to tell quite a story; veritably, a tale from Scheherazade! Dave, you see, was not our only visitor at that time . . ." She narrows her eyes. "Did you say that Dr. Montgomery would be expecting you, at Liendo?"

"Yes."

"But why do you imagine such a thing?"

"On account of his letter."

"A letter? Sent to you?"

"Actually, the letter was to a colleague of Dr. Montgomery's up in New York, but it contained a message for me. Dr. Montgomery invited me to come to Liendo, in order to impart some information regarding—" The puzzlement on her face stops him short. "But if you don't know anything about it, perhaps I shouldn't . . ."

"This colleague—what is his name?"

"Dr. Kringel. The publisher of *The Monist*."

Her expression darkens. "Dr. Kringel, did you say? Oh, dear!"

"What is it, Miss Ney?"

She shakes her head. "All very odd this is. Something wicked is afoot. Very wicked! This supposed letter from my best friend—what made you think authentically from him it came?"

Porter is taken aback. "He signed it. It was on Liendo stationery." He reaches into his jacket. "I have the page pertaining to me here in my pocket." He unfolds the piece of paper with unsteady fingers. Ney's inexplicable reaction has sent a tremor of dread through him. Has he come all this way, relived so many painful memories, all as part of some senseless hoax?

Ney takes the piece of stationery and squints at it. "But this is not even—!" She shakes her head and reads aloud in a rushed whisper. "'I have come upon the solution to an old mystery . . . discovered the person guilty of a most revolting series of crimes . . . murders of young women in the city of Austin . . . ended with the horrors of Christmas Eve, 1885 . . . responsibility never established, until *now* . . . details such that I cannot explain them here, but must deliver them in person. If Mr. Porter's memory of those events is hazy, then mention to him the name *Eula Phillips* . . . '"

She lowers the letter and gives him such an odd look that Porter feels hackles rise on his neck.

"Miss Ney, what is it?"

She walks to a nearby desk and rummages among a stack of papers, then returns holding two pages side by side, the one from his pocket and another. Both are on printed stationery, with *Liendo Plantation* set in handsome type at the top. There the similarity ends. The letter from his pocket is in a crabbed, highly stylized hand, all sharp angles and flourishes; the handwriting of the specimen from her desk is altogether different, flowing and elegant and airy.

"*This*, a sample of Dr. Montgomery's handwriting is."

"Then what—?"

"Fools of my best friend and of me he made—that wicked thief! And a fool of you, too, it looks. Where is the man who this letter gave to you?"

"Dr. Kringel? We came down on the train together, all the way from New York. We parted ways yesterday at the station in Hearne. I'm supposed to join up with him in Hempstead, at Liendo, tomorrow or the next day."

"Kringel? Come back to Liendo? Never would he dare! A wire at once I must send to Dr. Montgomery. He must to Austin come on the first train tomorrow from Liendo. Then all together, you and he and I, we shall think it out."

"But what—?"

"No!" she raises her hand. "No more of this until my best friend comes. Then an explanation we shall find together."

Porter is stunned. He feels utterly adrift. She sees his distress and her features soften. "You are alone in Austin?"

"Yes," he says. He has never felt more alone in his life.

"A place to stay you have?"

"A room at the Driskill."

"A hotel? No, no! Here you must the night spend. Dr. Montgomery tomorrow will come, and here you must be. Horace will I send with the buggy your things to fetch, and at the same time post a telegram to Hempstead."

He looks about the crowded studio.

She smiles. "Accommodation for you I have, in the tower. In a hammock you can sleep, can you not?"

The kitchen is in the basement. Their meal is roast beef, biscuits, string beans, and potatoes. Afterward, she gives him a tour of Formosa. The grounds cover a city block. The landscaping has been left mostly wild, with prickly pears, tall grass, and thickets. Waller Creek runs through the back of the property, shaded by trees, the banks traversed by a stone dam suitable for trolls to dwell beneath. As for the house, he has never in his life been in a dwelling so peculiarly laid out. The ground floor consists of two large studio rooms filled with Ney's work, both flooded with northern light. The larger of the two rooms has a curtained loft in one corner which serves as Ney's boudoir.

A flight of stairs in the foyer leads up to the second floor, most of which consists of a single large room that is evidently the domain of Dr. Montgomery. Set against one wall is a crudely made table strewn with laboratory equipment and scientific instruments, flanked by bookcases full of academic treatises and journals. *The Monist* occupies an entire shelf. Porter reaches for a copy and opens it to the masthead, thinking to see a familiar name, but the publisher and editor of the journal is listed not as Kringel, but as Dr. Paul Carus, a name he has never heard.

The man he deemed the best of all traveling companions is a fraud. Porter has been duped. But why? What can possibly be the point of such an elaborate hoax? Kringel extorted no money from him; Kringel paid for the trip! The fellow lied about editing *The Monist*. Did he lie about corresponding with Dr. Montgomery? Kringel had a copy of Montgomery's book. He also had a copy of *Cabbages and Kings* on the train. Porter remembers something odd. When he opened Kringel's copy to sign it, the title page had been torn out . . .

It is all very puzzling. The threads are too tangled for his worn-out mind to sort. He is exhausted from walking all day. He longs for sleep.

His accommodation is a chamber at the top of the tower, attainable only by a narrow, cast-iron spiral staircase. The tiny room contains a child-size chair and table, a miniature fireplace, a built-in bookcase, and a chamber pot. The oddly shaped room seems to have been designed specifically to accommodate the hammock hung from hooks in opposite corners.

A hammock, indeed! The last time he slept in such a thing was on a banana boat down in Honduras. He was younger then, and knew of backaches only by rumor. A night in a hammock will probably cripple him for life!

As he strips down to his underclothes and slips into the hammock, the odd angles of the room and the Lilliputian scale make him feel like a lost child in a fairy tale, put to bed in a weird, enchanted room. He would scarcely be surprised if a trapdoor opened and a gnome tumbled out.

The situation is absurd! He should gather up his things, find old Horace, Ney's Indian servant, and demand to be taken back to the Driskill. But the little room is actually rather cozy, and the hammock surprisingly comfortable. Having settled into the thing, it seems too much bother to get out of it . . .

3

He wakes at dawn, deliciously rested. His back feels better than it has in days. He shall write a letter to the railways, advising them to get rid of their sleeping bunks and install hammocks instead! His only dream had something to do with footsteps pacing back and forth on the roof above his head—a restless gnome, perhaps? Mice among the rafters, more likely.

Horace does not seem to be about. Porter hesitates to enter the studio where Ney's boudoir is located. He decides to take a stroll around the grounds.

He is drawn to the creek. Birds are singing. Sunlight glimmers on the leafy canopy. Water gurgles and splashes over the broken blocks of limestone. He takes a deep breath, delighting in the sense of solitude amid nature that was so much a part of his youth in Texas, that has become such a rare thing since he became a New Yorker—since he went to prison, actually, and learned to live without solitude, or dignity . . .

Through the underbrush he glimpses movement nearby. He sees a figure squatting on a bed of limestone over which the water flows in a rippling sheet. It is Miss Ney with her pantaloons down, relieving herself. He stands still and holds his breath.

Ney finishes her ablutions, splashes her face, then hikes up the creek bed. She is certainly spry for her age! He withdraws, not realizing that his winding path through the underbrush intersects with hers. They come face-to-face. Ney gives a start, and Porter abruptly finds himself staring cross-eyed down the barrel of a large pistol.

Ney gives a shriek of girlish laughter and lowers the gun. "Mr. Porter! So sorry I am! Oh, the look on your face!"

He reaches to his chest. He feels his heart pounding. "Miss Ney! Do you always carry that thing with you?"

"My mute escort?" She looks at the pistol fondly. "For many years has it been my safeguard. When Formosa being builded was, and I would ride up on horseback alone from Liendo, pitching my hammock by night where I would, with it beside me I would sleep. But nowadays not; only when I sleep outside, and even then not always. Who would molest such an old woman as I have got to be? And Texas is not so wild a place as once it was. But last night, knowing that Dr. Kringel was back in Texas . . ."

He notices a hammock strung between two trees nearby. "Do you mean to say, Miss Ney, that you slept outside last night?"

"As every night, when the weather is allowing. Inside is for out-of-the-rain sleeping. Even in cold weather I sleep sometimes on the roof, under bright stars and blankets. But best is here by the creek where my hammock I can hang. And you, Mr. Porter, did you sleep well last night?"

"Like a stone, ma'am, thank you. But let me understand—do you honestly think you need a pistol to protect yourself from Dr. Kringel?"

She hardens her jaw. "With that wicked man, anything is possible."

"It seems a bit far-fetched—"

"No, Mr. Porter, *you* have been far-fetched, if here he brought you all the way from New York under false pretenses."

"Touché," says Porter dryly. "But a gun—?"

"Do not worry. You also were protected."

"Protected?"

"Look there. Can you not see, on the tower top, Horace with his hunting rifle?"

Porter looks toward the house. Standing sentinel behind the crenellated battlements of the little tower is the old Indian, who waves down to them, then throws his head back and yawns.

"The gnome pacing over my head! I thought it was a dream! Do you mean to say the fellow was up there all night, standing guard?"

"In such a pretty pass, I could hardly have in my house a guest, without precautions taking!"

Shortly before noon, Horace goes off with the buggy to fetch Dr. Montgomery at the train station. One o'clock comes, then two o'clock, and still the buggy has not returned. Ney declares that they shall go ahead and eat lunch without her best friend. Porter can see that she is a bit fretful.

When the buggy finally returns around three o'clock, a well-dressed gentleman steps out. He has the distinguished air of a man of science, but is much too young to be Montgomery. He helps another man step out of the buggy. *This* must be Montgomery—yes, the old fellow is just as Porter remembered and imagined him, with his lofty forehead crowned by a mane of fine white hair, his long, ascetic face framed by white sideburns. He carries a knobby cedar cane. His wise old eyes glimmer with intelligence. He is the very image of the philosopher-hermit-sleuth of Porter's fantasy.

And yet, this is not the man who wrote the letter that resides in Porter's pocket, with its promise that brought him all the way from New York. The basis of Porter's expectations has turned out to be a fraud. But if not to this man, then to whom can he turn for an explanation?

Ney and Montgomery come together and clasp hands. "My best friend!" she says, offering her cheek for the doctor to kiss. "Late you are! But now I see why. Dr. Merriman!" She extends her hand to the younger man, who bows to give it a kiss.

"Yes," says Montgomery, "I thought it would save time in the long run to go to the lunatic asylum first, so as to fetch Dr. Merriman and bring him along. But when Horace and I arrived, the whole place was in an uproar—"

"A new patient, more violent than anticipated," says Dr. Merriman by way of explanation. "Straitjacket poorly tied—stupid nurse! Exhausting chase—"

"The lunatic asylum?" mutters Porter.

"Ah, my best friend, this is Mr. Porter," says Ney. "Dave Shoemaker's old friend Will, who has a writer made of himself in New York City. The one Dave talked of when he came to visit."

Montgomery shakes Porter's hand. "Yes, my dear, so your telegram reminded me. The author of *Cabbages and Kings*."

"Why, yes," says Porter, gratified to hear his title correctly cited, at least. The doctor still speaks with a hint of a Scottish burr.

"But I must confess," says the doctor, "the rest of your telegram was rather mysterious, Elisabet. Something to do with that Kringel fellow—"

"A sad case!" Dr. Merriman shakes his head. "A true test of the limits of our science."

"Please—I don't understand," says Porter, feeling like Alice down the rabbit hole. Is Kringel some sort of escaped lunatic?

"We are all mystified, Mr. Porter," declares Montgomery. "I propose that the situation is rather like the fable of the three blind men and the elephant. We have each grappled with a different part of the beast's anatomy— trunk, tusk, tail—so that none of us has a clear idea of the whole animal. Here, for example, is one piece of the puzzle." He reaches into his coat pocket and hands Porter a page torn from a book.

"The title page from *Cabbages and Kings*!" says Porter. "What's this, written by hand? 'To Miss Ney and Dr. Montgomery, this book by a long-ago visitor to Liendo, with gratitude and many fond remembrances, Dave S.' But—Dr. Kringel had a copy of *Cabbages and Kings* with the title page missing!"

The others look at each other knowingly. "Surely the same Kringel it is, then," says Ney. Montgomery and Merriman nod. Porter feels farther down the rabbit hole than ever.

They sit in crude cedar chairs beneath the shade of an ancient oak, close by the creek. Horace brings out a pitcher of lemonade and glasses, then sits cross-legged in the grass with the hunting rifle cradled in his arms, keeping an eye on the underbrush.

Porter has told them how he came to be there. Now he looks to them for an explanation.

"Where to begin?" says Dr. Montgomery. "With Kringel's arrival at Liendo, I suppose. That was several months ago. Elisabet was here at Formosa at the time. Kringel—or Dr. Kringel, as he called himself—appeared one day at my front door. A caller is a rare thing at Liendo. I should have been suspicious. But his clothing was impeccable, his manner gracious, his speech refined—but I need not convince you of the man's charm, Mr. Porter, since you, too, have been the victim of it. It didn't hurt that he had with him a copy of *Philosophical Problems in the Light of Vital Organization*."

Porter nods. "I'm acquainted with your book. Kringel had it with him on the train."

"The same copy he produced on my doorstep, no doubt. He praised it extravagantly. He said he had come to Liendo on a pilgrimage to meet its author. I was flattered, I confess. Artists like Elisabet become inured to the gushing enthusiasm of strangers, but to a hermit such as myself, it was rather overwhelming. And his flattery wasn't vapid; he had read the book thoroughly, had grasped its thesis, and posed some very subtle questions. Kringel seemed to me a widely read man of considerable intelligence, a citizen-scholar of the sort I once naively imagined I would encounter everywhere in the wilds of America. I realized how starved I was for intellectual conversation. The good citizens of Six-Shooter Junction can tell you the price of oats, but they are not much good at discussing Hegel.

"Kringel became my house guest, for some time. I never inquired too closely about his circumstances. This is America, after all, where a man's hygiene and sense of humor are more important than his pedigree. I think it would be fair to say that Elisabet harbored no more doubts about Kringel's character than I did."

"Off in a corner the two of you always were, discussing monism." Ney sips her lemonade. "Rather sweet I thought it, that a friend you had found."

Montgomery nods. "Then Dave Shoemaker came visiting from Chicago. He saw friends here in Austin first, and discovered that you had published a book of stories under a pen name. When Dave came to Liendo, he brought along a copy of *Cabbages and Kings*, which he presented to us very proudly. He reminded us of your visit to Liendo those many years ago. I presume that was how Kringel first came to hear of you, Mr. Porter.

"Dave reminisced about old times in Austin. One day he mentioned a series of murders that took place the year you and Dave visited Liendo— 1885, I believe. What happened next was very strange. The mention of those murders elicited a marked reaction from Kringel, who until then had been paying only passing attention. When Kringel realized that Dave had reported on those murders for the *Statesman*, his interest became even more pronounced. I found the subject distasteful, especially in the presence of Elisabet, but the two of them persisted in discussing it. Kringel's excitation increased even more when Dave informed him of a personal link between yourself and one of the murder victims."

"Eula Phillips," whispers Porter.

"Dave mentioned a trial. I vaguely remembered it myself, it was so much in the newspapers at the time. Dave said that you had been . . . involved with the murdered woman. 'She broke his heart'—those were his words. Kringel seemed beside himself with excitement. He wanted to know more. Elisabet and I excused ourselves. That Dave should be so knowledgeable about a subject so distasteful hardly surprised me, given his line of work. What took me aback was Dr. Kringel's appetite for it! I didn't know what to think.

"The next day, Kringel's door remained shut all morning. When the housekeeper ventured into his room, she discovered that his bed had not been slept in."

Ney joins the conversation, waving her hands. "Vanished into thin air— poof! Gone all trace of him, his clothes and such. Like a thief in the night!"

"Like a thief, indeed," says Montgomery grimly. "Over the next few days we discovered that a number of things were missing. Small, valuable things—a pocket watch, pieces of jewelry. And money! We had just received a sum sent annually from Europe, and had converted a considerable amount into ready cash. It was money we could scarce afford to lose."

"And also missing was the book," adds Ney.

"Yes, Kringel took the copy of *Cabbages and Kings* that Dave had given us, but tore out the title page and left it behind—for what possible reason, we couldn't imagine."

"Did you inform the authorities?" asks Porter.

"I would as soon not have done so," says Montgomery. "The episode was extremely painful, and not a little embarrassing. Kringel was my guest for weeks! It seemed impossible that a man capable of discussing the science of vital organization could be a common thief. But Elisabet insisted that we inform the sheriff in Hempstead. Dave said it would do no good, that we had been taken, as he put it, by 'a fakir of the first water,' who would know how to cover his tracks. The sheriff was able to establish that Kringel took the early train to Houston, but after that the trail vanished."

"Infuriated Dave was," says Ney, "very upset, especially as his visit was almost over and back to Chicago he had to go in a matter of days. But an idea he had! If this Kringel was a con man of any great repute, Dave knew men still in Austin who might know something of him—Marshal Lucy, Mayor Shelley, and so on. And so to Austin off Dave went with a promise to do what he could. And right he was! Not a week later comes Dr. Merriman to Liendo, who knows all about Herr so-called Doctor Kringel. A madman! A lunatic escaped from the state asylum! Under our roof for weeks, while in Austin everyone was told to be on alert!"

"It is rather disconcerting to think that I harbored him so long, without the least suspicion of his lunacy." Montgomery's brow darkens. "It makes a fellow doubt his judgment."

"You mustn't be too hard on yourself." Dr. Merriman puts down his glass of lemonade and leans forward in his chair. He is a thoughtful-looking man with mellow gray eyes, about Porter's age. "Kringel is hardly the raving lunatic people imagine when they think of madmen. He's of another sort. His appearance is harmless, even charming. He can seem as sane as any of us, I assure you. Indeed, there are some doctors at the asylum who are of the opinion that he's not insane at all, but a hoaxer.

"Let me recount for your benefit, Mr. Porter, a few of the things I previously explained to Dr. Montgomery and Miss Ney. Kringel was committed to the lunatic asylum about six years ago, after he had been observed wandering the streets of Austin, mumbling to himself and clearly out of his wits. His clothing was of good quality and there was money in his pockets, but the court could find no clue to his identity. A jury de lunatico inquirendo ruled him insane and committed him to the care of the asylum. Since that time, no relative or friend has ever come forward to claim responsibility for him.

"Under my care, Kringel gradually regained his wits. He became able to converse and answer questions, but some of his notions were so manifestly delusional that there could be no question of discharging him. He gave his name as Kringel, and his birthplace as Bavaria, and said he had lived in many places under numerous names.

"One of the previous identities he claimed was that of Dr. Frederick Augustus Fry, a phrenologist who lived for a while in Austin back in the 1880s. Kringel does seem conversant with old-fashioned phrenological theory. I managed to locate some people who had met this Dr. Fry when he resided here—all of whom insisted that Dr. Fry was blind!

"One of Fry's old acquaintances was kind enough to visit the asylum and meet with Kringel—William Pendleton Gaines, the former publisher of the *Statesman*. After conversing with Kringel for half an hour, Gaines couldn't say for certain whether the man was Frederick Augustus Fry or not. Gaines never saw Fry without dark spectacles, for one thing. For his part, Kringel made a great show of recognizing Gaines, recalling a visit to Bellevue, the house Gaines used to live in, and so on; but we all know how convincingly the skilled confidence man can feign acquaintance to gain the trust of others.

"For that is what Kringel must have been for most of his life: a confidence trickster. It seems he had a lifelong partner. The name he most often gave for that partner was Dr. Terry, and in fact there was a patent medicine bottler named Ephraim Ebenezer Terry associated with the blind Dr. Fry.

"As you can imagine, separating fact from fancy is a sticky business when dealing with a delusional patient. But I think it fairly certain that Kringel did have a partner for many years, whom we might as well call Dr. Terry, and that the proximate cause of Kringel's acute mental collapse was the death of this partner. According to Kringel, the two of them returned to Austin in 1900 after years of traveling, during which they supported themselves by playing confidence schemes on railroad passengers. Dr. Terry died, apparently by drowning in the Colorado River, and possibly as a result of suicide. Whatever the circumstances, the loss of Dr. Terry was so crushing that it caused Kringel to lose his wits; thus the condition in which he was found wandering the streets. I believe the two men shared what the French call a *folie à deux*, a 'madness of two,' a mutual edifice of delusion. Partners in crime tend to reinforce each other's alienation from the rest of the world; this was something more extreme than that, a wholesale reordering of the moral universe to suit the two of them. The loss of this partner in delusion was shattering.

"Since his commitment to the asylum, Kringel has gone through alternating spells of lucidity and derangement. Sometimes he seems to be a sane man feigning insanity. Sometimes he seems to be a madman pretending to be sane. He's a trickster by nature, and a chameleon as well. There have even been times when he calls himself Dr. Fry and plays at being blind with such conviction as to cause himself physical harm by falling down stairs and stepping in front of bicyclists.

"But most disturbingly, Kringel has repeatedly alluded to having committed murder. He avoids giving specific details, but claims to have molested and murdered any number of women, in league with his deceased partner. It is entirely possible that these claims are purely imaginary, the morbid fantasies of a diseased mind.

"Despite his madness, Kringel is a man of considerable intelligence, and a voracious reader. The asylum maintains a library for the patients; the more old-fashioned doctors still theorize that green gardens and vigorous walks and wholesome books can cure a troubled mind. Dr. Montgomery was kind enough to donate a copy of his new book, *Philosophical Problems in the Light of Vital Organization.* Kringel read it, and apparently took it into his head to meet the author. When he made his escape, the book disappeared with him; I fear that no one noticed at the time. We informed Marshal Lucy of his escape, but the authorities were unable to find him. I suspect he went off to Waco or Houston first, where he managed to con what he needed in order to buy a suit of clothes and put on a good appearance when he went to Liendo.

"He left Liendo flush with the money he stole from Dr. Montgomery and Miss Ney—quite enough money to travel first class to New York and back. He must have formed the intention to visit you, Mr. Porter, even before he left Liendo; that was why he stole some Liendo stationery, so as to forge the bogus letter from Dr. Montgomery which lured you back to Texas. That was why he tore out the title page of the stolen copy of *Cabbages and Kings,* for if you had seen the inscription from Dave Shoemaker to Miss Ney and Dr. Montgomery, what would you have made of that?"

Porter's head is spinning. He craves a whiskey but makes do with lemonade. "These murders Kringel claims to have committed. Do you think—?"

Merriman shrugs. "It is impossible to say whether they were real or imaginary."

Porter looks to Dr. Montgomery. "When Kringel and I parted ways in Hearne, he claimed he was headed for Hempstead. I last saw him in the telegraph office at the Hearne station, sending a wire—presumably to Liendo."

Montgomery draws a breath. "Ah, yes. As a matter of fact, a telegram did arrive the day before yesterday. At the time I had no idea what to make of it. It makes a bit more sense now. I think the telegram must be for you, Mr. Porter."

"For me?"

Montgomery pulls a folded scrap of paper from his coat pocket and hands it to Porter. Miss Ney and Dr. Merriman sit forward in their chairs. For their benefit, Porter reads the message aloud. "'To Mr. Henry O. Jones, care of Liendo Plantation, Hempstead: Please convey regards and sincere apologies to Miss N. and Dr. M. You and I must meet again. In Austin? I have a tale for you.' It's signed 'K.' The return address is given as Hotel de los Estranjeros, Coralio, Republic of Anchuria."

Dr. Merriman wrinkles his brow. "Anchuria? Is that somewhere in Latin America?"

"It's from *Cabbages and Kings.* It doesn't exist." Porter refolds the telegram. "I begin to wonder if Dr. Kringel does!"

4

That night he returns to the Driskill Hotel, over the protests of Miss Ney, who insists that he is welcome to stay at Formosa. Porter is tempted, but he suspects that the little room in the tower is where Dr. Montgomery usually sleeps. The efficient anonymity of the hotel will better suit his mood. He needs to be alone with his thoughts.

He dines in the hotel restaurant. Afterward he takes a stroll over to Guy Town. The old vice district seems to be intact. The saloons are plentiful, as are working women on the street. Guy Town survives despite the perennial efforts of politicians and preachers to shut it down. It seems that the moral crusaders and the prohibitionists will never have their way.

The district seems at once seedier and more quaint than he remembers. How enormous it loomed when he was young! This was Baghdad and Babylon, Sodom and Gomorrah, a dangerous, secret, magical city within a city, and all within walking distance of his boarding house! He has since seen parts of New York which put Guy Town to shame.

No doubt a bit of whiskey would give everything a rosier glow. He tries to locate the old Tin Cup, but it seems to have vanished. He settles for an establishment called the Buckle and Spur.

He has a shot of whiskey, then another. Inebriation does nothing to improve the surroundings; it only makes him maudlin. He suddenly finds himself, of all things, homesick for New York! He wishes he were in Pete's Tavern at that very moment, sitting in the booth reserved for him, with a deadline breathing down his neck, watching the Four Million pass by. What a small place Austin is, after all.

He puts down his shot glass and tips his hat to the bartender. On his way out, he passes a group coming in. They must be university students; they look like children to him, hardly old enough to order a legal drink. Laughing and ribbing each other, they make their way to the bar. Next to the old drunks, they seem aglow with energy. One of them in particular catches his eye, a ginger-haired boy with an intelligent face and a reserved manner. The boy looks a bit chagrined at finding himself in such a place, but his blue eyes are bright with excitement. Porter sighs. Guy Town is still Baghdad and Babylon, Sodom and Gomorrah, but not for him.

As he passes through the lobby of the Driskill, stumbling a bit, the desk clerk calls out, "Mr. Jones!" The assumed name fails to catch his ear. The clerk emerges from behind the counter. "Mr. Jones! A gentleman left this for you, not an hour ago."

It is a familiar brown leather satchel. The sight of it sobers him at once.

"And this, too," The clerk hands him a sealed envelope addressed to Mr. Henry O. Jones. Porter gives the man a quarter for his trouble and hurries up to his room.

He tears open the envelope. The note inside is on hotel stationery. Kringel must have written it at the front desk when he left the satchel. Porter recognizes the cramped, crabbed handwriting, the same as that of the forged letter which Kringel claimed to be from Dr. Montgomery:

Mr. Porter/Henry/Jones,
   The contents of the satchel are for you. You alone can do the tale justice. Such meetings as ours are arranged by Destiny! If you wish an interview, I shall be at the summit of Mount Bonnell at dawn tomorrow. Come by hackney cab. Send the driver away. Unless you come alone, I shall not appear, and we will not meet again.

                                                     Dr. Kringel/Fry/&c.

Porter undoes the straps on the satchel and empties it onto the bed. Out come two bulging scrapbooks with tattered covers, one red and the other blue. He opens the red one and leafs through the pages, which are full of brittle, yellowed newspaper clippings. Scribbled in the margins are notes in Kringel's crabbed handwriting. Some of the notations appear to be recent; others are faded and smeared. A confusion of arrows and dashes connect the jottings to the newspaper text and to each other.

The clippings are from newspapers all over Texas. He turns the pages and scans the headlines:

BLOOD! BLOOD! BLOOD!

A FEARFUL MIDNIGHT MURDER
ON WEST PECAN—
MYSTERY AND CRIME

ANOTHER SERVANT GIRL FOUND SLAIN

AUSTIN MURDERS BAFFLE POLICE—WOMEN
OF THE CITY TERRIFIED
SLAIN SERVANTS—OUTRAGE AND
DEMANDS FOR JUSTICE

THE DEMONS HAVE TRANSFERRED THEIR
THIRST FOR BLOOD TO WHITE PEOPLE!

DID THE HUSBANDS DO IT?

PHILLIPS FOUND GUILTY
OF UXORICIDE!

Porter's heart pounds in his chest. He turns back to the beginning of the scrapbook and scans the scribbled notations:

We decided to start with colored women, thinking it would be safer; soon we discovered we had a taste for the pretty things!

We met Mollie Smith by chance that very day; ascertained she kept no gun; ascertained the presence of her common-law husband, and so took the ax with us to deal with him. Dr. T. that afternoon had given her a powerful soporific for her megrim, which she must have taken, as she scarcely woke. Our first, and a complete success!

It was we who broke into the dentist's office and set the fire to cover our tracks. We intended Dr. Stoddard to perish in the flames. Alas, we made poor arsonists. The objective was to steal chloroform, which came in very useful!

Chloroformed Eliza Shelley and her brood—the thrill of taking her (each of us twice) while her sucklings slept nearby!
Irene Cross: chloroform seemed to have little effect. She put up more of a struggle than we expected. All the sweeter for it.

The 11-year-old girlchild was sweetest of all up till then. Terry wanted to take her mother as well, but I told him: "No beets when we have foie gras on our plates!"

Was there ever a man as stupid as Marshal Grooms Lee?
Why barefoot? Boots and shoes leave prints that can be exactly matched (by lawmen smarter than Grooms Lee, at least). Bare footprints are safer by far! I also came to enjoy a certain thrill in going about our business barefooted, like wanton savages!

Gracie Vance: We had dined with her employer, Major Dunham, discussing the dam proposal while the tender morsel served us and looked away whenever I smiled. (Pretty serving sluts never know what to make of the blind man who ogles them!) Used chloroform again; axed Gracie, Lucinda, and the man. Lucinda was burning with fever inside—a curious sensation. Gracie revived and almost escaped; Destiny put the brick close at hand. When I saw the newspaper report of the watch found on her, which I had stolen from Prof. Tallichet's serving girl, my heart skipped a beat. Thank God Grooms Lee was still in charge of the investigation!

Susan Hancock: We knew it was a risk, to take a white woman. What a shock her husband gave us when he came staggering out of the house, and we had barely finished our business.

Eula Phillips: First time I saw her was on a train leaving Austin. (I took a reading of her husband's empty head; Dr. T. lifted his pocketbook.) She looked very sad with her little Säugling in her arms, all pretty and blond and petite. At the moment of death, her expiring breath was like unearthly music.

Porter throws the red scrapbook on the floor. A loose piece of paper slips out and flutters to his feet. He stares at it for a long moment, then bends down to retrieve it. The slip is a standard form issued by the First National Bank of Austin, "Request to Remove Contents of Safe Deposit Box." In the blanks provided the number of a box is filled in, along with a signature that reads *Frederick Augustus Fry, Ph.D.*, initialed by a bank official. The slip is dated a few months back—immediately after Kringel's escape from the asylum. He must have retrieved the scrapbooks from his safe deposit box before he went to Liendo.

These, then, were the contents of the satchel always at Kringel's side on the trip from New York, the "work" which he had brought along, he said, to keep himself busy, but which he never produced in Porter's presence. Porter imagines the old man slipping out of their compartment in the dead of night, taking the satchel to the lounge car to pore over the old scrapbooks in secret and scribble in the margins, annotating his precious collection of clippings.

The blue scrapbook lies on the bed, untouched. He opens it. More clippings, more notations. More headlines about blood and murder—but not the Austin murders of 1885. These reports come from St. Louis, Memphis,

New Orleans, Chicago, Baltimore, Philadelphia, and elsewhere. The first clipping is from 1886. There are clippings from every year thereafter, all the way to 1900.

Murder after murder, scattered all over the country. One of the notations reads: "Austin taught us to bide our time and take our pleasure at irregular intervals—never twice in the same town—always discreetly."

Blank pages follow the last pasted clipping from 1900. That was the year they returned to Austin and Terry drowned in the Colorado. Fry must have stored the scrapbooks in the safe deposit box before he lost his wits and was committed to the asylum.

Porter turns the blank pages and discovers a loose clipping. The paper is still white, not yellowed with age. He recognizes the typeface and gives a start. The item was clipped from the New York *World*, where his stories appear every week.

A SHOCKING CRIME!

Early this morning, the body of Helen Carter, a known prostitute, was discovered in a room to let in the Bowery. The cause of death appears to have been a blow to the head, evidently delivered by a bloodied ax which police discovered in the room. Others in the building reported having heard a scuffle during the night, but no one investigated at the time. . . .

Scrawled at the bottom of the clipping is a note in Dr. Kringel's crabbed hand: *I feel like a man reborn!* There is also a date—the very day the two of them left New York to begin the journey to Texas.

5

The last stretch of the road to Mount Bonnell is as steep and bumpy as ever, and still stops well short of the summit. Porter pays the driver and sends him away. He peers into the dark underbrush, wondering if Kringel is watching. It is the hazy blue hour before dawn.

He scrambles up the rocky path. He has not slept a wink. He feels tired and punchy, exhausted physically and emotionally. He pauses to catch his breath and looks over his shoulder. In the hazy dimness the capitol dome is the size of his thumbnail. The dawning horizon is a hairline crack with scintillating yellow shining through. The sky directly overhead is deep purple, and toward the west, beyond the trees along the mountaintop, a few scattered stars still glimmer.

He recommences the climb, huffing and puffing. The satchel grows heavier with every step. Last night, by the glare of the hissing gas lamp beside his bed, he read the scrapbooks from start to finish. To sleep after that was impossible.

His pulse quickens. He breaks out in a sweat that has nothing to do with the climb. By the time he reaches the little clearing at the summit, his heart is hammering in his chest and his palms are clammy.

The clearing is empty. He walks to the precipice and gazes down at the river glistening like a black snake in the shadow of the mountain.

"So you came after all, Mr. Porter."

He turns to see Dr. Kringel step from the woods. In his long black coat with his mane of white hair, he looks like a symphony conductor, or a kindly grandfather, or a pleasant traveling companion. His expression is serene. In his right hand the man clutches a pistol, aimed at Porter.

He finds it impossible to speak. The climb has winded him. His back is in agony. His head is full of cobwebs.

"I see you brought the satchel, Mr. Porter. Did you read my scrapbooks?"

Porter stares at him.

"You must wonder why I brought you here, why I've given you my scrapbooks. Come, Mr. Porter, can you not speak?" Kringel keeps his distance but steps close enough to the precipice to look over the edge. "This was the very spot where poor Ephraim jumped, when the game was over for him. That was what he called it, the great game. We played it together, Dr. Terry and I. We dared to do the things that every man, deep in his heart, desires to do. We lived like gods."

Porter clutches the grip of the satchel until his fingers go numb. "Why Eula?"

"Ah, your beloved! We first saw her on a train headed out of Austin, with her baby at her breast. Even then, I knew that she would be ours someday. It was her destiny. Months later we saw her at May Tobin's house. I thought we might simply pay to have her; I would have settled for that. But she thought herself too good for the likes of us. Imagine!

"We waited until our time in Austin was up. A confidence man can stay in one place only so long, and the city had finally hired a marshal with more sense than Grooms Lee. We decided to give ourselves a parting Christmas gift: a white woman, and damn the consequences. We chose Susan Hancock. We had observed her from time to time, because her house was just around the corner from the Widow Tobin's. We were washing our hands at the water pump in the back yard when Mr. Hancock staggered out, blind drunk. We jumped the fence and ran to the Avenue, and what should we see, right in front of May Tobin's, but Eula Phillips leaving in a cab. We followed her home. It was destiny: that was the night, the hour, the moment we were meant to have her. We climbed the back fence. There was an ax by the wood pile.

"You, Mr. Porter—you patiently, politely waited for an invitation from Eula Phillips that never came. We saw our chance and took it. Did you never imagine doing what we did? Did you never nurse a fantasy of having your way with her, then snuffing out her little life in revenge for snubbing you? We only did what you would have done, had you the courage. Admit it!"

Porter trembles and shakes his head.

Kringel narrows his eyes. "What a great convulsion she gave, just as I spilled my seed. Inside her, inside them all, I touched a place that was neither life nor death. Only Dr. Terry ever understood." He gazes down at the river. "In the end, his manhood deserted him. His body betrayed him. He became impotent. When he made up his mind to come back to Austin, I knew what he intended. I saw him jump from this very spot. After that, I lost the thread. But now I've found it again—old as I am! You saw the latest clipping, from New York?"

Porter nods.

"So you *have* read the scrapbooks. Good! I first thought that Dr. Montgomery was the man to tell our story. But once I met him, it became obvious he would never do. His mind is too rigid, too limited. Then your friend Shoemaker visited Liendo—the very man who wrote about the murders for the *Statesman!* Montgomery was only a stepping-stone to Shoemaker."

The satchel drags at Porter's arm like a sack full of lead. "Why didn't you give these to him, then?"

"A newspaperman? To tell our story, we must have an artist! A great and famous writer, whose words will be read a hundred years from now—you, Mr. Porter! Can you not see how the web of destiny links us all together? You are to tell the tale."

"And you?"

"Did you not see the new clipping, from the *World*? The game goes on!"

"You didn't come here . . . to join Dr. Terry?"

Kringel laughs. "I assure you, Mr. Porter, I have no intention of killing myself. By this time tomorrow I shall be in another state, using another name. I have many years left."

Porter looks at the gun in Kringel's hand. He raises the satchel with both arms, takes a deep breath, and throws it as hard as he can. The satchel hits Kringel square in the chest. His arms close around it reflexively and he staggers back. He manages to keep his grip on the pistol. Pebbles fly off the precipice.

"I don't want your filthy scrapbooks." Porter backs away from the cliff, toward the trees, keeping his eye on Kringel. His heart pounds in his chest. He reaches inside his coat.

Kringel stares back at him with a stricken expression. He clutches the satchel. His jaw stiffens. He curls his upper lip. He awkwardly aims his gun at Porter.

A shot echoes across the Colorado and back, launching flocks of birds into the sky.

The recoil whips through Porter's arm and into his back, making him wince. The smell of gunpowder burns his nostrils. He has not fired a pistol since his cowboy days in South Texas. On his way to Mount Bonnell, he stopped at Formosa. Ney's "mute escort" packs a bigger wallop than he expected.

Kringel staggers back, a look of shock on his face. The satchel, still clutched to his chest, has a smoking bullet hole in it. He gives an abrupt scream as he loses his balance. His arms fly up. The satchel and the pistol go spinning. Kringel tumbles backward and disappears.

Porter runs to the precipice. On the way down, Kringel crashes through scrubby foliage that clings to the stone and repeatedly strikes the rock face, rebounding and somersaulting outward, releasing little clouds of dust and debris. Each time he hits the rock, a scream and a harsh thumping sound echo up. He finally makes a tiny splash in the water far below.

The satchel follows him. It strikes a crag and and bursts open. The scrapbooks shoot out and flutter in a downward spiral like frantic birds. They make two smaller splashes. A few pages fly free from the ruptured bindings and float downstream for a while, until the current sucks them beneath the surface.

Diana of the Hunt

NEW YORK CITY, 1906

*T*HEY meet at a table for two at an outdoor café at Madison Square Garden. Far above, the goddess Diana presides atop the tower, her golden bow lifted and her mantle unfurled.

Porter looks at the woman across the table. Within hours of his return to New York, she attempted to visit him. He told Lena to send her away. She came again the next day, and the next. She wrote cryptic, threatening messages, which Lena dutifully delivered. Still, he refused to see her. He was not yet ready.

This morning he sent a note to her posh house on Gramercy Park, saying he would meet her below the statue of Diana at a certain hour. Now they sit opposite one another, with steaming cups of coffee and an untouched basket of tea cakes between them. Delia is elegantly dressed and still quite striking. How ravishing she was twenty years ago, Porter thinks. At the time, he was too distracted by Eula's blond perfection to fully appreciate Delia's dark beauty.

"Your behavior since your return has been quite rude, Mr. Porter," she says coolly. "I've called on you several times. You refuse to see me."

What cheek the woman has! "I've been busy," he says simply. "Deadlines past due, editors threatening suicide, that sort of thing."

"Business is good, then?"

"Yes. My new book bodes to be a tremendous success."

"What is it called?"

"*The Four Million*. If everyone in the title would purchase a copy, I could move up to your part of town!"

She abruptly changes the subject. "You shouldn't have sent that note to my house. The servants gossip."

What nerve! A blackmailer complaining first about his manners, then about his mode of invitation! "Don't worry, I shan't be contacting you again after today. Nor shall you be contacting me."

"You have some money for me, then?" How like a fox she looks, with that glint in her eyes.

"No, Delia. I haven't a dime for you. Not a red cent."

"This is unacceptable, Mr. Porter."

"No, Delia, your blackmail is unacceptable. I shall no longer put up with it."

Her face hardens. "I have other acquaintances in the press, you know. They're always looking for bits of gossip—'the lowdown', they call it. What if I were to give them the lowdown about a certain embezzler I know?"

"Do so, if you must. I call your bluff."

Her nostrils flare. "I suppose you imagine you can checkmate me—conjure up something from my own past. I'm sorry to disappoint you, but my husband already knows about Jimmy's trial."

"I would never defame a dead man to get at you, Delia."

"What, then? If you even whisper the name May Tobin, I shall have you indicted for slander faster than you can dash off one of your stories."

"Delia, for heaven's sake! I have no intention of dredging up your sordid past, or anyone else's. The past is over and done with, finished, dead and buried. I simply said that I have no money for you. Now do what you will."

She stares at him for a long moment. "You called me here to make this declaration?"

"I called you here to be done with you forever—to be free of my past, once and for all. And I have something to tell you . . . about Eula."

She shakes her head. "What could you possibly say about Eula, after all these years?"

"I know who killed her."

Delia stares at him. Her aloof expression wavers. "Go on."

"It's a very long, very complicated, very strange story."

"With one of your requisite surprise endings?"

"Be quiet, Delia, and listen."

An hour later, the basket of tea cakes remains untouched. Delia's face has hardly altered expression, only now and then betraying a hint of sorrow, surprise, or regret.

"Afterward, I found Kringel's horse tethered amid the underbrush, not far from the top of Mount Bonnell. He had a saddlebag full of money and a ticket, under the name Jones, for the seven o'clock train to El Paso."

She considers for a moment. "Are you sure he was dead?"

"If you had seen him rebounding off that stone face, Delia . . ." He grimaces. "But I understand your concern. I wanted to make certain, too. When I got back into town, I kept my ears open for news of a body found in the river. Sure enough, Kringel was fished out that morning. According to the *Statesman*, he wasn't a pretty sight."

"But the bullet hole—what did they make of that?"

"It's the damnedest thing. There was no mention of a gunshot wound."

"But—"

"All I can figure is that the scrapbooks stopped the bullet. Even so, the force of the shot was enough to knock him over the edge. It was the fall that killed him, not the bullet. Dr. Merriman from the asylum identified his body. People assumed it was suicide."

"And the scrapbooks?"

"Nothing left of them, so far as I know. Swallowed by the river. So there you have an end of it. Can you imagine, he actually expected me to use those scrapbooks somehow, to spin a story out of them. He thought he was making me a precious gift. As if anyone would want to read about such a ghastly business! People like pretty stories with sad endings, or sad stories with pretty endings. Who would read a book about a monster like Kringel?"

She lowers her face. She presses a forefinger and thumb to her eyes. Can it be that Delia is weeping? He pulls the handkerchief from his breast pocket and offers it. She takes it and turns her face so that he cannot see her daub at her tears.

"All these years—" Her voice breaks. She takes a shuddering breath. "All these years, I was sure that Jimmy did it. He claimed to be innocent. I never believed him. How could I? We didn't speak for years, not since Father died. Now Jimmy's dead. I can never—"

He lays a hand on her arm. "The past is dead, Delia. Don't you see? It has no right to claim us. We're far enough along on the journey, you and I, to see the end of the road. We have so little time left! I won't spend it looking backward in misery. I'm free of Eula, free of Athol, free of Will Porter and all his foolish mistakes. I'm free of you, Delia."

She turns and looks at him. Her eyes are red. There is no disdain or rancor on her face, only sadness. It seems strange that he should ever have been afraid of her.

He withdraws his hand, sits back and smiles. "Do you know, I recently took out a lonely hearts advertisement, just to see what might happen. I've made the acquaintance of a most charming lady. Who knows, perhaps I shall even get married again."

Once Delia would have seized upon such words as revealing a weak spot. Now she merely nods, then stands and reaches for her handbag. "Good-bye, Mr. Porter. I suppose we shan't be seeing each other again."

"I suppose we shan't."

She manages a weak smile. "You'll at least pay the waiter, won't you?"

He nods. She turns and walks away. He watches until her figure is lost in the crowd.

The past is truly dead; he no longer has anything to fear from it. His only fear now is that the years remaining will not be enough.

What is it, to be alive? Where have all the dead gone off to? He will leave it to philosophers and lunatics to address such lofty topics. What story made of words on a page could recapture what he felt for Eula Phillips, or make him young again, or bring the dead to life, or right a single wrong? He will do what he does best. He will write stories for bank clerks and shopgirls, bored passengers and bedridden patients. He will be what he is, O. Henry— and let that be the end of it!

AUTHOR'S NOTE

⌇

*A*BOUT her novel of Australia, *The Timeless Land*, Eleanor Dark wrote: "This book has borrowed so much from history that it may be advisable to remind readers that it is fiction." I am tempted to say the same—yet equally tempted to invoke Thornton Wilder on *The Ides of March*: "Historical reconstruction is not among the primary aims of this work. It may be called a fantasia upon certain events and persons."

Dark and Wilder (savage names!) represent different approaches to historical fiction: strict adherence to known facts versus deliberate reordering of events. Because *A Twist at the End* takes both approaches, I feel obliged to point out what in the novel is fact and what is fantasia.

Had I written a novel about, say, Jack the Ripper, many readers could spot (or discover with minimal research) where I stuck to the facts or resorted to invention. But the series of murders which the young William Sydney Porter dubbed the work of "the Servant Girl Annihilators" have fallen into obscurity, even as a local legend in Austin, and no historian has ever seriously tried to make sense of them. I have portrayed those murders authentically down to the hour they were committed and the street addresses where they occurred.

Other factual aspects of the novel include the history of Senate Bill No. 79, the so-called Female Clerks Bill; the Alec Mack affair and its outcome; and the scandalous testimony which emerged from the trial in Part Four. If these events remind readers of current battles over affirmative action, of the Rodney King episode, or of a defense based upon the premise, "If it does not fit, you must acquit," I can only say that I would never have been so bold as to invent such parallels.

Also factual are the biographical details about public figures such as Mayor John Robertson, District Attorney James Robertson, *Statesman* publisher William Pendleton Gaines, Representative Taylor Moore, Marshal Grooms Lee, Marshal James Lucy, Comptroller William Jesse Swain, William Shelley, William Holland, Elisabet Ney, and Dr. Edmund Montgomery. Many of the other characters are based on lesser-known people who nonetheless appear in the historical record, including (besides the murder victims) May Tobin, Fannie Whipple, Sallie Mack, Hugh Hancock, Lem Brooks, and Delia Campbell.

Among the minor details, my passing mention of Tuna, Texas, is not fanciful; such a locality once existed ninety-five miles southwest of San Antonio (between Cotulla and Artesia Wells), as may be ascertained by consulting an 1885 railroad timetable. The statue of the Goddess of Liberty atop the Texas state capitol has recently been refurbished and restored to her original, if dubious, glory. Her contemporary, the monumental *Diana* executed by Augustus Saint-Gaudens, presided over Madison Square Garden until her tower was pulled down in 1925. She now resides at the head of the grand staircase of the Philadelphia Museum of Art.

The framing device of William Sydney Porter's journey back to Texas in 1906 is fictional, as are the relationship between Porter and Eula Phillips, Porter's visits to Liendo and Formosa, and the solution to the murders, which in actuality remains a mystery. In constructing this fantasia, it has been my method not so much to alter history as to take advantage of gaps in the record. The overall scheme is invented but not impossible.

Did William Sydney Porter deserve to be found guilty at his trial for embezzlement? O. Henry scholars have argued the question for almost a century without reaching a consensus. Porter consistently denied the charges. In New York, he made a secret of his past and worried obsessively about being exposed. The possibility that he was the victim of blackmail is not my invention, but was believed to be the case by Porter's intimates. In his 1921 memoir *Through the Shadows with O. Henry*, Al Jennings, who knew Porter in Honduras, the Ohio State Penitentiary, and New York, reports that the blackmailer was a woman Porter had known in Texas, who had since married a New York broker.

At the time of his death in 1910 at the age of forty-eight, O. Henry was a household name. When the secret of his convict past came out, the convergence of critical acclaim, untimely death, and criminal notoriety made him a literary legend. The legend has faded, but "The Gift of the Magi" and a handful of his other stories are still famous around the world. Many biographies have been written; I find Richard O'Connor's *O. Henry: The Legendary Life of William S. Porter* (1970) particularly astute.

Elisabet Ney at last became the subject of a thorough scholarly biography with *The Art of the Woman: The Life and Work of Elisabet Ney* (1988) by Emily Fourmy Cutrer. Three earlier books about Ney and Montgomery, *Elisabet Ney* (1943) by Jean Burton and Jan Fortune, *Two Romantics and Their Ideal Life* (1946) by Vernon Loggins, and *The Hermit Philosopher of Liendo* (1951) by Ira Stephens, are not without charm. Most charming of all is *Sursum!* (1977), a privately printed collection of Ney's letters edited by Mrs. J. W. (Willie B.) Rutland, which conveys a sense of Ney's unique way of thinking and speaking.

Austin: An Illustrated History (1985) by David C. Humphrey provides an excellent starting point for the study of nineteenth-century Austin. More specialized details can be found in *Dog Ghosts and Other Texas Negro Folk Tales* (1958) by J. Mason Brewer, *The Illustrated Self-Instructor in Phrenology and Physiology* (1855) by Orson Squire Fowler and Lorenzo Niles Fowler, *What Can a Woman Do?* (1883) by Martha Louise Rayne, and in the exquisitely detailed bird's-eye view map of Austin drawn by Augustus Koch in 1887 (reproductions of which are available from the Austin History Center). My re-creation of the trial in Part Four is based on the Statement of the Case in *Reports of Cases Argued and Adjudged in the Court of Appeals of Texas, Volume XXII* (1887).

The poem read aloud by William Holland in Chapter 13 is Walt Whitman's "Ethiopia Saluting the Colors." The sources for other extracts are as given in the text; in some cases, quotations from the *Statesman* have been considerably edited and condensed.

I conducted my research at the Bancroft Library and Doe Library at the University of California at Berkeley; in Austin, at the Austin History Center, the Travis County Clerk's Office, the Barker Texas History Collections at the University of Texas, and the Texas State Archives (special thanks to Bill Simmons for his help researching Senate Bill No. 79 of the Nineteenth Legislature); and on site at the O. Henry Museum and the Elisabet Ney Museum (Formosa) in Austin, and at Liendo Plantation near Hempstead, Texas.

Many people helped me in many ways during the writing of this novel. Michael Denneny wined and dined me at Pete's Tavern in New York. Rick, Oscar, and Hildegarde were patient and willing to travel. Barbara Peters pointed me to the Western bookstores in Scottsdale, Arizona. Penni Kimmel provided information about music and abortion methods in the 1880s and gave me invaluable feedback on the first draft. Andrew Holleran provided the Schopenhauer quotes on journalists and mustaches. Lawrence Schimel did site research for me in New York City. My agent, Alan Nevins, held my hand when I needed it most. Chuck Adams, my editor at Simon & Schuster, navigated me into port. I especially thank my hosts in Austin during the summers of 1996 and 1997, Tom Buckle, Gary Coody, and Anne and Debbie Odom.

I was inspired throughout the writing of A *Twist at the End* by epigrams from two plays of the same name written thousands of years apart. From Jean Anouilh's *Antigone* (1946), this existential shrug:

> And there we are. . . . And those who have survived will now begin quietly to forget the dead: they won't remember who was who or which was which. It is all over.

From twenty-five hundred years ago, the original *Antigone* of Sophocles provides a blunt rejoinder:

> Who died? Who did the murder? Tell us now.

That is what I have tried to do.